RAGE
of
QUEENS

Homeric Chronicles

JANELL
RHIANNON

Rage of Queens
Copyright 2021 © Janell Rhiannon
All rights reserved.

No portion of this book may be reproduced in any format
without the express permission of the author.

This is a work of fiction based on mythology. All characters are fictional. Any semblance to actual persons, living or dead, or actual events is purely coincidental.

Cover design and photography by Regina Wamba
Book design by Inkstain Design Studio
Edited by Melisa at There For You Editing

RAGE
of
QUEENS

For all the women I love.
And these most of all:
Amber
Anni
Bree
Miss Macy
Vandy
Verni

BOOKS BY
JANELL RHIANNON

HOMERIC CHRONICLES

Song of Sacrifice

Rise of Princes

Rage of Queens

The White Island (coming soon)

Catch my Podcast: Greek Mythology Retold

@Spreaker

@iTunes

@iHeartRadio

@Spotify

@Soundcloud

@Alexa (just ask her)

LIVINGSTONE SAGA
HISTORICAL ROMANCE SET IN 12TH CENTURY SPAIN

The Maker and the Gargoyle

WWW.JANELLRHIANNON.COM
For updates, check my webpage and sign up
for the *Myrmidon Crew Letter.*

Twitter @theravenangel
Instagram @janell_rhiannon
Janell Rhiannon Author@ Facebook
Janell Rhiannon on Goodreads
Janell Rhiannon @Youtube

Catch my Podcast: Greek Mythology Retold

CONSISTENTLY RANKED IN THE TOP 10 GREEK MYTHOLOGY PODCASTS

@Spreaker
@iTunes/Apple Podcasts
@iHeartRadio
@Spotify
@Soundcloud
@Podbean
@Google Podcasts
@Amazon Audible
@ Castbox
@Deezer
@Podcast Addict
@Podchaser
@JioSaavn
@Alexa (just ask her)

**For exclusive content become a *Myrmidon Elite Member Podcast Subscriber*

Only the dead have seen the end of the war.

PLATO

PART TWO
The Last Days

THE RAGE OF ACHILLES

War.
How do you begin?
Envy and greed.
Prophecy.
Rage.

War.
Where is your mercy?
Blood and bones
washed it away,
winging it to the heavens.

War.
Where is your victory?
Spears and swords
mutilated bodies bloom like spring flowers,
glistening guts sparkle in the sun.

War.
What is your legacy?
Death and destruction.
Memory.
Song.

War.
Who is your champion?
Death dropped a single name:
Achilles.

ONE

Vengeance

TROY—1238 BCE

Priam stood in the gray light of early morning, staring with red-rimmed and swollen eyes at his youngest son's lifeless form on the funeral pyre in the central court of his palace. The physicians had sewn Troilus' head and body parts back onto his beaten and bruised body. "My son. My precious son," he whispered to the gentle breeze sweeping along the stone. His raw grief dusted his eyes, squeezing his chest of breath. "Why have you allowed Achilles to defile my son? Innocent as he was of this war?" He tilted his head back, scanning the gloomy skies for a sign, but the gods gave no answer to the king. *Troy is now doomed.*

He closed his eyes, willing the sharp pain tearing his heart from his chest to stop. But, instead of relief, the past haunted him with images and sounds long forgotten. Hecuba's wretched sobbing when he ripped the newborn babe from her arms. The child's wrinkled, purpled face screaming up at him. Agelaus' wide-eyed disbelief upon hearing the royal command to expose the child. And worst of all, the seer's menacing and angry scowl that the babe wasn't being discarded quickly enough. *The gods curse me. Task me with killing one son, to save another. Where is the true choice in that?* Priam sighed heavily, his fists balled at his side, while a sliver of anger at the gods slipped to clench his jaw.

Hecuba, moving as a living wraith, whispered behind him, "This is all Achilles' fault."

Priam's head sank to his chest. "I do not know what else we could have done."

The queen's black gown trailed behind her like smoke, her veil a dark curtain behind which her icy voice cracked with new rage. "Achilles' life is forfeit for the pains he has brought to our household. The gods will not protect a defiler. The son of Thetis will not escape the wrath of Apollo's silver bow. Or my vengeance."

"Apollo does not care what Achilles has done. Look around you, wife. Do you see the god striding across the sky to smite the cursed Greeks at their beached ships? Does flame and smoke rise from their camp? There …" he pointed with a shaking finger at the pyre, "there lies our son! Dead. Defiled. Desecrated. Even at Apollo's feet, Troilus was not safe from that murdering, blood thirsty cur."

Hecuba stepped next to her husband's side, taking his weathered hand in her cold one. "Do not lose hope that the gods will deliver Achilles into our hands. Their ways are mysterious, unknown to us. Their will is whispered as a wind passing our ear … Do not lose hope."

Priam stared down at his wife. Her dark eyes were unusually calm. Lifting his free hand, he touched her pale cheek. "Strange words of comfort fall from your lips. Why do you think Apollo would help us now? Do you forget his will was the root of our sorrow? What scheme is brewing in your iron heart?"

"Justice. You may be king, but you do not possess knowledge of all things."

"Only the gods may weigh justice." The king shook his head. "You will bring more grief on our heads."

Hecuba's laughter rang shrilly against the stone. "Death and grief are the pillars of our threshold, or have you not noticed? Death and grief drink our wine and eat our bread, unwelcomed guests at every meal. I do not fear them. I intend to stop them."

"Please, Hecuba, I beg you—"

The queen slipped her hand from his, disgust dripping from her tongue when she said, "Do not beg. It is … *unkingly*." Turning abruptly, she walked away.

Priam watched her, floating like a cloud of doom across the courtyard until she disappeared into the shadows of the palatial pillars. He knew Achilles was to blame for Troilus' death, but he could not escape his guilt for bringing the war in the first place. What if he had not let Hesione go that day long ago? What if he had forced Paris to give Helen back instead of allowing her to stay? What if he had just killed Paris in the first place? *The gods fuck me with my lots. I cannot have vengeance or peace.*

For twelve days the Trojans feasted and held games to honor the youngest prince of Troy. And on the twelfth night the funeral pyre was lit. Hecuba stood alongside Priam as they watched the orange flames lick at the piled wood, growing into a roaring wall of fire, consuming the body of their beloved son. Neither the queen nor the king took their eyes from the horrific sight of Troilus disappearing into ash. The song of mourning flew from the lips of old women, floating into the dark night like a thousand cawing ravens. The shrill sound shivered up the spines of all who could hear their cries.

As the flames died, and the grieving crowd dispersed, Hektor watched his long-suffering parents reluctantly walk away, fading into the surrounding night. He wrapped his arm around Andromache's waist. Feeling the roundness of their child secure within her belly filled him with as much joy as fear. Theirs had been the lot of grief and sorrow regarding children, and now in the shadow of their youths the gods had granted them a final blessing. *Let it be, Apollo. Let me fade into song with a son to hear. Let him grow strong …*

Squeezing her tightly, Hektor asked, "How is your mother, my love?"

Andromache leaned into her husband's embrace. "As good as she can be for having lost everything."

"She has not lost all, my love. She yet has you."

The princess sighed deeply, her sadness evident. "I do not know if it is enough. Achilles murdered my entire family before her eyes. It haunts her still."

"In time, the horrors of war will fade. Trust me. She will heal and find joy again." He tenderly kissed her forehead. "We will find joy again."

"I hope these Greeks tire of war and leave us all in peace."

Hektor looked out in to the night, watching the dying embers fade. "That they will never do."

As they stood, surrounded by the growing silence, Hektor caught a glimpse of Paris and Helen behind a pillar. They were locked in a passionate embrace, oblivious to anything but themselves. He sneered into the dark. As the bloody war had consumed most of the Troad lands, he found that in his heart he blamed Paris most of all.

LEMNOS

Lykaon wiped his hands on his rough-spun chiton, and then picked up the tray of fat figs and plump dates. He carried them to Euneus, a portly man with a puffy face and a permanently pursed mouth.

"Hurry up, boy," Euneus demanded. "You move too slowly for my taste."

Lykaon cringed. Euneus' tastes leaned toward the despicable and depraved. Since he'd been in Euneus' service, he'd suspected many barbaric rituals. The rounded, dead eyed stare of slaves being led from mysterious chambers haunted him. Shrill screams and desperate pleading floated in his mind, even in the quiet of the day. And the blood he'd scrub away would discolor his hands for days. Some days, he worried that Euneus was plotting some nefarious deed involving him. Why else pay so much for a royal hostage?

"Apologies, my lord." The deference bittered his tongue. He silently cursed Patrokles and Achilles both for his current situation. *If not for them, I would be safe in Troy by now. Why? Why did I have to go at that moment for the branches?*

"I told you to clean yourself up, did I not?" Euneus growled angrily.

Lykaon looked down at his clothes. "Apologies, my lord. It is the only chiton I have without stain."

"Pour my wine. I expect my guest will be arriving shortly."

Ever a diligent servant, Lykaon did as he was bid, praying to the gods that he would remain unblemished and unsoiled by this man.

Do not let me die in this place, Apollo. Zeus. If either of you has ears to hear me. If any of you gods hear me. Lykaon recognized the name Eetion, and wondered what an ally of King Priam was doing traveling this far west. He'd been bought and sold several times between Thasos and Samothrace before landing in the house of Euneus back on Lemnos where his nightmare had begun years ago.

Before the quiet of morning turned to the bustle of mid-day, the expected guest arrived, a small caravan trailing behind him. Through a narrow window, Lykaon spotted Eetion. He was a thin man wearing the heavily curled beard of lower Mysia.

What does he want with Euneus? The bell rang for his service. *These fucking western barbarians.*

"I see your journey brings you well-endowed with ... ransom."

Lykaon's ears rang. *Ransom?* He stepped behind a tall, blue marble column at the chamber's entrance. A surge of hope heightened every sound in the room; the clatter of trays of fruit being passed between guests, the shuffle of the women's soft leather sandals on the marble floor. *Could he be here on account of me? By the gods, if he is I swear—*

Euneus cleared his throat grotesquely. "Lykaon!"

Lykaon hurried into the chamber. With his head bowed, he tried discretely to catch a closer glimpse of Eetion. "My lord?"

"So, this is Priam's son?" Eetion asked, plucking a date from a tray and plopping it into his mouth. A servant girl proffered the Imbrosian guest another cup of pale wine. "How do I know this is not some trickery?"

"I assure you, my *lord* Eetion, he *is* Lykaon."

"I have been chasing imposters of Priam's son around the Aegean. I must be sure."

Lykaon touched the slight dip in his chin, and lifting his head brought his full face into view. "I bear the mark," he said quietly.

Eetion set his cup down, and came forward. He examined Lykaon's jaw, turning it this way and that. His eyes widened, not so much because he knew he'd found the prince ... more so because of the wealth he stood to collect upon safe delivery of the young man. "It *is* the mark of Priam. All princes of Troy bear it, whether birthed by the queen or not. Who is your mother?"

"Laothoë, daughter of Aletes. Ruler of the Leleges people north of the Simoeis River."

Euneus clapped his meaty hands together, licking his thick lips in anticipation of extending his wealth. His ponderous weight rolled with his giddy laughter. "What is your offer, then?"

"Three hundred head of cattle."

Euneus sputtered. "That is all? No gold? Silver? Surely, Priam will pay handsomely for his return."

"He will. But my wealth is not inexhaustible. If you desire more, return him to Priam yourself."

"Fine!" Euneus grumbled. "Fine. Take him. He eats too much."

Eetion stood up. "Your hospitality grows thin, Euneus. Come, Lykaon. It is passed time you are reunited with your father."

As they walked from the courtyard of Euneus' home into the streets, Lykaon could scarce believe his fortune. "How long until we reach Troy?

"We must sail north and make our way to the Sea of Marmara, then south to Arisbe. If the gods are with us, we will make it to Troy unscathed."

"Why not sail straight for Troy? It is but a short distance from Lemnos."

Eetion shook his head vigorously. "Although the Black Shields and their commander remain in the south, Agamemnon has returned to the main encampment at the Bay of Troy. Their warships patrol the Dardanelles in the north. We must travel farther north. On land. Anything else is too risky. If they discover us …"

The hope Priam's son felt dwindled. "We will die."

Eetion laughed. "If we are fortunate, that is *all* that will happen to us."

TWO
truth in silence

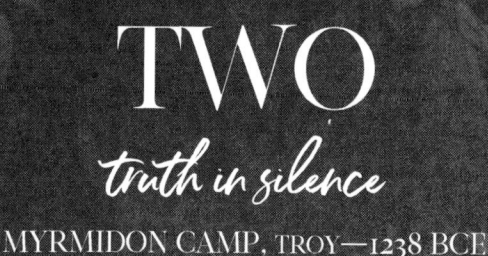

MYRMIDON CAMP, TROY—1238 BCE

Achilles eyed Briseis over the rim of his cup, as she pulled a slender thread through the soft wool of his tunic. He'd torn the hem sparring with Patrokles. "Your fingers … they're graceful."

"Callused."

"Did your mother instruct you to work the linen, or some other woman?"

Briseis didn't bother looking up, but continued mending. "I'm an expert weaver." She stopped, then met Achilles' gaze. "Was an expert weaver." She resumed stitching the seam.

"Why, then, do you not weave for me?"

"I do everything for you, Achilles."

The Golden Warrior sipped quietly at his wine. Her words rang true enough, but her tone pricked his heart. His instincts told him she hid some truth from him. He would flush it out, as a hound does a bird. "Why do you never speak of your life in Lyrnessus?"

Briseis bit her bottom lip. Achilles watched as her shoulders rose and fell. A brief silence spread between them. "Why do you care now, after all these years, about my life ... before all this?"

"What is *all this* to you, Briseis?"

"You. Here. All of it."

Setting his cup down, Achilles leaned back in his chair. Of all the women he had known, she intrigued him most. She shared very little of her thoughts with him. Her body most willingly, but never her full heart.

"I'll fetch more wine."

"No. I've no desire for more wine."

Briseis laughed softly. "Are you certain you're *my* Achilles?"

Achilles came around the table and stood before her. After taking the tunic from her hands, he set it in her basket. Then, he knelt, taking her knees in his hands. "Tell me, Briseis. Tell me everything." *How do I tell her that soon I will die?*

Tears filled her eyes. "I can't."

"You must."

Briseis pressed her lips tightly together, as a solitary tear escaped her eye. It streaked down her cheek, pooling at the corner of her mouth. "No," she whispered.

He brushed the tear from her mouth with his thumb. "I will begin for you." Reaching a hand to her face, he cradled her cheek as much in love as control. "I've kissed your entire body." His hand slid down the side of her neck, over her breasts, and then to her stomach. "I know you've carried children, yet my seed has never taken hold. I'm fairly certain I've fathered more sons than Neoptolemus."

More tears trailed down Briseis' stoic face.

Achilles whispered roughly, but not without tenderness, "I wish for there to be no secrets between us."

Briseis' body shook as memories she'd buried struggled to free themselves to the light. "When you took me from that life, you took the memories as well." Growing angry, because it was both a lie and the truth, she asked, "Isn't it enough?"

"No, it isn't."

Wiping her eyes, she said, "Tell me your truth first. Why now? You've never cared before, yet the past was there to probe. Why now?"

The fire in his blue eyes softened. *Truth. Tell her the truth.* "Because, Briseis ... Death is coming for me."

Briseis' chin quivered and she slowly shook her head. Grudgingly, she released the smallest truth, hoping it was enough. If she allowed the entire story to spill, she would die of heartbreak. "I had a daughter once. She died of a fever. There's nothing more to tell."

She has lost so much, because of me. "This is war, Briseis. You know I had no choice."

Achilles' lover scoffed at his thin regret. "There's always a choice, Achilles. War leaves only the bitter ones to swallow."

"When I'm gone, perhaps Patrok—"

"Say no more, Achilles."

He reluctantly released her knees. "As you wish. I am for bed. Come. Join me."

In the darkness of the tent, Briseis lay facing away from her lover whose gentle breathing told her he truly slept. Now, she was free to weep. Weep for the daughter she lost years ago. Weep because she would never feel another child inside of her. Weep for the life she had all but forgotten. However, her true torment lay in a truth burning inside of her heart whenever she looked at Achilles. One so private and painful, she dared only to dwell on it during the deepest, darkest hours of the night. She loved Achilles as she'd never loved Mynes. She loved him more than she'd loved anyone, save Phila. *Why do I love him?* She rolled to her back. *He calls me wife, yet I am not.* And that was the bitterest portion of her current existence to swallow.

THREE

dust of grief

BAY OF TROY—1238 BCE

The Great King reclined behind a huge trestle table of heavy timber. Menelaus, scowling deeply, sat to his right, while Nestor, enjoying the personal attention of his slave woman, Hecamede, reclined easily at his left. The lesser kings and princes—Odysseus, Diomedes, Ajax of Telemon, and Ajax the Lesser—sat on either side of Agamemnon's brother and chief counselor. Achilles and Patrokles, enjoying the company of each other and already into their second cups of spiced wine, sat at the far end of the table. Piles of fresh bread, platters of split figs drizzled in honey and dusted with ground almonds, and bowls of dates stuffed with soft cheeses lined every table. Torches burned brightly against the growing night. Slave women danced bare breasted with golden chains jangling about their waists. The men grabbed at their flesh as they swirled by, scenting the air with jasmine and roses. Men hungered for the honeyed treasure between their legs. The whores' tents would be full when the stars' brilliance waned in the purple dawn.

When Chryses, flanked by Apollo's priests bearing staffs wound with wreaths and fluttering golden ribbons, approached Agamemnon in the royal pavilion, the horde's silence was so heavy the crackling sound of the spits roasting fatted meat could be heard carrying on the soft wind. A sea of Greeks surrounded Apollo's chief priest, enough men to drown him in his own blood, yet he'd walked without fear as those with the Shining God's favor did.

The priest bowed deeply to Agamemnon. "I have traveled far, Great King, to speak with you on my daughter's behalf."

Agamemnon nodded. A thin slave boy whispered into the Great King's ear. "Indeed, you have. Chryse is far to the south." The king swept his hand across the assembly. "What do you wish from me, priest of Apollo?"

"I ask only for the return of my daughter, Great King." He bowed more deeply than before. "She is precious to me, as are all daughters to their fathers."

The priest's words stung the old wound of Iphigenia's sacrifice. In a flash, her blood soaking the sand at Palamedes' feet, her frightened eyes begging him for mercy, and her final glance of resignation rose up as a ghastly reminder of the price of war. *She knew my iron will would not be moved. She knew me, in the end. Who I am in the darkness of my heart.* "You ask a great deal."

Chryses indicated to the chests laden with treasures that his subordinate priests carried. "I have brought the ransom of a princess to prove my good will and that of the god, Apollo. I swear by the god's silver bow that I will pray and sacrifice daily on behalf of you, Agamemnon, and your brother, Menelaus. That you will bring the city of Troy to its knees and reap the harvest of gold within her vaulted, shining walls ... sailing safely home to your own lands."

"All this for a woman?"

"My *only* daughter, my lord. Returning her *honors* Apollo, son of Zeus."

The assembly rose up in cheer, each man thinking not so much of his share of the gold, but more so the blessing. Perhaps, with this priest on their side, the war would soon end and they could return home. For home had become more alluring than gold to men weary of a war without end, and the passing years had turned their *true* wives into goddesses in their memories—their beauty and voices growing softer as the desire to sail home grew stronger.

"Take the gold!"

"Accept it!"

"We can sail for home."

"Defeat Troy!"

"Apollo! Apollo! Apollo!"

The men pounded their eager fists on their tables, jostling wine cups and bouncing bread from platters. Their unified voices rose up, shaking the quiet fury of their king.

Agamemnon, flushing crimson with anger, stood slowly from his seat. He gazed out at his men. *Traitors, all of them. They abandon me on the thin promises of a stranger.* Far across the pavilion, he caught sight of a pale saffron gown fluttering in a ghostly breeze. *Iphigenia?*

Her silver voice rang in his ears. *"Will you let me die for nothing, Father?"*

He froze, as his hardened eyes stung with unshed tears. He ground his jaw tightly shut, blinked, and looked again. The specter had vanished. Raising his rough hands, ringed with gold and gemstones, he quieted the assembly.

"Who are you, Chryses, priest, tempting me and my men with your honeyed words? You would pray for our demise once your daughter was returned to you. I know you hate us, as much as we despise you Easterners. I will not return Astynome. Why should I? Every father would beg every one of my men for return of their family. It is our right to take as slaves those we capture. You wish my men to give up this right? Take their prizes from them? She was given to me by right of my valor."

The priest stepped back, astonished by Agamemnon's refusal. "But, my lord, she … *Apollo*—"

"Where was your god when she was taken? If he intended to save her, he would never have allowed her capture."

Nestor squirmed uncomfortably, visibly shaken by the king's blasphemy against the shining god. "My lord, perhaps, caution—"

The Great King wheeled on his advisor, his crimson cape swirling about his waist, and roared, "You take the side of this priest over me?"

"No … no, but the gods—"

Agamemnon spat. "Speak no more on my behalf, Nestor. And as for you, *Chryses*, get out of my sight with your beggar's words and your dull god. I will *never* give up the girl. She will die an old maid in Mycenae in my palace far from this pitiful place, weaving my cloth and wrapping her legs around my thighs." He took his seat, staring intently at Chryses, who'd paled whiter than sea foam. "And leave your gold," he sneered. "I have need of it."

The priest signaled his acolytes to set the ransom chests down. They eyed him with suspicion and surprise. "Do as he commands." Without a word Chryses backed away from the royal dais, until he and his entourage faded into the darkness beyond the feasting

Greeks. He was in no position to challenge the Great King. Retreat and plead his case to Apollo were now his only recourse.

Since Queen Mira's ransom and return by Achilles, she'd been guested in King Priam's palace, attended by the royal physicians and priests. The horrors of the day Achilles sacked Thebe tormented her, and she could find no peace in wakefulness or sleep. Her son-in-law, Hektor, had ordered guard hounds to protect her at all times, giving her some measure of security. Standing there, on her balcony, with ragged-furred beasts lazing at her feet and Apollo's light warming the air, the echo of death coming for her lost city haunted her. The rows of rooftops and refugee tents stretched out as far as her eye could see, and beyond that she imagined the swirling dust to be Achilles' Myrmidons. She shuddered in the bright light of the new day.

A gentle knock at the door stirred the hounds to growl and saunter into the main chamber. Queen Mira turned. "Who is there?"

"It is I, Mother," Andromache answered.

The queen called the hounds to her side. "Enter."

Andromache entered quietly, careful not to startle the beastly guards camped near her mother's feet. "It is good to see you up and about your day."

The queen embraced her daughter, cupping Andromache's cheeks in her thin hands. "It is always good to rest my weary eyes on your lovely face. You're all I have left tethering me to this world. You and this child." She placed her hand on Andromache's belly. "He is healthy and fat."

"The midwife says it will be soon. But, for the rest, do not speak such dark words, Mother. You will call down the gods' wrath. You frighten me."

"The gods have already unleashed the worst on our family. You did not witness ... with my own eyes ..." Queen Mira's face contorted in agony, but she spilled no tears. *My grief is dust in my mouth and in my eyes.*

Andromache took her mother's hand in hers, leading her to the couches set near the hearth. "Let us not speak of that day. Of Achilles. Or anything unpleasant. Shall I pour you a cup of wine?"

"It is the only pleasure left to us, is it not?"

"Mother," Andromache laughed nervously, "that is not true."

Taking the cup of pale honeyed wine mixed with cinnamon from her daughter, Queen Mira drank deeply. "Then, you have more gratitude for this life than I."

Andromache shook her head in concern. "You trouble me with your heavy words. What have the physicians revealed regarding your illness?"

"That only time and the gods would still my racing heart."

"Small comfort, their words."

"Small indeed."

The two sat sipping their wine in silence. Joyful times of extended feasting had long since faded into memory. The city had grown too poor caring for the ever-growing numbers of refugees to host extravagant events. Mournful ballads replaced the boastful songs of the glorious deeds of heroes. The sound of weeping and wailing swept through the air most days as word inevitably wound its way to the citadel of recent deaths at the hands of the Western invaders.

"Do you have any word from Hektor about when the war will

end?"

Andromache sighed into her now empty cup. She pressed a palm to her temple to still the mild dizziness. "No."

Queen Mira shivered as thunder cracked and the lightning flashed above her. "Did you hear that, my daughter?" she asked, her voice shaking with fear.

Andromache strained to hear anything out of the ordinary. "I hear only the fire crackling in the hearth."

But the lost queen stared with glazed eyes at her daughter. *Why does the shadow of death swallow my beautiful girl? Who wields the bloody blade?* Her wine cup slipped from her fingers, clanging loudly against the tile.

"Mother!" Andromache screamed, as the guard hounds rushed to their mistress' side. "Mother!"

Within moments, Hektor's men filled the chamber.

Andromache commanded sharply, "Get the physicians! Call Hektor to me!" She cradled her mother's head in her lap, freely weeping. "Mother, don't leave me. I beg you stay with me." She gently brushed a stray lock of hair from her mother's pale cheek. In that moment, Andromache became once again a young girl desperate to remain at her mother's side, frightened of a world without her. "Stay with me."

FOUR
Apollo's silver bow
OLYMPUS—1238 BCE

As Apollo pulled his sacred chariot across the sky, breaking a new dawn with streaks of rose and gold, a clamor of prayer assaulted his ears. *Apollo, I pray most ardently for your revenge.* He cast his glittering eye down through misty clouds to the blue and green sphere below. Focusing his godly sight, he landed on the priest, Chryses, slaughtering fat rams and cattle on an altar trimmed with fresh olive branches. Beyond the altar, he saw a hundred spits roasting the rich offerings of the priest. *Hear me, Lord of the Silver Bow. If ever my sacrifices pleased you, I pray you hear me.*

The god focused closer on the priest, seeing his face clearly now in his mind. "Chryses, I hear you." Apollo, having set his blazing orb aloft and freeing the mighty stallions from his chariot, flew down the high rampart of Olympus, through the downy layers of the heavens and over towering pines, to the south of Troy.

He found the priest bent over a bloody altar, sweating and

weeping as he pulled his blade across another goat's throat. *"I hear you, Chryses."*

The hairs on the back of Chryses' neck stood on end, as a heavy presence pressed his shoulder down, forcing his eyes to remain shut. "My lord," he whispered hoarsely.

"Speak, mortal, for I am pleased with your offering."

"I wish the return of my daughter, Astynome."

The Shining One dug heavy fingers into the priest's neck. *"Astynome, yes, I have seen her. Who has taken her?"*

"The Great King, Agamemnon."

The god laughed against his ear. *"He will not appear so great when I am done with him. He will beg for mercy and return your beloved daughter."*

Apollo released Chryses, disappearing into the night.

The priest collapsed at the altar, rubbing his neck from the shooting pains down both arms. "Gratitude, my lord, Apollo."

TROY
THE GREEK ENCAMPMENT

The shining god bore down on the beachhead stacked with rows of bleached hulls resting idly along the sandy shore. His blazing eyes scanned the camp on the verge of waking. Men wiping the dullness of wine-induced sleep from their eyes stumbled from tents to relieve themselves, pissing away the night's wine. Women bustled about cook fires, roasting fish and fowl and stirring steaming pots of gruel. Children darted from tent to tent, waking the men still abed.

Apollo knelt against the firmament, removing his mighty bow from his sacred shoulder, and pulled three stinging arrows from the quiver at his hip. With icy fingers, he pulled the first of thousands of fatal strikes taut against his glorious cheek. He unleashed his plague on mortals and beasts alike. The god's laughter shook the ground; boulders tumbled down the craggy cliffs before the Greek's camp, while the ocean churned in chaos behind them.

Death and darkness waited for them all like a coiled snake ready to strike from the shadows. *Agamemnon! Your pride and doom walk hand in hand! All shall know me and fear me.*

Queen Hecuba entered Apollo's temple, her veil of black gauze fluttering behind her like smoke trailing from a fire. With bare feet, she stepped into the sacred chamber of the god. The queen stood before the golden statue of Apollo. "I pray you hear me, Apollo, the Shining One. Cause of my misery and my joy."

An old priestess appeared. Her wrinkled hands reached for the queen's garments. "Prepare for the ritual."

Hecuba stepped back from the altar, extending her hands at her sides. The priestess silently undressed her. She folded the queen's clothes, placing them at the statue's feet. The attendant sprinkled myrrh into a basin of warm water, then bathed the queen with it, covering her entire length with the fragrant liquid.

"He will hear you, my lady," the priestess said, as she finished.

Hecuba shivered in the empty chamber. "Gratitude."

The old woman smiled wryly. "Apollo provides what he will, and takes with equal relish." She indicated to a section of black marble floor. "Lie down. Close your eyes and keep them closed, unless he commands you otherwise."

The queen obeyed without argument. As she settled into position, a sliver of fear chilled her heart. *What if he refuses me? Will he remember what he sowed within me?*

Flames leapt from the silver bowl at the statue's feet, catching on the queen's gown, burning it to cinders and filling the chamber with thin, gray smoke. The ground beneath her vibrated and shook, until slowly Hecuba's body rose into the air. The heat of a thousand burning tongues licked her flesh, and heavy hands pressed into her soft flesh. She felt her thighs being pried open, as a warm presence shifted between her legs.

The god's silken voice enticed her. "You seek the pleasure of my pain a second time?" He slid a hot hand between her legs, slipping his fingers inside of her. "Not a virgin, but still beautiful to behold, Queen Hecuba." He tasted her nectar on his fingers. "As sweet as I remember."

Hecuba fought to keep her eyes closed against his blinding presence. Her voice croaked with the smoke and heat when she replied, "I am grateful for your favor."

"As you should be." The god bent his head to Hecuba's sacred flesh, dragging his tongue through the delicate folds. Hecuba moaned, arching her hips to meet his touch. "Your husband should not have abandoned you for his whores and concubines." Apollo yanked her body to the edge of the altar and plunged his full length into her.

Hecuba screamed in ecstasy, as she wrapped her legs around his buttocks, his skin burning hers, and pulled him into her. "Fuck me, Lord Apollo."

The god growled his pleasure, plowing his sacrifice until her entire body shook with pain and pleasure, and her love flow spilled against his cock, dripping onto the altar. Only then did he release his fiery silver seed into his willing vessel. "You have pleased me, once again, sweet queen."

Hecuba lay before the god, sweating, aching, and exhausted. Her voice a mere whisper, she pleaded, "Help me with my revenge. For *our* son."

"Troilus," the god said. "I regret that I could not save him from Achilles. That was Athena's doing. I could not risk open war with her." Apollo extended a hand. "You may look upon me, Hecuba."

Apollo's skin shimmered in the golden light. Curls of silver-veined crystal tumbled about his shoulders. His eyes shone with azure and orange flame. Hecuba gazed upon his naked form, as his seed oozed between her thighs.

"You gods have your wars, as mortals do. Let me be our son's avenger."

"Achilles is chosen by Zeus. Protected by Athena. Only Aphrodite hates Achilles … perhaps, because he is more beautiful than Ares and she cannot bed him." He laughed. "Even we immortals have our weaknesses, it seems."

"Help me, Lord Apollo. Help me be the instrument to bring Achilles to his knees. He has killed our son. *Your* son."

"I had no hand in raising the boy. Priam believes him to be of his flesh and blood?"

Hecuba nodded. "I spoke to no one of our union, as you commanded." She recalled the sadistic ritual Apollo performed with her. The dancing flames of blue and gold, entwining limbs with strangers, and the pulsing cocks of hooded priests building within her a great need, until the final ecstatic union with Apollo. Her belly had swelled with Troilus after the encounter, for only a god could have stirred her withering womb to life. The child had been her last and greatest joy, even more so than the return of Paris. Over the years, since Paris' return, she'd come to realize why Apollo had commanded the child be killed. The abandonment of her babe had marred her very soul, yet his return brought only bitterness and a different regret. But Troilus, he was a gift from the Shining One and didn't deserve the cruel death inflicted by Achilles.

Apollo sighed, if a god can sigh. "I will do as you request. But come no more to my temple. What we conspire is against the Father, and that is a war I cannot win."

Hecuba rose from the altar and approached the god, his silvery seed still dripping between her thighs. Kneeling, she kissed his bare feet. "Gratitude, Lord Apollo. I will hold you forever in my heart."

Apollo laughed, taking her head in his hands, and lifted her face to his. "Hecuba, your heart is iron. Go. Speak of this no more."

The chamber light flickered to darkness and the god disappeared from sight. Hecuba stood, naked and used and grateful. *Achilles will be mine.* She laughed as the priestess cleansed her body. *Achilles will be mine.*

Paris admired the wide expanse of clay roofs and bustling streets winding around the lower city. He had never imagined such greatness when he was merely a bull herder. Idle thoughts of the golden city with towering walls were nothing more than that. "Perhaps, I should bring the boy here. I don't even remember how many seasons have past since his birth."

Helen's eyes widened slightly. "Why would you bring your son here? Is he not like his mother? A child of the woods and streams?"

Staring out at the golden glow of Apollo's light spreading across the city below, Paris shrugged and hung his head. "He's my only child."

Helen clenched her jaw. "Are you blaming me for not giving you more sons and daughters for Troy?"

Paris turned to face her. "I'm not blaming you for anything. But have you never wondered if this isn't a curse from the gods?"

"Hektor and Andromache have no—"

"You compare us to them?" Paris scoffed, "By the gods, my brother has no great love for me, but how can I blame him? Look at us, Helen. Look at what we are. What has Hektor ever done to the gods that he and Andromache should suffer so much?"

Angry tears stung Helen's eyes because the truth couldn't be denied. Their love was tainted by the goddess. Her entire life had been tainted by Aphrodite's gift of beauty. And her beauty had only wrought misery and death. *If only I could bear a son for Paris.*

"I'll send a messenger for Oenone in the morning."

"What? And drag her to the city with the boy in tow? Have you forgotten we are at war? Do you really think your son is safer here, than under the protection of the woods? The Greeks care nothing for the empty forests and meadows. However, if they should discover you have a son, his life … wouldn't it be in jeopardy?"

"Troy won't fall to the Greeks, Helen. Ever."

"Yet, how many years have past and still they remain. More ruthless. More vicious. More hungry for home." Helen laughed softly. "If you believe Agamemnon will leave before Troy is looted of its treasures and smoke fills the skies, you are more ignorant of war and the Greeks than I supposed."

"Behind your beauty, Helen, you are the cruelest woman."

"One of us must remain level headed."

Stretching out his hand to her, Paris beckoned. "Come. Lay with me and I will show you a level head."

Reluctantly, Helen obliged his offer to once again fuck their miseries away. It's how they resolved all their pain and frustrations. *I can't tell him about Corythus now. He will cast me aside for that nymph … send me back to Menelaus. I can never go back to Sparta. Ever.*

FIVE
arrows of war
TROY—1238 BCE

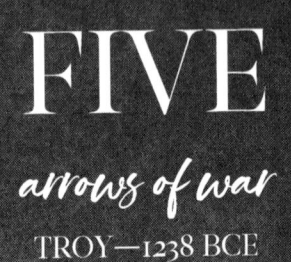

Queen Mira reached a pale, fragile hand to her daughter's cheek. "I still see the shy girl praying before Hera. Fearful Prince Hektor would not love her. How strong you have become since then."

"That feels a lifetime ago," Andromache said softly. "So much has happened since then."

"I never thought to outlive all my sons and your father. Knowing his murderer burnt his armor with him gives me no peace."

Andromache placed a cool, damp cloth across her mother's forehead. "Shah, Mother. Do not dwell on those dark days. The sadness saps your strength."

The queen placed her hand on her daughter's. "It is more than sadness, my sweet girl."

"What do you mean, Mother?"

"I pray the gods bring a quiet end to my days."

"No!" Andromache shook her head. "You must not ask for such a thing."

The queen caught sight of her pale reflection in her daughter's eyes. "I have no desire to witness more death."

Andromache shivered with the faint flash of dust and glittering gold. "Troy will not fall."

Queen Mira's eyes, gray and grief-stricken, filled with compassion for her daughter. She realized her prayer would place the burden of heartache on Andromache. "You have suffered much, my sweet girl. Too much. We all have."

"I understand why you wish for death. But I am yet here. Troy stands strong. Hektor will prevail. He must."

"You have not seen this Achilles." Queen Mira managed a weak smile. "I have lived long enough, my gentle daughter, to see that you have earned the respect and love of the Golden Prince. His love for you shines clearly in his eyes. That is enough for me." The queen sighed. "Andromache, light the torches."

The princess glanced around the chamber. "Mother, they are all lit."

The queen shook her head weakly against the pillow. "I am coming! Some days he has no patience."

"Who has no patience, Mother?"

Annoyed, the queen pulled her hand from her daughter's. "Your father. Who else? Always pressing me to hurry. The wedding wagons are loaded. Are you ready, my girl?"

"Mother," Andromache said, cautiously, "that was years ago."

Reaching toward the foot of her bed, Queen Mira said, "You know how your father hates waiting." The quietness of death settled over Andromache's mother, the life-light faded from her eyes, and her hands slid slowly to her sides.

The torch flames flickered wildly then stilled. Andromache sat silent for a moment, disbelief weaving through her. "No. No. No. Nooo!"

Hektor found his wife draped over her mother's body, weeping like a child. The royal physicians stood helplessly watching. The prince wrapped his arms around his wife, pulling her tight into his embrace. Andromache's tears wet his tunic and her sobs filled his own heart with tender sorrow. "Be at peace, my love. She suffers no more."

Andromache looked up at her husband, her face blotched with anguish. "How can I ever have peace? I am alone in the world now."

"You will always have me, my love, and our child. You will never be alone."

Andromache sobbed against Hektor's shoulder, sinking fully into his embrace. "I pray the gods will it so." Again, the flash of dust and gold burned behind her eyes. Her mother's fear of Achilles unnerved her. If he was as terrifying as she said, then Hektor might not survive. *I beg you gods keep my husband safe from Achilles. I beg you.*

A searing pain ripped through her belly. "No, by the gods, no. Not now," she cried out. A warm gush of water splashed the floor.

Without word or question, Hektor lifted his wife in his arms and carried her to their chamber. His voice boomed through the halls for the midwife and court physicians.

Corythus inhaled the sweet scent of Helen as she leaned across him, reaching for the wine on the table. His loins pulsed to life at the slight brush of her soft breast against his chest. Even through his chiton, he could feel the tip of a hardened nipple. He hated himself for being drawn to his father's wife. He'd heard many whispers about her, and none of them flattering. The entire court knew that Queen Hecuba held her in disdain, as much as Paris loved her. But watching her full lips part over the rim of her cup made him wonder what kissing her might feel like. Taste like.

Helen sipped her wine, wiping a small red drop at the corner of her mouth with a delicate fingertip. "How is your training going?"

Corythus shrugged. "It is not easy, Helen." Her name rolled smoothly over his tongue.

"No, I should think not. But, your father needs a warrior for a son, not a flower gatherer."

He bristled at Helen's not-so-subtle reference to his mother. "When will I be ready to meet my father?"

Helen sighed. "Soon, my son. Soon."

Picking nervously at the leather cuff on his wrist, Corythus asked, "What if he refuses to accept me?"

Helen smiled brightly, lifting a single eyebrow. "How could he not accept you? Handsome and strong as you are." She placed a hand against her flat belly. "You'll be his heir," she said, reluctantly.

"I don't care for his riches."

"No," she said, abruptly. "No, you would not."

Corythus hung his head slightly. "I must return to my training…"

Helen stood, her gown falling like sheer water over her body. "Yes. Go. I'll summon you again." She extended her hand to him, letting a delicate finger slide down his forearm. "Come, training is not as harsh as that."

He took her hand and stood. Before he realized what was

happening, Helen leaned up and kissed him. Against his will, his lips parted and his tongue darted quickly into her mouth. He'd wanted this, but had resisted such thoughts by pushing them into the dark. He pulled back, flustered and embarrassed. "Apologies … I—" Corythus ran from her.

Helen watched his chiton billow behind him in his haste. Maybe Paris was right. The gods cursed her womb. A single tear slid down her cheek. *It's not my fault the goddess filled me with false love.* She wondered if Paris regretted leaving the nymph and his son behind. If only she could get with child. Pouring more wine, she walked to the sunlit balcony. With the rise of Apollo, her bloody flow had began, dashing her hope, once again, that Paris' seed had at last taken hold within her. Recalling Corythus' awkward kiss, she smiled coyly to herself. *Perhaps, the son can do what the father cannot.*

Achilles grunted to himself. *I fight alongside them all. Worry over them as a mother worries over her children. Yet, I'm helpless to protect them against the gods.* Achilles glanced up as the sky brightened, as Apollo spurred his horses at a furious pace, raking the sky with the blood-red fingers. *Another deadly dawn.* He scowled. For days, death had stalked man and beast alike. First, the dogs and then the mules and horses fell to a bloody flux, ending only when their eyes rolled back, revealing the yellowed orbs. After the first beasts laid yet unburied and unburnt, the men fell with the same illness. *Fucking gods*, Achilles thought as he piled wood into funeral pyres to burn the bodies. The stench of vomit, shit, and death fouled the air, sickening the living who stumbled about with fever and loose bowels. "Nine fucking, stinking days!" he roared, throwing the last of a few logs onto the most recent pyre. He shouted at men passing by, "Where is your *Great King* now? Abed? Asleep? Drunk on wine while we suffer, sending the dead to the Underworld?"

A swirl of sand pelted him. The hairs on his arms stood on end. Achilles grinned wickedly, as he snarled, "What do you wish this time, Athena?"

"I am not Athena, but Hera."

"You are all the same to me."

"Dangerous words from the mouth of a mortal."

"Look around you, Goddess. You have worse in mind? Better Zeus finishes us off with a flash of his lightning bolt, than let us suffer more of this."

"Apollo, not Zeus, sent this plague."

The Golden Warrior bellowed, "Why? What have we done that the Trojans have not?"

"I have no desire to continue your suffering. Call the Myrmidons and the others to assembly. Call Kalchus to speak."

Achilles balled his fists at his side. "What prophesy can he give that you cannot?" He waited for a response, but none came. *The fucking gods*, he thought, storming off across the camp in search of Patrokles.

He found his companion among the sick and dying, administering poultices for fevered foreheads and water for parched throats. "Patrokles. A word."

Patrokles glanced up from a patient whose mouth hung dryly open.

Achilles noted the fat flies buzzing above the man's face. Peleus' voice echoed in his mind, *"Close your mouth, Achilles, or flies will put worms in your belly.*"

"You should press his lips together with wine."

Patrokles returned to squeezing the greenish ooze from a cankerous sore on the man's arm. "He does not need wine, cousin."

Achilles shrugged. "It's the flies."

Patrokles grinned as he wound a strip of fresh linen over the wound. "Peleus had an aversion to flies, as I well remember. Are you here to put your training with Chiron to use, or have you come to lecture me on the finer points of flies?" He tied the split end of the bandage into a neat knot and laid the injured man's arm gently at his side.

"I come for advice."

"By the balls of Zeus, he comes seeking answers instead of barking orders."

Achilles pulled the tent flap angrily shut, blocking out the light Patrokles needed to see his patient. "Why so hot, *cousin?*"

Patrokles wiped his sweating brow. "Apologies. I haven't slept in two days." He reached for a stale piece of bread on a wooden platter. "What troubles you? Is it Briseis?"

"No, it is *not* Briseis. I have ordered her to remain inside of my tent until this sickness passes."

"Wise."

"Hera has spoken to me."

Patrokles sat back on his stool, and the sick man coughed, startling the flies communing on his chin. He wiped the man's chin with a damp cloth. "Are you certain?"

"I am."

"Prophesy or warning?"

Achilles clasped his hands behind his back. "Is there a

difference?"

"What did she want?"

"She told me to assemble the men and call Kalchus to speak."

Patrokles stood and poured two cups of spiced wine, handing one to his cousin. "I see your dilemma."

After draining the cup, Achilles wiped the back of his hand across his lips. "I'll have to call Agamemnon."

"Yes, yes you will. And risk widening the gulf between the men."

"Hera said it was *Apollo* who unleashed this sickness on us."

Patrokles sipped his wine. "Apollo? Hmm. That would explain much." He drained his cup as well. "You mustn't ignore the goddess."

"No, no I cannot. But still …"

"Is there more?"

Achilles remembered the last time a goddess demanded his obedience. The pitiful sight of Troilus clinging desperately to Apollo's statue's feet in the temple yet haunted him. It mattered little that he'd been commanded to do what he'd done. In the end, it was his hand that drew the knife. He'd wrestled with the knowledge that he was little better than Agamemnon. It galled him to be on as low a plane as the Fat King. "This war will take everything from me."

Patrokles crossed his arms across his chest. "You have benefitted more than most. What has it truly cost *you*, beloved of the gods on both sides of the Trojan Wall?" His words were bitter. "You still have your freedom. Your family is safe. Your men revere you, though to hear you speak like a whining child, they might reconsider."

"You presume too much," Achilles said, his anger seething beneath the surface. "Speaking with you was a mistake." His footsteps showered sand as he abruptly turned and stormed from the tent, flinging it wide open.

Patrokles watched his commander disappear into the rows of tents and men. He turned to his patient again. "Chiron should have forced him to play the lyre more often."

The half-dead man croaked, "Then we'd have been dead years ago."

Patrokles closed the man's mouth. "Shah. The flies."

Princess Andromache grabbed the midwife's arm, her eyes pleading for the truth. She was old for childbearing, she knew it, yet the gods had allowed Hektor's seed to flourish. "Will he live?" Another pain shot through her, tearing a scream from her throat.

"Calm, my lady. All is well," the midwife said firmly, stroking the princess' damp forehead. "You will hold your son."

A tear slid down Andromache's cheek. "I could not ... could not bear it, if—"

The midwife placed her cool hands on either side of the princess' belly. "Shah, my lady."

"I am old. What if ..." Andromache's fears refused to let her be. As each labor pain engulfed her body, her heart prepared for the worst. "Is Hektor nearby?"

"Aye, my lady. He is. In the hall. Waiting."

"He should have cast me aside and taken a fertile woman to wife." Another pain gripped her hips, changing its course and purpose like a river running rampant over a flat field. "I feel him coming." She wept, but not for joy. She wept for fear the child would be born without breath. "Eleithyia, Goddess, I beg you—" Andromache tilted her head back, groaning with the effort to bring the child to light.

Across the chamber, a breeze fluttered the privacy curtains at the balcony. The midwife turned, catching the flash of silver and bronze. Her eyes widened as the specter grew larger, moving silently into the center of the chamber. The other women attending fell to their knees before the goddess towering before them.

In a voice of honeyed silver she commanded, "Bring me the blade." She turned to Andromache. "Long have you suffered in fruitless labor, my daughter. Your womb carrying its precious burdens only to end in blood and empty arms. No longer will your bed be one of sorrow."

"Goddess," Andromache whispered. "I'm grateful."

Eleithyia pulled the linen covering from Andromache and lifted the princess' gown. She placed her hands on the mound of child, pushing and pulling gently. "Your discomfort should be less. Now, daughter, push. Push because his life depends on it."

Hearing that her son's life hung in the balance, Andromache roared and pushed with all her might.

The goddess smiled, encouraging her. "Aye, daughter, that is the way. Push like a warrior locked shield to shield against a common foe."

Again, the princess bore down, her legs shaking with her effort, tears streaming down her face.

The goddess knelt between Andromache's bent knees. "His head is crowned in your glory. He will be blessed for a short time. Now, push him to the light."

Andromache gripped the back of her knees with her hands, bearing down with what effort she had remaining. She felt a burning, then a quick tug, and quite suddenly, relief as the babe slid from the birth canal into Eleithyia's waiting arms.

Deftly, the goddess took the sharp blade, slicing the life cord. "The water basin," she commanded sternly.

The midwife gasped. "He's purple."

Andromache panicked. "He's not crying. What's wrong?"

The goddess calmly swept the child's mouth with her finger. She placed her lips over his nose and mouth and blew a gentle breath of air. The child threw his hands out, stretching to life, screaming at the top of his lungs. His skin color turned a healthy pink. Eleithyia gently scooped fresh water over the tiny body, cleaning away the muck of birth. She cradled the boy, now quiet in her arms, and handed him to the princess.

"Gratitude, Goddess," Andromache whispered, feeling the weight of her love with Hektor in her arms for the first time. "We are truly blessed," she beamed. All of the pain she'd suffered over the years, all the children she'd buried with their small malformed bodies, all the humiliation she'd carried suddenly faded. The warm bundle in her arms was her salvation, her most ardent prayer come to life. She looked up at Eleithyia, her sparkling eyes and gown of stars, and nodded. "I will not forget."

"Blessings fade in time," the goddess said, before her glittering image disappeared into thin air.

Hektor burst through the door. "I heard the cry!" He rushed to his wife's side, pushing the astounded women aside, and then stopped for sheer joy when he beheld the sight he'd longed his entire life to see—Andromache cradling their child as it suckled at her breast. He wept without shame.

Andromache was glowing with pride and sweat. "Astyanax, this is your father."

Hektor's tears washed into the crease of his wide smile. "A son."

He laughed softly, then louder with joy. "A son."

"Our son."

The Golden Prince bent to kiss his wife on the lips. "The gods favor us, even into our late age."

Andromache kept the veiled warning in Eleithyia's words to herself. Nothing would make her steal her husband's joy. She'd learned, over the drawn out years of the western invasion, that war was fought one battle at a time, and a man's heart must have something to fight for, that he mustn't despair too often. No, she would keep the warning to herself, giving Hektor his happiness without blemish. She owed him that much at least for all the years of his faithful devotion to her and to the city. She would be his strength from this day forward, bearing the burden of her secret silently, so that he could continue to fight valiantly for Troy.

Besides, she reasoned with herself, she had no clear idea what the goddess meant. Likely, it was another harbinger of doom regarding the shining citadel. And that, if it was true, couldn't be stopped if she spoke the warning aloud. No, better to end the final days of life as if hope existed, as if the skies would again brighten, and as if Troy would once again be the shining, free city of the east.

SIX
losing love
TROY—1238 BCE

The feast, sparsely set upon the trestle tables, drew the few men able to stand and walk. Roasted meat and stale bread were passed around as the captains argued, sickness and fear gripping all in attendance.

"Kalchus must be allowed to speak," Achilles said.

The seer shook his head vehemently. "I prefer silence."

Achilles plucked a plump fig from the tray before him. "Even when you know the gods give you the answer to ending this plague?"

Kalchus shuddered. "I cannot."

Achilles popped the ripe fruit into his mouth, savoring the sweet, grainy texture on his tongue before addressing the thin assembly of Myrmidons and Greeks. "I vow to protect you, Kalchus, whatever your words reveal."

The seer, leery of the long days of war, slumped in his seat. "Words, always words, son of Peleus. Words that fall on deaf ears or worse bring the edge of a blade to one's throat. If you vow on the life of your sacred mother, I will speak what the gods have hammered into my restless mind."

Achilles nodded. "On Thetis' life."

Kalchus dared a sideways glance at the Great King. He pressed his shaking fingers to the base of his throat, imagining the blood tricking down, staining his tunic. He swallowed the bitter fear of death. "The gods have answers that our King Agamemnon may wish … remained unspoken, or said in private."

The Golden Warrior scoffed. "Who among us can choose what the gods wish or do not wish on our account?" He gestured to the gathering. They had all seen the bitter days of war and death. The camp sickness was heaping more agony upon those already suffering with no end in sight. Not even the physicians, not even Patrokles, not anything he'd learned from Chiron had worked to staunch the plague. "Who among you holds the sway of his destiny before the gods?" *Death, will I choose death?*

The seer pressed his sweaty palms together, blurting out the vision Hera had burned into his mind. "Agamemnon has angered Apollo by refusing to return the priest's daughter, Astynome." Kalchus immediately bowed his head, uttering a quick prayer that Agamemnon wouldn't sever it from his shoulders.

Agamemnon slammed both fists onto the table. "You vile tongued cunt! Always prophesying by birds shitting on rocks and rotten entrails on altars. Your words *never* favor me. You only tell me how the gods will fuck me!" The Great King's cheeks quivered with fury. "If I allow the return of one girl, how will we ever be victorious? Where would our honor be? I'll tell you. We will have cast it to the winds of Aeolus. How is it right to allow foreigners to break hospitality oaths and steal our women? Our treasures are justly won, are they not? I hear you gripe and complain about my brother. But surely what happened to Menelaus could've happened to any of you had that fucking Trojan prince guested at your homes instead. Or are your wives too hideous for a prince to consider bedding?"

The men sheepishly glanced at one another, each one thinking Agamemnon was right. It was a glaring truth they ignored, allowing them to blame Menelaus for the war in general. Agamemnon's wrath, however, was nothing to trifle with and for that reason they remained silent. Only Achilles was brazened enough to goad Agamemnon. And he wished the men would rise up and slit the fat king's throat.

The Great King continued bellowing, spittle flying with his ferocity. "Now you tell me it's the god's will that I should return Astynome? You all know I prefer her to Clytemnestra. That cold bitch is probably plotting against me at this very moment. But if I must give the girl back to save all of you, I'll do it. I only ask that I'm compensated. I am king of this army. I deserve my portion of geras."

Rage raced through Achilles' veins. He stood slowly, gripping the table's edge with war calloused hands. Disgust for Agamemnon dripped from every word. "You expect the men to simply give up their measly portions because you, the Great King, want more? You've already been given more than you deserve. How many battles have you won that were not aided by thousands standing beside you? Do you suppose these soldiers have hidden wealth beneath the sand like the treacherous Palamedes? All that *we* have won with *our* blood has been portioned out. Give back the girl, Agamemnon. Are you blind to the suffering of your army? I've fought alongside my men. Broke bread with them. I build no barriers between myself and them. I've protected them like a mother bear protects her cubs from predators. I've held their hands as death claimed them. What comforts have you ever offered your men? Let the priest have his daughter and I will see that you are given her worth three times over once we bring Troy to its knees."

Agamemnon's face quivered. Hatred poured from his eyes. "You always seek to cheat me of my due, Achilles. At every chance, you dishonor me by your absence at my table, your lack of greeting, and your stinging words. You think it fair I give up my prize, while the rest of you keep your own? The only reason you want me to hand over Astynome is so you can laugh behind my back as you fuck that dark-haired beauty, Briseis, every night."

Achilles roared, pushing his table over, scattering the men beside him who had no desire to be in the wake of his indignation.

The Great King laughed wickedly, goading Achilles' fury. "We all know how that camp whore keeps Achilles in check, don't we? By the balls of Zeus, you'll compensate your king for what he freely gives up to save you from Apollo's lethal arrows. Why should I wait, Achilles?" Facing the warrior he hated the most, he said, "Maybe, I should take your woman, Achilles! Teach you your proper place in *my* army. Surely, you won't mind if it means ending the camp sickness for the men you say you care for most? I will send Astynome back to her father and end this plague in our camp. Odysseus, take our fastest ship and our best rowers. Deliver the cursed girl to her father. Take sacrifices to please the priest and his god."

Achilles kicked at the broken table on the ground, sending a shower of sand into the air. "You can't dismiss me with a threat." His chest heaved. "You forget who I am, Agamemnon. Look at you, standing there high on your shrinking dais, commanding the King of Ithaka as if he were your slave, destined to do your business, righting the wrongs you inflicted on all of us. Did Odysseus offend Apollo? You're a fucking coward of a king." Sweeping his hands out before him, he said, "I ask all of you here: Why do we fight at all? To save the honor of a cuckolded dishonored King of Sparta? And what have the Trojans ever done to us? To me? Did they steal my land, my grain, my woman? Look where we are after years of war on account of your cursed family. What do we have to show for our efforts? Some pottery and a few sacks of gold? Surely, some god urges you on to threaten me. You believe you have the strength to take my prize? The woman who I love as much as any of you love your Greek wives? At least I fought for Briseis myself, you fucking coward. My men handed her to me for my valor on the field. How long did Odysseus and I wage war in the south for your benefit? Your head is bent with a crown of undeserved glory. The rest of us get the scraps after you take the lion's share, you greedy cunt. I should take *my* ships and *my* Myrmidons back to Phthia and let you try to win the war by whatever means you can muster."

"Go ahead, Achilles. Get on your ships and unfurl your dark sails. Desert us if you feel you must. I will not beg you to stay, you ungrateful bastard! Why the gods favor you, I cannot fathom. I despise you. You won't catch me begging you. You're *nothing* to me. Your pitiful whining is unworthy of song. You always forget that I'm the king of this army, not you. I command the men, not you. I determine the portions, not you. I promise you this, by the balls of fucking Zeus, I *will* take your Briseis." Agamemnon pointed an angry finger at the assembly. "Any man daring such brazen speech against me will see his prizes snatched from his tent just as I'm going to take Achilles.'"

Those soldiers, who had stood in support of Achilles, quickly settled back to their benches. They were too sick and weary to fight back, even if Achilles was right. None of them wished to risk their own small gains for a woman, not even for Achilles' sake.

Achilles' fingers itched to cleave Agamemnon's head from his shoulders. As his hand gripped the pommel of his silver sword, partially unsheathing the lethal blade, Achilles was halted by a violent yank on his braids. He spun, expecting to find Patrokles or Odysseus, but was instead blinded by a golden light. He held a hand to shield his face from the glare. "Athena. Come to watch me slit his fat neck?"

"Achilles, save your black vengeance for another time."

The Golden Warrior seethed. "I did not take you as a patroness for Agamemnon."

"I come at Hera's request. She hates the Trojans, and so by default, must love all you Greeks equally. She would not have you kill Agamemnon, dooming her to lose the game."

Achilles spat and sheathed his sword. "The Fat King dishonors me with his threats. If he takes Briseis, he steals my glory and my honor."

"Do not fear, Achilles. You will be rewarded thrice over. Obey Hera. Obey me."

"By your command, I will do as I must. But I do not have to honor Agamemnon." The muscle at Achilles' jaw twitched. He turned to the king. "You lead an army with your perfect bronze plate barely scratched. I swear by all the Olympians, and on my sacred mother's heart, that your men will beg for *my* return to battle, when Hektor cuts you down like so many beasts to slaughter. Then, you will regret disgracing the best of the Greeks."

Nestor rose quickly from his seat, raising his hands to quell the growing tension. "Calm your anger. Cease this arguing. We cannot defeat the Trojans if we have no peace within our ranks. Listen to an old man. I have seen many battles, many heroes … I speak from experience, if you will heed my words." The wizened counselor faced Agamemnon. "My lord, think of the morale of your men. Achilles' presence on the field gives them courage."

Agamemnon slammed his empty cup on the table. "Wine!" he bellowed, as a scrawny boy scurried to obey.

The king's counselor extended a hand to Agamemnon. "My lord, you do not need the girl. You have more women at your feet than your faithful wife will allow, once you are home again. And, Achilles, it is not fitting you should speak so disrespectfully to a king ordained by the will of Zeus. I beg you both, listen to me. End this feud."

Agamemnon leveled his eyes at Nestor. "Achilles speaks as if *he* is the king, not *I*. If he will yield—"

Achilles laughed in Agamemnon's face. "Look around you, Fat King! What do you see? Men half-dead and pale as wraiths? What chance do you and your ragged army have against the singing swords of Troy? Content yourself with commanding others, but by fucking Zeus, you will never again command me. You wish to take my rightful prize, take her. I will not fight the likes of you for her." He took one menacing step in Agamemnon's direction. "But if you dare take a single piece more of my stores …" Achilles smiled wickedly. "I will slit your throat."

The Great King roared and tossed his table over at the threat, but too late, for Achilles' iron heart had turned against their common purpose even as he swiftly strode from the gathering. The assembly sat aghast. If Achilles left them, how could they win this war? How would they ever reach the safety of their homes? The men murmured amongst themselves, bewailing their now uncertain fates, fearing the worst now that the Myrmidon commander and his men had abandoned their ranks.

In his fury, Achilles disregarded courtesy, flinging open Patrokles' tent flap. "Cousin!"

A woman moaned in the darkness. Achilles squinted into the shadows, spying long, black hair falling across a man's arm. In a single stride, he was at Patrokles' bedside, his anger and jealousy flaring.

A hand shot out from beneath the linens, grasping Achilles by the wrist with a grip as iron as his own. "If you lay a hand on her, you will regret it, cousin," Patrokles said icily.

Achilles yanked his arm away and scoffed. "You can try. Everyone is full of challenges for me this day."

Patrokles slowly sat up; the woman now awake lay cringing against his body. The reason for Achilles' rage dawned on him. "Did you suppose I would take what belongs to you, behind your back?" Rising from his bed, Patrokles handed the woman her chiton. "Dress and be gone." The woman grabbed her clothing and ran naked from the tent into the night.

Achilles sank heavily into a chair. "I have lost her."

Patrokles slipped on his chiton, taking a seat at his table and lighting an oil lamp. "Who have you lost?"

"Briseis."

"Now, I know you are drunk, cousin."

Achilles clicked his jaw tight. "I am not drunk, but soon will be." His words seethed over his teeth.

"Has she escaped you, or left camp on her own accord?"

"Agamemnon has taken her."

Patrokles' confusion flared to crimson anger. "Fucked by the gods! Take her back! You know what that bastard will do to her. How could you let him take her?"

"I did not *let* him take her, cousin. He took her by right in place of Astynome, who Kalchus swore must be returned before this plague kills everyone. When I pulled my sword to kill him, Athena's hand held me back."

"*Athena*," Patrokles repeated under his breath. "I cannot believe Agamemnon would be so bold."

Achilles pressed his palms against his temples. "I have quit the war, Patrokles," he mumbled miserably.

Patrokles sat back, eyeing his cousin. "Quit the war?"

Achilles looked up, his eyes blazing blue fire. "I will not fight for him. And neither will any of the Myrmidons."

Rubbing the dark stubble on his chin, Patrokles said, "You will abandon the men for pride?"

"I abandon nothing but this unworthy cause." Even as he said the words, he bemoaned the prospect of an ignoble death. *If I do not fight, I cannot die with honor or song.*

"Why interrupt my fucking a warm, gentle woman to tell me this, when you have no plan to save Briseis?"

"You must deliver her to Agamemnon. I cannot."

Patrokles slammed his fists against the table rattling the lamp. "You are truly an iron-hearted bastard. Do your filthy deed yourself."

Achilles stood slowly, approaching his cousin with a few

measured steps, his blue eyes boring into Patrokles'. "You *will* do as commanded. Or you will die."

The dark twin of Achilles sneered, his voice dripping with disgust. "Does she know?"

"Not yet." Achilles made to leave. "Give me time enough to say farewell, then come for her." He strode quickly from the tent, leaving behind his most trusted companion to contemplate his reasoning.

Achilles hoped that Patrokles would offer Briseis comfort in the near future when he could not. *Will not.* A war waged between his head and his heart as he walked the lines of tents to his Myrmidon encampment. His fury cooled in the chill night air. As he approached his tent, he saw the familiar sliver of light where the tent flap rested askew. He stopped, standing alone in the darkness, contemplating his life in small moments, all of which he now realized were but steps in a long farewell to life and love.

His days in Troy would be his last; he'd known that since the day on the beach in Skyros when he heard the eagle screeching above him. Until that moment, he'd questioned the dual nature of his fate. And now he longed for more time, because swift-footed fate was closing in on his heels. Soon, the hot sands of Troy would swallow his mortal frame and the wind would sing his song.

It angered him that his end might be one of dishonor at Agamemnon's hand. He hadn't thought that a possibility, until this very moment staring at his tent, knowing his woman, the wife of his heart, waited patiently for his return. *Not so patient, Achilles. Not Briseis.* Her touch, her words …

He laughed. Angry words as much as loving … comforted him in this dreary place. He'd spent most of his life brushing away soft feelings, love in particular, into the dark recesses of his mind, locking them away to forget. But this woman ... this woman held the key to open everything his iron-heart sought to keep hidden from the world. Love was weakness. Before Briseis, affection had been enough to sustain him, untamed sex enough to preoccupy him. He'd cared for Deidamia with great affection. The pleasure he found between her thighs had occupied many a lonely day in his prison on Skyros. He adored his son, Neoptolemus. The love he bore his mother and father was pure enough. But his feelings for Briseis, that was something else entirely.

Once his prisoner, Briseis had found her way through his heaviest armor. Her spirit remained indomitable in his presence. She would not be conquered, as Odysseus had warned him. He'd decided after first making love to Briseis that love was no game of war, but one of attrition. *Has enough time passed for her to forgive me? To love me?* She was the calm in the midst of his storm. She'd kept his counsel and held his heart. Agamemnon had struck him a near fatal blow with his pronouncement, placing Briseis as a pawn between the Fat King and his own honor. Achilles had no wish to lose her before his final day. *Yet, I must let her go.*

Briseis looked up from her mending when Achilles entered the tent. She smiled warmly, as he sat heavily into a stool near the table.

She set the garment and threads aside. "I know that look. It is never good. What is troubling you, Achilles?"

He avoided her eyes by examining his feet. "There are matters, Briseis, which I must speak of before the moon passes into dawn."

She shivered, pulling her himation tighter across her shoulders.

"I have never known you to sound so … fearful. What is it? Tell me."

Achilles' shoulders rounded slightly. His eyes nervously found hers. "Do you remember the first day I saw you? In the temple?"

Briseis nodded. She wanted to vomit at the recollection. She tried never to think of the time before. It does not matter now, she reasoned, as she mended Achilles' clothes, fetched his water, and satisfied all his appetites. She'd grown to love him, but it was complicated by pain and guilt and what-ifs. "Why do you bring up old wounds? It is … different now."

"You said I would never claim you."

She closed her eyes, willing the tears to stop before they fell. The hairs on her arms rose. "I did." The words stuck dryly in her throat. "What has happened?"

Achilles leaned forward, resting his forearms on his knees. "It was the first time I recognized that I, Achilles, son of Thetis, had a mortal weakness." He reached a calloused hand toward her. "For all the protection my mother had endowed me with, this she could not protect me from." He dropped his hand back to his lap.

She pressed her lips fiercely together, yet her chin still quivered. "Maybe, I don't want to hear what it is …"

"I must speak." He stood up, closing the gap between them. Kneeling before her, he wrapped his arms around her knees in supplication. Pressing his lips against her soft thigh, he whispered, "On that day, Briseis, I loved you first."

Briseis kissed him on top of his head, his words forcing her quiet tears. "I never thought to hear those words uttered until the last. What sorrow do you bring to me, Achilles? Do you go to battle?"

"No."

"I do not understand? Are you ill?"

"No, I do not have the camp sickness."

Briseis tilted her lover's head to face her. His forehead was deeply furrowed, his eyes gazing at her with a softness she'd never seen before. "Then, what has brought you to your knees? Please, get up. I want no more heart break."

Achilles stood slowly, pulling her with him. "Woman, you will always have my affection. In the days to come, you will doubt that I have loved you. But it would be wrong to forget the truth between us. No other woman has heard those words fall from my lips. Not even the mother of my son. They are not spoken lightly."

"In the days to come? What are you talking about?" She pushed him away. "You tell me of your heart, yet sound like you are casting me aside?" Her heart pounded. "Why be so cruel and speak aloud the only words that could pain me more than living each day? You are heartless." She collapsed back into her chair and buried her face in her hands.

Standing before her, Achilles brushed her cheek with his unsteady hand. "That is not my intent," he said hoarsely. "Come, wife of my heart." Briseis allowed him to lead her to their bed where he laid her gently down beside him on the coverings.

"I want to memorize every part of you." His hand traced a line down her arm, his touch as soft as carded lamb's wool. His kisses landed sweetly along her neck and shoulders. The tenderness was foreign to her.

"You kiss me as a wayfarer kisses the feet of a goddess."

"Shah, woman." His tongue explored her mouth more deeply, running it against her teeth.

"Where is my Achilles?" she asked, her breath shaky.

"He is not here, my love. It is only me. A man. Imperfect." He pulled her close, wrapping his heavy arms around her. "Promise me, Briseis, that you will remember me this way."

She wept freely now. "I promise."

Achilles kissed her eyes, her cheeks, her lips. "For me there is only death or love. I can't live in both worlds."

His confession pierced her defenses. She'd always known it was true, but she'd silently hoped she was wrong. Their love would break them both no matter what they chose. They needed each other for divergent reasons, but they were real none-the-less. There would be no escaping the war to come and its aftermath.

"War is no place for a woman … or for such softness as I feel for you." His hand slid slowly up her side, tracing the soft, round curve of her waist, finally cupping her breast in his hand. "I am sorry the gods have kept the joy of a child from your breast."

Briseis buried her face in Achilles' neck. "As am I." She had longed and prayed for a child, but each moon the gods denied her. She had not longed for a child to claim him, but to have a small piece of life that was hers alone.

"My days are few, Briseis."

She looked up, desperately searching his eyes for comfort. She found only confusion. "No one is your equal in battle. I have *seen* you dance in the blood of your enemy."

"You are more than a beautiful spoil of war. There are no words to beg the forgiveness I would ask. And no heart should grant after …" A tear caught in his eye. "After what I have done."

Briseis turned away from him in his arms. "Speak no more of that day. Or of your last days. You will live out the war, if any mortal can. Patrokles has promised to marry me, if you would not, when we return to Phthia. I must believe it is possible to survive this, or every sacrifice has been for nothing."

"My fate is set in the stars now. And if I had the might of the gods, I would scatter the stars so I might begin anew. This time knowing that *you* were coming to me." He pulled Briseis back into the crook of his arm. "Let us not waste this night." He mounted her slowly, pressing deep into her flesh, each thrust bringing her agonizing pleasure. They cried out together, collapsing as one flesh.

Achilles kissed her again. Sweetly, like a new lover. "No matter how this war breaks us, you will always be the one."

A loud commotion sounded outside of the tent and tore the sacred shroud of their lovemaking. Achilles spoke quickly. "Agamemnon has ordered me to give you over to him. Compensation for his loss. He has demanded an equal prize."

Briseis sat up, her eyes wide and horrified. "What? What do you mean?"

Achilles roared and threw the linens from their bed as he got up. "He has demanded you to replace the priest's daughter."

His words stunned her. "You are handing me to Agamemnon?" Then it dawned on her. A terrible knowing in the pit of her stomach. "You did not even fight for me."

"It was not as simple as that," he snapped angrily.

Patrokles' raised voice carried on the night. "You fucking bastards have no right!"

A rough voice growled back, "We have every right. Stand aside."

At least a dozen armed guards pushed into the Achilles' tent. The biggest one, Talthybios, spoke with as much confidence as his shaking spear. "You know why we have come, my lord."

Patrokles pushed passed the intruders. "I am sorry, cousin," Patrokles said through his clenched jaw. "They insist they follow

Agamemnon's command."

The shorter guard, Eurybates, trembled before Achilles. "We're here for that woman."

Briseis instinctively pulled a linen sheet up over her nude body. She pleaded with her lover, "Tell me this is a mistake, Achilles."

"I cannot," was all he said.

There he was, the warrior returned. She recognized the stony scowl and cold eyes. The love so tenderly expressed moments ago had vanished like some magical mist.

Achilles picked Briseis' chiton up from the ground and tossed it at her without even a glance in her direction. "Put this on, woman. And you fucking cock-holes remember this day. Soon, you will need me in battle, and I will not be there. Tell Agamemnon I hope his bloated pride is satisfied."

With tears streaming down her face, she reached for the garment and slipped it on over her head. She now understood what his words meant. Remember him with love, because he'd known death was coming for both of them. Terror filled her with what Agamemnon would do to her. He hated Achilles, and would surely take that out on her, Achilles' prized possession. No matter the sweet words that fell from his lips, she was and always would be nothing more that— his spear-won prize.

Achilles turned to look at her now, holding her eyes with his as he lifted her gently from their bed. "She is ready." Then, without warning, he pushed her toward the guards.

"Wait! Wait!" Briseis screamed. "I beg you, Achilles!"

One of the guards slapped her across the face, leaving a burning red mark on her cheek. "Shut your mouth. You're nothing but a whore slave in this camp."

Too late Achilles heard Patrokles' blade slide from its scabbard. His cousin was at the guard's throat, pressing his gleaming blade to bone. The man's blood gurgled from the gaping wound at his neck. In shock, the guards nearest Patrokles and the dead man backed up, but before Patrokles could grab the next man Achilles seized his cousin tightly around the shoulders. "No more, Patrokles. I command it!"

Patrokles continued struggling, but couldn't free himself from Achilles' grasp. Slowly, Achilles released him.

As they dragged Briseis from the tent into the night, the sound of her weeping and screaming trailed to silence. Patrokles stared after them, before unleashing his rage on his companion. Turning into Achilles' body, Patrokles took them both to the ground. The dark warrior wrapped his arm beneath Achilles' chin and his leg around Achilles' waist. He pulled back with all his might, furious that his cousin had allowed Agamemnon's men to take Briseis. Achilles, ever quicker, twisted from Patrokles' hold and shoved him roughly against a stool. They lay panting and exhausted on the hard sand.

"Why?" Patrokles roared in anguish. "Why did you let them take her?"

"You are a fool if you believe I would let her go willingly. Hera forbids me to raise my hand to Agamemnon. I cannot fight to keep her, by will of the goddess, so I must let her go."

Patrokles' gray eyes burned with angry tears. "The gods curse you at every turn. You do not deserve her."

"No. I don't. But she deserves your friendship and comfort. And that you must give. She will be lonely and frightened."

The dark-eyed cousin of Achilles shook his head in disbelief. "I will be as I always am for her sake."

Achilles pulled himself up to his elbow, looking his cousin squarely in the face. "You think I do not know you love her?"

Patrokles stood, brushing sand from his arms and legs, the hurt evident in his eyes. "I have loved you both more than you know. But she will not have me for love of you."

"When this war ends and I am gone, you will be the one to comfort her into old age."

"What is your meaning? You of all mortals will not die in this fucking war."

"Still, promise me, you will be her protector, when I am dead."

"On my life."

Achilles stood and grasped his cousin's shoulders firmly. "Go then. Begin your vigil on her behalf."

Patrokles nodded. "I will never forgive you for what you've done to her."

The Myrmidon commander watched his cousin disappear into the night and hoped he'd not broken their bond forever. Scanning the tent empty now of *her* presence, his heart finally cracked, flooding his love for her into his chest. He beat his fist into the growing ache. He hadn't realized, until this empty moment, how much Briseis was woven into the tapestry of his world. He would no longer hear her singing quietly as she mended his garments. He would no longer feel her hands stroking his furrowed brow and cheeks. He would no longer smell the sweat and salt of her skin as they made love. Would he be able to win her back and keep his honor? Would she want him?

Patrokles' words already haunted him. He knew he didn't deserve her and was certain now that Patrokles loved her the way he could not. He loved Briseis because the war had placed them together and she comforted him, but Patrokles loved her despite the war. His threat of marrying her, if Achilles did not, sprang from his heart; his words were not for convenience or for Achilles' sake. She was a rightful princess, a queen. And he had made her a slave, and worse, had given her to his enemy without explanation. Patrokles fought for her, when he would not. He had to let her go, so he could die as fate decreed. For the songs that would be sung. He sat staring into the quiet space of his tent.

Achilles poured a cup of wine and drank deeply, the nectar bittering on his tongue. "Glory is empty for the living." He then drained the amphora. "Nax!"

The young servant, ever faithful, scurried into the tent. "Yes, my lord." His eyes fell to the dead body on the sand, a red tide spilling from it into the thirsty sand. He stepped back, hesitating to approach Achilles in a murderous mood. "My lord?"

Without meeting Nax's gaze, he snapped, "Get rid of it."

"Yes, my lord." He hesitated. "Briseis—"

Achilles groaned, throwing pottery across the tent. "She is gone. I will say no more." He strode from the tent, leaving his servant to clean up the mess he'd made of everything.

Restless and miserable, Achilles wandered to the beach far from the Myrmidon ships beached deep into the foreign shore. The silver moon hung high above him, casting its eerie glow on the foaming waters of the bay. Many an evening, he'd brought Briseis here to lie beneath the stars. "Briseis," he whispered into the wind, as he sank to his knees. *What have I done? Mother ...*

For the first time since he set foot on Troad lands, he freed the darkness of his deeds to the light and regret filled him. Deidamia's sad eyes as he knowingly abandoned her and their son. Iphigenia's dead eyes staring up at the sky. Peisidike's horrified eyes pleading for her father to save her. Troilus' wide-eyed terror just before his blade slit the young prince's throat. Countless thousands of pairs of eyes had been dimmed by his hand. And now, he added Briseis to his private agony. How many more eyes would look up to see their futures dashed at his hand? War roared within his blood, he could not deny that, but no one had cautioned him that the weight of it would crush his mortal soul and steal one of the two people who tempered the storm inside.

Achilles sat staring out to sea, his mind bent on grief and his heart torn by lamentation. *My days will end without peace. I was a fool to love.* The thin line of moonlight shimmered on the water, catching Achilles' eye. He wiped his tears on the back of his hand. *Mother ...*

Thetis rose, shrouded by a mist from the gleaming sea.

The nymph walked serenely from the gentle waves to bend her knees at Achilles' side. "What a wretched man you have become, my son. This world is too harsh for one with so short a life." She stroked his cheek with a cool finger. "Your pain pierces my heart. What has happened? Is it the woman?"

"I can hide nothing from you, Mother."

Thetis smiled sadly. "I would hear your grief though you were on the highest mountain top. And I would find my way to you. Tell me, my son, what troubles you?"

"Agamemnon has taken Briseis from me."

"Why would you allow it? She carries your love, does she not?"

A flicker of hot rage rose in Achilles' chest. "I did not allow it," he snapped. "Hera forbade me to interfere."

Thetis sat back, stunned by the unexpected and unfortunate revelation. "Hera," she whispered. "What does *Hera* care for your woman?"

"A priest of Apollo came to camp, begging Agamemnon to return his daughter. A woman called Astynome. We took her, by right of victory, at Thebe. Gave her to the Fat King when we rejoined the main army. The men would have given her to me, but … I have no need of other women. And Odysseus …" Achilles shrugged. "His queen can say he is a faithful man."

"Agamemnon refused Apollo's priest?"

"He did, and Apollo laid waste to us. With each dawn more death. With each dawn more bodies to burn. The stench … the living cannot escape the smell of rotting flesh and shit. Hera came to me unexpected. She commanded that I encourage Kalchus to speak. That he had some reprieve for us. I did all the goddess commanded. The seer spoke, angering Agamemnon with his words."

Thetis traced a circle in the sand. A shield. "And what did the son of Atreus demand?"

"He relented to the old man's words. What could he deny standing there before the assembly? Yet, he raged he would not remain without his share, even though everything of worth has been awarded. I interceded on behalf of the men, vowing to pay him many times over once Troy falls. But he would have none of it. He said he would take my woman as compensation, so I drew my sword—"

"The goddess held you back."

Achilles nodded. "She told me to save my wrath for another day."

Thetis wiped the shield sketched in the sand with the palm of her hand. "You cannot disobey Hera. You were right to do as she commanded. She is ruthless in her revenge."

An angry tear skidded down Achilles' golden cheek. "What am I to do then? How am I to win her back?"

"My son, my sweet son. Even in grief you are too beautiful for this world of mortals. Did I bear you to endure agonies of the heart? To weep the last days of your life away? I am a pitiful mother."

Achilles laughed then. "*Sweet*. There is a word I do not recognize."

"I see you as the babe at my breast as clearly as I see the man before me ... despite the passage of time, despite the blood you have spilled."

Regret filled Achilles. "My days are quickly leaving me."

"I cannot change Agamemnon's mind. And I cannot persuade Hera. What would you have me do, my son?"

"Persuade Zeus instead."

The nymph brushed her hands together, the sand catching in the wind. "If Hera should discover me ..."

"All my life you have told me how you saved him when all the other gods turned against him. He will hear you. Take his knees. Beg him to avenge your only son, whose days are swiftly winging him to Hades. Beg him to show Agamemnon who is lord of all. Beg him to inspire the Trojans' courage and beat the Greeks back to the sea. Only then will the Fat King see that he cannot disgrace me."

Thetis searched her son's face, shifting between his grief and his rage. "If I do this, my son, it cannot be undone. Thousands will fall to satisfy your pride."

"So be it. Only then will they see Agamemnon for who he truly is. A wretched coward, undeserving of song."

"Careful you do not lose your way with the son of Atreus. This war will take everything from you."

"Do not fear, Mother. I will not lose my way. What more could this war take from me?"

The nymph rose, her pale skin shimmering in the moonlight. She reached a hand to smooth her son's tumbled hair. "In twelve days, Zeus will return to Olympus. I will press his favor then. Promise me to stay far from the fighting until I send you word."

Achilles stood also, embracing his mother in gratitude. "I will do as you wish."

With the promise secured between them, Thetis returned to the sea, sinking beneath the tide. Her caution rang in Achilles' ears. *"Do not lose your way in this war with the son of Atreus."*

SEVEN
reunited
FAR SOUTH OF TROY, CHRYSE—1238 BCE

Odysseus stood mid-ship, watching the jagged coast line of Chryse loom before the bow with its wide-painted eyes now faded with the years. White foam sprayed along the hull as the wind bore the galley swiftly toward its destination. His brow furrowed as he contemplated how best to beg the priest's forgiveness and gain Apollo's as well. *Athena, give me the words to persuade him.* Odysseus had no intention of returning to a camp mired by a wasting sickness. Even the salty sea mist couldn't wipe the stench of the dead and rotting flesh from his nose. Seeing a thin curl of smoke rising skyward on the distant shore, he pointed the spot out to his crew. "There is where the priest has made his altar. Antilochus, ready the girl."

The youngest of the Greek warriors leapt from the rail, swinging down from the rigging with a single hand. "Aye, my lord!"

"Make haste," Odysseus shouted after him. He could see why

Achilles had taken an interest in Nestor's son. He was eager and strong, noble enough to know his place among his betters. "We land there. In the bay, below the smoke." He scowled into the wind whipping about his face, for he knew the gods to be fickle and cruel. Athena was the only steadfast deity he held in esteem. Her guidance had never failed him. Casting his eyes skyward, he squinted for a god-sign and called upon the goddess. *Athena, help me.*

The blue expanse remained ... blue. Odysseus then commanded, "Pull in the sails. Ready the bow stones."

"My lord?" asked Eurylochus. "We don't row for the beach?"

Odysseus stood firm. "I'm not certain of the dangers that lie ahead. I won't beach our ships in this strange place. We may have need of a swift retreat." Before Eurylochus stepped aside, Odysseus grabbed his arm. Pulling his second close, he whispered harshly into his ear, "If you believe our blood ties give you leave to question my command, well, think twice. Never overstep with me again." Odysseus released his iron grip on the man's arm.

Eurylochus bristled at the rebuke, but bore his indignation silently. "As you command, *lord* Odysseus."

"Then, we understand one another. Gather some of the men and bring the cattle up from below. We will have to lower them into the water and swim them to shore."

"Would it not be easier to—"

Odysseus bellowed, "Do as I command!"

At the captain's raised voice, men scurried to tie down the sails and hurled the bow stones over board, securing the ship in shallow surf. One by one the cattle brought to Chryse as sacrifice for penance owed Apollo were lowered and guided carefully to the sandy shore. Antilochus brought Astynome to Odysseus. The captain bowed to her. "My lady, our deepest apologies for your rough treatment. Soon, you will reunite with your father. You should never have been kept from his side."

The young woman, her wheat-colored hair a ratted mess falling about her shoulders, stood defiant before Odysseus. "I will not forget you." She spat on the wooden deck. "You with that Achilles brought me to my shame. You handed me to the crude king, who defiled my body. You made a slave of me, as much as did he. No, I will not forget you. The gods will curse you for what you have done."

"Take her to shore," Odysseus said quietly. *I am already cursed.* He recalled the days, years ago, when the oracle warned him that when he left, he would not see home for many years. He hadn't believed her. Now, as each year passed, the weight of her truth stung not only his pride, but threatened to bury his heart as well. Briefly, his mind flashed to Penelope's graceful hips swaying—

"Aye, my lord," Antilochus said, looking to his captain. "My lady, Achilles is not at fault. Agamemnon is rough with all who defy him."

Astynome laughed icily. "You think Achilles is not already cursed among mortals? His fate will be the cruelest of all."

Antilochus escorted her in silence to the railing, before securing her by a rope and lowering her into a smaller boat and the waiting hands of the soldiers below.

One by one, the crew of the sacred expedition jumped into the surf, some swimming and some in smaller craft, making their way to the shore.

Odysseus had marked a path in his mind from the beachhead to the trailing smoke above the shore. It was a difficult hike over rocks and shifting sand, herding cattle along the way. Streaks of violet and gold swept the heavens by the time the entourage reached the altar

Chryses had erected for the God of Plagues.

Apollo's priest spoke, "I have been expecting you, Odysseus. Before your sails appeared on our horizon, Apollo told me you would come."

Odysseus narrowed his eyes, thinking of what the girl said to him. He could not shake the fear of more curses falling on his head now that he stood before the priest. "I have come at Agamemnon's command to return your daughter and make sacrifice to Apollo so he will end his plague."

"All could have been avoided had your king bent his pride because of a father's love for a daughter, but he murdered of his own flesh and blood for war, did he not?"

Odysseus, cautious in response and not wishing to anger Apollo or the priest, answered, "He did only as Artemis bid."

The priest mocked the partial honesty of the wily tongued commander. "Only because he'd offended her first. You Greeks follow a fool."

"No doubt the Great King has erred more than once," Odysseus said. "But this evening we seek to make amends on his behalf, if you will accept our offering of cattle for sacrifice." He gave the signal, and a veiled woman was led from the rearguard forward.

Chryses fell to his knees, overcome with relief and joy and dread. "Astynome," he whispered desperately.

At the sound of her father's voice, Astynome tore free from Antilochus' arms, her veil flying into the air as she rushed to her father's side. "Father, Father!"

Chryses wept openly as he embraced his daughter, his flesh and blood, returned because the shining god had willed it so. He kissed his daughter's red-rimmed eyes and her swollen cheeks. "My beautiful girl," he whispered over and over. He lifted a lock of her tangled hair to his lips. "That you are safe." His hands shook with joy at the touch of a loved one returned as if from the dead. Slowly, the two rose from their knees to face the Greeks waiting nervously for a sign the sacrifices would be accepted.

Odysseus stepped forward. "We offer these cattle, if it will move Apollo to pity us wasting away, burning our dead in foreign lands."

"Have your men line the beasts up before the altar. We will sacrifice them, sending your smoky offering to the shining god. We will know soon enough if he accepts," he said solemnly. "But, if you believe Apollo is a god of mercy, then you surely do not know him."

Chryses approached his altar, sticky trails of blood staining the piled stones, and hefted a silver blade to the sky. "Lord of the Silver Bow, Shining God of Olympus, hear my prayer of thanks." He signaled for the first beast to be led forward. With a swift slice, the priest slit the throat of the bull. It stood dazed, bleeding its life onto the earth. Its legs shook as it struggled to live, but death brought the animal to its knees. "Light the fires. Butcher the sacrifice. We feast tonight to Apollo's glory." Blood soaked Chryses hands and arms, as he signaled for the next bull and the next.

The melting fat of roasting meat spat and crackled on a hundred spits set up in lines around the perimeter of the holy place. Songs praising Apollo rose with the smoke into the night. The wine jars hauled up the trail, gifted by Agamemnon, were emptied. The Greeks and priests drank deeply of the red nectar, and as the warmth spread into their blood and bones, their songs rose more boisterous and sincere. In wine, it was told, truth will flow.

And far above the feasting, Apollo heard their winging words. Sitting upon a golden rock, fletching new arrows for the next bloody dawn to unleash more death on the wretched Greeks, the shining god paused to listen. Warrior voices rose in songs of praise. *Apollo. Apollo. Apollo.* He swept his hand before him, clearing the scattered clouds from the sky. Clearly, he observed the spotted cook-fires and inhaled the essence of roasting meat. He rose like a mountain from a long sleep. Set down his arrows. *It is finished, then. Let the Greeks live.*

As the last of the bulls was butchered and the fatted portions set to spits and the wine emptied into their bulging bellies, the pilgrims seeking Apollo's pity made the long hike back to their ship. With torches held aloft in the dark of early morning, Odysseus and his men stumbled with wine-hazed eyes, cursing the entire way. Once they reached the shore, they waded into chilly water to reach the ship. There was little rest for all.

A rosy dawn greeted Odysseus and his crew as they awoke bleary eyed, cold, and exhausted from feasting the night before. The captain surveyed the sky. Discerning an auspicious wind, he gave word to pull up the bow stones. The crew silently settled into their places, rowers to their well-worn benches, and riggers to their ropes and sails. If they were fortunate, they would return in a few days time to a camp without sickness.

EIGHT
two queens
ITHAKA—1238 BCE

The aroma of roasting meat wafted from the kitchens into the central hall of Odysseus' palace. Servants scurried about, setting fresh greenery and blooming field flowers on tables. Penelope surveyed the hall with an eye to detail. "Eurycleia!"

The faithful maid servant appeared as if from the shadows. "Yes, my queen?"

"Have more wine brought up. Good wine. I've heard my cousin drinks wine like a king. Are there any roses blooming?"

"I'll send one of the maids to gather any that are."

Satisfied, Penelope said, "Good. You always know what needs to be done. What would I do without you?"

Eurycleia nodded and disappeared to her tasks.

Some fresh-faced slave girl pressed a cup of wine into Penelope's hands. "Eurycleia," she said aloud.

"No. That is *my* doing."

Penelope turned to see Anticlea standing there with a cup of her own. "You startled me."

"You've made the hall a cheery place once again, if only for a short while."

"I'm having more flowers brought in … and more wine."

Anticlea scoffed. "I wonder how many will be in the queen's retinue?"

"The messenger said only the queen's immediate family would be attending. They stay but a week. The hospitality won't be over much."

"I'm curious about why *she* wishes to visit Ithaka."

"As am I." Penelope sipped her wine. "This is an excellent quality, Mother."

"Laertes' vines."

"I'm not surprised. Have you seen Telemachus?"

"No. Perhaps he's about his chores?"

Penelope drained her cup and handed it back to Anticlea. "Only if the gods prodded him in the back."

"You must be firmer with the boy. Soon it will be too late to influence him at all."

Telemachus enjoyed his time with Eumaeus, the ancient sheep herder, because he didn't nag him about chores or study or sword practice. The young prince preferred to accomplish his tasks as he saw fit. Eumaeus granted him the freedom to roam without guilt or pressure to be more than just a boy. Walking the hills, Telemachus could pretend he wasn't the Prince of Ithaka facing a future looming with responsibility to fulfill.

"Come on, Argo. Old boy. We're almost there," Telemachus said, stepping across a shallow stream. Argo's muzzle was graying but his tail still wagged like a pup's. He panted happily along behind his young master. They came to a meadow, its tall grasses swaying and winged bugs floating magically in the air. Apollo's light beamed brightly against a cloudy blue sky. "Eumaeus told me that Pegasus comes here." He scratched the dog behind the ears. "He swears that when he was a boy, he saw it here. It must be a special place … if it's true. Eumaeus is *old*."

Pulling a wrapped hunk of bread and cheese from his shoulder bag, Telemachus said, "I bet you're hungry."

Argo tilted his head to one side, drool dripping from his mouth.

The boy laughed. "You're always hungry." He ripped a piece of bread off and tossed it to the hound. "We have guests this evening. Mother says I must play the prince to my cousins. I don't even know them. More strangers." He tossed another piece of bread to his furry companion. "Be polite. Hospitable. Charming. Like my father, she says."

Argo begged for more, pawing his young master's thigh. Telemachus absent-mindedly tossed him more bread.

"I hate when she says that. How am I supposed to be like a man I've never met? Be like my father. Do him proud. He left when I was a babe. How am I to know him at all? And this past week, Mother was constantly checking my chin for beard hairs. She's like a fat fly buzzing around my head."

Telemachus only knew the ideal of a man crafted for him by others. People who missed and loved the long-absent king: Mother. Grandmother. Grandfather. Eumaeus. Eurycleia. They all painted an image of a man so tall and foreboding, Telemachus often wondered if his father wasn't actually a god. All his life, he loved and hated this man named Odysseus. This stranger off to war. Some days, he didn't care if this Odysseus ever returned, but other days a dull ache carved a deep hole behind his heart. It was as if a part of him was missing. When that happened, he squeezed his fists into tight balls, willing the pain away. A hawk screeched above, shaking the troubling thoughts away.

Something moved in the grass, catching Argo's attention. The dog's ears perked up. Slowly, the scruffy hound stood, tail pointed. The grass rustled unnaturally again. Before Telemachus could stop him, Argo bounded off across the meadow.

"Wait! Argo! Get back here!"

It was too late. Argo had caught the scent of the small fox and was off on the chase.

Oil lamps burned brightly, filling the hall with a warm, golden glow. A lyre player plucked a sweet song of love. Olive garlands graced two trestle tables set with platters of roasted beef and goat. Servants carried out bowls of fresh cheese, figs and dates, and rounds of bread. Bowls of olive oil steeped with thyme and rosemary were set by each plate.

Penelope rose from her seat as Clytemnestra swept into the hall wrapped in a fine-spun purple cloud, her dark hair intricately pinned about her head. Glittering gold dangled from her earlobes. A chain of hammered gold stars sat gracefully around her long neck. She was followed by a boy who looked to be Telemachus' age and an even younger girl.

"Welcome, cousin." Gesturing around her, Penelope said, "We hope you will be pleased."

Clytemnestra's lips curled up, slightly. "Your hospitality has warmed our hearts."

The Mycenaean queen took her place with the grace of a woman practiced in royal etiquette. Penelope wondered if Clytemnestra was so poised, how much more so was Helen by now? The stories she heard of Helen bore little resemblance to the girl she ate apples with beneath a tree.

"I understand Palamedes paid Ithaka a visit. I trust his words fell on barren soil?"

Anticlea blurted out, "Most certainly. My son is more honorable than—"

"Than … Agamemnon?" Clytemnestra's eyes swept to Anticlea's, her smile wicked, but knowing. "Any man is more honorable than that *murderer*."

Penelope shifted uncomfortably in her chair. She cleared her throat. "Have some wine." Clapping her hands, she signaled the wine stewards to pour. She stole a glance at her mother-in-law, and gulped half her cup. "How does Mycenae fare with its king away?"

"We have managed. As I see you have as well, cousin."

"With fields and orchards and livestock, we stay quite busy."

"And raising a fine young prince, I see? Telemachus. Is that correct?"

Telemachus was busy eating a chunk of meat, but looked up at hearing his name.

Clytemnestra narrowed her eyes ever so slightly. "How old are you, boy?"

Straightening in his chair, he squeaked, "Thirteen." The heat of being scrutinized rose to his cheeks. He took a sip of watered-wine. "Thirteen," he managed, with more baritone in his voice than an adolescent boy.

"Indeed," Clytemnestra said, pleased that the young prince had attempted to impress her. "Do you ever think of marriage, Telemachus?"

Penelope and Anticlea blurted in unison, "No."

Clytemnestra's laughter unnerved both women. "You believe your son too young for such discussion? Is he not a prince? To rule, one day, after his father?"

Penelope scrambled to find the words. "He is … Telemachus is … is too young. Of course, he will be king … Odysseus will return before—"

"Your son is grown? How can you be so certain of that? How many years have passed already with little to no word from any man? I say they are lost at Troy, or will be."

Anticlea sighed, choosing her words carefully. "We pray that is not the case for my son. What mother doesn't wish for her son's safe return?"

"I understand your feelings, Anticlea. More than you might know. I only speak to the fact that as the years pass, it is less and less likely any of our men will return. War makes and breaks men. We must do what we must to maintain our kingdoms and prosperity. If the war drags on much longer, rivals will rise to claim what is ours from our children. That's what I seek to prevent. Losing the worlds we've preserved in the absence of our … *kings*."

Clytemnestra's word dove into Penelope's chest, wrenching her most private fears from the shadows. She'd brushed Odysseus' words away that day, long ago, when he'd forced her to promise to take another husband if he didn't return by the time their son was a man. The thought of lying beneath another man wasn't as frightening as the thought of her son losing his position as the next king. If she chose too soon, Telemachus would lose his birthright. If she chose too late, Telemachus might not survive at all.

Penelope knew the daughters of Tyndareus were able strategists in ways women could be. "Then, you've come with a proposition?" Penelope asked.

"I have."

Curiosity got the better of Penelope. "What is it?"

"That we bind Mycenae and Ithaka together through marriage. My daughter, Erigone, to your son, Telemachus."

The young prince of Ithaka coughed with his mouth full. Anticlea choked on her wine. Erigone smiled blissfully unaware she was being bartered. Aletes stared disbelievingly at his mother. Only the two queens retained their stoic composure.

Penelope looked Erigone over, sitting there dipping her bread in olive oil. She would be a great beauty someday. That would please Telemachus, perhaps. But, the beauty of Tyndareus' house had only brought strife and war. She wasn't certain that was in Ithaka's best interest. Provoking Clytemnestra wasn't in her current best interest. Better to deal with the present, when the future, whether she wanted to admit it or not, was uncertain. "Your daughter would become Queen of Ithaka. Eventually."

"Eventually," Clytemnestra echoed. "And if Odysseus should return, I think he would approve of such a match. If not, perhaps, your wifely wiles can bring him to reason. There is no more powerful or prosperous kingdom than Mycenae."

Penelope lifted her cup. A maid filled it. "Agreed."

Anticlea rolled her eyes, murmuring discontent to whichever gods would listen.

Telemachus was mortified. "But, Mother! I don't want to get married."

Penelope reached to pat her son's arm. "It wouldn't be for several years to come. It is a good match, Telemachus. Don't you agree, Mother?"

Anticlea had recovered her senses. "If you think it best for Ithaka, then it will be."

"It seems, cousin, we have an agreement between our households," Penelope said.

"Good." Clytemnestra pushed her chair from the table. "Suddenly, I'm quite tired. I think it best I take to my bed. May I leave the children to finish?"

"As you wish, cousin."

As Clytemnestra left the hall, Anticlea whispered across the table, "She's with child again. If I'm not mistaken. She took very little wine."

Penelope agreed. "Unexpected to say the least." She silently wondered who was fathering these children while Agamemnon was away. Whispers spoke of Zeus, but Penelope wasn't so sure. No god was stalking the halls of Odysseus seeking to impregnate her. Although, if one did, she might not resist over much. Her husband had been gone for so long that her desires pressed her to find some satisfaction without fear of bastards running loose. She cringed thinking what a nightmare Anticlea would make her life if that happened. Odysseus' mother loved her son more than her own husband. No, Penelope could never give in to another man.

Tired from the dinner and a little too much wine, Penelope allowed her two hand-maids to help her with her gown. They pulled the shoulder pins and carefully folded the sheer garment and stowed it away. They slipped a thin sleeping chiton of pale blue linen over the queen's shoulders, before they attended her coiffed hair. Pulling golden pin by golden pin, her honey-wheat tresses tumbled down her back. Penelope fingered a lock of hair, noting some gray. *When he returns, what if Odysseus does not find me as beautiful as he once did?* Then she shuddered. *If he returns.*

As the women turned to go, Penelope's hand lingered over one of the maid's. Without making eye contact, Penelope walked to her bed and lay down. The maids glanced at each other knowingly and followed, climbing into bed with the queen. Penelope lay back against the pillows with a maid settling on either side. They kissed her on the neck, their hands roaming softly over her. The woman with dark, silky hair slid down to her breasts and suckled them, pulling the nipples gently between her teeth, teasing them to tight buds.

The other moved her kisses down Penelope's belly to her sacred flesh. The queen moaned, moving her hips provocatively, encouraging the woman to explore the soft folds with her tongue. Penelope's legs quivered with anticipation. With one sucking at her breasts, and the other sucking at the tiny bud below, it wasn't long before Penelope's entire body shook with pleasure.

For a moment, the three lay entwined, one maid resting her head against the queen's breast, the other resting her head against her thigh. Penelope lay naked between them. "Go," she whispered softly.

The dark-haired one with golden eyes dared to lean down,

kissing Penelope on the mouth, gently biting the queen's bottom lip. Warmth flushed through Penelope at the exchange, a small flame of desire reigniting. "You may stay."

Once they were alone, the maid removed her chiton. "If I may, my queen?"

Penelope nodded against her pillows. "There is something in that box there." She pointed across the room.

The maid pulled the lid off. Inside was a phallus of fired and glazed clay. She carried it to Penelope like a lover, eyes full of fire and hands ready to explore the world of her queen's body. Leaning down, she pressed her warm lips against Penelope's ear, whispering words in a foreign tongue.

Penelope uncharacteristically grabbed the maid's head in her hands, bringing them face-to-face. With eyes locked, the lonely queen pulled their mouths together, deeply kissing the other woman. Pleasured moans rose between them as they pressed their nude bodies together. Penelope reached to touch the maid's sacred flesh. A flash of heat surged through her as she pressed her fingers into the wetness there. The maid handed her the phallus.

Taking it in one hand, Penelope pushed it into her lover, who moaned with delight.

Grasping her breast, the woman asked, "Will you suckle?"

Penelope, leaning on an elbow, slid up to reach the woman's side. She'd never felt a woman's nipple in her mouth. She tongued the brown circle, until it rose like an almond. Then, she suckled like a babe pulling milk. Penelope was overcome by the need to satisfy the woman, and rammed the phallus deeper over and over again until the woman beside her groaned and her legs quivered. Once the maid regained her composure, she returned the passion. Sweating and rubbing together, they passed the night.

When Apollo's light filtered through the window, Penelope woke with the maid's arms wrapped tightly around her waist. Caressing the woman's hair, she said, "You must wake."

The dark-haired beauty's eyes fluttered open.

"Go before the rest of the household is about their chores."

Without a word, the woman got up and pulled her chiton back on and left the chamber.

Penelope appreciated that this maid never made demands of her, or tried to steal private moments. The first time the queen had allowed such intimacy, was after Nauplius departed. Anticlea had convinced her that the old man was nothing more than a liar and a fool. But, the encounter had dredged up her loneliness, and with it, the ache to feel a man make love to her. To feel his arms wrapped around her. To feel the weight of him as he pressed into her, claiming her as his own. One evening, she had dismissed all her maids save one. She'd taken her by the hand into the private royal chamber.

Penelope had sworn it would never happen again, but her desire for physical touch only grew after that. And with no word from Odysseus, no end in sight of waiting…

She never spoke to the women who privately serviced her. What she did was simply an act of passion to quell the ache of loneliness inside of her. But this night, Penelope wanted to wrap her legs around someone. Kiss someone deeply. Have her body filled and used for pleasure. She wanted to chase the darkness and sadness away by making love to this woman, this nobody, who was everybody to her in the moment.

NINE

lost boys

ITHAKA—1238 BCE

"But I don't want to marry that little girl."

"Her name is Erigone." Penelope pulled a blue thread through the curling ocean waves on her tapestry. "She won't be a girl when you marry her. She'll be a woman."

Telemachus grimaced and rolled his eyes. "Gross."

Sighing, Penelope plucked a piece of lint from her design. "You say that now. Trust me, son, in a few years you'll be begging to marry."

"No. I won't." He rubbed at his smooth chin. "Is that why you're always checking to see if I have a beard? To see if I'm old enough to marry?"

"It's more than that, Telemachus."

"Tell me, Mother."

Penelope's eyes, sad and distant, met her son's. How could she expect him to understand what was at stake? "If your father doesn't return by the time you grow a beard, he made me promise I'd take another husband."

"What does that have to do with me?"

"Everything, Telemachus. Everything. Look around you. This palace. The lands. The people who depend on us for prosperity and protection. If your father doesn't return to *all* of this, your *birthright* will be forfeit."

"But I'm your son."

"Exactly. You're my son, which may spare your life. But, you're also Odysseus' son, which might demand your life. Do you understand? If the elders don't see you as a capable king, a man, then neither will the people of Ithaka. Rivals will come to take what belongs to us. Force me to marry someone else, for with my hand, the kingdom would pass peacefully to the next king. Have no doubt such a man would likely want his own children to rule after him. That is why you must marry. Why we must talk of these things. Let it be known. In doing so, the elders will know you take your duties seriously. As only a man can do."

Telemachus shifted his feet and stared out the window, avoiding his mother's intense gaze. "I don't want to be the king."

Penelope stood abruptly, spilling her basket of colored yarn. Standing before her son, she raised his chin roughly. "You say that now without knowing what it is to be king. I have labored too long and sacrificed much for you. More than you can ever realize. If I ever hear you utter those words again, I will slap them from your mouth myself."

Unaccustomed to his mother's anger, Telemachus stared at her in stunned silence.

"Now, leave me. In the morning, I'm sending you to your grandfather. Maybe you will listen to his reason."

Telemachus walked out with tears in his eyes.

The queen resumed her weaving. She pulled a bleached thread through a small needle and set to work on a cresting wave. Skillfully, Penelope frosted each one with white foam. When she finally put her work down, Apollo's light had begun to fade. *Odysseus, please return soon. Athena, I beg you bring him home.*

PHTHIA

Deidamia ran a hand across her cheek. The distorted image of the polished silver reflected an aging face. "Has it truly been that long?"

There was a knock at the door. Deidamia signaled one of the chamber maids to open it. A young boy, nervously wringing his hands, entered.

"Well? Have you a message?"

The boy nodded. "King Peleus says to tell you he is here."

Deidamia stood, reluctantly satisfied with her appearance. She fussed at a few pleats on her gown before sweeping gracefully from the chamber and rushed down the corridor.

The great hall was lit with oil lamps, and the central hearth roared with sunset flames. Garlands of olive curled around every column and hung around every table. Center pieces of rosemary and fresh flowers spilled from vases, spicing the air. Deidamia stood at the entrance looking for her son among the crowd.

"Neo has not arrived," Chiron said, as he clopped up next to her. "You are his mother, are you not?"

"I am," she whispered, awestruck. "I never thought to see a … you among these guests."

Chiron laughed. "Indeed. I wouldn't miss this reunion for anything."

"I can scarce believe eight years have gone by. I've missed my son more than he knows."

"He is no longer the boy you sent away."

Deidamia pressed her lips to a straight line. "It wasn't my choice to send him away."

Chiron clicked his tongue. "I've seen that look on Neo's face many times. Do not be angered by my words." He placed a warm hand on Deidamia's shoulder. "His father's blood runs hot through his veins. If it is at all possible, I believe Ares favors Neo more than Achilles."

"Are the stories about Achilles true?"

"Which stories? There are many."

"That he … that he stoned a woman to death?"

"Yes."

"I never would have believed my husband was capable of such violence."

Chiron folded his arms and studied Deidamia's face. "You still regard Achilles as husband? Interesting."

"He may yet return," Deidamia said, defiantly. "To us. To me."

"Ah, look, Neo arrives."

From across the hall, a man taller than all the others entered. His shoulders were wide and his gate long and confident. He wore a simple bleached chiton with a black cape pinned over his shoulders. A short sword strapped at his waist.

Deidamia rushed to him. "Neo! Neo!"

Chiron quickly followed.

Neoptolemus turned in her direction. "Mother."

She embraced him warmly, but his cool reception confused her. "I've missed you. All these years. You were just a boy—"

Neo's look of disdain spoke volumes. "I do not miss the boy I was."

"What has Chiron done to you?"

"Prepared me for my destiny."

"What destiny? Surely, you intend to come back with me to Skyros. Or … or remain here with your grandfather in Phthia." All the fears she had about Achilles never returning flooded her. The rumors that he'd taken another wife in the camps. *I can't lose my husband and my son to this war.*

Peleus approached just then, greeting his wayward grandson with a hearty embrace, oblivious to Neo's coolness. "Of course, he will remain here. Become commander of the Myrmidons as we await his father's return."

Neo squared his shoulders. "You are both wrong. I will join my father when the time comes. Chiron has seen it."

"But, surely the war will soon end." Peleus looked to Chiron for answers. "What is he saying?"

The centaur squinted an eye at Peleus. "Old friend, where's the wine? The good wine. Neo, I trust you will regale your mother with stories of your training. You may not miss the boy you once were, so let her know the man who you have become in his stead."

"Very well, Chiron."

As Neo led his mother to a table, Peleus signaled his personal slave to bring the good wine.

Once they'd quaffed a cup of the god's nectar, Peleus pressed for an answer. "What have the gods revealed to you of this Trojan War that the rest of us do not know?"

"It will be over soon, but not before great losses are doled out to both sides."

"What kind of great losses? Ships? Treasures? I hate when you speak in circles. Get to the point."

"I can say no more. Enjoy your time with Neo. He's not long for Phthia."

"You steal my joy, Chiron."

"I've been told that many times. The truth is rarely pleasant. And deception so convincing."

TEN

wine over water

CAMP OF AGAMEMNON, TROY—1238 BCE

Thin fingers of fog coiled around the quiet tents in Agamemnon's main encampment. Odysseus dreaded meeting with Agamemnon. He shivered beneath his wool cloak, thinner now than when he'd left Ithaka years ago. Penelope had woven it, so he'd refused to discard it for a newer one. Dogs scavenging for scraps around burnt fire rings scattered, as he made his way toward the king's pavilion. A few babies cried for feeding. A few women piled wood beneath cook fires. *Colder days are upon us. Gods help us if we must see another winter here.*

Royal guards crossed their spears before Agamemnon's tent, barring him from entering. "The king has commanded that he not be disturbed," said the helmed man on the left.

The King of Ithaka scowled, recalling Achilles' stinging words hurled at Agamemnon about how the Great King ordered his captains around like slaves. He flexed his jaw and bit the truth on the tip of his tongue. "Tell him Odysseus has returned with news from Chryse."

The guard quickly ducked into the tent, returning moments later. Without word, he stepped aside, allowing Odysseus to enter.

Agamemnon stood, hair unbound with his disheveled robe hanging open, leaning over several scrolls and charcoal-sketched leather maps scattered across his table. "Our supplies run low. If we do not breach that fucking wall before the cold sets in, we will have to wage another southern campaign to replenish our supplies."

Odysseus helped himself to the wine on the table. He sipped from the silver cup, again thinking of Achilles' insults. There was much truth to what he said, even if in anger. Agamemnon did take the largest portion, but he was the high king, and it was his due. *Or is it?* Odysseus brushed the question away for the time being. The camp was on the verge of a civil war and all he wanted was to go home. He secretly wished he could leave with Achilles and his Myrmidons and quit Troy altogether. "Ask Achilles to raze another city—"

"I'll ask that miserable dog for nothing."

"He's the Sacker of Cities. He and his Myrmidons can secure supplies more readily than—"

Agamemnon's fist crashed down on the table, sending marking stones flying in all directions. "Achilles has abandoned us," he said angrily. "He's chosen to turn his back on the entire army ... the entire campaign because of a slave woman."

"Give her back. Apologize. Blame it on too much wine. We need Achilles and you know it. I know it. The men know it."

Agamemnon roared back, "And let Achilles lord it over me that he controls the army I command? Who will follow me after that?"

"But you took Briseis—"

"She is a camp whore. Nothing more. I liberated him from a distraction. He never made her a proper wife, but now he is free to find one."

Odysseus shook his head. "All these years you two have been at one another's throats. Each denying the other his due. Now, it's your pride that's doomed us. Have you forgotten Kalchus' prophesy? Without Achilles we will lose the war and our way home."

Agamemnon's cheeks quivered with his growing irritation. "I will not be second guessed by a—"

"A king?" Odysseus asked. "Perhaps, Achilles was not entirely wrong after all."

"You tread dangerously close to treason, Odysseus. Do not force me to make an example of you as well."

"If truth is treason, then we are already lost." Odysseus set his cup down. "You have more women than any other man and a proper wife waiting for your return. Yet, you take the only woman of your greatest captain? To what end? Give her back unharmed." Odysseus swallowed hard. "You ... you have not defiled her, have you?" *Achilles will slit his throat if he has, king or not. Then, we are lost for certain.*

"I have not touched the girl ... yet," he said. "But I *will* take her for all the trouble she's caused me."

Odysseus stared unflinchingly into Agamemnon's eyes. "My lord, you have brought this upon yourself." He turned and left Agamemnon to his maps.

I must find Patrokles. He will know Achilles' mind.

Odysseus walked among the Black Shields' camp, searching for Patrokles. He found him in the healing quarter, hovered over a sick child. "It would seem Apollo has accepted our offering."

Patrokles looked up, his eyes dark and deadly. "Agamemnon's offering."

"Either way. The plague has slowed its course."

The physician turned back to the child. "Here, drink this, little Molus." Patrokles lifted the boy's head to the rim of the bowl. The patient drank slowly, sinking back again to the bed. "Those who were afflicted yet suffer. The plague takes its toll, although your words are true enough. I haven't been called to attend new victims of Apollo's wrath."

"Whose son is this one?"

"There are several possibilities, but it doesn't truly matter, does it? Not unless a man was brave enough to accept him as his own. Or desperate enough."

"I've heard what Agamemnon did … to Achilles."

Patrokles' scowled. "Again, your words lighten the deed. What Agamemnon has done to Achilles?" He spat on the hard sand. "What he has done to Briseis. She suffers most."

"Why did Achilles let her go?"

"His pride? His glory? What does it matter? He let her go. There's nothing to be done about it now."

"Did you expect him to fight a war within the very heart of our camp? So near the end of this campaign?"

Patrokles stood, towering over Odysseus, wiping the grime of sickness from his hands on a scrap of linen at his belt. "Achilles is *Achilles*. Who among these many captains, yourself included, could stand against him? Who would wish to stand against him? You have seen him striding, sword in hand, cutting men down as a farmer cuts his wheat. With ease. Precision. Briseis claims she saw Ares side by side with Achilles that day in Thebe. And yet, *he* let her go. He alone could have prevented her humiliation." He poured fresh water into another basin. "I tire of this war, Odysseus. If you seek Achilles, then look to his ship. No doubt he's sulking there blaming everyone else but himself for his loss."

Odysseus left Patrokles to his work. The rift between the two men surprised him, but then, he recalled their dispute at Thebe. At the time he'd believed Patrokles had been simply goading his cousin to marry the woman. Now, he realized the truth of it. Patrokles was in love with Briseis, perhaps more so than Achilles. *How did I miss that?*

Walking to the far side of the bay, Odysseus headed for the galleys farthest from Agamemnon's fleet. Achilles' hull rested high above the rest, even buried partially in the sand. Its dark hull faded. The round, menacing eyes gracing the prow had recently been repainted. *Keeping busy.* Odysseus called out, "Achilles!" But the Myrmidon captain gave no response. "Achilles!" He looked within the modest tent spiked along the side, but the Myrmidon commander wasn't to be found.

"You are returned from Chryse," Nax said from behind him.

"Aye. Young Nax. Where's your master?

Nax cast his eyes at his feet. "My lord is best ... left alone."

"He'll see me, one way or the other."

A shadow fell over Odysseus and Nax from above. They looked up against the sky to see Achilles, shrouded in light, standing naked on the rail. His eyes were dulled with too much wine and his hair a wild mane about his shoulders. His cape hung askew. "Achilles is not here," he called down. "He has left this miserable place."

"I will come up," Odysseus said, grabbing a jug of water from Nax. "He will need this."

Achilles jumped onto the wooden deck, shouting over his shoulder, "Do as you wish, King of Ithaka. You are not my slave to command about. I am no Agamemnon."

Climbing the rope ladder up the galley's side, Odysseus found Achilles in a crumpled heap of linens and furs, surrounded by empty amphorae. "I see Nax has kept you well supplied." He proffered the container in his hands to Achilles.

The Golden Warrior took it and drank deeply. Instantly, he spat it out, showering the deck with the clear contents. Achilles bellowed, "What swill is this?"

"Water. Drink it."

"I enjoy being drunk."

"You are a wretched drunk, Achilles. It doesn't suit you."

Achilles laughed bitterly. "You're wrong, Odysseus." He tossed the water aside, reaching for a fresh amphora of wine. He pried the lid off with a small blade and drank the crimson liquid until it ran in thin rivers down his neck. "If I am to die in this unhappy place, I refuse to remember it."

"That is the wine speaking, not the Sacker of Cities."

Achilles' eyes narrowed to slits. "You are mocking me, King of a Rock."

"Peace, Achilles. I haven't come to mock you."

"Why have you come, then?"

"To see the truth with my own eyes."

Achilles slammed the clay container against the wood, sending shards flying across the deck. "What truth?"

"That you've withdrawn your Myrmidons from the fight."

"Aye. That I *have* done."

Odysseus squatted next to Achilles. "Why, Achilles? Why take your men from battle?"

"Because Agamemnon has humiliated me, or do you believe I prefer to stay away from the song of swords clashing?" Achilles grabbed Odysseus' arm with fingers as strong as iron bands. "Because he took *her*."

"It was his right."

Achilles sneered, jerking his hand away. "It is my right to sail home. I took no oath like the rest of you fucking goats."

Odysseus bristled at the insult. "You should've married Briseis properly, as you said you would back in Thebe. None of this would have been possible. This is your fault, Achilles."

"Get. Off. My. Ship!"

"As you command," Odysseus said, annoyed by the entire conversation and turn of events. He stood and made for the railing. "We can't win the war without you. Think of all the men depending on you." Not waiting for an answer, he leapt down into the soft sand.

What do the gods wish from us? Maybe they seek to fuck us as Agamemnon claims. He immediately thought of the Oracle and her haunting words. *I cannot be gone for twenty years. It has been too long already.* He thought of Telemachus. *Almost a man.* Then, he thought of Penelope. Her radiant smile was almost all he could clearly recall. The exactness of her face was fading. He recalled her tears as he made her promise to marry another if he didn't make it back before Telemachus reached manhood. *I must make it back to Ithaka before my world is lost to me. Despite Achilles and Agamemnon.*

PHTHIA

Neoptolemus woke before Apollo set the new day on fire and began his ritual training. His years with Chiron had honed him to be hard and unforgiving, even in regard to his own comforts. He took no pleasure in sleep, wine, or the tenderness of women. His heart longed only for battle and blood. The centaur promised it would be soon, but refused to say more.

He heard his mother's foot falls before he saw her approach. He relaxed his sword at his side. "I am here, Mother."

"Did you sleep well, Neo?"

"Yes."

"You're no longer plagued by troubling dreams?"

"The dreams remain."

"But they no longer bother you?"

Facing his mother, he decided to smile. "I'm not afraid of anything, anymore."

"I see."

"I must thank you, Mother."

"For what, Neo?"

"Sending me to Chiron."

"You were just a boy—"

"Aye. A boy who needed to become a warrior."

"You're not angry, then? That I allowed Peleus to send you away? The things you told me of your training …"

Neo softened, uncharacteristically. Wiping sweat from his brow, he said, "It was best. I was unruly. Undisciplined. Without Chiron's guidance, I'd not be ready for my fate."

"You mentioned that last night. Can't you tell me more? Of what Chiron has foretold?"

"Only what the gods allow."

Deidamia looked to her son for an answer. A chill shivered through her heart. "Your dream of a burning city … was Troy?"

"Aye. It was."

"It all makes sense, now, I suppose." She wanted to cry for all the lost time. It seemed that it passed more swiftly with age and that was certainly a curse of the immortal gods for whom time made no difference. In Deidamia's mind it was only yesterday Achilles had smiled sweetly at her and had played the lyre, making songs of love for her. Neo, a nearly-grown man standing before her, was a virtual stranger. All her memories of him were simply that: *hers*. Likely, Neo recalled other things more important than a mother's hugs and kisses. Thetis' pain struck her like thin lightning. The nymph had missed most of her son's life. How had she managed to live with the pain of not knowing and always wondering? Thetis had unsuccessfully tried to prevent Achilles from going to war, and here she was wishing to do the same for her son. "May I watch you train?"

Flashing his mother a brilliant smile, he said, "As you wish."

Neo slashed and parried with his sword, swinging his shield lightly about him. His feet moved like an elegant dancer. The resemblance to Achilles was striking. A wave of longing and dread washed over Deidamia. Yes, her little boy truly belonged solely to her memory now. She'd been sitting long enough on the hard marble for the pain in her hip to throb. *I am becoming an old woman. How long has my husband been gone?* She tried to recount the years in her mind, and realized she couldn't even keep the memories made in Achilles' absence in order. Then, it struck her with horrifying certainty. *He's never coming back for me. I have lost my entire life to this war.*

ELEVEN
beguile and betray
PALACE OF PRIAM, TROY—1238 BCE

The cool air chilled Helen's skin, as she made her way down the dark hall. She walked alone and without a torch, for secrecy required stealth and quiet. After several turns, she came to the simple wooden door. She tested it to see if Corythus had obeyed her command to leave it unbarred. She smiled as she softly pushed it open.

Corythus lay on his side sleeping in the dimming light of a sputtering oil lamp. The chamber was small and dank compared to hers, but it had been too risky to provide him with a more sumptuous accommodation. She had no desire to give her secret away before she was ready.

Helen walked to his bed. Standing there for a moment, she silently contemplated how like Paris he appeared. *Handsome.* She undid the clasps at her shoulders and her sheer gown slipped to the floor before she slid into the bed next to him.

Corythus moaned in his sleep as he turned over, draping a heavy arm across her breasts. Helen wriggled her hips into his soft cock, rubbing him until it sprang to life. While Corythus slept, she gently rolled him onto his back. She took his swollen cock in her mouth, expertly twirling her wet tongue around the hard ridge of its head. He moaned against the linen and furs; a stray hand found her head, pressing her face closer. Helen sucked and stroked him. A few short pulses told her Corythus was on the verge of releasing his seed, so she straddled him.

His eyes fluttered briefly as she sheathed him within her. A few wet strokes and his eyes flew completely open. Though darkness shrouded Helen's face from his full view, he knew her by the smell of honey and myrrh. "What are—" He groaned and grabbed her hips, grinding his cock into her as the warmth of their union shot through his entire body.

Helen covered Corythus' mouth with hers, keeping the roar of his pleasure from echoing across the chamber. She swept her tongue across his teeth, tangling it with his. He reached for her waist, and with his arm expertly pulled her beneath him.

Corythus' voice was a husky, desperate whisper, "Helen—"

"Shah," she said, pressing a silky finger against his swollen lips. "It is best not to speak." She moved her hand to the wetness between them, feeling his renewed readiness. "Take me once more." Her thoughts flew to the first time she laid with Paris in Sparta years ago. They'd been overwhelmed by desire and fucked in a filthy stable. The sting of Paris' confession that Aphrodite had somehow spurred their unnatural passion had never left her. Resentment crept like a fog around her heart. Often, she found herself weighing the life she had in Troy against the life she left behind in Sparta. Although mothering felt foreign to her in her youth, now, as age began to settle her beauty, her thoughts turned more and more to legacy. For a time, she hoped the goddess would grant them children, but that had not happened.

As Corythus kissed her neck, a sweet pleasure filled her belly. *This is pure and real.* She wrapped her legs around his thighs, urging him to plant his seed deep inside of her. She moaned as her release shook her legs, and quickly Corythus followed.

"I love you," he whispered against her ear.

"Do not love me."

"It is … too late." Pulling her into his embrace, he threw a leg over her hip. He kissed the side of her neck, before drifting off to a contented sleep.

When Corythus' breathing slowed, Helen slipped from the bed. After picking her chiton up from the floor, she fastened the shoulders together. She smoothed out the gentle pleats, and then slipped quietly from the chamber, disappearing into the dark hall.

King Telephus signaled for his army to march ahead. Troy was but one more rise of Apollo away. He was relieved they'd avoided any interference from Agamemnon's army so far. And Achilles. Especially Achilles. The rumors of the Golden Warrior's ruthlessness chilled him to the bone. Although a skilled healer, which he knew first hand, Achilles was merciless and cruel. Telephus massaged his thigh, running his finger along the raised scar. "This war should have been finished years ago."

Korei, the king's faithful second, nodded. "It would seem the gods love these Greeks."

Telephus scowled. "Precisely what I'm afraid of."

"Do you think the whispers of the Spartan Helen true?" Korei asked.

"That she's bewitched them all?"

"Aye."

"It's possible. The tales of her beauty persist. If I were Priam, I'd have thrown her back to Menelaus the moment she stepped foot in my kingdom. No woman is worth so much death and dishonor as she has brought."

Korei wasn't so sure. "I would have killed a thousand men to save my wife."

"That was different. She was a faithful wife. A valiant woman."

"We should march all night. The moon is full. We won't be safe until we reach the walls of Troy," Korei said.

"Agreed. Where is Eurypylus, my son?"

"A camp woman has given birth. He attends her."

"Find him. Remind him not to fall behind. I'll not have my son butchered by Achilles because he worried over a slave's child."

Patrokles waited until darkness descended on the camp before making his way into Agamemnon's rows. He knew where Briseis had been taken, and so far, the Great King had denied his requests to visit Achilles' prize, claiming the woman was his by right. No doubt a punishment meant to hurt Achilles. When the campfires burned to embers and the men stumbled off to their tents, Patrokles moved as a wraith. Keeping to the shadows, he found Briseis' quarters, nestled among the other tents spiked for Agamemnon's women. A single guard sat on a stool outside the entrance, his head nodding in a dream. *One less death this night.* Without a sound, the dark cousin of Achilles slipped behind the tent and beneath it.

An oil lamp glowed thinly in the dark. He squinted into the shadows, finally finding Briseis. Patrokles' heart ached to see her huddled and frightened and alone. He knew her heart, as well as his own, broke with Achilles' betrayal. "Briseis," he whispered, stepping into the view.

She sat up, startled by the sound of a familiar voice. She pushed a lock of tangled hair from her face to see better in the dim light. "Patrokles?"

"Aye, my lady."

Briseis leapt from the rumpled bed and into his arms. "Patrokles," she whispered desperately into his neck.

Her sobs wracked his body with a pain, tender and sweet, as he'd never known before. His heart pounded as though headed into battle, yet...*yes, it is a battle and I will lose.* For the first time, he held the woman he'd loved always from afar. He wrapped his arms tighter around her, feeling his arms press into her curves. He inhaled the salty honeyed essence of her skin. "I am here, Briseis."

"Why? Why has *he* done this to me?"

Patrokles pulled back to see her face swollen with grief. He kissed her damp cheek. "I do not know this Achilles. I do not recognize this man. Are you hurt? Has Agamemnon—"

"No. He has not touched me. Perhaps, I am safe?" she offered hopefully.

"Perhaps, for now ... but he did not risk the fury of Achilles to place a woman with camp whores and not use her." Patrokles took her face in his hands, searching her eyes, and knew, in that moment, for the rest of his life he'd love no other woman the way he loved her. "If the gods had granted me such a prize, I would have fought a thousand Greeks to keep you at my side." He leaned his head down, his lips hovering just above Briseis' mouth. *It is wrong to love her.*

Her lips parted, and he could hold back no longer. His mouth descended on hers, and he kissed her tenderly, years of yearning for her touch inflaming his body and soul. When her arms wrapped around his neck, pulling him closer, his heart leapt within his chest. A tear slid from the corner of his eye with the agony and the joy of the moment. His kiss deepened, and his tongue found hers. He breathed her air, tasting the salt of her tears at the corners of her mouth.

Patrokles picked her up and took her to the makeshift bed. With her head resting against his pounding heart, they sank into the furs and linens. He kissed her lips, her cheeks, and her neck. "You hold my heart, Briseis."

She wrapped her legs around his thighs, pressing their bodies together as one. "Take me, my lord."

"If he should discover—"

Briseis placed a tender finger against his lips. "He has discarded me for all to see. I belong to no one now."

It was enough. He sat up, pulling his chiton over his head.

Briseis reached a trembling hand out to touch his chest. "Untie your hair," she whispered.

Without taking his gray eyes from hers, he reached a hand behind his head, sliding the knotted leather tie from his hair. His dark locks and braids spilled about his shoulders. Briseis' eyes widened at the beauty of the man kneeling over her. "Patrokles," she said, smiling.

"My lady." He undid the shoulders of Briseis' tunic and slipped it from her body. "I never thought to see you as you are, so beautiful ... and mine, if only for tonight." *Do not forget.*

"Come to me," she whispered, needing the comfort of his body and his love.

Patrokles lay beside his love, showering her body with kisses, his hands delighting in her every curve. *How can I dismiss her?*

"Patrokles," Briseis whispered against his ear. "Do not think on him. We both know we are not destined for one another, but we have this night. Our bliss amid betrayal."

He slid on top of her, spreading her thighs with his hips. "You know my mind so well, Briseis. You are right, my love." He pressed his cock into her body, both moaning with forbidden desire.

Briseis wrapped her legs tighter around the back of his legs, her heels digging into his buttocks, urging him to take her deeper and harder. "Patrokles ..."

He rode her in silence until he sensed her body stiffening before her climax, then he smothered the sound of their mutual release with a passionate kiss. He lay atop her, their mouths devouring each other's, while his cock pulsed slowly inside of her, and their lovemaking spilled onto the furs beneath them.

Patrokles rolled to Briseis' side, pulling her into his strong embrace. "I will keep you safe, even if he will not."

"If he ..." she said, quietly into the shadows.

"He will try to kill me."

"You must not—"

Patrokles kissed her swollen lips. "Shah, my love. He will never know. I have no intention of dying by Achilles' hand."

TWELVE
an ugly truth
MYCENAE—1238 BCE

Orestes broke the seal on the thin scroll and opened it, scowling as he read the contents. "I wondered why Mother was so hasty in visiting Ithaka."

Elektra watched her brother toss the scroll to the floor. She thought he looked like Agamemnon just then with piercing dark eyes and a wide jaw. So many years had passed since she'd seen her father that most of her memories of him were fading to the shadows. "Does it say when she will return?" Elektra asked, hesitantly.

"She's already well underway. My messenger had a faster ship. Better rowers."

"If she discovers you have been spying on her …" Elektra shivered. "She'll … I don't want to think about what she'll do." As the years passed, her mother had become increasingly secretive and withdrawn. She was less a mother and more a distant relative who wielded her fate. While she'd grown more fearful of her, Orestes had become quite bold.

Orestes laughed. "I'm not afraid of her." He picked up the scroll and tucked it away on a shelf behind him. "She has secured a betrothal for Erigone."

Elektra scoffed. "Erigone? But she's only a girl of five seasons. To who?"

"Telemachus, the heir apparent of Ithaka."

The news rattled her confidence even further. "That would make her a queen."

"And you have yet to have a suitor."

"I am aware," Elektra snapped.

"Don't be angry with me, sister. I am not the one keeping you from a proper life."

Orestes' words stung as much as angered her. She was already considered old by tradition. If her father returned soon, he could arrange a match. *Any match is preferable*, she thought, *to being a lonely woman without children to comfort me.* That was the way of a woman's world. Voiceless in public, but around the hearth, a wife and a mother wielded some power. And that was far better than none or being under her mother's eye for the rest of her life. Without her parents' backing, who would want her, except an old man? She shuddered inwardly. "Why would she do this? Without father's consent?"

"That's exactly why she did it. To usurp his part in it. Join me by the fire."

Orestes took the couch closest to the hearth, gesturing to his sister to take the one opposite. "I believe she's planning something, when or *if* Father returns."

"Of course Father will come home."

"Dear sister, what do you know of war? The gods will dictate who returns and who does not. Mother is preparing for all possibilities. Which means, she's preparing to push the true heirs of Mycenae, you and I, aside."

"What do you mean? 'True heirs'?"

"Tell me you don't believe the whispers that our mother bears children by Zeus?"

It was another stinging insult to her lack of suitors … that her mother remained fruitful, while she had yet to experience the joy of motherhood. "How else do you explain her being with child at her age?"

"If a man plows a field often enough, some wheat is sure to grow."

"You hate her that much?"

Orestes ran his tongue over his front teeth before he spoke, his mouth curving wickedly with poisonous words. "I hate her with good reason."

"The gods will curse you for such thoughts."

His laugh was sharp and cold. "Do you think the gods have not already cursed this family? I believed, and still believe, there was a purpose behind father killing Iphigenia. There's also a reason the gods keep the war from ending. There is a truth echoing in these halls that you ignore."

"What truth?"

"Aegisthus is the father of Aletes and Erigone."

Their mother had guested their uncle for long periods of time over the years. If it was true, then they were doomed by the gods. Their mother had made sure of it. Little by little, small things began to make sense in her mind. How Aegisthus was always here when her younger siblings … cousins were born. How could she have missed something so obvious beneath her nose? *I am still naïve and stupid*, she thought. "How could she do this to our family? She disgraces all of us."

"Why do you think she is aligning her bastard daughter with a true prince and not her eldest legitimate daughter?"

Elektra fumbled for words, for connections, for answers. She had none.

"She plans to push us aside, sister. Planting her children by that goat in our places. She hates Agamemnon—"

"But she loves us."

"Not more than she hates our father. And because of that, she will put her children, not his children, in power. That is the only way she can maintain her control of Mycenae."

"Father will return. He can undo any harm she does."

"If he returns. If. I'm not sure what our mother has planned for our father, but her actions prove to me that she has a plan either way."

Elektra thought for a moment. "It won't come to that, Orestes."

Her brother laughed angrily. He clapped for a servant. From the shadows, a young woman emerged with head bowed and hands clasped behind her. "Bring wine. And cups." The girl nodded, disappearing as silently as she'd entered.

"How old is Telemachus?" Elektra asked.

"As old as the war is long."

The serving maid entered, poured the wine, then handed them each a full cup.

Orestes dismissed the servant with his hand. Waiting until he heard the chamber door shut, he leaned toward his sister and whispered, "She secures a strong ally in Ithaka. King Odysseus has but one child." Orestes rubbed the stubble on his chin. "We must discover her plan."

"Do you think we should tell grandfather?" Elektra could see Orestes' mind scheming. She feared Tyndareus. He was even colder than her mother.

"Not yet." Orestes drank his wine thoughtfully. "It was prudent of him to arrange a betrothal between Hermione and I. Tyndareus is shrewd. He may see mother's actions as working in his favor. No, I can't go to him unless I have proof his daughter works against him. Better to wait."

"Perhaps, you should go to Sparta. Visit your future bride?"

"She's still too young to wed."

"True. But you could go on pretense of showing grandfather you honor his plans by gifting the girl a small token. Then discover what he's thinking regarding our mother."

"You surprise me, Elektra."

She smiled wanly, shrugging her shoulders. "I have good ideas … from time to time … I think."

"I'll make arrangements to leave before Mother returns."

They reclined on their respective couches, watching the hearth fire burn down to glowing orange embers. Elektra wondered how she would face her mother when she returned. Knowing now that her younger brother and sister were also her cousins disgusted her. When would the curse be lifted from her family's house? If Agamemnon were to die at Troy, Orestes could become king by right. He was old enough. But she knew their mother too well. Orestes could only claim his birthright by civil war. *We are as wretched as the Olympians themselves.*

Clytemnestra, wrapped in a woolen himation, reclined on a small couch at the stern of the ship. The sails billowed with strong winds and rowers sat at the ready. The heavy gray sky threatened rain, or worse, a storm. She'd been pleasantly surprised that Penelope had agreed so quickly to her proposal. Although curious about the Ithakan queen's agreement, she never pressed for reasoning. In the end, it didn't matter. Mycenae and Ithaka would be united by marriage and eventually by blood.

"Pardon, my lady."

Clytemnestra turned to face the nursemaid flanked by her children. "Yes?"

Glancing at each child, the nursemaid said, "They wish to sit with you a while."

"Come, my darlings. Come." The queen pulled a linen blanket over them as they settled next to her. "You may go ... what is your name again?"

"Sara."

"Sara. See that provision is made for their midday meal."

"What did you think of Ithaka, Erigone?"

The little girl shrugged. "It was breezy. More breezy than Mycenae."

"It's surrounded by ocean. I'm sure there is always wind to keep the air cooled."

Aletes asked, "Will we see our cousin again?"

"Yes."

"When?"

"Soon."

"How long is that? Don't we have to go back so Erigone can marry Telemachus?"

Erigone piped up, "What do you mean, brother?"

"Mother and Queen Penelope promised to marry you to Telemachus."

"I don't think I'm meant for that."

Clytemnestra reached for her daughter's hand, wrapping it in hers. "You'll be ready when the time comes."

"Who will you marry me to?" Aletes asked.

The queen thoughtfully extended her other hand to her son. "One day you will rule Mycenae. That is when we will choose a bride for you." Clytemnestra saw the questions in Aletes' eyes. "That is our secret. Do you understand?"

Aletes nodded.

"Never speak of that to anyone. Not Neola. Not Aegisthus. And especially not Orestes or Elektra. No one. Do you understand?"

Aletes nodded more vigorously.

"Good. Now, go with your nurse …"

"Sara," Erigone said.

"Sara. Yes. Go."

"How many days until we reach home?" asked Aletes.

"At least five, if this storm doesn't break our course."

When she was once again alone, Clytemnestra's thoughts turned to the child she was carrying. She pressed her hand gently on her belly. In her bones, she knew the end of the great war loomed on the horizon. She could not let Agamemnon return to Mycenae. Not now. Not ever. If he were to make it home, he would without a doubt hunt her and her children down. He would never be satisfied with their banishment. He had too much pride. Under the stormy skies, she promised herself that she'd kill Agamemnon by her own hand, risking the retribution of the gods, before she let him touch any of her children ever again. A bolt of Zeus' lightning ripped across the sky. The wind picked up, and the sea surged with power. It was time to finalize plans with Aegisthus.

THIRTEEN
lost son returned

PALACE OF PRIAM, TROY—1238 BCE

Lykaon's horse plodded slowly along the cobble stone streets of Troy. The citadel was unrecognizable. Refugees filled the side alleys with their tattered tents and crowded around the public fountains. Excrement from men and animals alike dried in the sun, scrapped away only here and there. The air was stifling and putrid. He fought the urge to vomit as he and Eetion of Imbros pressed deeper into the heart of the royal city.

"Does my father know the decrepit state of Troy's streets?" Lykaon asked.

"Nothing passes Priam's attention," Eetion answered, digging his heels into his horse. "These people have nowhere else to go. And there is nowhere for many of them to stay, except on the streets, or wherever they can find a corner."

Lykaon gripped his horse's reigns, wringing them into his palms until blisters formed. "What if he does not accept me into his household?"

"The king will not refuse his own flesh and blood a place at his table."

"What if he—"

"I suggest you stop talking, until it is clear you must speak."

The streets were noisy and chaotic, but they rode on in silence, passing a dozen or more make-shift tenements. They rode past the curved street of bakers, then the wide lane of skilled leather workers, and finally through the quarter of potters and metal smiths. Upward the streets stretched on, upward toward the shining palace of Priam … and hopefully, home. *Pray the gods I am welcomed.* Lykaon feared his father's rejection after his long absence, but dreaded the queen's icy reaction most. She held the key to his existence.

It was Queen Hecuba, jealous of Priam's concubines and whores, who ruled the palace with the power to send anyone away, including Priam's bastards and their mothers. He recalled the day she sent his mother, Laothoë, back to her father, King of the Leleges, in disgrace. Lykaon's royal lineage provided little protection in Priam's court. The children of Hecuba ranked highest in honor and privilege, of that there had always been no question.

Eetion spurred his horse to trot. "Hurry, boy." He pointed ahead of them. "See the citadel there? Soon, I will be a wealthy man, for all the troubles I have endured on your behalf."

As Apollo's light descended, they arrived at the gate of the palace. They'd traveled far and under precarious circumstances. Lykaon was certain they looked little better than the ragged refugees over-running the city.

A guard on the rampart hollered down to them, "What is your business with the palace?"

Lykaon nervously eyed the guards flanking the pillars of the gate. His horse, sensing his unease, whickered loudly and shook its head. He imagined Hecuba glaring from behind the guards.

Eetion called up, "I have urgent news for the king's ears alone. He is expecting me. Let me pass."

The guard's laughter rang heavy, like an avalanche of stone. "Every man believes he's entitled to see the king whenever he pleases. Do you carry a missive from the king?"

Lykaon shouted, "I am Lykaon, a son of Priam, returned from captivity."

Eetion glared sideways at Lykaon. He should have known he would blurt out who he was. "I have rescued this boy and I'm here to return him safely into the king's hands."

The heavy, wooden gate opened, and six guards appeared to escort them directly to the great hall. The courtyard was shaded by citrus trees, tall, shaggy palms, and tented pavilions. Small children played together at the fountain, watched over by their nursemaids fanning themselves beneath an arbor. A few older boys practiced with wooden swords. He remembered when he was one of them. Carefree and oblivious to what it truly meant to be the second level of Priam's sons. It seemed a lifetime ago since Lykaon had laid eyes on the impressive pillars and brightly painted walls of Priam's palace. He took a seat at a bench near the central hearth. His body was now weary from the long and sometimes dangerous journey from Lemnos to Arisbe, and then south to Troy.

There was a great commotion at the northern entrance to the hall. A cortege of men and women followed closely behind an anxious king and queen. *My father has aged.* Lykaon spied the tall warrior armored in gold, an azure cape fluttering behind him, as he strode like a god behind Priam. *Hektor, Prince and Defender of the citadel. I have little in common with my half-brother.* In fact, he wondered if the strength of Priam's line didn't arise from Hecuba's blood. Beside Hektor was his wife, carrying a tiny babe in her arms. And bringing up the rear of the solemn procession were Paris, Deiphobus, Cassandra, Helenus, and Polydorus and Polites.

Priam greeted him with open arms. "I would know that face anywhere. My son is returned."

Relieved, Lykaon rushed to his father's embrace. Grateful tears flooded his eyes and he was helpless to stop them. The long months of slavery had almost broken him, and now, in his father's presence he felt safe enough to weep for his misfortune.

King Priam, empathy burning in his eyes, sought his eldest sons' faces. "This is why we must drive the invaders back to their lands. How many more of my sons, your brothers, must suffer?"

"The women suffer as well," Hecuba said, feigning compassion for Priam's bastards. "Each of your sons has a wife … and mother. Tell us, Lykaon, what happened? We are privy only to the rumors."

Queen Hecuba's interest caught Lykaon off guard. "It was Achilles, my lady."

"Tell us everything," Queen Hecuba said, taking her place at her high chair on the dais. Priam sat beside her, and his siblings gathered close by, sitting on steps and benches.

Lykaon was nervous now with all the eyes on him. Family they were, but not always friendly. "A dozen of us were in an orchard cutting fresh branches for the chariot master outside of Lyrnessus. We did not even know the foreigners were close to the city, until they were on us, screaming that we throw down our weapons. But, of course, we would not. That's when we were ambushed by Achilles and his Myrmidons. They dragged me through the mud by my hair. Humiliated me."

Hektor grew intrigued by his encounter with Achilles. "You met Achilles face to face, yet live? I would have thought he'd kill every son of Priam he laid his hands on."

"They spared me for the gold."

Queen Hecuba got up and paced a few steps, her violet gown flowing behind her like a bubbling stream. "They make a profit of selling our people into slavery. It is reprehensible." She knelt before Lykaon, tilting his dimpled chin up so he could see the revenge burning in her own eyes. "What do you seek, son of Priam?"

"I want Achilles to pay for what he did to me. I was sold by his word, humiliated by his commander, Patrokles—"

Hecuba nodded. "Revenge. You wish for revenge."

"I do, my lady."

The queen stood, staring each of her children in the eye. "And he shall have it."

Eetion cleared his throat. "Now that I have returned your son, I will take my reward and return to my own home. If it pleases you, of course, King Priam."

Priam clapped his hands. "First, we celebrate my son's safe return." Servants and slaves brought in trestle tables and benches. Wine flowed. The sweet, smoky aroma of roasting meat filled the air. "Lord Eetion, you will have your gold after we feast."

"How can I refuse?" Eetion said, accepting a cup brimming with red wine. A slave pulled a bench, set with luxurious linens and pillows, behind him.

The king clapped him on the back. "You cannot."

As the royal family settled into their couches, the queen raised her alabaster cup. "We give thanks to Apollo for your return." A quiet cheer rose for Lykaon, and behind the smiles and well wishes, they all questioned Queen Hecuba's toast. It was known she usually avoided any mention of Apollo. Her recent change of heart left her family wondering what had happened. Why raise Apollo above the other gods? Why Apollo at all?

When the palace settled into sleep, Priam entered his wife's chamber. The oil lamps were still lit and he found her sipping wine on her balcony. "Hecuba."

"Priam."

Coming up beside her, he said, "You surprised me this evening."

Glancing at him with a rare smile, she asked, "How so?"

Priam's elbow brushed hers. "Your praise of Apollo. After all these years, I thought—"

Hecuba placed a cool hand on his. "Clearly, husband, you do not know everything about me."

"You confuse me, woman."

"Come to bed, Priam."

"With you?"

Hecuba, her eyes sparkling, took Priam's hand in hers and led him to her bed. She used Priam's body as Apollo had used hers—complete abandon, void of love. Knowing that she would bring Achilles to his knees excited her and this was the only way she could share her secret. Men fought war with weapons forged of bronze, but women must use the weapons of the flesh. She'd brought a god to her side, not by sword or spear, but by the power she wielded between her thighs.

MT. OLYMPUS

Thetis, her heart heavy with her son's grief, marked the passing of the twelfth day by the brightest star in the heavens. She burst through the cresting waves as soon as Apollo's light swept the azure sky with amethyst and gold, making a swift ascent to the farthest peak of Olympus. She knew Lord Zeus would be perched on his high seat of power, gazing at the mortal world ensconced below his feet. Long gone were the days that the Lord of Thunder would seek her attention at her private inlet. Long gone were the days of his tender and hungry kisses. She hoped that the love he bore her then would serve her now in her son's time of need. A son that should have been his own.

The fresh snow crunched lightly beneath Thetis' feet as she approached. Her damp hair crisped in the cold. Crystals formed about the hem her gossamer gown. "My Lord of Thunder." Her clouded breath hung in the thin air.

Zeus exhaled a small breath of mist and rain. "Why have you come here, Thetis?" His heart ached in her presence. The mighty lord of Olympus balled his spear hand at his side. "You are forbidden."

The nymph flung herself at his feet, grasping him about his knees in supplication, overcome by her sorrow. "My lord, if ever I have pleased you, I beseech you hear my prayer."

The god's hand reached for his former lover's head, hovering slightly before laying it against her hair. The heat of his touch melted the snow from her long locks, releasing the dark tendrils to the wind. "You are as lovely as I remember."

"Does our ancient love hold meaning for you still?"

"What troubles plague your heart, sweet nymph?"

"It is Achilles, Father Zeus."

The god knelt down, cradling her head and lifting her chin so his eyes could find hers. "What of the Golden One?"

"He should have been ours, Lord Zeus, but you commanded me to marry a mortal. Had you loved me more, he would have been yours and his suffering would not exist."

Zeus bristled at the reminder. "I could not allow it, no matter how much I loved you then."

"I am alone in my grief. Cast from the palace of the mortal who planted Achilles in my belly. And now, I alone must plead for the life of my shining son."

Moved by pity, he said, "Tell me what has happened."

"Agamemnon has humiliated Achilles before the host of Greeks. Taken his prize, but she is more than that to him, I know it. It is hard for a man condemned to brief years to love, yet I know Achilles loves Briseis. As much as he can love, because war is in his blood. And Agamemnon has taken her."

Zeus sat in silence, neither acknowledging her or her words. Then he asked, "What would you have me do?"

"Punish Agamemnon. Let the Trojans push the Greeks back to their ships. Give the Trojans victory after victory, until they see how much honor is due my son." Thetis pressed her cause; Achilles' life and legacy hung in the balance, and only Zeus could help him now. "Bow your head and make it so, or deny me. Do you fear Achilles now, son of a mortal? The prophecy you feared cannot come to pass. Am I to be the most dishonored immortal of them all?"

Zeus brushed her hair with his hand, curling a long lock of it around his finger. "You do not fathom my life here." He gestured to the pointed mountain tops of Olympus. "See how my heavenly realm extends beyond your sight? Out there is a world you do not know. There is more ... but no matter. What you ask of me sparks open war with Hera. She gives me no rest. Always accusing me of aiding the Trojans. Leave me, Thetis. Before she discovers that you have come with arms wrapped about my knees."

Thetis reached a hand up, gently cupping the mighty god's chin. "I beg you, my love, who was never my true lover. We know the truth, even if Hera does not accept it. I beg you, grant Achilles this honor."

Zeus grasped her wrist, pulling it from his face. "You do not know the entire consequence. What you ask ... what he asks—"

"He is to die at Troy. What else is worse than his death to endure?"

"I pity those who love him." Zeus caressed Thetis' pale cheek. "I have loved you, Thetis. Try to remember that when the end has come."

"I promise," the nymph said.

"All that you desire for your son will come to pass."

The God of the Thunderbolt bowed his head and the peaks of Olympus trembled with his power. Snow shook free of the narrow peaks, sliding in blinding white waves down the sacred mountain.

As Thetis dove for the sea, the god's words echoed in her ear. *"I have loved you, Thetis. Try to remember that when the end has come."* She feared what he meant, but if Achilles' died with his honor, she promised herself she would find a way to live out her days of lonely sorrow.

Zeus returned with the speed of the wind to the shining hall of his palace where the crippled God of the Forge had prepared a lavish feast. The Olympians rose to greet their father, smiling and raising their crystal drinking cups in his honor.

Hera seethed behind her cup, because she had spied Thetis entreating Zeus. Touching him intimately. She was certain they hatched some plan together without consulting the rest of the gods. So she crooned silkily, "I see you are of a gentle mood, Lord Zeus. Lord husband. What can be the cause, I wonder?"

Zeus bristled at her words, his jaw twitching. He knew better than to trust her. "Clearly, wife, you aim to enlighten me on some matter."

Hera's eyes narrowed dangerously, full of accusation. "I saw you settling secrets with the nymph, while we all awaited your return. No doubt she seeks your influence for her son, Achilles. Your favorite."

"You forget your place, Goddess. Why attempt to know my thoughts? My heart? They are jealous and unchanging. Unable to reason without flying into a rage. I must seek peace away from my own halls. If I decide to plot a course without you, it is none of your business."

Hera softened a bit, so Zeus would listen. "I know the affection you have for Thetis. I know you gave her up to save us all from despair. That is why I fear any oath you make with her. Have you agreed to her request to aid Achilles and destroy the Greeks, while they sit idle at the beach without the shining commander to lead them in battle?"

"And if your suspicions are right, Hera, what can be done about it? Do you claim the power to change a course I have set in motion? You are too suspicious. If I have made a plan with Thetis, then it is my will to do so. Although you are sister-wife to me, I command you to obey me. Now, sit down and speak no more against Thetis and Achilles." The god's icy stare scanned around the table, ensnaring each deity and filling them with dread. "None of them will protect you and hope to live, if I decide to choke you with my own hands."

Hera sat in silence at the threat, knowing Zeus was right. None of them would lift a finger to help her, risking their positions on Olympus and their very existence. Zeus possessed the might to destroy them all. He had, after all, defeated Cronus, ushering in the reign of the Olympians. What would come after them? She had no idea, and didn't wish to know.

Hephaestus leaned into his mother, whispering urgently to her, "What disaster are you trying to bring down on us? If you two are at each other's throats over one mortal man, there will be war here, in the heavens. Seek Zeus' good graces, I beg you. For all our sakes. Push aside your jealousy of the nymph. What is she compared to you?" He reached for a silver cup. "You recall what happened to me when I dared defend you? He threw me like a heavy stone, and I plunged toward Gaia for an entire day. My body smashed and broken in the dust below us. If not for the mortals on Lemnos, who healed me, you would be less one son."

Hera knew he spoke the bitterest truth. She took the proffered cup from her son. She saw the horror of that dreadful day in Hephaestus' eyes. Bitter tears glistened unshed her eyes. "You are right, my son. I will not risk your life again, nor any other Olympian."

Hephaestus smiled, refilling Hera's cup to the brim with sacred nectar. "Let us eat!" he cried out. "And sing! Apollo, brother, pick up your golden lyre. Grace us with your silver voice."

Apollo laughed. "For you, brother, I will play." The shining god plucked the taut strings. He beckoned the Muses to sing with him, and soon the melodies of the stars and sea filled the Olympian hall.

When night descended on Olympus, the gods drifted to their private chambers and abodes. Hera followed a drunken Zeus to his bed chamber carved into the crystal walls of the mountain.

As the Thunder God fell into his bed of furs and linens, he caught sight of his sister-wife. "I have no will to argue, Goddess. Go. Sleep elsewhere."

Slyly, Hera enticed him, "I have no desire to sleep, lord husband."

"What do you wish then?" he asked, propping his enormous frame up on his elbow.

Hera pulled the golden brooches from her shoulder seams, and her gown fluttered to the marble floor. She stood in her naked glory before her god. "To make love to you until the mountain quakes with your pleasure."

Zeus' hunger for Hera grew, his divine cock swelling with his need to possess her. "You are a temptress, Goddess. Beguiling in your beauty."

She approached him, swaying her slim hips provocatively as she went. Her delicate hand slipped to her sacred cross as she walked. She slid a single finger down the center of her glorious slit, bringing it up to her lips before licking it. "Would you taste me, lord husband?"

Zeus roared his desire for her. He reached out a hand, yanking her roughly before him. Positioned at the side of his bed, Hera stood, legs slightly apart as Zeus' tongue explored her. He licked and sucked her sweet inner lips, finding the engorged bud of her center. He caught it delicately between his teeth, teasing Hera with the tension of pain and pleasure.

The goddess' hand gripped Zeus by the head, pinning his face against her. As his tongue brought her to a raging climax, her legs gave way beneath her.

Catching her fall, Zeus laughed at her weakness. "I command you to stand. I am not finished with you, Goddess. Your insolence and meddling will be punished."

Hera obediently stood, her legs still shaking. She felt the wetness of her desire drip down her inner thighs.

Zeus spread her legs once again, slipping a warm finger inside of her. "You shall not challenge me, Hera," he said, as he pressed another finger into her willing body. He slowly pumped his fingers in and out, slipping them out far enough to circle her sensitive bud. Hera moaned under his expert touch.

"Please, lord—"

"Do not speak, Goddess," he warned, menacingly. Hera rubbed her center against his hand. "Not yet." He slid his hand from her, and pulled her to his bed, bending her over the edge. He stood, now, taking position behind her. The goddess' round buttocks beckoned for his attention. He punished her ivory skin until it shone red with his wide palm prints. Then, Zeus gave into his own pleasure, plowing his enormous cock into her. He groaned loudly with the sensation of her glistening cave, engorged and wet, wrapped around him.

"You will obey me," he commanded.

"I promise," Hera gasped between thrusts.

Zeus grabbed Hera by her hair, tilting her head back as he pressed his entire length into her. It was true that he loved the flesh of mortal women, but they were incapable of receiving his divine form. Always with them, he had to hold back, descend in a lesser form to take them. But with Hera, he could unleash all his passion and power. As Hera's body once again shook with her pleasure, Zeus spilled his silvery seed into the goddess.

He broke their sacred union abruptly, pushing her to their bed. "You will sleep next to me this night." When he wrapped an iron arm around her supple frame, Hera turned her head and kissed his chest. As they both drifted into the sleep of deities, he whispered, "I know you lie."

Zeus lay staring into the deep purple sky twinkling with silver stars. Thoughts of Thetis had woken him from his slumber. Stroking Hera's side, he plotted against the Greeks she loved so much. He sighed. *Pathetic that I should love a nymph more than my own sister-wife. Thetis could never receive me as I am, but she …*

He kissed a lock of Hera's silver hair. Bedding his wife brought him pleasure, but his heart remained unmoved. *Thetis. It will always be Thetis.*

He thought of the shining boy, Achilles. Watching him fight alongside Ares thrilled him. Achilles' blade glinted like a god's, his beauty among men and women unquestioned and unparalleled. *He could have been mine.* The mighty Lord of Gods rolled to his side, facing away from Hera. *Mine. What if he had been mine? Would I have been as Cronus, slaying him before he came of age? Would he have challenged me? Would his mother's love have tempered us both and we ruled the high mountains as father and son? These fucking mortals force us to play these games as if we gods have no hearts.*

He sat up, sliding quietly from his bed. His nude form glistened in the cold starlight, as he stepped to the edge of his chamber without walls, staring down at the world of men. *How do I keep my word to Thetis and raise Achilles' honor among the Greeks?* Gazing through the clouds into the Greek's encampment, he knew what he must do.

FOURTEEN
abandoned and alone
ITHAKA—1238 BCE

"Your mother tells me you do not wish to marry that girl from Mycenae."

Telemachus reached for a cluster of olives over his head. The ladder shifted precariously. "Erigone. She's Agamemnon's daughter."

Laertes clicked his tongue and scoffed. "Hold tightly. Agamemnon's child, she says?"

Telemachus narrowed his eyes, hearing the disdain in his grandfather's tone. He plucked the olives from their silver-green stem and stuffed them into the satchel at his hip. "What's wrong, Grandfather?"

"He's been gone too long to father those brats of hers."

Defensively, Telemachus said, "Erigone wasn't a brat."

"The girl is not Agamemnon's. He's been gone as long as your father. Your mother, faithful as she is, isn't breeding children in his absence."

"Then who is her father?"

The old king brushed at the leaves on his chiton. "I have no idea."

"I did hear the servants whispering about it..."

"What did you hear?"

"That Zeus fathered them all, including Erigone."

Laertes laughed out loud. He laughed until reason once again settled on his usually stoic face. "That's the story of all the whores of Sparta. That Zeus chooses them over all other women." He snorted. "Ridiculous. Lies. No wonder the gods curse the House of Atreus. I won't allow this marriage to take place."

Telemachus' eyes brightened at the thought. "Truly? You can stop it from happening? When? How?"

"When the time is right. But say nothing to your mother. Be agreeable when she speaks of it." Laertes playfully rattled the ladder. "Perhaps, if the gods allow, your father will return and intervene before I must. He knows better than any man the joy of marrying a woman he loves and who loves him equally in return."

Telemachus' smile quickly faded to a frown. "Grandfather, do you believe the gods will send my father home?"

Laertes squinted up at his grandson, as Apollo's light hit his eyes through the silver leaves. "Hand me that cluster," he said, pointing just beyond Telemachus' head.

Obeying, Telemachus clipped the tender stem with the blade of his pruning knife. He tossed the olives down to his grandfather. "Do you?"

"Youth is persistent, if nothing else." He smashed one of the darkened fruits between his fingers. He lightly tasted the purple juice, then spat it out. "These are perfect. Not too soft."

Telemachus smiled, wryly. "My mother says as much. About being young, not the olives."

"Is that why she sent you? Come down from there."

Telemachus climbed down the rickety ladder, jumping to the ground, skipping the last two rungs. "You should get a new ladder."

Laertes laughed out loud and put his arm around his young grandson. "There's nothing wrong with that one."

"It creaks. It wobbles."

"As I said, there's nothing wrong with it." He bopped his grandson on the nose. "Perhaps, it's you who wobbles."

Telemachus brushed his grandfather's hand away, annoyed. "One day it will fall apart when I'm on it."

"Well, then, that will be the day for a new one."

"What about my father?"

Sighing, the old king said, "Are you hungry? I am famished for bread and wine."

"Will you never answer me, Grandfather?"

"Let's go back." Together they walked beneath the shade of ancient cypress trees lining the narrow road. "What do you know of war, Telemachus?"

"Only the stories. How men fight with honor. Kill their enemies."

"My son, war is … *war* is so much more than that."

"How can I learn when Mother refuses to let me truly train? Achilles went to Chiron when he was younger than me. And his son is there, I could train with him. I'll never become a man if I can't fight."

Laertes knew Chiron was an excellent trainer of young warriors, but he wasn't sure it was the right place for Telemachus. The men trained by Chiron became hard, insensitive brutes. "You believe war makes a man, a man?"

"Aye. A man must fight to protect his home. His family." Looking up at Laertes, he asked, "Is that wrong?"

"You've grown taller since last I saw you."

Telemachus laughed. "Mother says that, too." Glancing at the ground as they walked, he timidly asked, "Do I remind you of him? My father, I mean?"

"You miss him." It was a statement, not a question. "I miss him as well."

They walked on in silence for a long while. Laertes mulled over the burning question in his grandson's heart, for it was also a question haunting his mind these many days. Did the gods keep Odysseus safe? Would they return his son, the king, to Ithaka? Who could know? And what to tell a fatherless boy?

"Sometimes, when you are laughing, I hear him."

"Truly?"

"Truly," Laertes said, smiling at his grandson. "When you ask me a thousand questions without breath, you also remind me of him."

Telemachus laughed out loud. "Does it bother you? Mother groans when I ask too many. I'm just curious about everything."

"So was your father. There is nothing wrong with being curious. A good king must ask many questions, before he can make a wise decision."

"King? I won't be king until …" Telemachus hung his head. "Until …"

"Don't worry. Your father will return, Telemachus. I have no doubt."

"When? When will he return? Why has he abandoned me for so long?"

"War never follows a plan. No matter how strategic the commanders. Ares loves the blood and gore too much. The gods pitch men against one another. The winds blow or grow quiet. You father has not abandoned you, Telemachus. He is at war. That is what war is. To be separated from your family. Do you believe you're the only boy who must grow up without a father?"

"It feels that way."

"When your father left, he took many men with him. They left wives and families behind as well."

Telemachus kicked at a rock. It skidded ahead of them while they walked.

"Loneliness and waiting are the hardest part of war. That, and not knowing."

"Mother weeps all the time."

"Can you blame her? She suffers more than you can imagine."

"How do you mean?"

"The love she and your father share is difficult to live without."

"Why do you live here, alone, without Grandmother?"

Laertes laughed. "Too many questions indeed. But, when your father returns, you must be prepared for a ... *complicated* man."

"What do you mean?"

"War changes a man."

"How?"

"Death squeezes the best and worst from a man's soul. War is death. Death to dreams. Hope. I live alone, Telemachus, because it's the only way I find peace in living. Blood filled my hands, washing my mind with its curses. The sight and smell of it are never far from me. I've never been able to chase away the nightmares from behind my eyes. In solitude, here tilling the soil, I find peace. The nightmares are less. Only the shades of the dead haunt me now ... but I am glad of them. They bring strange comfort that I, too, one day, will be able to return to their company."

"You make war sound like a burden."

"Because, it *is*."

"Why can't King Agamemnon defeat Troy? Aren't we better than the Trojans? We have *Achilles* and the Myrmidons."

"Don't forget your father. And Ithaka's finest. The army Agamemnon commands is the largest ever to go to war. But it would be wrong to assume the enemy is weak and unskilled. Clearly, they are not."

Growing tired of talking about war, Telemachus yawned. "I am hungry after all."

Laertes hugged Telemachus. "Good. We're almost home."

SPARTA

"I'm afraid to see Orestes, Grandmother."

"No need to fear him, Hermione." How swiftly the false words fell from her lips. No woman was safe when her life could be bargained away for gold and power. Or lust. Not even the gods kept one safe. Leda feared for her granddaughter's future. A future controlled by Tyndareus. The man who unflinchingly destroyed his own daughters' lives, who married Clytemnestra to Agamemnon, who bargained Helen to Menelaus, and now designed a plan for young Hermione. How could she stop the inevitable? Her eldest grandson was a man capable of deciding if he would stand by his grandfather's decision.

"Do you think my mother left with that prince, or was taken?" Hermione asked.

Leda shook her head. "Is that what you're afraid of? Being taken?"

Hermione shrugged nervously. "A little."

"I knew that one day you would ask about the rumors."

"It's hard not to listen, when servants whisper."

"What have you heard?"

Hermione avoided making eye contact with her grandmother. "Nothing … really."

Leda asked sharply, "Then, why are you asking now?"

Hermione shrugged again, as children do when they do not have the words. "I was only wondering."

Taking her granddaughter's chin in her hand, she admonished her, "We keep no secrets between us, Hermione. What did you *hear?*"

"Apologies, Grandmother. I have no wish to upset you. It's just that I heard someone say that my mother was seen with him … that prince, doing unspeakable … things."

"Lies," Leda hissed. "Ill-tongued slaves speak too freely and unkindly of their queen. Mind you, when she returns, she will reign once again. And they will all be sorry."

"Why doesn't she come back?" A tear slid from Hermione's eye. "Why has my father not offered a ransom? Bring her home? Do you think she loves me?"

Placing an arm around Hermione, Leda pulled her close. "It's hard to understand why the gods allow these tragedies. Of course, your mother loves you. She was taken by that traitorous cur. The stakes are beyond what any ransom could purchase. The promise of wealth from war is too tempting for men to abandon. You know, it wasn't the first time your mother was kidnapped."

"It wasn't?"

"Unfortunately, your mother's blessing of beauty has been more of a curse. Have I told you about Theseus?"

"No. Who was he?"

"The King of Athens."

Leaning into her grandmother's side, she asked, "What did he do?"

"He stole your mother away to Athens, when she was just about your age. His intention, marriage. But your uncles, Caster and Pollux, rescued her. The gods be thanked. Because of that, your grandfather decided to marry her to your father."

"Is that why I have to marry Orestes, then? So I'll be safe?"

"So Sparta will be safe. We're merely pawns in his game for control and power. Never forget that truth. Our value lies in alliance building. Marriage. However, I'm not so sure your aunt will allow what Tyndareus proposes." *By the gods I hope she finds a way to halt this union.*

"Aunt Clytemnestra frightens me. She's cold and never smiles."

Smoothing a stray lock of Hermione's hair, Leda thought of the day Clytemnestra was forced to marry Agamemnon. "She has reason to be distant. Your grandfather has made her life … *difficult*. Learning the craft of ruling your world as a woman requires a heart of iron. A Spartan heart."

"What should I say to Orestes when he arrives?"

"Be charming. Be sweet. Be guarded." She brushed the tip of her granddaughter's nose. "Observe him without him knowing. How he looks at others. Who he looks at. Listen to his words, but remain as silent as you can. And tell me everything. Between us, we may be able to discover his intensions. For a man of his standing is not here out of undying love for a girl, not yet a woman. Promised or not." Leda's heart screamed at the thought that Orestes, grandson or not, would take her beloved granddaughter from her. Abuse her under his weight. Violate her with his hands. Scar her with his unwelcomed tongue.

Tyndareus took the proffered cup of wine, dismissing the servant without a glance. Sipping his wine, he observed his grandson over the rim. "I was … *surprised* by your message wishing to visit Hermione."

"Is there something wrong?"

Narrowing his dark eyes, he tried to discern a deeper truth behind Orestes' fixed smile. "How do you find life in Mycenae these days? How fares your mother?"

"Mycenae prospers. My mother is … my mother."

Tyndareus laughed. "Clytemnestra should have been born a man. Tell me, has she indicated when, or should I say *if* she intends to relinquish the crown to you?"

Under his grandfather's scrutiny, Orestes squirmed in his chair like a small boy. "No, we rarely speak of it." One of his grandfather's bushy gray eyebrows shot up. "I mean, we never speak of it … really."

"Indeed," Tyndareus said, rubbing his palms together. He grabbed an amphora of wine, pulled the wax plug, and tossed it on the table. "She's plotting. I knew it."

"I think she's waiting for our father to return."

"Is that what you think? She has kept the power of Mycenae for herself, instead of giving it to you. I'd rather you were on the throne than Agamemnon. I'd force him to stay away if it kept you in power.

But your mother ... now there's a puzzle. I can't unseat her. She's my flesh and blood. Neither will she reason with me. If she is waiting for Agamemnon, it's only to kill him. After that, who knows? And that is what concerns me."

"Do you honestly believe that?" Orestes asked, shocked by his grandfather's candor.

"Clytemnestra is devious and determined. Never forget that about your mother. She won't allow anyone to take the power she's grown accustomed to. I know I would not." The king sighed wistfully. "If only she were a man."

"What should I do? What is your advice?"

"Kill her bastards." Tyndareus leaned forward on the couch, his stoic gaze piercing Orestes' insecurities. "Then, kill her and take the throne for yourself. That is, if Agamemnon does not return. If he does, he'll kill her himself. And you can leave him to me."

"I was not expecting—"

"What? Such a drastic solution to your problem?"

"But, I didn't say I had a problem with my mother—"

"Of course, you do. Or why else would you come to see a young girl you've no interest in marrying?"

Orestes opened his mouth, but Tyndareus shook his head. He already knew the excuses his grandson would utter. Weren't they all the same in the end? "Do as I advise and you'll be happier and safer."

"Safer? From my mother?"

"Aye. Make no mistake, Orestes, she will stop at nothing to carry out whatever plan she has devised. And since she has not shared it with you, you can be assured it works against you."

FIFTEEN
gods and dreams
GREEK ENCAMPMENT, TROY—1238 BCE

Agamemnon woke with start. Had it all been simply a dream? Or was it more? He slid his weary body from his bed, tossing the linens over the naked woman beside him. He glanced down at her. She was no Briseis. He couldn't even recall her name. He'd pleasured himself with her body several times before the restlessness within calmed. *This night*, he thought, *I take Achilles' woman as my own.*

He poured a cup of watered wine and sat heavily into his chair. *This dream. What is the meaning?* "Boy!" he hollered gruffly. "Boy!"

A young man scurried in, disheveled and wide eyed. "My lord?"

"Call the heralds and my generals," Agamemnon ordered.

In a blink, the boy disappeared. The Great King's mind raced with images of Nestor directing him to waste no more time and attack the Trojans. *The end is near.* His heart pounded furiously. *Nine years. Nine.* He slipped his leather sandals on, secured his belt and sword, and fastened his crimson cape around his shoulders. He strode from his tent, his bronze cuirass blinking in the early morning light, walking as tall as a god. As he passed the rows of men, they bowed their heads to him. His heart swelled with thoughts of final victory. *Mine. Troy shall be mine. Zeus has shown me the way.*

When all his war chiefs gathered around his table in the royal pavilion, he signaled the slaves to serve them wine and warm bread. They broke their fast at his behest. No one asked about Achilles' empty chair or the bench beside it where Patrokles kept his cousin's council. The clash between the Great King and the Myrmidon commander had struck discord throughout the army. Some sided with Agamemnon, but the masses sided with Achilles, secretly bemoaning Agamemnon's greed.

Outside of the tented meeting, nine heralds awaited their orders to address the horde. They shifted nervously on their feet, eager to run like the wind with the king's words. Within, the captains grew anxious, wondering what Agamemnon believed so important.

Odysseus, eager to get on with it, finally asked, "Why are we here?"

Agamemnon flashed a rare smile from beneath his heavy beard. "I had a dream from Zeus. It concerns us all."

Murmurs and questions swirled around the table.

"How so?"

"Tell us."

"Do not keep us in suspense."

The Great King raised his silver cup, calling for quiet. "The mighty Father came to me as Nestor." He gestured to his loyal counselor. "And told me the gods had ceased their bickering, calling a truce among them. He urged me now was the moment to strike at Priam and bring Troy to ruin. He promised this would be the beginning of our great victory. When the dream was over, I slept as peaceful as a newborn sucking at its mother's tit."

Telemonian Ajax smashed his fist on the table, sending war markers flying from their strategic points on the huge, leather map. "We are finally going to take that accursed city."

Agamemnon nodded, still smiling. "You will be the one the troops look to for courage since the Myrmidons remain withdrawn."

Odysseus shook his head, knowing what it meant to battle without the Myrmidons. "There is only one way to appease Achilles."

The Great King frowned. "Is he king of this horde, or am I? There can be no truce if he continues refusing my authority. Let Achilles and his Myrmidons rot for all I care. We have men enough to defeat the Trojans. And we have Zeus on our side. How can we lose?"

"My lord, think of the men," Odysseus implored.

"No more talk of Achilles. He has made his choice. But first I will test the men's resolve. I must know they are truly with me, or we cannot win. Stand your ground so I may know their true hearts."

Nestor laid his hands on the table. "My king, do you believe that wise? The years ... surely, if anyone else had claimed a dream from Zeus, we'd not believe it. As king you are closer to the gods than any man here. But, tempting the men, now, after nine long years?"

Agamemnon bristled at the implication. "Do you think that without Achilles the men will not fight for me? Their king?"

Odysseus sneered behind his hand. "On this, I agree with Nestor. It is risky to dangle their dream before them, expecting they will not grab it."

The Great King stood, laying his hands on the table. "I will hear no more. Zeus has spoken to me and, if the gods are for me, then no mortal man may stop me." He eyed the captains gathered around him. "You have followed me this far. Obey me in this." He signaled his servant. "Boy, tell the heralds to call the army to the far field." Agamemnon marched out of the pavilion with his captains falling in behind him.

Thousands of soldiers swarmed the field before the Great King's dais, the ground quaking and groaning as they marched to hear the king. Rumors swirled in the early morning, winging words of home and the end of war. Heart-sick of war, they prayed the rumors to be true, to hear it from their king's own mouth they were bound for home. The heralds quieted the crowd, and soon an eerie silence spread across the sea of men.

Agamemnon, encouraged by their eagerness, believed that for the first time the men honored him. With Achilles out of the way, the men had finally turned to their rightful leader. He raised his hands, holding high the king's scepter. "Zeus has tricked me," he said. A rumble of confusion spread across the crowd. "Zeus bowed his head to me that we would bring the Trojan walls to rubble. That we'd return home triumphant with ships weighted to the waterline with geras untold. But that was all deceit on his part. He now commands we return to our homes empty handed. Give up the assault on the Trojan walls. He commands we leave the city unburnt."

"We should have outnumbered them, but their foreign allies stock their army with more men than we can count, with more chariots than we can make. Foreigners keep us from victory. Our ships rot on the sand and under the harsh sun. The wood gives way and the ropes snap. Meanwhile, our wives and families wait for our return. Yet, here we linger. A never-ending war before us. I say it's time to return home and forget the Trojans and their riches. Have we not collected geras enough to share? I say let's make for home!"

Before Agamemnon's final words sounded in the air, the men stampeded for the ships, cheering as they stumbled over each other in their joy. Sand showered the air in their haste. Soldiers, thin and weary by prolonged war, found strength in the promise of home. They pulled stocks from beneath hulls and began digging the creaking ships from their sandy docks.

Agamemnon stood shocked and angry. "Cowards, all of them," he seethed.

Menelaus exhaled in exasperation. "Your captains tried to warn you this might happen. What are you going to do?"

Agamemnon growled, "Zeus must have a purpose. To be made a fool of before my army ..." *This would never happen to Achilles. That Fucking Phthian. Even in his absence, he mocks me.*

From her silver chair, Hera watched the tragedy play out on the beach. "Although I love the Greeks best, Agamemnon is a fool. Challenging the men to choose between home and war. Look, Athena, see how they scurry like ants to a crumb of bread?"

Athena knelt at the Queen of Olympus' feet. Gazing down through the wispy clouds circling the peaks of the sacred mountain, she saw clearly the Greeks running about their ships. "They make ready for departure. So soon? The war is not won."

"We cannot allow this to happen. Leave Helen, that conniving bitch, safe in Troy living as a queen. How many of our faithful Greeks have died on her behalf? No, Athena, you must help me stop this."

"Why would Agamemnon wish to test his men?"

"I do not know. But, you must fly to Odysseus. Speak to your faithful servant. Use stealth, daughter." She grabbed Athena by the arm, squeezing it tightly. "Zeus must never know we interfere."

"I understand. I fear whatever bargain he struck with Thetis is now unfolding. We risk rebellion …"

Hera released her daughter's arm. "If Zeus should turn on us, we will not survive his wrath."

"Have no fear, I know what I must do." Athena grabbed her shining spear and glittering helm, and leapt from the mountain, flying to the beach in search of Odysseus, King of Ithaka.

Athena found Odysseus hanging back near a horseless cart. She moved behind him, pressing her holy hand onto his shoulder, speaking directly into his ear. The hairs on Odysseus neck stood on end. "Goddess, I know you are here."

"I cannot fool you, Odysseus."

"What wisdom do you have for me, Athena?"

"Shameful how these men run from their king. Run from battle."

"What can I do? Agamemnon's words gave the men hope of home. I cannot blame them."

"Leaving Helen of Sparta for these filthy Trojans would be disgraceful."

"What can be done? Agamemnon has brought this catastrophe on himself. Always striving to prove he is the best of us. Fool."

"Do not be so harsh, Odysseus. A man cannot help but be who he is

born to be. Look at you, as stubborn in your old age as when you were a boy."

Odysseus sighed heavily. "Laertes often chided me for being so. Yet, what am I to do now?"

Several men ran past him half carrying, half dragging their belongings toward the ships.

"Too many have lost their lives on account of Helen. Speak up. Persuade them on Agamemnon's behalf. Remember there is no safe return without Achilles. If you leave now, you are all doomed."

Athena's heavy hand released Odysseus' shoulder, sending his cape fluttering to the ground. The bronze rings of his cuirass clinked as he ran to the Great King's platform. He grabbed Elephenor, captain of over forty ships from Euboea, along the way. "Friend! Why are you running with your men? Are we not princes and kings of our own lands? Agamemnon was wrong to test the men like this, but we know better. We must stay and fight these bastards."

Elephenor's wiry eyebrow lifted in surprise. "You of all men should be running for your fast ships. You and your constant talk of home." He grabbed at his cock. "And your faithful Penelope."

Ignoring the crude gesture, Odysseus encouraged his fellow captain. "Soon enough we will hear Agamemnon out. We heard his plan at the captains' table to test the men. We all know his jealousy of Achilles standing among the men. Likely he wished to raise his own esteem in Achilles' absence. Come, man, you know the rage of kings is strong, but the rage of princes, such as we are, beneath Agamemnon's rank, is stronger still."

Elephenor nodded consent. "You and your silver tongue. Always knowing what to say, how to change a man's mind."

Odysseus clapped the old man on the shoulder. "Help me, then, get these soldiers back to the field. They must give the king a chance to win back their fighting spirits."

Together, they grabbed men running by and chastised their weakness, calling them deserters and cowards.

"You are fools," Odysseus yelled as they ran passed, bashing random men with the broadside of his sword, as they scurried toward the ships. "By the balls of Zeus, you should be struck where you stand for your mutiny. You know Agamemnon wouldn't abandon us."

Slowly, the tide of discontented men ebbed and they reluctantly returned to hear the Great King's message. Some grumbled that the king's test was cruel. Others grumbled that old age would kill them before they ever saw victory. As the men clamored together by the thousands, one voice refused to be silenced.

Thersites, an ugly mess of a man, unwisely continued to rage on against Agamemnon. He shook his wrinkled fist at the Great King. "What more do you want from us? You have the bulk of all the geras, the best of the gold and the women. But still you aren't satisfied, are you? Where would any of you captains be without the likes of us? We tend your fires, tend your horses. Mend your armor. We live in the sand and dirt, while you sleep on furs and walk on carpets. But you want more? And you, Great King, your greed is boundless. You weren't content with a hundred beautiful women to warm your bed, you … you had to have one more. You dared to take Achilles' woman. We all know how he regarded her, took her as a wife to live in his quarters. Achilles is a better man than you, because he's let the insult go. Otherwise, he'd have slit your throat the moment you took her."

Odysseus pushed his way through the throng, making directly

for Thersites. He grabbed him by the neck, squeezing as he spoke. "Who are you to speak to kings? Hunched over and broken, you are hardly worth a shit in battle. Only cowards abandon their king and commanders. Do you think you know more than me? More than Agamemnon about war and strategy? Has Zeus taken to speaking to lowly men like you with no hair and skinny arms?" He released his grip on the old man and tossed his sword at Thersites' feet. "There, heft my sword if you are able."

Thersites stooped to pick up the heavy blade, and his arm shook as he held it out. Odysseus easily batted it from the man's hand, and it fell to the ground. "You are not even strong enough to wield my blade, so shut your mouth. If I ever hear you spouting such filth again, I will strip you naked and whip you all the way back to the ships myself, or call me Telemachus' father no more."

Athena rose behind Odysseus, heralding his voice like thunder. "Agamemnon! The men betray their oaths, true enough. Wishing to return home, be reunited with their proper wives. I know how all of you tire of hearing about my Penelope." A rumble of laughter spread through the horde.

"But can you blame them? Lesser men than this mob would have betrayed you after a mere month. Yet these men, look at this ragged bunch of warriors! They've served you for nine years. True fighters! Hold out a while longer! Hold your courage close so we may see Kalchus' prophecy spring to life. Aulis is but a breath away in time. Were we not just there, yesterday? Young and eager for war? Our cocks hardened by the thought of gold? Did Kalchus not divine by bird devouring snake that we would be gone nine long years, but in the tenth seize our victory? Here we stand, in that very moment armored for war and victory!"

As a mighty cheer rose for Odysseus' winging words, Athena's presence slipped from Odysseus' shoulders. His smile faded, knowing his patron goddess had once again disappeared.

Nestor spoke then. "Such a disgrace watching the best of you running before the final battle. Before claiming the victory we know is ours by right. Did not Zeus give his blessing to us when we left Aulis years ago? Striking lightning on our right? And what of your youthful oaths that now as men you are honor bound to fulfill? I tell you this with a heart bent on war and victory. Do not abandon our mission to strike back at Troy for dishonoring our traditions. Stay and fight until you have a Trojan woman beneath you as payment for your pains of war." A cheer rose from the throng of men. Nestor continued, "Agamemnon, Great King, stay your course. But arrange your men by their clans so that you can know with certainty who is truly for you, and who is against you. Wherever you lose ground on the field, you will know where the true cowards are and who to punish."

Agamemnon's chest swelled with pride, looking out at the ocean of men. "If I had ten men such as Nestor, sitting around my war council, Priam's precious citadel would fall in a single day." The Great King then stepped forward to address the crowd, his bronze cuirass flashing brightly in Apollo's light. "True that Zeus throws obstacles in our path to victory. Who can fathom the ways of the gods? It is true, as you have heard. I did take Achilles' woman. His lack of respect was … It is no matter now. The deed is done. If *he* could just work with me, as my commander, try to see eye to eye with me, we would have sailed home long ago. Now, we must make our final push against the shining towers of Troy. Zeus has shown me in a vision that we must move quickly. Go to your tents and ships and prepare for war. Polish your shields and fill your bellies. But I tell you this, if I catch any man trying to hide from this battle, I will feed him to the dogs and birds."

The heralds called out for the men to obey their king. The horde, once again eager for battle, hurried to ready for the end.

"Come," Agamemnon commanded to his captains of war. "Sacrifice with me to Father Zeus."

They followed their king, Idomeneus and Nestor close behind Agamemnon with Telemonian Ajax and the Lesser, then Diomedes, son of Tydeus rounding out the entourage. Odysseus and Menelaus walked in silence behind them all.

Odysseus brooded about how the battle would go without Achilles, knowing how the men depended on the Golden Warrior for courage in the field. When limbs tired and hearts fell, one glance at Achilles dancing in the gore and blood with his golden helm glittering in the sun could encourage even the faintest of hearts.

Menelaus scowled knowing that soon he would have to face the woman who cuckolded him before an entire world.

Priests prepared the fattest bull for Agamemnon's offering to Zeus. They each grabbed a handful of barley from the bowl passed between them, as they circled the sacrifice. Agamemnon prayed, "Hear me, Lord Zeus, Father of all gods. Command Apollo to slow the day, keep his light high above us as we fight the Trojans to the death. Let there be light enough so we can finish them off and I have shredded Hektor's corpse on the field before his father's eyes."

But Zeus' ear was deaf to his prayer. The god was secretly bent on keeping his word to Thetis.

A slender priest approached, holding aloft his sharp blade, ready to honor the gods. With Telemonian Ajax on one side and

Diomedes on the other, the holy man slit the wide neck of the bull and its crimson blood spurted onto the ground, some catching in a silver basin. The beast's eyes rolled into its head and it crumpled to its knees. Within moments, the bull collapsed completely. The commanders stepped back as the sacred work of cutting the sacrifice and burning the fat began. Lesser priests skewered the fatted strips of meat wound in lengths of fat and roasted them. Agamemnon and his captains filled their bellies with the sacred meal.

When the final call for battle rang out, and the men marshaled into clan cohorts, shields and spears readied, Odysseus' keen eye caught the golden glint of Athena's shield and helm, as she strode between the men, whipping them to bravery with her cold whisper. The men marched proudly now for war; their earlier cowardice forgotten as the thrill of battle filled them. The ground shook beneath thousands of feet marching to the Scamander Plain and to the Gates of Troy.

SIXTEEN
ash of betrayal
MYRMIDONS' CAMP, BAY OF TROY—1238 BCE

Thousands of black shields rimmed with hammered bronze lay idle, stacked against sandy ridges and quiet tents. Tall spears tipped in bronze glinted in Apollo's light. A blanket covered Achilles' chariot, and his mighty horses, Balius and Xanthus, chomped the thin sea grasses along the camp's border, their tails swishing at biting flies. The sacred beasts gifted by Zeus to Peleus and then to Achilles longed for battle, as much as the Myrmidons.

When the Greek horde marched from their base camp, a dust cloud spiraled up, nearly blocking Apollo's light from the sky. The Myrmidons, accustomed to leading the forces, remained unhappily behind with their prince. Although they understood Achilles' rage at Agamemnon, their hearts longed to join the fight. Some mused that the Great King was fortunate his head was still attached to his neck. Others wondered why their captain, the greatest of the Greeks, would allow his woman to be taken. But the whispers of the rift between Achilles and his second on command, Patrokles, troubled them the most.

Why were these two, as close as brothers, at each other's throat? Every morning for years, they walked along the ships and rows, greeting the men and planning strategy. Since the taking of Briseis, they passed as strangers to one another. Whispers of Achilles' drunken days spoiled their morale.

As the Myrmidons waited for final orders, they busied themselves packing up their ships and idling in the surf. Although Achilles had promised they'd sail for Phthia, he'd made no real attempt to do so. With the rest of the army marching out to face the Trojan forces, they passed the time with wine and women, secretly hoping Achilles would change his mind.

Achilles preferred the company of no one, keeping to his ship and temporary tent. Swaying with too much wine, he gripped the dry deck railing and stared out across the sea. "I have been a mother to my men. Given the best of myself on the field. Yet, here I am, the mighty Achilles. Empty handed. With nothing I desire."

Twelve days had passed, leaving him to wonder what plan Thetis had devised with Zeus that he might win back his honor. *And Briseis.* The dark surf, stretching out as far as his eye could see, glittered under the sun, yet his mother failed to appear. *Strange. I cannot even hear her.*

The sting of losing Briseis remained a fresh welt across his pride and heart, his rage kept in check only by wine followed by more wine. His Myrmidons arrived periodically in small groups seeking his audience, yet he refused them all. The only one he wished to see was the one who stayed away. *Patrokles.* His cousin's words, sharpened by truth, cut more deeply than any sword. Only he would dare speak with such honesty.

"I do not deserve her," Achilles said into the wind. He hung his head, dizzy from wine. A single tear escaped his eye, before he rubbed it away with the back of his hand. "I do not deserve her." Stumbling back to the deck of his galley, he collapsed in a wretched heap, reaching for yet more wine. "How can I live without my honor? And without her love, and Patrokles? I am empty." Achilles cast his gaze to the heavens. "Patrokles was right. *You* have cursed me." After pulling the wax plug from the jug, he took a huge swig before falling flat on his back. "Briseis, forgive me. Patrokles, forgive—"

Achilles closed his eyes against the brightness, his heart burning to ash knowing that Agamemnon would delight in claiming Briseis as his own. *Athena! Why not let me slit the Fat King's throat?* In his stupor, he half expected Zeus to hurl a thunderbolt, a welcome mercy to this agony. He threw the amphora across the deck, shattering the pottery against the opposite rail, splashing wine in all directions. The dry, wooden planks drank the crimson liquid like a thirsty beast. *Will Briseis understand?* His cousin's words haunted and hacked at his soul. In this miserable state, he passed into a black and dreamless sleep.

As he slid the linen strip down his blade, Patrokles thought of the soft curve of Briseis' hip. His memory drifted to the dip at the base of her neck and the erratic pulse beneath his lips. The gentle touch of her fingers as she cupped his face in her hands tortured him. The honeyed kisses and sweet moans that escaped her lips while they lay together echoed in his memory, breaking his heart. Exhausted by the memories, he laid his sword across his knees.

Outside of his tent, Myrmidons walked passed, leaving him to his peace, perhaps fearful of him. Since Achilles had retreated to his ship in a perpetual drunken stupor, he'd become a recluse himself. He knew the men likely thought it was grief at losing Achilles' constant companionship. They would never guess the truth of his absence.

"Patrokles? Are you in there?"

"Leave me be, Knaxon."

"I have fresh bread and wine."

"Enter then. But I'm in no mood for company."

Achilles' servant pushed through the tent flap carrying an amphora under one arm and a loaf of bread under the other. "I'll put them on the table."

Patrokles didn't look up and remained silent.

"Will you go to see him?"

"No."

"But he needs—"

Looking up, Patrokles' gray eyes smoked with anger. "Why should I care what he needs? Why should any of us care? He deserves whatever misery he's heaped upon his own head."

Knaxon backed up toward the tent opening. "I only thought—"

"I know what you thought. You think I can bring him back to us. To *you*. I've seen the way your hungry slave eyes watch him. You think I don't know you desire him?"

"I-I never—" Nax stumbled to escape Patrokles' growing rage.

"He gave away his woman! Do you think he would treat you so differently? No." Patrokles scoffed. "He has forsaken all of us. He's cursed by the gods. Be thankful he's not among us. We deserved better from him. Especially Briseis. Now, get out of my tent."

Nax ran.

A moment of silence passed, before Patrokles put his weapon aside. He sat at the table, poured a cup of wine, and broke the crust of the bread. A thin cloud of steam rose from inside of it. Eating held little joy since his world had scattered to the winds. "She was mine for a moment," he whispered quietly.

Confessing his love to Briseis hadn't freed him of the burden he'd not-so-secretly carried. The moment of ecstasy between them now burned him to ash. *She is right. We are not destined for one another.* Achilles would always be the man she carried in her heart, not him.

And although he disapproved of how Achilles handled Agamemnon's demand, he knew in his heart that Achilles loved Briseis however roughly and ineptly. *How can I look him in the eyes knowing what I have done? He will know I have betrayed him. How can I return to Briseis now?*

He ate and drank as his mind raged with regret, grief, and longing.

Briseis languished in her tented prison, fearful that at any moment Agamemnon would burst through the opening and take her by force. *I will not be his whore!* Yet, she studied her sparsely furnished tent. The piss pot in the corner. The thin furs and linens on a mattress. The small, wooden table with a single stool. *I am a whore.* Her memories of the time before the Greeks came to Lyrnessus had faded as her life with Achilles overshadowed the world she'd known before. The world where her father had lived and her mother sat at her weaving were lost long ago. Only Achilles remained. He was her anchor in the swirling storm of blood and war. And now, he also had abandoned her. *I have nothing left except Patrokles. And even he stays away.*

She lit an oil lamp next to her mattress. Shadows danced gingerly on the tent wall. "Patrokles," she whispered. "I don't deserve your devotion."

Making love to him was a moment of reprieve for them both. It seemed the only way to make sense of Achilles' decision to discard her and abandon the war. When Patrokles tenderly confessed his love for her, as a woman, she knew that if they made it from this war alive, he'd never leave her. He would wed her in Phthia as he promised long ago. Maybe that was enough to live for. A tear slid down her cheek, and she brushed it away with a dirty hand.

Earlier, she heard the distant rumble of thousands of warriors leaving the camp. *Perhaps, all will be over soon.*

Death lurked in every corner and dishonor loomed before her. An uncertain future loomed before her, as she sat in the dank, dark tent of a lowly slave.

SEVENTEEN
brazen and bold
GREEK ENCAMPMENT, TROY—1238 BCE

Before Apollo pulled the light into the heavens, Hektor had called for the army to assemble safely behind the wall. A sea of polished bronze filled the lower streets and alleys. Men waited nervously for orders, thinking about death, and praying that today was not their time to greet the dead. Polites, son of Priam, took his watch on the lower ramparts with his men. Apollo's ascent into the heavens split the sky with gold and blue. He inhaled the salt and jasmine of the cool, morning air. As the plain brightened beneath the renewed light of day, he stared hard toward the Greeks' encampment. In the distance, a thin trail of dust rose as a lone rider raced into view. "A scout," he called down to the tower watchmen. "Open the gate."

Moments later, the wide-eyed scout panted his warning out. "They're coming. The Greeks are coming."

"How many?" Polites asked.

"All of them, my lord." He bent to catch his breath. "All of them."

"The Myrmidons?"

"There were too many, my lord."

"Pray the gods are not against us. If the Myrmidons take the field, the worse the battle … for us." Polites called down to the guards, "The Greeks are coming! The Greeks are coming!"

The alarm sounded throughout the sleepy city. Women wailed and children cried. They knew it was only by the gods' graces that their loved ones would be spared or killed or worse, butchered and maimed.

Helen rose from bed and walked to the balcony overlooking the city. She swept the linen curtains aside. "Do you hear, Paris? The cries of a city going to war grow louder."

Paris rolled over, blinking as the harsh light of morning stung his eyes. "The Greeks must be on the move again." He pulled the blanket over his head. "Close the curtains."

"You should get up," Helen said brusquely. Paris' lack of urgency annoyed her. The people grew to resent her and Paris by the day, why would he not take action to protect them from hurtful rumors? He was a pale comparison to Hektor.

"One more fuck, then I will rise to my duty."

Helen wrapped her himation tightly around her shoulders. The pull of Aphrodite dissolved her growing resentment. "I hate myself for all of this."

Removing the covers from his face, Paris asked, "For what?"

She lay beside him, desire filling her and clouding her mind. She fought to cling to her own thoughts, not give in to Aphrodite's curse. "That I would lie with you, fucking, when I know you should be gathering with the army."

"My first duty is to love you." Paris grabbed Helen by the shoulders, pulling her beneath him. He yanked her gown up over her hips and greedily plunged into her. His thrusting fully awoke Helen's passion, and soon her body completely betrayed her. Sweating and moaning, they climaxed in unison.

The curse slowly lifted, and Helen began to cry. Angry tears spilled down her cheeks. "Go. I'm sure Hektor has already sent a guard to find you."

"What do I care if the guards find me abed with my wife?" Paris kissed her forehead. "Don't cry, Helen. Any other man would do the same."

"But you aren't any other man. You're a prince of Troy. You should be armed and at Hektor's side. I won't have word reach him that they found you in bed, after the call to arms sounded."

Paris flung the covers off. "You wish me to go to my death so quickly?"

An urgent knock sounded at the door. "Prince Paris?"

"I'm coming! Tell Hektor I'm on my way."

"My lord," the voice behind the door sounded apologetic, "Hektor commands I bring you straight to him."

Helen glared at Paris. "I told you to give a care what your brother thinks. If you Trojans win this war, he'll be king someday. Do not add kindling to his burning hatred of us."

Paris laced his sandals and then strapped on his greaves. "What do you mean, 'you Trojans'?"

"Nothing."

He picked up his breast plate and positioned it over his chest. "Help me with the shoulder buckle."

With nimble fingers, Helen made quick work of the task. She

placed a hand on his arm. "Fight well and bravely, husband."

"I will fight to return to your side, my love."

With those parting words, Helen watched as he grabbed his bow and side-quiver, spears, helmet, and his leopard skin cloak before exiting their chamber. Only then did she dissolve into a heap on the floor. Years ago, she fled Sparta because she believed in her heart that a life with Paris, in Troy, would fill her with the love she desperately wanted. But, it had all been a lie woven into her stars by Aphrodite. Even the freedom from responsibility was bitter. No one loved her here. No one adored her. She was no cherished daughter of Troy, except to Priam. He alone accepted her. But that, too, was tainted by Hecuba's loathing for her.

Then, there was Corythus. His passion for her was real. Helen pressed her hand to her abdomen. Startled, she looked down. Her hand rounded over a slight swell. She counted back the days. A knowing smile spread across her face. The son had managed to do what the father could not. *Paris will think it's his. But so will Corythus.*

She pulled a small box from beneath her bed. Blowing dust from the lid, she opened it with trembling fingers. Oenone's letter was undisturbed. Helen clutched it to her breast. *I can't let either of them know the truth. I must send Corythus back to his mother.*

Hektor stood alongside King Telephus on a terrace overlooking the commanders below busily organizing the allied troops among the Trojans. The cacophony of many languages blended in a single song. "I owe you my gratitude for returning to help us, as you promised years ago."

Telephus clasped his hands behind his back. "The Greeks are a menace to this land. I will do my part to send them back into the sea. I am curious, however, if the rumors are true or not."

"What have you heard?"

"That Achilles and his Myrmidons no longer fight for Agamemnon."

"It's true."

Telephus stroked his beard, twisting the beads braided into the ends of it. "Why did he withdraw?"

"No one knows."

"Why hasn't he returned to Phthia?"

"I have no idea."

"I don't like it. As long as he remains in the Troad—"

"If Achilles rejoins the army, we will fight them all the same. Ah, my errant brother arrives."

Telephus turned his head to see Paris approaching. He was almost as tall as Hektor, and bearing a remarkable resemblance, except that Paris' features were slightly more refined. "So, *he* is the one who brought Helen of Sparta."

Paris nodded to Hektor. "Greetings, brother."

Hektor's face remained stoic. "What delayed you?"

Paris said, "I was saying farewell to my wife."

From across the rampart, a lookout's voice rang clearly with the dreaded warning. "The Greeks are here! The Greeks are here!"

All heads turned toward the plain. A cloud of dirt and sand rose above the approaching enemy. The faint sound of thunder rumbled in the distance.

"So, it begins again," Hektor said. "Look to your army, Telephus."

The gates opened wide and the guts of Troy spilled through. The battle cry of thousands echoed and shook the ancient walls. One by one the ordered ranks of Trojans and allies fell into their positions with Hektor, tall and shining, leading them all.

As he rode toward war, Paris couldn't shake the guilt inflicted on him by Helen. Since he revealed the truth to her about Aphrodite's promise, their life had shifted in subtle ways. Her becoming more distant and him more demanding. He relied on the curse more and more just to be close to his wife. It was clear that Helen no longer respected him, her love a cold thread pulled taut between them. *All our joy is now only bitterness.*

The Trojan forces halted with an audible jolt, taking up their final formations. Horses nervously pawed at the ground. Men murmured beneath their helms. Paris cleared his mind of his troubles with Helen. He watched as the entire Greek army approached without a single shout or cry. The only sound they made was the thunder beneath their feet and the clanging of their shields. They marched as one, unwavering and uncaring of any odds. Their spears glinted in the rising sun.

Agamemnon's army halted close enough that each side could see the faces of the other. Both sides stared at one another. Paris, shaking with pride and guilt, slid from his horse and strode into the gap between the armies. His slave scurried to hand him his spears. In a voice like a rolling river, he asked, "Who among you dares to fight me?"

A voice cried out from the Greeks, "To the death?"

"To the death!" Paris roared.

Hektor quickly rode to Paris' side. "What are you doing, brother?"

"What I should have done long ago. I will make this right between the Greeks and us."

Hektor smiled beneath his shining helm. "Finally, your Trojan blood is revealed."

A clamor rose among Greeks, as Menelaus leapt from his chariot tall, broad, and ferocious, shouting, "I will fight you!

Paris' heart chilled when he saw Helen's former husband step forward.

"I will fight you, you fucking wife stealer."

The blood drained from Paris' face and he stumbled backward. *What am I doing?* The courage that filled him a moment ago fled, and his feet followed. He pressed into the front line of the Trojans behind him, disappearing from view.

Menelaus taunted, "Are all Trojans so brave?"

Behind Menelaus, the entire Greek army broke out in laughter.

As Paris melted into the ranks, Hektor caught him by the shoulder of his cuirass and shook him angrily. "Is your *only* skill, brother, stealing other men's wives? Your eyes, your smile, your charm are no use to Troy unless you stand and fight your own battles. I spent my whole life praying the gods would lift our mother's grief and now, look at you! A groveling coward. You are a disgrace to Troy, to all of us. All my prayers were wasted. Wasted! I wish you'd never been born. That you'd died on that holy mountain." He released Paris' armor, shoving him to the ground.

Hektor slammed his spear butt into the dirt. The shaft quivered in his hand. "Can you hear the Greeks laughing at you? You're brazen, Paris, not brave. You will be the ruin of our father and Troy.

You're no match for Helen's true husband. If our father had known what disaster followed on your heels, he would have stoned you that day in the arena instead of embracing you. We'd have rid ourselves of your curse forever."

The surrounding Trojans murmured their agreement. Indignation and denial burned at the back of Paris' throat. "You should have. I was forced to give up my life. My wife. My son. For what? Scorn? Pity? I was happy before I came to Troy. I never asked for any of this!" He spat blood.

"Yet, here you are," Hektor said.

"Are you that eager to see me die, brother?" Paris realized that Helen had been right all along. Because of what they'd done, what he'd done, no one in Troy would truly accept either of them. Without Aphrodite's protection, they were doomed to a life of misery and rejection. *My lust has brought me to this. A slave to the goddess' whims.*

Hektor's horse shook its massive head, but the Golden Prince gave no reply.

Paris said, "It's not my fault Aphrodite blesses me. I will fight if you wish me to. Let the armies watch." His shoulders heaved with heavy breath, weighing his pride and prowess. "The winner will take Helen and all her treasure."

Satisfied, Hektor nodded. "So be it." He signaled the Trojans to set down their weapons and sent the interpreters to each ally so the united forces understood what was about to happen. Hektor slowly rode his mount into the gap between the opposing armies.

A rain of Greek arrows speared the ground before the Trojan Prince. He raised his arm for peace.

Agamemnon cried out, "Hold!"

Hektor thundered, "Paris wishes to meet Menelaus in hand-to-hand combat."

"What is the prize?"

"Helen. And all she possesses."

"This is a fight to the death, Prince Hektor. Does your cowardly brother understand?"

Hektor nodded. "He stands a coward no more."

Menelaus moved to his brother's side and shouted, "We have all lost too many men because of this fight between Paris and me. Let this final battle end the strife so the living can return to a peaceful life. Let's sacrifice to the gods to prove the honor of our words. Bring a white ram and black ewe. We will bring the same. Bring Priam to bear witness whether his son will be an oath keeper or not."

"Agreed," Hektor shouted, before returning to the ranks of his men.

Men on both sides sighed in relief as they removed their heavy helms and unbuckled their armor. They sat wiping sweat from their faces, waiting for the King of Troy to arrive and for the sacrifices to be made. By the time Apollo emptied the sky, the war would be over.

Princess Laodike, urged by the goddess Iris, flew to Helen with the news. She burst into the weaving room, heaving for air to deliver her message.

Helen glanced up from her loom. "What's wrong? What's happened?"

"It's Paris. He's going to fight Menelaus."

"Alone?"

"Aye. While the armies watch."

The blood drained from Helen's cheeks. "I spoke harshly to him this morning. Had I known—"

"They fight for you."

The spool of crimson thread in Helen's hand fell to the floor and rolled to a stop. "For me?"

"Whoever wins, takes you as his prize forever."

"I see."

"And all your treasure."

"I did not think this day would come so soon."

"What do you mean?" Laodike asked.

"The day when I would have to return to Sparta."

"But the battle hasn't begun yet."

"You don't know Menelaus like I do. Paris is no match for him."

Laodike shrugged. "They're waiting for Priam to bring the sacrifices."

"I should go," Helen said softly. "I should be there when—"

Laodike was gone.

Helen stood taking in her well-crafted work. She prided herself with the crimson cloak she wove for Paris. On it were all the stains of her existence. The abandoned child in Sparta. The stolen treasure of her grandfather's, for truly it was his, not Menelaus' or hers. The thousand ships sent across the sea. The death of Troilus. And above all the chaos and death, shining Aphrodite, Goddess of Love. But not for her. Aphrodite was goddess of doom and destruction. She represented all that she wished she could change, but could not.

Carefully, she tucked the fine threads into her basket, uncertain she'd ever return to finish the cloak. She ran her hands along the raised embroideries on the even warp and weft. Helen allowed herself to think of her old life with Menelaus. *Was it as awful as I imagined it to be?* Her hand absently caressed the new child growing within her. Corythus' child. *Was I wrong to leave Hermione?* Doubt clouded her memories. She wasn't sure what she wanted any more. Everything she believed she wanted slipped like ash between her fingers.

All her worries trapped her in a tangled net. An urge to see Menelaus gripped her fiercely. Helen wrapped her white himation tightly around her shoulders, as a fit of weeping overtook her. By the end of Apollo's light, she would lose a husband. Which one, she could guess. Menelaus had been many things, but none could fault his skill with a spear or sword. He was far better than Paris at warfare. In her heart, she knew Priam would be forced to hand her over as the prize. Wiping her tears away, she rushed to the Scaean Gates.

When she arrived, Priam and the city elders were waiting. "Come, Helen. We were just debating on your beauty."

"How so?"

"Whether or not your image rivaled the goddesses or not."

Helen glanced at the sky, then shivered. "You should not tempt the immortals with such talk. I fear I have brought enough danger and death to Troy."

Priam's eyes softened with sadness. "My son is going to fight for you."

"I know. Everything is my fault. Whatever happens."

The king put his arm around her shoulders to comfort her, as a father comforts a child. "Others may blame you, my daughter, but they do not carry the pain I do. My past is not unblemished. When I think of Hesione, my sister taken by Herakles … well, I don't blame you. It's the gods who bring everything to pass. Let them shoulder the burden of blame for this war." Pulling her to the rampart's edge, he said, "Come, tell me the names of some of these men afield."

Pointing to the tallest man in the front lines, Priam asked, "Do you recognize him?"

"He is Agamemnon. It would be hard to miss him, even from a great distance."

"And that man there? He has tossed his armor to the ground and walks like a king through the men. His shoulders are wide enough to be a bull."

Helen blocked the sunlight with her hand. "That is Odysseus, King of Ithaka."

"They have a giant, as well," Priam said, pointing across the way.

"Ajax. Ajax of Telemon. Sparta guested him many times."

Priam stiffened. His mouth puckered with the sour taste of the name. "Telemon."

Scanning the assembly below, she said, "I do not see my brothers, Pollux and Caster. That surprises me. I have never seen so many Greeks assembled in one place in my life."

A messenger approached. "My lord?"

"Have the sacrifices been readied?" Priam asked.

"Aye, my king, Hektor waits for you on the field."

"I'll be there shortly." Priam looked at Helen with tears in his aging, milky eyes. "We both know I will lose Paris for the second time." He turned and walked away.

From the rampart, Helen watched as Priam joined Agamemnon between the armies. It pained her that Priam, who had shown her only kindness, would be one less son by nightfall. And it was her fault, whether he blamed her or not.

BATTLEFIELD BELOW TROY

Agamemnon and Odysseus led the Greek offerings to the makeshift alter followed by Priam. Priam's slave poured cleansing water over the hands of the three kings, then poured the wine in a communal cup.

Agamemnon pulled a dagger from his belt, grabbed the white ram roughly by the horns with his other arm, and slit the stunned beast's throat. Its blood gushed like a river undammed. He sent up a prayer to Zeus. "Bear witness to false words, Zeus, Lord of the Heavens. Menelaus and Paris fight to the death over Helen and her treasures. We plead for no mercy, only fairness and honoring of oaths. Should Paris kill my brother, Menelaus, let him have her and all her possessions. And we will all return home. If Menelaus should kill Paris, then the Trojans must promise to return Helen and all that was taken from Sparta. If the Trojans dishonor this oath, I vow before you, Zeus and all assembled here, that I will remain here, until I receive what's owed by oath and burn Troy to the ground."

A slave brought forth the other animals and Agamemnon slit each one's throat. As the sacrifices lay grossly gasping for air, the Great King continued. "I swear to you, Zeus, that if either side violates this oath that the violators will be struck down and their women, mothers, wives, and daughters be raped until they bear the children of the enemy."

King Priam looked to Hektor with grief-stricken eyes. "I'm going back to the city. I'm too old to stay and watch my son fight to the death with Menelaus. My heart cannot take the strain."

"As you will, Father."

As Priam's chariot pulled away, Hektor and Odysseus marked

the fighting area with a deep groove gouged with the butt-end of their spears.

Odysseus asked Hektor, "Should we draw lots to see who throws their spear first?"

Hektor nodded. "That would be the most fair."

Stooping to pick up two rocks, Odysseus said, "The red one for Menelaus. The gray one for Paris. Hand me your helmet."

Hektor narrowed his eyes.

"No trick. It's for the lots. My helm is over there on the ground." He indicated with a head nod.

Unbuckling his chin strap, Hektor slowly handed his prize armor to the enemy.

Odysseus placed both rocks inside and shook them. Holding it out to Hektor, he said, "Choose."

Hektor was aware that his brother stood nervously behind him. He regretted his harsh words, knowing the moment of his brother's death had arrived. He put his hand in and pulled out the gray rock. "Paris. Paris has first throw."

"Clear the circle," Odysseus yelled. "Paris casts his spear first!"

A rumble of curiosity rolled through the armies, as the two opponents took their places. Glaring death at one another, they readied their spears in their hands.

Paris took two steps back, then swiftly hurled his weapon with a roar. The shaft flew like a god-inspired tool, hitting dead center on Menelaus shield, but the blade tip bent and the spear fell to the dirt.

Menelaus quietly prayed, "Grant me the vengeance I deserve. Let me crack his skull so his brains spill. No one will ever dare to break the hospitality of Sparta again." He threw his spear with all his anger and skill. It flew like a screaming bird of prey, piercing

Paris' shield cleanly through, the tip glancing off his enemy's ribs.

Paris, stunned by the sheer force of his opponent's throw, glanced down at the thin line of blood seeping through his tunic. Panic surged through his body and his legs lost their strength. Before the blackness engulfed him, a heavy hand press down on his shoulders.

"Have no fear, Paris. I am beside you."

"Aphrodite," he whispered in awe and confusion.

The King of Sparta reached for his sword. Wielding it high above his head, he slammed it down with all his might on Paris' curved helmet crest where it shattered into three pieces.

Paris' ears rang, but his fear was melted by the goddess.

Looking up to the sky, Menelaus raged, "You gods curse me, not him?" Turning his attention to Paris, he sneered, "I should have killed you with that blow!"

Angry at being cheated, Menelaus leapt to Paris still on his knees and yanked him by the chin strap of the remaining section of his helm, jerking him from his knees, and started to drag him back to the Greeks' side.

Paris choked as the helmet strap caught beneath his chin.

Aphrodite, unseen and determined, snapped the leather. Paris slipped from his helmet and from Menelaus' fury, scrambling for safety toward the Trojan ranks. Menelaus flung the helmet into the ranks of Greeks and charged after Paris, intent on killing him once and for all, when a blinding mist swirled about him. He couldn't see anything or gauge his direction. Batting his arms at the mist, he yelled, "Paris! Paris!"

Also blinded by the strange mist, choking and coughing, Paris clawed his way in the dirt, praying he was moving away from

Menelaus and toward the Trojans.

The mist cleared as quickly as it had descended, but Paris was gone.

"Where is he?" Menelaus roared. "Where is he?"

Hektor stood stunned. He glanced around frantically, looking for Paris to be hiding behind anyone. "I don't know. By the gods, he's … vanished."

Agamemnon stepped forward, shaking his head in disgust at the Trojans. "I should have known to expect trickery from you Trojans. Your brother broke his word to Zeus. I declare Menelaus the victor. Turn over Helen and the treasure she stole from my brother." He dared a step closer. "If you do not, Prince of Troy, I will burn your precious city to the ground. You have until tomorrow."

PALACE OF PRIAM

Up on the rampart where Helen had been watching the duel, she blinked and Paris was gone. She could see Menelaus raging between the armies. He was definitely shouting. "What has Paris done?"

"Nothing, daughter, that I did not intend."

Helen bent under the weight of the goddess' hand on her shoulder. "Aphrodite."

"Go to him, daughter. He awaits you in your chamber. I've anointed him with scented oils."

"Why do you torment me, Aphrodite? You elevate me only to be enslaved by my desire and another man's craving? Take Paris for yourself if he is so precious to you. Leave me be. How can I go to him now? He's abandoned the field, left the other men behind. The women already laugh behind my back. I'm scorned enough. And Hektor. He hates me. So does Hecuba. I don't need more enemies within these walls. Your gifts are a burden."

Aphrodite squeezed Helen's arm, burning her perfect skin with her immortal touch. *"You wretched little bitch! How dare you speak to me with such ungrateful words."* The goddess pressed her hot lips to Helen's ear. *"Do not tempt me to hate you, for my affections can be easily forgotten. And your miserable life ruined. Now, go to him, who I chose for you."*

Helen pulled her himation closer and ran from the goddess to the palatial quarters she shared with Paris. Brushing pass guards and slaves, she hoped to find that Aphrodite only tested her resolve and obedience. She held her breath and closed her eyes, as she pushed the door open.

"Helen?"

Helen's eyes flew open at Paris' voice. There he was reclining sensually on the bed, glistening as if fresh from the bath. A bright smile on his face. His armor, renewed and gleaming, hung on the wall. His spears were propped up in the far corner.

Avoiding his face, she said, "You don't appear to have been in a battle at all. I wish that you had died at Menelaus' hand rather than disgrace us both by quitting the fight."

"Don't blame me for what the gods contrive for us. Menelaus had Athena on his side. I had Aphrodite on mine. What of it? Can we fight the gods?"

Shaking her head, Helen said, "I don't know. Maybe we should and end it all."

Paris got up from the bed to take her hand. "I know you

don't mean any of the harsh words you say. We are both trapped in Aphrodite's will. She's bound our stars." He wiped Helen's tears away with his thumb. "Don't cry, my love. There will be another time to challenge Menelaus."

She looked up. "Why can't I fight this urge?"

"Do not." Taking her hand, Paris led his wife to bed. "Let's stay in bed until the dawn." He kissed her slowly, pressing his tongue passed her teeth.

Helen softened against his body, wrapping a leg around his hip. "Fuck me, Paris. Fuck me until I forget this day ever happened."

As Paris took her, tears of desperation escaped her eyes. Aphrodite owned her body and her love to Paris. There was nothing real to cling to anymore. Her body betrayed her heart and she climaxed with her husband. In her grief and disgust, she turned away from him. Rage filled her heart at what Paris' judgment had cost her; a life in Sparta, a daughter, an honored position as queen beyond anyone's doubt. But it was Aphrodite who had planned it all and she could not fight a goddess. It was easier to allow her hate of Paris to grow instead.

Hecuba and her second son broke the night fast alone. The queen signaled the slave to take the stuffed figs away. The smell nauseated her this morning. "These are rotten." She sipped at her honeyed wine to calm her stomach. "I fear some illness has overtaken me."

"Would you like me to call a physician for you, Mother?"

"No. It will pass." Her womb fluttered. "Where is Helen?"

"She refuses to leave our chamber."

"Little wonder why. After Menelaus."

Paris rested both forearms on the table, leaning over his platter. "It was not my fault. It was Aphrodite's will."

Again, Hecuba's womb fluttered.

"Mother? Are you sure you don't require the physician?"

"I told you, it will pass," she snapped. "I'm just … tired. Aphrodite, you say?" Hecuba remembered with awe and horror the day the goddess appeared when Paris wed Helen. Her commands were clear regarding Helen. "She saved you from Menelaus?"

"I was on the ground. My head was pounding. I couldn't get up. I was crawling like some wounded dog. The goddess sent a fog and everything went dark. When I opened my eyes, I was in my chamber. That's where Helen found me."

"The goddess did you no favor. The world now believes you're a coward."

Paris slammed an empty palm on the table, jostling the bowl of fruit near his elbow. "I will get the chance to save my reputation."

"For much of my life, I mourned you. Your absence destroyed my peace. Now, your presence brings the doom that was foretold. I can't help but worry what will happen to Troy, to all of us, if the Greeks can't be broken. It doesn't matter if your reputation is one way or the other. If you don't find a way to bring down Achilles, the army will be scattered. And the women … you know what will happen to us. Tortured and raped, praying for death."

"That won't happen. Besides, Achilles doesn't even fight."

"So, you lose in his absence? What is worse, I wonder. If the enemy is victorious, our fate will be a certainty."

"I've lost my appetite."

"So have I." Hecuba rested her palm against her lower belly.

Apollo. What have you done?

Paris pushed away from the table. "I'll go to Hektor. He may be angry, but he needs me in the war to come." He dismissed himself, leaving Hecuba alone at the table.

"I'm too old for this," she said to her bread. "*Too old.*" In spite of the obstacles and improbabilities, she smiled wanly. It made sense to her that Apollo would use her again. Even the gods desired offspring.

As Paris walked through the lower garden, Apollo's light warmed his neck. It soothed his sour mood. Everyone he passed avoided meeting his eyes. No one greeted him, as they did before.

Lost in thought, he nearly missed spotting Helen. He stopped mid-stride, watching as a strange man backed her against a wall, talking intimately with their foreheads pressed together. The man brought his hand up to gently brush Helen's cheek.

"*She does not deserve you.*"

"Aphrodite." Paris' shoulder sagged under the immortal's presence. His heart was desperate. "Why did you give her to me?" The goddess forced him to watch as the man leaned down to kiss Helen passionately on the lips. "She makes no effort to stop him." Desperation snapped to jealousy.

"*She tires of my gifts.*"

"She's an ungrateful …" his breath tore is chest and his teeth clenched, "whore."

The goddess laughed in his ear. "*She has caused much trouble for you. Take your revenge.*"

Paris sprinted across the stones and grabbed the man by the

throat. The stranger's blue-green eyes swam with confusion. The man's mouth contorted awkwardly, so Paris squeezed harder. It wasn't until he felt the neck bones pop beneath his fingers that he heard Helen screaming for him to stop.

He roared in anger. "You wish that I save your lover's life?"

Helen fell to her knees beside Corythus, stunned. "No. No … not like this. I was sending him home." She looked up at Paris, horror and grief etched across every part of her face. "You don't know what you've done."

Paris sneered down at his wife. "I've become the man you wished me to be. Ruthless and brutal like Menelaus. A killer."

Gripping Corythus to her breast, she sobbed. "It's my fault. All of it."

"Who was he?" Paris stood watching his wife grieve. "How many times have you been with him?"

"This has Aphrodite's hand on it."

Paris grabbed her roughly by the elbow, yanking her to her feet. Corythus' head hit the hard ground. "You disgrace our marriage by mourning justice done? I should kill you. Who would miss you?"

Wrenching her arm free, Helen ran to their chambers, weeping hysterically with Paris on her heels. When they reached their room, Helen collapsed on the bed.

Paris slammed the door behind them. "Tell me who he was," he demanded. "Tell me!"

Helen's face was stained with shame and sorrow. "You will hate me more, when I tell you." Reaching under the bed, she grabbed the box with Oenone's letter, pulled it out, and held it out to her husband.

"What do you mean? What is this?"

"Open it. *Read* it."

Paris' fingers shook slightly as he unlatched the lid. Inside, he saw the papyrus. "A letter?"

"Read it, Paris."

Pulling the scroll out, he unrolled it. His eyes scanned the first few lines.

Is it you who is reading my letter? Or has the golden-haired woman prevented it? I suffer because the gods have united against me. What did I do to deserve this punishment? Remember when I taught you to about the flowers and the forest? When you took me beneath the heavens as your wife? When you carved my name upon a tree? If only the rivers could run the opposite direction, and the days roll back to make you mine again.

Paris glanced up, confusion marring his handsome brow. "Oenone sent this? When?"

"Almost a year ago."

I am forsaken, yet the Forgotten Prince lives on. When I saw your ship sail into the harbor, and your arms wrapped about the golden-haired woman, my heart broke. My sad fate sealed by your choice. Do you recall when you first left for the west? You did not want to leave me, kept calling me back for sweet kisses. You asked me if I would live in Troy, knowing I could not ever be held by stone and mortar. We wept in each other's arms.

Am I not worthy of a prince's love? Is the crown of flowers bestowed on me not equal to the circlet of gold you wear? Is the golden-haired woman loyal? Faithful as I have been? She turned from her husband easily for you. Does Hektor hold her in high regard? Or your royal mother? Once a woman has been unfaithful, she will always be unfaithful.

Tears ran down Paris' face. "Why didn't you tell me? Why would you keep this from me?"

"Jealousy, Paris."

"Of Oenone?"

Helen looked away. "That she gave you a son and I could not."

Paris continued reading.

Is this the ruin Cassandra dreamt? That you told me of in our secret cave? That you would bring the doom of Troy by ship hauling the wife of another, forsaking your own? I beg you take pity on my loyal heart. I loved you before you were a prince, when the sky and fields were enough for you. Before you longed for gold and glory. I am yours, my love, since our youthful days together. Remember me, Paris. Come back to me. Take care of our son.

"My son? My son is here? In Troy?"

"Yes," Helen choked on the word.

"Where is he? I want him brought to me at once."

Helen's mouth twitched unevenly; her chin quivered. "You will have to build him a funeral pyre as a greeting."

Time stood still. Like the day he made love to Oenone. The woodland magic brought to Troy. It dawned on him in bits and pieces. The dimple. The eyes. The stranger kissing Helen had … *Oenone's eyes.* "Wait." Paris collapsed to his knees, holding his head in his hands. He swayed precariously. "No. Tell me that wasn't Corythus. I beg you. Tell me."

Helen whispered, "I cannot."

"The way he was kissing you. Corythus was your lover? My … son was your lover?"

"Yes," the confession stuck dryly in her throat.

Paris howled his heartache to the heavens. Rocking on his knees, he cried bitterly. "My son. My son." His features twisted in anguish and disgust. "What have you done, Helen? What have *we* done?"

Helen knelt beside Paris, her body yearning to be close to him. "We have broken everything around us. Our world is now as broken as we are."

Paris' cock stiffened against his thigh. "No." Even in his agony couldn't resist the curse of Helen's nearness. "What is this madness Aphrodite inflicts on us?"

Tears melted Helen's cheeks. "I can't fight it." She reached for his face and pulled him into a passionate kiss. "I hate myself," she whispered. "I hate us."

"I know," he said, pulling her to him.

In the middle of their chamber, they stripped their clothes as their torment had stripped them of everything. Their bodies as naked as their souls.

Paris whispered, "Fucking is all the gods have left us."

EIGHTEEN
heavenly discord
OLYMPUS—1238 BCE

The immortals of Olympus assembled under the blinking crystal stars, sipping nectar from golden cups. The war game played out below them. Clearly, both sides had retreated to shade and respite.

"Aphrodite plays unfairly." Athena eyed her sister across the fine table. "Menelaus would have killed Paris if you hadn't interfered."

Hera agreed. "Now, look what confusion you have wrought on both sides. Neither knows what to do."

Zeus held up his hand for silence. "Wife, we all know your hand in this. You defend Menelaus. Aphrodite, you favor Paris." The gathering of gods looked nervously at one another. "Paris should have died by Menelaus' hand, but you prevented that."

"But, I was cert—"

"Enough." Zeus sighed heavily. "Only one question remains. What should we do now? What is done is done. How shall it end?"

The secret he kept for Gaia crossed his mind. "Should we inspire continued war or push for peace? Should Priam's city stand or fall? Should Helen be returned to Menelaus?" *Gaia would push for war.*

"You may end the fighting whenever you choose, husband," Hera replied. "We all know you are capable to bend the minds of men. Why do you interfere with our pleasure in the game? What is it to you, who wins or loses?"

"It is curious, *wife*, that you desire the Trojans wiped from the earth. Surely, this is not because Paris chose Aphrodite? I wonder if you would be so eager to kill them had the judgment ended differently."

"I have my reasons." Hera gestured around the table. "We all do."

Ares looked up to his father, a scowl on his face, and said, "We all know you favor Aphrodite."

"Is that why you feel justified in defying me?"

The God of War narrowed his eyes, and then diverted them from Zeus' intense gaze.

"Just as I thought. Either way, Hera, you will never be content with my decision. The city of Troy has always honored me." Zeus leaned into the table, his eyes burning into Hera's. "Know this … when the time comes, I will take a city beloved by you. And you will keep your wicked words from my ears."

"Do as you will. But send Athena down. Let her encourage the Trojans to break the peace."

Zeus leaned back into his chair. "So be it."

Athena stood from the table, grinning. "Are you certain, Father?"

He waved his hand, and the goddess leapt from Olympus, falling from the sky like a shooting star burning gold to silver.

TROJAN BATTLEFIELD

Both sides had found shade and rest apart from one another. Trojans and Greeks alike sat unarmed under skinny trees and tall bushes, while others used their shields as shade. Murmurs of confusion about what had happened to Paris traveled lightly on the warm, dry breeze.

Pandaros caught Athena's eye as he sat inspecting his arrows. She smiled to herself. "Here is my man." She was at his side in the blink of an eye.

Leaning down to his ear, she urged softly, *"Earn Hektor's gratitude and strike Menelaus through the heart with one of these."*

Pandaros startled as his piled arrows magically clacked together. "What mischief is this," he nervously whispered. "Who's there?"

"Athena."

Sweat beaded across Pandaros' forehead. "By the gods. Athena?"

"What are you waiting for? Don't you wish honor and glory for your house?"

The Trojan nervously picked up an arrow and stood. He scanned the enemy scattered here and there across the field.

"There. Do you see him?"

"The man with his hand on a horse?"

"Yes. Make true your aim."

Pandaros glanced around at the Trojans lounging about, escaping the heat. The low chatter carried in bits and pieces. A pregnant goat. A marriage proposal. A leaky roof. But mostly he heard talk of Paris and what would happen now. There was no one to stop him. Grabbing his bow, he quietly nocked an arrow. "Apollo, I *mean* Athena, guide my arrow." He pulled the bowstring back and released it. A war song whistled through the air straight for Menelaus.

Men from both sides looked up in surprise at the familiar, but unexpected whoosh.

In an instant Menelaus' side burned with pain as he fell sideways into a prickly bush. He'd heard the dull clang of his armor and fell back as something knocked him from his feet. Nearby men scrambled to help him to stand. A few gasped. Menelaus looked down to see an arrow sticking awkwardly from beneath his golden belt. Blood blossomed through his armor, spilling down his thighs. "Help me to some shade," he said in disbelief.

Agamemnon hurried to his brother's side. "Let me see him. Get out of my way."

"I am fine, brother. It's only a scratch really. My armor took the worst of it."

The Great King knelt beside his brother, assessing the wound for himself. "The Trojans have broken their word. There's no longer a reason to wait."

"I agree." Menelaus groaned. "Maybe I should see the physician."

"Take him safely away from here and see he's attended to." The sound of men drew his attention. He looked across the plain. The Trojans were on the move. "Quickly. I will not have our legacy become dust in the wind."

Three men carried Menelaus away as ordered.

Agamemnon addressed his troops, "My brother was denied his honor by that scum, Paris. That Trojan coward. Now …" He paused, making eye contact with those closest him. "Now, they have broken the peace between us. We've been at war for so long, many of us have grown gray in the beard. We miss our homes. We miss our wives." Nervous laughter rippled through the ranks. "We will fight these bastards and we will win. Arm yourselves for battle."

A cheer of ascent went up, as men strapped on their armor, slung their shields across their backs, and picked up their spears and swords. They marched in quiet determination, intent on making a final stand, the idea of home a beacon of hope.

The Trojans and their allies advanced line after line. Behind them a giant cloud of dust rose with the rumble of their voices. Hektor signaled for the horde to halt. Astride his horse, facing the Greeks, he recalled when he was a boy riding Ares across this very plain. *Ares, you were swift and fearless, as I was.* That boy had longed for war. His mother had tried to warn him that war broke more hearts than killed men, but he hadn't understood until this very moment what she'd meant. If he should die, it was but a single passing moment of agony, but the devastation his death would cause was heavier. Death would be kinder than the life his family would be forced to face without him. "We cannot lose," he murmured to himself.

Across the chasm a giant emerged from the ranks of the Greeks. He raised his arms and let loose a terrifying roar. The hairs on Hektor's arms rose. In a flash, the giant's spear flew with the speed of Apollo into the Trojan front line. A swirl of dust circled skyward like sacrifice smoke rises to the gods, as the target crashed dead to the ground. A Trojan spearman took aim and missed the giant, but his arrow found a home in another chest instead. Death drew blood on both sides.

Hektor cried out in fury, and the Trojans raced to meet the Greeks. The great armies crashed into each other like waves on a rocky shore. Bones cracked and splintered under spears, blood splattered shields and helms. Soon a sea of death threatened to drown the living on both sides. The gods unable to sway one side against the other.

Sensing doom, Hektor cried out, "Fall back! Fall back! Pull the dead with you!" Wheeling his horse about, he signaled his commanders. Interpreters scrambled to spread the word among the allies. Soon, both Greeks and Trojans were dragging the dead and wounded to safety.

From a nearby hilltop, Hektor surveyed the chaos below. His horse nervously stamped a hoof into the rocky ground. "Easy." He reached a hand to the beast's neck. "Easy."

"Why do you quit the fight, Defender of Troy?"

Every hair on Hektor's body rose as the cold words washed over him. "Ares?"

Sardonic laughter filled his ears. *"Do you not recognize your patron god, Hektor?"*

"Apollo. Forgive me. I am weary." He spoke half a lie. He was weary, but that wasn't the cause of not recognizing the Shining One.

"Why pull your army from the field?"

"I've lost too many men in a single day."

Apollo squeezed Hektor's shoulder. *"The Greeks will lose this war. They have lost their greatest weapon. Achilles. That fool lies drunk on his beached ship mourning the loss of a slave woman."*

"What of all the fallen?"

"More will fall."

"How is that encouragement? Even from a god?"

"If you do not fight, Hektor, Defender of the City, all of Troy will suffer. Cassandra has always been right, you know." The god squeezed tighter. *"But, you will forget that before long."*

Athena spied Apollo as he slid behind Hektor. "Putting his venomous tongue to work no doubt. Spreading his vicious lies."

The goddess swept down among the Greeks as they wept for their dead. She whispered past their ears like a cool breeze. *"Fight. Fight. Fight. The gods are on your side."*

By afternoon, the dead of both sides were heaped in mounds and more still lay scattered on the battlefield like rocks cast into the shit and gore of war. Zeus had indulged Hera's desire, but denied her clear victory. Fate would always have the final say.

PRIAM'S PALACE

"I recall seeing him train from time to time," Paris said. His eyes, empty of tears, burned. "I never guessed he was … Corythus. Why would Oenone send him here?" He reached for his dead son's hand. "When he was a boy, he begged me to stay. I walked away, Helen. I just took his arms from around my neck and walked away."

Helen stood mutely, watching her husband mourn his son. Her guilt and grief had drained everything from her. "I understand what it is to lose a child."

Paris wheeled on her, his eyes full of anger. "You haven't lost a child! You left a child behind. She's alive. My son is dead. You have no right to equal your pain with mine."

A knock sounded at the door and a chamber servant opened it at Paris' signal. Hecuba entered. "I came as soon as I—" She stopped dead in her tracks when she saw the body lying on the table. "What is this? What has happened here?"

Paris answered with a ragged voice, "He was my son, Mother."

Hecuba's step faltered. "Corythus? By the gods," she whispered. "I had no idea he was here."

"Neither did I." Paris looked to Helen. "She's known all this time."

"All this time?" Hecuba faced her daughter-in-law, her moment of weakness gone. "You?" Rage shook her to the core. "Why didn't you tell anyone?"

Helen's eyes grew large. She fought the urge to run from the room and keep running until she was beyond the citadel. "I wanted … I hoped he would—"

"What?" Hecuba shrieked. "What did you hope to gain by such a secret?"

"When that old man brought him, he said—"

"What old man?" Hecuba's anger cooled slightly. "Tell me."

"Agelaus?" Paris asked. "My foster father? Is there anything else you haven't told me?"

Helen shook her head. "He brought Corythus here to keep him safe from the Greeks."

"Only to place him in the hands of a viper," Hecuba spat. "I have watched you time and time again ruin my son with your … your disgusting displays of love. All you have brought to him is pain. That's all you've brought to Troy. I remained silent because Aphrodite demanded it so." She was in Helen's face with a flurry of her linen gown. "But I no longer care if the goddess hears my thoughts. Priam should cast you from the wall and let the birds pick your bones clean."

Helen back away. "I had no idea this would happen. It's not entirely my fault. The gods—"

"All of it is your fault," Hecuba screamed, her eyes blazing with hate. "Get out." Helen scrambled backward toward the door. "Get out!"

Paris stood stunned by his mother's reaction. All the prophecies and bad omens washed over him. "What have I done, Mother, that the gods cursed me from your womb? The priests were right. You should have let me die."

Hecuba winced inwardly at the words. She knew all too well the anguish Paris was experiencing. "You were ripped from my arms. From my breast." She shook her head. "I wish everything had been different. I never wanted you to die."

"Do you regret that I didn't?"

Placing her arm around her son's shoulder, she said, "We love and we lose. That is life. We regret. We accept. We move on. I don't know what else to say." She could not bring herself to utter the words aloud that, aye, she wished he had died. She wished he'd never returned to Troy. What did it matter now to say the words? What was done was done.

Paris looked his mother in the eyes, his face lined with fresh grief. "Corythus did not deserve …" the truth stuck in his throat, "deserve any of this. He was safe with his mother." He grabbed Hecuba's arm. "Why? Why would he come here?"

Hecuba's lower lip twitched. "Who knows?" The lie tasted sour. This was her doing, she knew. She had encouraged the nymph to send the boy, but she had not intended this. "The war has taken everything from everyone. What are you going to do now?"

"Send his body back to Oenone."

"I'll see that it's done."

"Gratitude, Mother."

"Go. Arrange the proper rites for your son. He was a Prince of Troy after all."

When Paris left the room, Hecuba decided she'd send a messenger to Agelaus, commanding him to stay away from the city and her condolences to the nymph. It would be easier, safer. Looking at the young man on the table, she knew Paris would be forever changed by this. Losing a child was like ripping a part of your soul out. And this war had brought her more grief than any mother should ever have to bear. Hecuba placed a hand on her rounding belly. The new life swam beneath her palm. She welcomed this parting gift of Apollo's, because the unborn child sealed the agreement she had with the Shining One. She kissed Corythus' cold forehead. "The war rages on even now, as you sleep in death. I only knew you briefly, but I promise I will have my revenge on Achilles for all of us."

NINETEEN

gods among mortals

TROY—1238 BCE

Aeneas watched the Greek called Diomedes swing his sword, bringing a swift death to every Trojan in his path. Bloody corpses and body parts lay strewn behind him. "The gods are with him. Take him out with an arrow, Pandaros. We should stay a safe distance—"

"Look, look how he moves, Aeneas. By the gods, he could rival Achilles. Every time I try to hit him with an arrow, it bounces off or flies safely passed him. A god must be beside him."

"But which one? Their fickle favor never gives us the fucking upper hand for long." Aeneas leapt to his chariot. "Let's charge him together." His grin invited reckless glory. "For Troy."

Pandaros leapt on the chariot platform beside Aeneas. "For Troy."

Aeneas snapped the leather reins and the horses bolted, sending up a dust shower behind them. Pandaros reached for an arrow, braced his thigh against the chariot, then brought his bow up to nock the arrow in. Aeneas maneuvered the horses over and around the dead and wounded.

Seeing them coming, Diomedes barreled toward them like a bull on fire.

Pandaros' aim faltered. His arrow glanced off the enemy's armor once again. "Who is protecting him?" he yelled. Aeneas careened the chariot around for a second charge. Diomedes rushed forward on foot, and as the chariot neared, he leapt with the wings of a god. His sword caught Pandaros at the jaw, sending the lower half of his face flying. Broken, he fell from the chariot.

Aeneas reined in the horses and jumped to defend Pandaros' body. "You won't defile him or strip his armor," he screamed, pulling his sword from its scabbard. "Never."

Diomedes sneered. "We'll soon find out." He stooped to pick up a small boulder and hefted it with all his might at Aeneas. It slammed into the Trojan's thigh instantly shattering the bone, sending Aeneas to the ground.

Aeneas screamed in agony. Looking down, he saw his ragged bone poking through a bloody wound. "Fuck!" He slumped to the ground, unconscious.

Diomedes laughed wickedly. "Prepare for the Underworld, you Trojan fuck." He advanced, but was instantly met with a blinding mist. "Athena, what is this? Why do you block my victory?"

"Look."

Diomedes squinted through the mist. He saw a very tall woman carrying Aeneas off the field. "Who is she?"

"Aphrodite. His mother," Athena whispered.

"What can I do against a goddess?"

"Trust me. Go after her." Athena kissed Diomedes on the mouth, filling his body with her strength.

Prying a spear from a nearby dead man's stiff hands, Diomedes raced after Aphrodite. His feet never carried him so swiftly before. The sound of men and horses dying surrounded him. But still he ran. Closing in on Aphrodite, he hefted his spear as he ran. Just paces behind, he hurled it at her. The blade-tip nicked her hand. Instantly, she dropped her son's body, but her scream startled Diomedes to the bone. He stumbled, skidding across the ground. With dirt in his eyes, he struggled to find his footing, as a dark cloud whipped around the fallen Aeneas.

"What trickery is this, Athena?" He searched for Aphrodite, but his keen sight granted by the goddess had vanished. In frustration, he threw a handful of dirt at the air. "Fuck!" he screamed. And fell to his knees in the dust.

Seeing Aphrodite stumble under Diomedes' blade, Apollo flew to her and pulled Aeneas to safety.

"How can I repay you?" she said breathlessly.

Apollo leaned his dark chiseled face so close to Aphrodite's she could feel his breath on her cheek. "Keep to lovemaking, sister. You don't belong on a battlefield. You of all of us were not made for war."

"I could not leave my son to be slaughtered." She swayed precariously to the side. "My hand is bleeding."

"Find Ares. He will get to Olympus. You cannot be helped here. Go."

Aphrodite was not a doting mother, but she cared for the Trojan man. "But Aeneas—"

"I will get him to safety. Now, go. What are you waiting for? It is not safe here."

Hektor surveyed the bloody field and consulted with the ally commander, Sarpedon. A tall man with a broad round chest. The sharpness of his honesty never missed a mark, not even with a king. "Every strategy I plan is thwarted. It's as if the Greeks know our every move. What am I not seeing?"

"Your bravery is what's missing, Prince Hektor. My army fights harder for your lands than your own brothers who hide like hunting dogs fearful of the lion. Who is hunting who?"

Sarpedon's words chilled Hektor's skin. "You are not Sarpedon. What god is here?"

"It is I, Ares."

Hektor bowed his head, his helm dipping to the god. "Tell me what to do."

"Kill them all, Prince of Troy. Fight!"

Without second thought, Hektor leapt from his chariot. "Men! We must fight! Ares is with us!" His commanded was echoed down the lines of his army. Men groaned with effort to reengage the Greeks.

Ares threw up his wide reaching arms, raising a heavy dust cloud to block the light. Infused with purpose, the Trojans fought from their hearts. The God of War unleashed a fierce war-cry, shaking the ground beneath the feet of all men. Trojans as well as Greeks stumbled; men covered their ears, and dropped their weapons. Fearing a god's wrath, the Greeks, retreated in fear, sheltering behind shabby trees and dusty dunes.

OLYMPUS

Ares' bloody call reached Hera far above the rampage of men below. She knew that once unleashed, savoring the taste of death on his tongue, the God of War would be nearly impossible to stop. She would risk what she must for her Greeks. Containing her irritation, she approached Zeus immersed in a tragedy far from Troy. "Will you allow Ares to blatantly disregard your wishes?"

Reluctantly, Zeus pulled his attention from below. A flash of annoyance crossed his face. "What would you have me do, Wife?"

Hera took his knees in her arms. "Allow me to take matters into my own hands, for once."

Zeus laughed without humor. His lip curled beneath his shimmering beard. "You have always done as you wished. Only when I shake the mountains free of snow do you cease your machinations against me." He leaned his face dangerously close to hers. "And then you start up again when you have used my desire for you against me."

Hera tilted her head up, kissing Zeus on the lips. "It is our way, is it not? You would tire of a docile wife. I beg you; give me leave to stop Ares."

Zeus waved a hand, clearing a view of the raging battle below. Resignation settled on his face. "Go, then. Do what you must."

Bowing her head, she kissed the god's hand and flew to Athena's side. "Daughter, do you see what is happening? We must not let the Trojans and Ares take the day from us. From the Greeks."

"Why do you worry so much? He only knows to slash and spill gore."

"He pushes the Greeks back across the plain. Soon, they will be huddled like frightened rabbits hiding at their ships."

Athena scoffed. "Not for long. Ready your chariot, Hera." Athena reached for the sacred aegis and slipped the garment over her golden gown. The Gorgon's head on the back of it rolled its eyes and the scales woven about the skin shimmered with unleashed terror. She donned her helm and gripped her spear. Together, mother and daughter sped to the Trojan plain to engage the Greeks and stop Ares from stealing the day completely.

The goddesses moved like the wind among the Greeks, whispering words to raise their blood lust. *"Be ashamed the Trojans push you toward your ships. Are you so ready to sail for home? Are you so weak in battle without Achilles? Raise your spears or the enemy will if burn your passage home. Fight back. Push them to their precious citadel and empty it of all its treasure."*

Courage spread—slowly at first, and then with swift blades.

Diomedes called out, "Athena has returned!" His cry alerted Ares from afield, who pivoted, aiming his war-lust at the giant. Ares with his eyes aflame charged Diomedes, but Athena had taken notice and swept to Diomedes' side unseen. Diomedes' spear jerked wildly in his hand. In a flash, the tip of Diomedes' spear slid across Ares' war belt, piercing the god's flesh.

Ares' thundering roar of pain shook the earth once again. Greek and Trojan alike searched the sky, expecting Zeus to appear and strike them dead where they stood. A dark cloud spread around Ares and he escaped the battle for high Olympus. He made immediately for Zeus' crystal chamber, dripping a trail of sacred blood behind him.

Before he could speak, Zeus held up one mighty hand. "Keep your complaints to yourself. You love war and all the hardships that come with it. You revel in death. Do not forget that I have seen you dance in blood with Achilles. You will not suffer long. Go find the healing balm you require."

Sighing, in exasperation, Zeus said, "I have had enough of all of you immortals whining and begging for this side, then that. I command you all to return to Olympus and let the mortals fight amongst themselves."

TWENTY
burdens of war

TROY—1238 BCE

Agamemnon yelled, "What are you waiting for, brother? Kill him!" The king pushed his way to his brother's side, pulling a spear from a dead body, and ran it through the man cowering before Menelaus. "He doesn't deserve your mercy. Or mine. I won't rest until Troy is obliterated from memory. No one but the gods will remember this fucking place." Agamemnon put his foot on the dead man's chest, crunching the ribs, twisted his spear, and then pulled it free of the mangled flesh.

Menelaus stammered, "I-I don't know why I—"

Agamemnon scoffed. "You think too much."

Menelaus leaned against his spear. Blood and mud caked all the way up his legs. "I don't think all our forces took the field, brother. Many are dead, but I would have thought more based on our numbers. This come-and-go as you please to battle won't win this war." They stood watching the crows and ravens already feasting on the dead and able-bodied soldiers scavenging for weapons and trinkets.

"Obviously, it's not *my* strategy, brother. Just fucking chaos." The Great King signaled for a messenger. "We need to pull back. Regroup."

"Agreed," Menelaus said, pulling his spear from the slippery ground.

TROAN LINES

Hektor unbuckled his helm and embraced his younger brother, Helenus. The years of warfare insulated Hektor from many of his siblings for much of the time. If he wasn't fighting alongside them, they drifted to shadows in the endless halls of the citadel. "What news?"

"Hektor, you've aged. Your hair is grayer than I recall."

Placing a hand firmly on Helenus' shoulders, Hektor leaned close and said, "War is the great equalizer of men. Tell me, what news? Good or bad, I must hear it." Then he winked.

"Brother, my dreams plague me on your behalf. On the city's behalf. The gods refuse to show us their constant favor. By all the stories past, these Greeks should have given up and left long ago. But they remain. Stubborn. Determined. As if they believe they are the chosen of the gods." Helenus stepped closer, lowering his voice. "Brother, I have seen the city in ruin for myself. Our women dragged to their ships. Children skewered on spears. Your men lose heart and you must settle them before we lose everything."

Hektor rubbed his beard. "That cannot happen." The prophecy

of Paris crept through the crevices of his memories. *Troy's doom trails behind my brother, wherever he goes. They should have let him die.*

"You speak of Paris."

Hektor jerked his head up. Surprise etched his face. "How did you … how did you know my mind?"

"I know a great many things, Hektor. Most of them unpleasant. Helenus' eyes bore into his elder brother's. "You must find a road into their hearts. Go to our mother. Persuade her to offer the richest treasures, a jewel-encrusted robe, to Athena. And sacrifice a dozen sacred cows. Perhaps then Athena will show mercy on Troy. Protect us from Diomedes, who has become the new Achilles."

"Your words echo Cassandra's of long ago."

"You may not like what I say next, brother."

Laughing, Hektor said, "Don't hold back now."

"Bring Paris to the field. He has a part to play, yet. Despite the conflict raging in your heart."

Hektor shook his head. Paris had been a bull herder. He'd danced fearlessly and gracefully with the beasts as a youth. However, since his parents had embraced their lost son, it had been nothing but a slow descent into madness and misfortune. The whispers of Troy's demise trailed behind Paris like a thin smoke. "I will do what I must." He jumped into his chariot and sped to the city.

When Hektor crossed the threshold of the inner gates, a throng of anxious women rushed him, eager to hear news of their men. He addressed the women he knew. The ones he did not, he offered sincere apologies. "Pray to the gods," he said to one and all.

The palace was oddly quiet. No one came to greet him. He grabbed a female slave carrying a basket of bread across the courtyard. "Where is the queen?"

"Weaving." The startled woman rushed off without another word.

Hektor hurried to Hecuba's private chambers. He wanted to make the request and return to the field before his men noticed that he'd gone. He knocked softly.

"You may enter."

"Mother," he said.

Hecuba's back stiffened, then she turned to face him. "Are you some trick of the gods sent to haunt my waking eyes?"

"No, Mother, I am here."

With tears shimmering in her eyes, she said, "I had not dared to hope that I would see you before the end. If at all …" She had no need to speak more of her thoughts aloud, for both of them knew what she implied. Hektor would return victorious, or he would be dead and Troy captured.

Hektor crossed the space between them. "Neither did I, Mother. But I'm glad I have come." He wrapped his arms lightly around her, while she clung briefly to him. His armor was filthy and smudged with war.

"Why have you left the battlefield? Has something happened?"

"I come at the request of Helenus."

She pushed against his chest, wiping her hands on her gown. "The news can't be good, then. Neither he nor your sister, Cassandra, have pleasant words to share with anyone. Ever. Tell me, does Achilles fight?"

"No. No one has seen him or his army. The rumors prove true. He battles Agamemnon in some feud or other. Unfortunately, a new threat has emerged to take his place."

"Who?"

"They call him Diomedes. He rages like a wild bull. Helenus calls him the *new* Achilles."

Hecuba clicked her tongue. "Well, that is sour news indeed. Wine?" She signaled for a servant to pour the honeyed mixture. "You must be thirsty. Tired. Rest a moment since you're here."

"No amount of wine will help me now. I must keep my wits sharp. But," Hektor sat on a soft stool, "I am weary."

Hecuba sipped her libation. "How is the fight going?" Sighing, she ran her finger around the rim of her cup and then set it down. "If you're here at Helenus' request, it must be … unwelcome."

"He says you must make an offering to Athena. That you are to take the elder women with you to her temple. He says you must lay your most exquisite robe at her feet. And sacrifice a dozen cows. If Athena is pleased, perhaps she will slow Diomedes."

Hecuba's lip pressed to a thin line. Shaking her head, she said, "I will do as you ask. But the gods tend to do as they please."

"I must bring Paris back to the field, as well."

"There is a surprise. He fights, and then is whisked away on a goddess' whim. I am confused by everything."

"I am beginning to worry that the prophecy—"

"Shah. Do not say it aloud."

"I'd rather the earth swallowed him whole for all the misfortune he's brought to Troy. If I could send him on his way to the Underworld, I would rejoice."

"Be careful what you say, for our words may be taken as a prayer used against us in a way we had not intended."

Hektor rose from his seat. "Gather the offerings as quickly as you can. I will find Paris—"

"No doubt abed with Helen."

"And get him back to war." He kissed his mother on the cheek. "Until I see you again."

"My heart will rejoice on that day." She reached up, taking his face in her hands. Her eyes searched his. "So blue, my son."

He smiled wanly. "Farewell, Mother."

Hecuba watched his powerful frame leave the chamber. His presence had filled the lonely space if even for a few moments. She drained her cup. "Farewell, my son." Her only hope was that Apollo would follow through on his promise to her and bring Achilles to his knees. Whatever kept him from battle, kept him safe from her vengeance. "The bastard must return to war." A flash of gold and dust blinded her from behind her eyes. She shivered. "You have work to do," she reminded herself.

As she crossed the threshold, a chill of another kind stopped her dead in her tracks. "Goddess?" she whispered.

"Athena."

Panic rose in the queen's heart. *Was the goddess listening all this time? Had Athena heard her speak?* "I am making my way to your temple as Helenus requested."

Athena's cold laughter filled Hecuba with dread. *"You think Apollo will help you, old woman?"*

Hecuba stood, struggling under Athena's heavy hand like a wild doe caught in a hunter's trap fearing for her life and her fawn.

"Do words fail you?"

"My apologies."

"You need not bother, Hecuba. I will never abandon Diomedes. Childbirth at your age will kill you, if you should survive the Greek's victory."

Athena's presence evaporated as quickly as it had come. Hecuba shivered again. "Please, Apollo, do not forsake us."

CHAMBER OF PARIS

Hektor's long strides carried him swiftly across the courtyard to Paris' chamber. He didn't knock, but bust through the door, all politeness gone. Paris sat in a chair polishing his weapons, while Helen sat in the corner sewing finery with a few of her maids.

"Men are dying beyond the wall. Dying, because of your selfish desires. How can you remain in your chamber while war rages all around us?"

"My heart is heavy, brother. Aphrodite has placed me here. What good is a man's will against a goddess? But, if you must know, Helen has been encouraging me to fight."

"A Trojan warrior needs no encouragement from his wife. He already knows his duty."

"I know my duty. I fulfill what I must. Besides, the gods show neither side favor, so what's the point?"

Helen rose from her soft chair. "Hektor, I know your love of me is thin, or," she paused, licking her full lips, "perhaps it doesn't exist at all. Paris deserves some small measure of your grace. The hardship that befalls Troy is my fault. It would have been better for everyone had Leda drowned me at birth. Aphrodite has brought this upon all of us. If Menelaus had been a different man … But that is not what the gods handed me." She leaned closer, taking Hektor by the arm, steering him to a private corner. "Paris is what the gods and fate have made him. The same as you or I. We don't choose who or what we are. And your brother, he's more like a flowing stream, ever changing. He's not made of the oak you are. Sit a while—"

"I'll not sit here wasting time." Hektor shook his head in disgust. "My brother has no use for our father's legacy. Nor songs. What will they sing of him? That he stole a queen and ruined a city? My city."

Helen dropped her hand from Hektor's arm.

Hektor's angry gaze found his brother's. "Once this war is over and our city is safe, *if* you are still alive, I will kill you myself." He turned and left, leaving the chamber door wide open and Helen's mouth agape.

He quickly passed through the main hallways, before exiting the main palace for his private quarters on the palatial hill. Bursting through the main entrance, Hektor yelled, "Andromache!"

A startled maid ran to greet him. "My lord." She bowed her head. "We weren't expecting you."

"Where's my wife?" he asked brusquely.

The maid's eyes widened in fear. She stammered, "Sh-She is ... she is o-on the w-wall, my lord. With your son."

"Why? Why would she go to the wall without sending word?"

"Forgive me, my lord, but whispers reached us that the Trojans were failing. That the invaders were too many. Too strong. She took the babe and ran for the tower. Hoping, I think, to catch sight of you."

Hektor bolted from his home, panic gripping him as he ran.

Andromache pushed her way through the small crowds dotting the upper sections of the wall. Astyanax's arms clung tightly around her neck. "We are safe for now, little one. Perhaps, if the gods are willing, we will catch sight of your father."

Her name carried across a short distance. "Andromache!"

She turned. There he stood, helm shaking in the sunlight, tall and beautiful in her eyes. "Hektor!" she cried out and rushed toward him. His embrace became her entire world in that moment. All her fears melted in tears down her face. "I heard you had come. I was afraid—"

Hektor brushed her cheek with his thumb. "Afraid I wouldn't come to you?"

"If you had business with your father, or the elders …"

"My love, I will always come for you. Never doubt that. Never doubt my love."

"Then why have you returned? The war rages on. I fear …"

"What do you fear?"

Andromache swallowed hard. How could she voice the words that haunted her dreams? Give light to the darkness creeping into her mind, whispering of his doom? "What if you … what if you don't return from the battle?" She dared to meet his eyes. "You are the Defender of the City."

"Andromache —"

"No. Let me finish. You know what's coming. I've seen it in your eyes a hundred times." Lowering her voice, so only he could hear, she said, "Troy will fall because of Paris and what he's done."

"Not as long as I am alive."

"That is what will be our undoing. If you fall—"

"I will not fall."

"Can you read the mind of the gods? Will Achilles stay away forever? Why do the gods allow us to suffer as we have?"

"We will push the Greeks into—"

"The sea. Aye, I've heard you say that a dozen times."

Hektor grabbed her arm, steering her away from the eyes now lingering on their passionate conversation. "You will frighten the boy."

Andromache could see the hurt in her husband's eyes. The aftermath of war lingered in her mind, pushing her to the edge of madness. For the first time, she understood her mother's wishing to die. To end the fighting forever. "I am more frightened by what will happen to us when you're gone. It would be better for you to take our lives now, than face this life without you. Our son will be fatherless, as I am. We will have no protector."

"Know that I love you, Andromache, and our son. If I don't fight, these fears of yours may very well become reality, not just for you and Astyanax but for all the widows and children left behind. One day Troy will fall, Andromache. When, I don't know, but one day. If I should fail what would become of you and our son? You'll be a slave to some foul-mouthed Greek, forced to weave another woman's loom—"

"Stop, Hektor. We both know what comes after. For me and Astyanax."

"I'd rather be dead than hear you cry out for me as they dragged you to their ships." He reached for Astyanax, but the babe cried.

"Look at you, Hektor. Armed for battle. He's frightened of your helmet."

Hektor laughed and removed it, then scooped his son into his arms. "He's getting so heavy. A true Trojan prince." He smiled, tears glistening in his eyes. "I pray the gods make him a better man than I have been. A strong king, when I am gone."

Andromache knew in her bones that Hektor would never be king, nor would their son rule Troy. She believed her husband to be the most valiant warrior and yet even under his leadership the

Greeks had not been defeated. Worse yet, the gods themselves shifted favors, so no victor emerged. So many had lost so much how would their world recover? She wondered if these days of war would end Priam's line forever, and if her husband shared her mind. "I beg you. Position men at the lowest section of the wall where the invaders have tried scaling it—"

Hektor placed their young son in her arms, pulling them both into his protective embrace. "Do not let fear control you. Fate will lead all of us, brave or weak, down our intended path. My soul will not wing to the Underworld if it is not my time. Let me worry about the war."

Andromache met Hektor's gaze. "If you think your safety and the welfare of the city are beyond my concern, you're wrong. Who keeps the home while the men are away? Who births and cares for a man's legacy? We do. We bear the brunt of your wars. For you, your death would be a relief from endless fighting, but it will ruin me in every way."

"Believe me, Andromache, I know. Why do you think I fight so hard for Troy? For you? Prepare for my return, wife. Nothing fills me with more courage than the thought of your arms wrapped around my neck and your sweet, hungry kisses." Hektor kissed her firmly on the lips. He studied every line of her face before placing on his helmet. "Farewell, my love." He turned and hurried from the wall without looking back.

Andromache, holding Astyanax tight, cried watching Hektor disappear from sight.

After donning his shining armor, Paris ran from his chambers to find his elder brother, knowing he'd be making his way swiftly to the field of war. He caught sight of Hektor as he was descending the tower stairs. "Brother!"

Hektor stopped and turned. He waited, spear in hand.

"Brother, I told you I would come. Did you not believe me?"

"You fight as hard as any man once the battle has begun." Leaning against his spear, Hektor's azure eyes pierced Paris'. "It's your lack of urgency to fight and win that concerns me. How many Trojans have died simply because you draw breath? How many wives have lost husbands and children their fathers because you chose Helen? Do you even know? But, there's no more time to talk, brother. If we drive these Greeks from Troy for good, then we will find our way to being brothers once more. If that is even possible."

Paris nodded mutely. He could no more explain why Helen tore him from his duties, than he could explain why he returned to her bed even after all that had happened. There was nothing more to say. They descended the stairs, making swiftly for the plain and the war.

TWENTY ONE

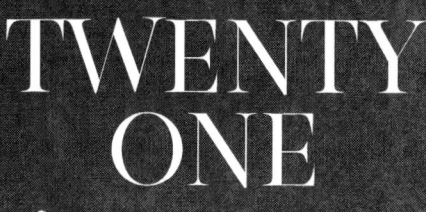

long-shadowed spears

TROY—1238 BCE

The sky burned deep blue with the length of the day, when Athena saw Hektor and Paris in their shining armor sending up their war cries to rally the Trojans against her beloved Greeks. Anger rose in her chest like molten rock. "Fools," she seethed. She blazed down the sacred slopes, taking refuge beneath an oak to strategize how best to defeat the Trojans once and for all.

"What are you hiding from, sister?"

"Go away, Apollo."

The Shining One rested his back against the tree trunk. "Not very friendly of you."

"Don't you have a temple to fly off to? A hapless mortal to fuck? Or mutilate?"

Apollo laughed wickedly; his crystal locks shook and his blue-orange eyes blazed. "And miss whatever mayhem you're plotting?" He licked his lips. "Against Zeus' wishes? No, I wouldn't miss this for all the virgins on my altar."

Athena stood to her full height, eye to eye with Apollo. "You know why I'm here. But what is it, I wonder, that you hope to gain?"

"Aren't you tired of this war already? It's tedious." He casually folded his hands behind his back. "Why don't we *just* … end it?"

"How do you propose to stop nine mortal years of battle? Ride across the sky west to east?"

"Not a bad idea." Apollo shrugged, as if he was actually considering the idea. "We could inspire a man-to-man combat to end it for good."

"That hasn't worked so far. Paris—"

"Aphrodite loves him too much to see him suffer. She has her reasons. I have another in mind. *Hektor.*"

"Hektor?"

"Yes, let him raise the challenge. We'll see which Greek of yours will accept."

Athena was skeptical of Apollo's intentions. She knew he was capable of lying just to steer matters into his favor. "And no interference?"

"None."

"Agreed."

Apollo sped to Hektor's side, whispering his will, *"Call a challenge, Hektor. Call a challenge and end the war. You will sleep soundly in your bed tonight next to your lovely wife."*

Hektor moved by the god's inspiration bravely marched to the front of his army and called out in a booming voice, "Greeks! Let us end this war. Send your best to fight me. The loser's body will be treated with respect and be housed in Apollo's temple as a reminder of the Greek brave enough to challenge Hektor and lose." The army shuffled nervously behind him. "Well, where is this brave Greek?"

Menelaus stepped forward and shouted across the chasm. "I hope you are no coward like your brother."

Hektor's heart pounded. He bellowed, "Come find out."

Agamemnon leaned into his brother, and said, "You are no match for Hektor. Even Achilles had some reservation fighting him. I won't risk losing you now. The men would race for the ships."

"You'll make me the coward, then," Menelaus fumed beneath his helm. "I have no wish for the men to see me as the weaker brother."

"Better the weaker brother, than dead."

Menelaus ripped his helmet angrily from his head. "Fuck!"

Agamemnon and Menelaus folded back into the ranks of their army.

Hektor cried out, taunting them, "Is there no one brave enough? Why don't you just leave now? Come, send your best man … or is Achilles still playing the coward to your fight?"

Ajax of Telemon, brilliant in his bronze-ringed armor, pressed through the ranks of men to face Hektor. His strides were confident and long. He moved like the God of War himself. "Pray for me, friends, that I take this bastard's life quickly so we can claim our victory." Facing Hektor, he smiled cruelly and shook his spear. "I will eat your beating heart while your dying eyes watch. Then you will know who is victorious and who will fuck your wife by sun down. I always wanted to fuck a princess." The Greeks cheered their champion.

The Trojans trembled for their prince. This giant of a man was no Achilles, but he was close in stature. Many had witnessed Ajax's savagery in the field. Hektor's heart pounded against his ribs as the call to fight filled him with red fury. He would see the challenge through and not cower like Paris did in the face of Menelaus.

Ajax moved nearer his opponent. "Let all you Trojans be assured the best of us are here on this field, not moping about like a child on a ship. I accept your challenge. Apollo will gladly take your body, as I will happily take your armor to my tent. Best ready yourself to die."

Hektor replied, "I know the dance of blood and death." Hefting his mighty ash spear, he cast it, piercing Ajax's shield down to its last layer. The giant set his shield edge on the ground and smashed down on the protruding spear shaft, snapping it off.

Ajax laughed aloud. "Your arm is weaker than I thought, Prince of Troy." With an arm like lightning, he loosed a spear toward Hektor. It pierced clean through the Trojan shield.

The tip of Ajax's blade bit Hektor below the ribs. Dropping his ruined shield, Hektor drew his sword, undeterred. He leapt at Ajax, sword extended to jab the Greek's shield. His sword tip bent back like a soft river reed. Ajax hammered Hektor in fury with his sword; the clanging song of blade on blade filled the air. With a mighty strike, Ajax caught Hektor's unprotected neck, slicing just above the collarbone. Hektor fell to his knees. A roar went up from the gathered Greeks. Crimson spilled down Hektor's shoulder. Reaching for a heavy rock, he threw it at Ajax, but it clanged off his shield.

Ajax laughed to the sky. "This is the man who defends Troy? It is a wonder we did not storm the walls years ago!" He stooped to pick up a small boulder, for his hands were much bigger than Hektor's. He spun once, then again, picking up speed, and loosed his stone at Hektor. Hektor fell straight back with the force of the blow, gasping for breath.

They fought back and forth, no clear winner and neither giving ground. Apollo's light faded from blue to gold. Exhausted and dripping blood and sweat, both men rested a moment, leaning in spears and staring at one another.

Hektor said, "Night is approaching. And the gods appear content to declare no victor between us."

"You challenged me, Hektor of Troy. Call the fight if you wish. As for me, I will fight beneath the stars."

Hektor reluctantly removed his helm, sweat dripped down his face and into his eyes. "Go feast at your camps. We Trojans will do the same. War will wait until the dawn. Perhaps, the gods will choose a victor with the new day."

Men on both sides gathered up their weapons and armor, silently retreating to their respective sides. Both armies, tired and hungry, secretly longed for food and sleep more than they wanted to watch Ajax and Hektor trade blows into the night.

PRIAM'S PALACE

Fires lit the ramparts as women and children sang in the winding lanes of the citadel. The dark mood of the city lifted beneath the stars. Every household celebrated the returning men, and Hektor, Defender of the City, most of all. As long as he survived the war, there was hope for everyone. Hope that the Greek invaders would be defeated and sent back across the sea.

In the halls of Priam's palace, the feasting was bittersweet.

Hecuba took her place beside her husband. She smiled at Hektor and Andromache. Their marriage brought her joy in her dark moments. Paris and Helen sat across from Hektor. She couldn't understand why Aphrodite demanded the acceptance of Paris and another man's wife, when clearly the first husband wished for her return. She signaled for her wine to be poured. She glanced down the table. Cassandra and Helenus whispered together. Polyxena sat alone, quietly picking at the figs. Hecuba sighed and her heart ached to see the empty chair that belonged to Troilus. At the farthest end, Melita, Priam's most recent wife, sat with her son, Kebriones.

Her eyes wandered to Priam. Despite the fine tunic and the gold and lapis lazuli draped around his neck, she couldn't help but notice that war had aged him. She smoothed her hand over the slight swell of her belly. She worried that age had caught her as well, and that Apollo's gift would claim her life in the end. Soon, she would not be able to hide the child growing inside of her.

Helen's silver laughter caught the queen's attention. It sickened her stomach seeing her second son engaged in intimate conversation with the whore from Sparta. "How can you laugh, Helen, when the tragedy wrought by your own hands hangs above you?"

Hecuba's barbed words quieted the polite chatter at the table. The royal family looked to one another. "Well?" Hecuba prodded. "The boy's bones can hardly be cooled. Yet, you sit here among his family, mirth tumbling from your lips."

Helen opened her mouth, and then closed it.

"What tragedy do you speak of?" Hektor asked.

Paris looked at his mother and shook his head. "Another time, brother. I have no wish to dwell on the grief in my heart."

"I have never dismissed such heartache so easily," Hecuba said her words as sharp as any blade.

"What are you talking about?" Hektor asked.

Hecuba simply said, "Ask Helen, she knows exactly what she's done."

Priam mercifully intervened. "For the sake of what may be our last meal together, Hecuba, stop hounding Helen. You've made your disdain clear enough over the years. Her wrongs have been righted and sealed by Aphrodite herself."

At that, Antenor spoke up, "Why do we continue to risk our city for Helen?"

Priam's cheeks flush red. "I will have no more talk of Helen."

Antenor stood up, resting his hands on the table. "As your counselor, it is my duty to advise you as best I can. Why do you refuse to see the truth, Priam? Paris dishonored a king by stealing his wife away. Then, compounded that dishonor by fleeing the field like a coward, breaking a sacred oath made before the gods, the Greeks, and his own people. Send Helen and her possessions back. It will go bad for us, if we do not." He looked at Paris with stone cold eyes. "You know in your heart, what you must do. Haven't you had enough of this bloody war?" Antenor sat in a heated huff.

Paris stood. "I tire of everyone pushing me to give Helen back to Menelaus. She has been my wife for years. Is it because she has given me no sons that you all continue to reject her? You expect me to throw her away as if our life together has no meaning? Well, I refuse. If you wish, return her possessions. For me, it was never about the treasure she enriched our city with. My brothers and their wives have never complained when her wealth provided them more luxury or weapons. Or have you all conveniently forgotten that?" He took his seat. "Give the gold back. But I will never give back Helen.

Never."

Priam sank deeper into his chair. Despair was his constant companion these days. His family fought amongst itself as viciously as they fought the enemy at the gate. His shoulders sagged under his burden. "I'll send a messenger with Paris' proposal at dawn. I will also ask for a reprieve so we can give proper rites to the fallen. The foul air wafts to the city. I will not have that for my people."

"Why did you defend me, Paris? After … everything. After," Helen choked out, "*Corythus*."

"His death is as much my own doing as yours. I never should have abandoned him. If I had stayed, he would be alive. If I had brought him here instead of chasing a life I never wanted, he would be alive."

"It would be easier for you to send me away and never look on me again."

Paris took Helen's face in his hands. His blue eyes searched hers. "We both know it is more complicated than that. Aphrodite will never allow us to part. If we did, it would insult her."

Helen could read the deep sorrow on his face. Her desire to produce an heir for Troy, securing her position within the royal family had withered like a broken branch. Now, she questioned everything about her life. With Corythus, she knew her passion was genuine. It was hers, not the goddess influencing her to love. She found that she craved that connection with her lover. "She will never be satisfied, until we are dead."

"We agree on that." Paris released her and sat heavily on the edge of their bed. "His body is in his mother's care by now. It's a small comfort knowing that she will honor him."

Helen nodded, fresh tears spilling down her cheeks. She heaved a heavy, shuddering sigh.

"Why did you do it? What could he give you that I could not?"

"The truth will not bring you comfort."

Paris' eyes flashed with anger. "Tell me." His tone grew sharper. "Tell me why you had to sleep with my son."

"He loved me, Paris, for me, not because of a promise by a goddess. We both know if it wasn't for Aphrodite, we would never have met … and I would never have come to Troy. There would be no war."

Paris lay back on the bed. "I have truly brought the wolf to the gate. Oenone tried to warn me that this day would come. But I refused to listen."

"Why?"

"I believed I could save my life with her, if I obeyed the goddess. But then I saw you."

Helen lay back beside him on the bed. She entwined her fingers with his. "I believed our life together would be different than the one I lived in Sparta under Menelaus' watchful eye. I am no better off than any woman taken prisoner and used against her will."

Paris stared at the ceiling. "You truly believe you are nothing more than a war prize to me?"

"There is no other way to see it. You only desired me because of Aphrodite. And I abandoned my virtuous life, the life I could never quite embrace, for the same reason. The goddess stole our wits and played her games with us. For her prize. To be the fairest."

Paris' thumb brushed hers. "We are both wretched fools, Helen."

Helen turned her head to Paris, her eyes seeking his. "Perhaps, I should go to Menelaus and end the war."

"I believe the Greeks would fight on. They've been here too long. Suffered the loss of too many men. You may have been a true concern in the beginning, but *now* ... it would never be enough."

Helen got up and glided to the balcony, pushing the privacy draping aside. "It is a beautiful night. Do you suppose it will be our last?"

From the bed, Paris said, "It's hard to say which way the gods will lean. Come to bed."

Helen turned to see the familiar look of lust in his eyes. "We can't."

"Why not? What if it is our last night together?"

"No."

Paris was up from the bed in an instant. He crossed the chamber in a few long strides. Taking Helen by the waist, he turned her to him. "I will not be denied, Helen," he said huskily. Her body softened in his embrace. "You want this as much as I do. I don't care if it's some trick of Aphrodite's."

"It's wrong."

Paris' mouth hovered over hers. His warm breath warmed her lips, before they descended in a desperate and searching kiss.

Helen wrapped her arms around his neck, pulling him closer. Her tongue probed his mouth. The familiar need to have Paris inside of her coursed through her body. "Take me, then."

They reached for each other beneath the stars, satisfying their passion on the balcony. Once they were done, sweating and miserable, they untangled their bodies and went to bed.

In the dark, Paris said quietly, "I was angry at Agelaus for many years after I came to Troy."

"Why?" Helen whispered softly.

"My whole life I wanted only the truth."

"And now?

"I wish only for the lie."

Andromache tucked the purple-striped blanket around Astyanax sleeping soundly in his cradle. Turning to Hektor, she said, "I thought I'd never see you again after the wall."

"I told you I would return. What can I do to ease your fears?"

"End the war. Come home and never fight again."

Hektor took her hand. "Come." He led her to their balcony. Above them the stars winked against a cloudless night. "We will endure, my love."

She leaned into his strong embrace. "I can't survive without you. Neither will our son."

"For reasons we are blind to, the gods wish Troy to suffer for now. But this city … *Listen*. Do you hear that, Andromache?"

"Yes."

"That is the sound of our stories already being sung. The heart of Troy is strong. Our walls have endured generations." He turned Andromache to face him. "Trust that we will prevail."

"But what if—"

"Do not speak words of doubt." Hektor's eyes darkened. "If you do not believe in me, then I am lost. Do you understand?"

Swallowing her doubts, Andromache managed a weak smile. "You are my everything." She pressed her cheek to his chest. "When this is over, promise me, no more war." Hektor's chest rose and fell.

His heart beat steadily in her ear. "Promise me."

"I cannot."

A silent tear slid down her cheek. "Make love to me, Hektor," she whispered, desperate to cling to him.

Sweeping her from her feet, he carried her to their bed. Their hands and lips explored the known territories of each other's bodies. And when they lay together, satisfied and sweating, Hektor pulled Andromache into his arms and slept.

In the darkness, Andromache wept quietly.

Priam entered Melita's chamber unannounced, startling her. "My lord, I did not expect you."

"I wanted to … to see my son before the dawn."

"He is here. Out on the balcony."

"May I speak with him? Alone?"

"As you wish." She paused before leaving. "Come find me in the garden when you are through."

Priam nodded, as she closed the door behind her. Crossing the room slowly, he carefully thought on the words he wanted to say. He stepped onto the balcony. "Kebriones?"

Kebriones turned to face Priam. "My king."

Priam took in his bastard son's appearance. Dark eyes, unlike the children he fathered by Hecuba. But the dimpled chin was a clear sign. His long, black hair curled in ringlets to his shoulders. He was as handsome as any of his legitimate sons. "What do you see when you look out on Troy?"

"An unconquerable citadel."

"I understand Hektor requested you fight alongside him?"

"He is running short of brothers."

"I am running short of sons." Priam sighed heavily. "I never knew a man's heart could break so many times in one lifetime. For once, I'm grateful I am mortal."

"Why, my king?"

"I know that one day, perhaps soon, the agony will end."

Kebriones remained silent, looking out into the night. "Hektor fought bravely against Ajax."

"Our hopes and those of Troy are bound to his victories."

"Do you believe the Greeks will allow a day of rest to collect the dead? Or that they will take the offered gold for the Spartan woman?"

Priam eyed Kebriones. "Even you hate her." It was not a question. "The city blames her."

"And Paris," Kebriones added.

The old, festering wound stung renewed by the fact that Paris' life had brought about their impending end. Cassandra had been right all along, but there was no way to change the past. "It was an impossible decision. I pity them both."

"He was your second-born. More important than your bastards."

With an old, wrinkled hand, Priam took his vibrant son's hand in his. "I have always loved all my children. I am glad you are here. And will fight alongside Hektor tomorrow or the day after. As for Paris …" His voice trailed away to silence. "Kebriones?"

"My king?"

"This city is as much yours, as it is any of my sons. Fight bravely when the time comes. You will be rewarded." He turned to go, and then unexpectedly embraced the tall warrior. His tired eyes filled with tears. How strong Kebriones felt against his growing weakness. The years had worn him down, the prolonged siege war sapping what little vigor he had left. Priam patted Kebriones' shoulders. "Call me Father from now on. I'll go now. Your mother asked to speak with me."

Kebriones watched King Priam leave. He wasn't certain how he felt about the overdue acceptance into the royal family. Priam had mostly ignored him his entire life, until he needed him. He would fight, because he was a Trojan warrior. He was honored to fight with Hektor, because there was no one braver in battle that he'd ever seen. "Father," he whispered into the night. The word tasted bittersweet on his tongue.

Melita nervously picked at the embroidery on her linen belt, while she waited for Priam, uncertain he would even show. Life as a wife to King Priam was little different than when she was a lowly concubine. Queen Hecuba marginalized all Priam's women at the edges of palace life, clearly wishing no interaction, except for the children as they grew.

"Greetings, Melita."

She stopped fiddling with her belt. Her stomach lurched. "Husband."

"Our son has grown to be a fine man. You have raised him well." Priam took a seat next to her on a stone bench. "I shouldn't be surprised."

"Kebriones has your blood."

"The seasons have come and gone more times than I can count.

But these last, with the enemy banging against the gates, beached on our shore … this is not how I envisioned my final days."

"I feel the same."

Priam took her hand in his. "The gods."

"The gods."

"What did you wish to say to me, wife?"

Melita blushed like a young woman. Since she'd returned to the palace, long buried feelings for Priam clawed their way to the light. She'd sworn to never resurrect them, but they had a life of their own. She bit her bottom lip.

"Do you ever miss the time we spent together? When we were more … *youthful*."

Pulling her close, he said, "I do."

"Would it be wrong to ask …" Melita examined her hands in her lap. "Do you find me too old?"

Guessing at her question, Priam shook his head. "No, you are as lovely as when I met you." When Melita remained silent, he asked, "Is that what you wanted to ask me? If I find you too old?"

Her eyes searched his in the dark. "May we lay together, Priam? Like we were young once more? Unless, the queen—"

"Hecuba prefers to sleep alone." He lifted her hand to his lips. "But I do not."

GREEK CAMP

Under the stars, Agamemnon's army feasted. Musicians played. A singer sang songs of the day, of Ajax and the Trojan Prince. The boisterous sounds of drunken men rose to the heavens. Nestor drank deeply from his cup, the wine warming him as it traveled down to his full belly. To his right, Odysseus and Ajax sat. Opposite him was Diomedes. And to his left, the royal brothers of the House of Atreus. He sat back, taking in the rare moment of peace.

"He hits like a bull. I hadn't expected such strength," Ajax said, holding his cup up for more wine. "I must be twice his size. A god had his back no doubt."

Diomedes laughed with a mouthful of bread. "The Trojans believe Hektor to be their Achilles."

Silence. Not even the slightest breeze brushed against the tented walls.

Diomedes glanced around the table. All eyes were fixed on him. "What? It's true."

Odysseus raised his eyebrows at Diomedes. "We almost made it one evening without speaking his name. Was that too much to ask?"

Agamemnon's face turned sour. "We don't need that traitorous bastard or his fucking men."

Odysseus muttered to Ajax, "Here we go."

Diomedes sounded in his own defense. "I was only saying—"

Nestor stood abruptly. "We must collect the dead."

The ripple of quiet spread from the commanders' table to the entire army. Banners snapped in the crisp breeze. Torches flickered. The silence deepened.

"They deserve proper rites. We must burn them and wrap their bones."

Agamemnon leaned back in his chair. He rubbed at his beard. "What do you suggest? Call off the battle in the morning?"

"Aye. The Trojans will want their dead carried home, as well."

"Do you agree, Ajax?" Agamemnon asked. "It was your

agreement to finish the fight with Hektor in the morning."

Worried that Ajax would disagree, Nestor spoke quickly. "We must also build a wall surrounded by a ditch deep enough to keep the Trojans from advancing into our camp."

Eyeing Nestor, Agamemnon asked, "The gods have spoken to you?"

Nestor slyly answered, "If we do not, the Trojans will run us into the sea."

Agamemnon scowled. "Very well. With Apollo's light, we send word of a truce to gather the dead."

Ajax inquired, "What about Hektor?"

Odysseus gripped Ajax by the shoulder. "Better not to tempt the gods into handing you death. Hektor may kill you. As you said, a god backs him."

When Apollo's light stretched broad fingers across the blue sky, Agamemnon gathered his commanders still reeling from the festivities of the previous night. The king signaled for watered wine to be served with bread and honeyed figs. "I see you are all in fine form."

Odysseus groaned. "We need better wine."

Ajax said, "Or more. Bring me a cup of wine, boy." A young servant boy scurried to the giant's side and poured a full measure. "A man can never have enough wine."

Diomedes openly mocked Odysseus. "The King of Ithaka appears to have had enough."

"Can we please not speak of wine?" Odysseus stuffed warm bread into his mouth. "Water, boy. Bring me water."

"While you recover your wits, I have news from Troy," Agamemnon said.

Menelaus scoffed. "They offer a pittance of what we can take."

Odysseus raised his aching head. "What do they want?"

"A day's truce to collect the dead," Agamemnon said.

Leary of a Trojan initiated truce, Odysseus probed, "How convenient. By Menelaus' face, I should think something more."

"Our immediate departure … for the return of the gold taken from Sparta with Helen."

Menelaus growled, "Everything but the surrender of my rightful wife."

"We should take the deal and sail for home, before we are too old to make the journey. Or our families forget our faces," Ajax said.

Diomedes eyed the elder commanders around the table. His cup clanged noisily as he slammed it down. "By the gods! Don't even consider taking the treasure. It's clear the Trojans know they are going to lose. Why else would they make such an offer?"

Agamemnon asked, "Do any of you wish to return home without taking Troy?"

"Even if they offered to double Menelaus' gold, it would not be enough to satisfy each man. If we take Troy, our reward will be much greater for all the efforts we have made," Odysseus said.

Menelaus had sat the entire conversation sulking, because the one thing he wanted could not be shared. So, his complaints always went unheeded. "I want my wife returned."

Agamemnon asked, "We agree to a truce to collect and prepare the dead, and refuse the offer of gold?"

A collective, "Aye!" sounded around the table.

"So be it," Agamemnon said. "Odysseus, I task you and your

men to build a barricade around our camp. We may need it once the fighting begins anew. The Trojans have come too close for us to believe victory will come easily or without great cost."

"That will take days," Odysseus complained.

"You don't have days. You have one."

Odysseus groaned. "Fuck my lots."

To ease the burden, Agamemnon said, "I will have … better wine this evening."

"How did you manage that?" Ajax asked.

"It's from Lemnos. Euneos, the son of Jason, sent it. He was very pleased with the last shipment of slaves."

Under the toiling heat of day, both sides collected their dead. Men slipped through slick, bloody earth and gore to carry their dead to their respective sides. Women wept and washed the corpses of countless men. Men gathered what wood they could to build great funeral pyres, sending flames and ashes shooting into the lengthening day.

In the Greek camp, when the fires burnt low, they gathered the warm bones in bundles, marking each one. When they returned home, if they returned home, the dead could finally rest.

Above the wailing and honoring of the dead, Poseidon scowled at Odysseus' work. He complained to Zeus, "Look at their disrespect of us."

Zeus leaned over the edge of night to see what his brother moaned about. "I see tired men and fires. What is so disrespectful?"

Poseidon pointed. "The wall surrounding the Greek's camp."

"A defensive move. It is war, brother. No gods intervened."

"You sent Apollo and me to toil, among the Trojan mortals for an entire season building their sacred wall. We earned our honor back with the task."

Growing annoyed with Poseidon's complaining, Zeus snapped, "How does the Greek wall offend you?"

"They offered no sacrifices. Asked no permission or for godsigns. They disregard your will with their arrogance. They believe their flimsy structure will protect them. That *we* will protect them because of it." Poseidon leaned closer to his brother. "There will be fighting among us, if you do not even the field for both sides."

Zeus leaned back in his crystal chair, thunder rumbling across the sky as he contemplated the fate of the men below. "The wall must fall."

TWENTY TWO

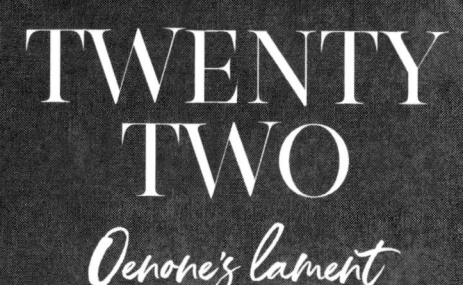

Oenone's lament

TROY—1238 BCE

The winds whispered to Oenone of her son's death and that his body was being carried back to her. Standing in the field filled with white blossoms, she waited for him. It would not be the reunion she dreamt of ... sweet embraces and gentle kisses. It was a nightmare from which she couldn't wake. Memories of Corythus' boyish smile and joyful laughter filled her heart, breaking it over and over. Yet, she could not stop the onslaught of beauty mingled with the pain. Crystal tears slid down her cheeks like glittering ice.

With the rising light of Apollo, Oenone caught sight of the Trojan party bearing Corythus. She recognized the man leading them across the field. It was Agelaus, stooped and gray, but it was him. *My beautiful boy is coming home.*

As they neared her, her hands tore at her gown of flowers. "Father, I do not know what to do. I cannot bear the pain."

The river god answered on the wind, *"You must, daughter."*

Oenone straightened, her eyes brimming with agony. Her chest heaved and her breath caught in her throat. Her shoulders shook. *How could I have let him go?*

Agelaus greeted her with dark and sunken eyes. He bowed his head and took to his knees. "I never dreamt of this day, fair Oenone."

"Agelaus," Oenone managed a weak whisper.

The men set the golden litter down at the herder's signal. The flowers bent toward Corythus' body like women weeping for their sons. Bird song ceased. A cloud of pale-winged butterflies whirled past.

Oenone took one tremulous step closer to her son's body, before collapsing next to it. She pulled the fine linen from his face. Corythus' eyes were closed and he appeared to rest in serene sleep. Lifting a trembling hand to his cheek, Oenone brushed her thumb across it. "Death is colder than I imagined." She looked up at Agelaus. "Quieter." Leaning down to kiss her son's forehead, her grief rose in a raging wave. The ancient pain of mothers who bury children rose in her chest, unnatural and primal. She clawed at the flower crown on her head, flinging it to the ground. An anguished howl escaped her throat and she yanked out locks of her dark hair in bloody clumps.

Agelaus fell to his knees, weeping for her loss and the memories of a young boy he'd raised, years ago, who now had caused such disaster. He wept and beat the ground with closed fists. The Trojan litter-carriers backed away from them and made their way across the field, disappearing from sight.

Oenone's voice rose with her agony. "Our life was sweet and

simple, my beautiful son. Your father's love sheltered us. The world outside of the three of us did not exist. There was only love. Tenderly, I watched over you, keeping you safe beneath my wings like a mother bird. Until the day arrived when the fledgling must fly away from her. I watched you go with pain in my heart, knowing one day your father's blood would call you to fly from me. I accepted you would grow apart from me as children do, seeking their own path. With a heavy heart, I released you. I always believed you would return to me, but not like this."

Once her sobbing eased, she asked in a ragged voice, "How did this happen, Agelaus? Why did Paris not keep him safe?"

Agelaus kept his eyes to the ground. "P-Paris," he choked. "Paris killed him, fair Oenone."

The meadow spun beneath her. "What are you saying?"

"He did not know it was his son. He discovered Corythus was Helen's lover …"

"I do not believe you."

"Why would I lie, fair Oenone?"

Her heart pounded as disbelief crumbled to rage. Each breath ached. "How?"

"That's all I know."

"What power does the Spartan woman wield that would cause a father to kill a son? Was it not enough that she stole my husband from my arms, but to take my son as well? What curse is this from the gods?"

"My lady, you should not speak of the gods this way."

"Who are you to question my wrath? Is it your son laid pale and lifeless before you? No, the son you raised sits safely behind the citadel's tall walls. But, Paris knows that I have seen his end and that he will ask for me. He will need me in the end, and my ears will be deaf to his pleas. May the gods take all that he loves and burn it to the ground. Let the world forget that Paris of Troy ever existed."

Oenone turned to her beloved son. "But you, my beautiful boy, Corythus, let your song be sung until the gods abandon this world for another."

TWENTY THREE

battle of the gods

TROY—1238 BCE

At dawn, Zeus gathered the Olympians. His patience had worn thin and his dark mood still rumbled through the sky below. "You have all taken great pains to follow the war below … Trojans and Greeks alike. However, they are mere mortals. Beneath us in all ways. At our mercy. At *my* mercy. You are all here at my mercy, or have you forgotten who rules these crystal halls?"

The gathered gods and goddesses said nothing out of fear.

"There has been bickering and dissension among us on account of mortals and their war. But no more. I forbid any of you from lending your skills or whispering strategies from this moment on." Zeus' voice lowered to a terrifying pitch. "For if you disobey me, I will bind you and drag you across mountains and oceans. And leave you in dark Tartaros *forever*."

Athena's golden gown flashed with her movements. Her helm gleaming, she spoke up, "Father, we all recognize your dominion over us. We have no desire to quarrel with you. But, some of us pity the Greeks … far from home and loved ones. We hear their prayers. See their sacrifices. I beg you, Father, don't take away everything from us. Leave us the whispers, at least. If they listen, it is well. If they do not, then it will be as if we had remained aloof and silent."

Zeus gazed at Athena, then around at the hard, glittering eyes of his family. "My threat is only to keep us from tearing each other apart. Look what has happened already. Aphrodite has been injured and Ares, as well. I will not have us divided and at one another's throats … over the war of men and gold."

"And Helen," Hera muttered.

"It is not my fault. How could I see Paris' choice would start a war?" Aphrodite screeched.

"Enough!" Zeus blasted the goddesses with his irritation. "It is as I have said. This war divides us almost as much as it does the mortals below."

In truth, Zeus had grown weary of the war, but he would honor his word to Themis. He strode to his golden chariot and leapt aboard the platform. With a roar, the horses flew to a high peak far from Olympus, their golden manes glistening in the wind. His foul mood misted about him like a shroud. Peace. That was all he desired. Peace and *Thetis*. Whenever he stole away for solace and solitude, his mind always toiled on the nymph. The heavens darkened and his turmoil rumbled through the gathering clouds.

He cast his piercing gaze toward the war. He watched as the

Trojans scattered across the plain like ants roughly disturbed from their mound. The fighting on the ground was fierce. The blood of hundreds poured into the sand. "A choice must be made," he said to the clouds about him. "Fate must decide, for I alone cannot. I shall never have peace if the others think I have elevated one side over the other."

Apollo's light burned through the mist, when Zeus manifested the Scales of Fate in his hand. Holding the golden instrument above the melee unfolding on the field, he bent his will on the outcome. The Greek's portion hung low. "So be it. This day belongs to Troy."

Odysseus scanned the rumbling heavens. Darkness crept into the clouds as lightning whips cracked overhead. The god-signs were ominous. He signaled his men to return to the camp, fearing nothing good would come of remaining afield. From the corner of his eye, he saw Nestor's horse skid into the ground, Paris' arrow piercing its eye. He ignored Nestor's cry for help. All the other commanders followed his lead, except Diomedes.

Diomedes yelled, "Get on my chariot, old man. Together we will chase Hektor down."

Nestor leapt up to the platform despite his years, eager for vengeance. His old bones screamed, but his mind was bent on war.

"Take the reins," Diomedes roared in the old man's ear.

Nestor gripped the leather straps and snapped them across the horses' backs. They surged forward, chasing at breakneck speed after Hektor. Diomedes leveled a spear at Hektor's charioteer. His aim was true, and the Trojan fell from the chariot, sending up a dusty cloud. Another charioteer leapt to help his prince. Diomedes wheeled his chariot around, making another deadly pass at Hektor. A flash of blinding light hit the ground in front of his chariot, filling the air with the stench of rotting flesh.

"By the gods," Nestor screamed, dropping the reins in fright. "There will be no victory or glory for us today, Diomedes. We can't fight the will of the gods."

"What are you doing, you fool?" The chariot careered wildly side to side. Diomedes grabbed the reins flopping against the side of the chariot. "What songs will our people sing if I abandon the fight now? That I cowered in fear before Hektor? I'd rather die than hear my humiliation as a camp song."

"No Greek will ever say that of you. Who cares what Trojans will say? The Trojan widows and fatherless boys know your skill."

From across a small distance, Hektor yelled after Diomedes' retreating chariot, "You'll never take Troy! You'll never take our women. You're a coward. Unworthy of glory."

Diomedes snapped the reins, urging the horses in retreat. "Easy for him to say when he knows Zeus favors him today."

Hektor's voice boomed over the retreating enemy. He urged his men and the allies closest him to chase their retreating men. "Look! Zeus grants victory to us. The time is right to crash the wall they dared to build on our lands. Jump their ditch, whatever it takes. Set fire to their ships. Let the smoke choke out the light." He turned to his charioteer and said, "If I can take Nestor's shield and Diomedes' breastplate, we may well scare these bastards to set sail for home."

Watching from a secret place, Hera's anger intensified. Gathering all her grace and power, she approached Poseidon. "Zeus may be lord of us, but we are gods after all. We have our own wills. How can you stand to watch Greek blood being spilled?"

Poseidon shook his head. "You wonder why Zeus is always at your throat. Did you not hear him? He forbids it."

"I recall a time when you would not have shirked from such a challenge."

"Even gods may change."

"They bring you worthy gifts and sacrifices. I have seen the spark of satisfaction in your eyes when they honor you."

"Be quiet, Hera. Before your tongue drags us into war with Zeus over some mortals' fucking conflict. They built that wall without proper sacrifices. They deserve to be put in their place. But I won't risk Zeus' justice."

Hera bristled at Poseidon's indifference. "If you refuse to help them, I will risk the wrath of my husband."

Poseidon opened his arms to her. "By all means, provoke him. But leave me out of your devious plans."

Hera stormed off, leaving Poseidon to watch the skirmishes below.

As Hektor pushed the Greeks back toward their ships, Hera flew down to intervene. Moving like a cool breeze, she found Agamemnon standing bewildered on the deck of Odysseus' beached ship. "We are trapped against the sea. We need a strategy or they will overrun what barricade we have." Below, on the sand and around Agamemnon, men gathered to hear their orders.

Agamemnon rubbed at the hair rising on his neck. "What is—"

"Speak to them of courage lost. Did they not all brag to you of their prowess just one eve ago?"

"Athena?" the Great King whispered in awe.

"Hera."

"Zeus is on our side then, if you have come on his behalf."

"Remind your men of their wine-courage."

Agamemnon's chest rose with renewed vigor and determination. Gathering his crimson cape in his arms, he signaled the army to gather near the ship. The signal was passed along the growing ranks filing toward the shore lined with their ships. They packed close together; the stench of their sweat and open, bleeding wounds stung Agamemnon's nose.

"Men," he bellowed above the low chatter of voices filled with the fear of death and defeat. "Men, do not lose faith that the gods are with us."

The assembly quieted.

"Tell us, Great King, what the gods intend," a lone voice shouted.

Men nodded, hopeful yet reserved.

"Hera has whispered in my ear. We should take heart that Zeus will help us carry the day."

"Why do we lose?" another lone voiced rose up in question. "How does death surrounding us prove that?'

"Where is your boldness now that the wine has drained from your bodies? How many of you bragged about the legions of Trojans you would slay before Apollo's light faded? Yet, now you run in fear from the very men you swore in your cups to kill. Hear me, Zeus! We know that you are with us! You will not let them push us into the sea!"

A cheer rose from the assembled men. Above them an eagle soared and dipped its wing toward the ground. Hundreds of voices whispered a single hope, "A god-sign."

The commanders—Odysseus, Diomedes, Ajax, and his brother, Teucer, son of Hesione—made their way to their men and headed out to face the Trojans. The thunder of their horses and rumble of thousands of foot soldiers sounded in the close distance.

Ajax and Teucer marshaled their troops, meeting a wave of Trojans. They fought side by side, shields blocking the deadly blows of spears and swords. The clash soon separated the brothers. Teucer found a broken chariot wheel to hide behind and pulled an arrow from his side quiver and nocked it, waiting for a chance to take lethal aim of Hektor. He waited patiently as Hektor's chariot flew toward him. Teucer steeled his courage and his strength. In a flash, his arrow took flight, only to glance off the Trojan prince's golden helm. He quickly nocked another arrow and let it fly; the arrow flitted like a moth and struck Hektor's charioteer instead. His limp body fell from the platform, sending up a swirl of dust.

A tall warrior leapt onto Hektor's careening chariot and grabbed the reins. Teucer heard Hektor cry out the man's name, "Kebriones!" Hektor jumped from his moving chariot, picking up a spear on the ground next to the body of a man who was not quite dead.

To Teucer's horror, the Trojan prince charged straight at him.

His usually quick fingers fumbled with an arrow, as he tried to nock it. In a blink of his eye, Hektor's spear smashed through the chariot wheel barrier and shattered his collarbone. Teucer screamed and fell back in agony. Hektor advanced like a bull. Out of the rising dust, a roar rose of such fierceness, Hektor stopped dead in his tracks. The hairs on Teucer's body rose. "Please gods, let it be."

Ajax, flanked by two warriors, appeared with his spear readied, and blood in his eyes. "Hektor! We meet again." Skidding to a halt at Teucer's position, he used his giant shield to protect his younger brother. "You will have to take me first, before I will let you take my brother. Your cousin."

Hektor's spear arm relaxed just slightly. "That could only be, Teucer. Hesione's son."

A mighty roar rose from the Trojan ranks behind them. Hektor turned to his opponents. "Another time, Ajax. Seems we are close to breaking through your flimsy wall. Best prepare to die, or sail back across the sea."

The noise of men drew Hera's attention. Glancing down at the war below her heart raged as Trojans pushed into the Greek's camp. No matter what she did, Zeus' wishes prevailed. "Athena," she whispered to herself. "She loves the Greeks." She went to search her daughter out.

In an evergreen meadow surrounded by tall, swaying trees of oak and pine, Athena was tending to the owls of Olympus. "Greetings, Hera." Athena did not turn to face her mother, but had seen Hera's reflection the large, yellow eyes of the owl perched on her arm.

"I am surprised to find you here," Hera said.

Athena turned around; the owl stretched its neck to see beyond Athena's shoulder. "Why should it surprise you? You know I care for these creatures."

Hera approached slowly. The owls were wild, and unaffected by the gods' power. "May I?" She lifted a slender hand to stroke the owl.

"It is up to her."

Hera gently ran her fingers over the owl's head. It closed its big eyes and fluffed up its feathers. "What is this one's name?"

"This is a Glaux."

"She does not seem so small." The owl opened its eyes. Hera withdrew her hand. "Will you join me, daughter?"

"If you have come to speak about the war, go back to the palace. Why do you think I spend my long days here? With the birds?"

"What about the Greeks? They continue to make sacrifices and beg for your help. Will you keep turning a deaf ear to their pleas?"

Athena pushed her arm up, encouraging the bird to fly to a nearby tree. "What would you have me do? Defy Zeus? Not all of us have the protections you do."

Hera took Athena by the elbow, steering her beneath a large oak. She glanced about them. "*Your* father, *my* husband, is doing all of this to honor his word to … *Thetis*. He loves her, because he cannot have her. I know this. You know this. We all know this, but *he* thinks we cannot see how he favors the nymph, who wishes to hurt the Greeks we love."

"Because Achilles sulks like a child over a woman."

"Zeus allows the Trojans to pummel the Greeks time and time again, so Agamemnon will regret his decision. When he begs for Achilles to return, Achilles' honor will be restored."

"So, he favors one side, while forbidding us from doing the same?" Hera smiled. "How is that fair? Are we not gods, as well?"

"Odysseus," Athena whispered. "How has he fared?"

"You should see for yourself."

Athena knew the dangers, yet how could she allow her favorite patrons to suffer? "If I do this, Zeus will never forgive me."

"Perhaps not."

"If we stand together, Mother, Hektor and his forces could not withstand us."

"No, he could not."

A breeze swept across the meadow, swirling about the conspiring goddesses. Their hair caught in the air. Their skin chilled. Their eyes locked, knowing they'd been discovered before they could enact any plans. "Athena," a voice whispered. "Athena."

"Iris, what is your message?" Athena asked.

Iris materialized before Hera and Athena. Her glittering silver robe floating about her as if in a sea. "You have angered Zeus, Athena. He bids me say this: I expect Hera to conspire against me, because she is conniving."

Hera bristled. "He brings it on himself."

"He bids me say: If you help the Greeks, if you go against me, I will send a deadly sickness to kill all the Greeks' horses and livestock. I will allow sickness to kill them all. If you love the Greeks, then obey me."

The messenger flew off then, leaving Hera and Athena alone to consider the threat.

"It is impossible to go against him. His eyes and ears surround us here," Hera said, defeated.

"What shall we do, Mother?"

"Nothing. Nothing at all."

Upon returning to the crystal halls of Olympus, Zeus was already there, waiting. "Sit," he commanded.

The goddesses took their seats with apprehension, both fearing punishment. They avoided his eyes and did not utter a single word.

Zeus' silver hair floated about his face. Anger etched his sharp jaw. He was both mesmerizing and terrifying. "What is wrong with you, Hera? Athena? If you would have stepped a single sandal on that battlefield, I would have killed you before you had a chance to beg my mercy. Your disobedience would turn my heart iron against your pleas."

Athena looked up, meeting her father's hard gaze, but she said nothing.

Hera's temper could not be contained. "You have the power to send us into dark oblivion or slavery. We know very well how you love to punish any of us at your whim. But you, dear *husband*," bitterness dripped from her tongue, "you have underestimated how deeply some of us care for the Greeks. Your concern for Thetis and her son drives a wedge between us all."

Zeus growled and narrowed his eyes at his wife, a thin smile spreading across his face. "Defy me and you will wake to a bloodbath below. I will pluck the life of every Greek before you sip your nectar of the dawn. Know this, dear *wife*, Hektor's fury will continue his victories until Achilles leaves the prison of his ship. And that will not happen until Patrokles' death. Fate decrees the order of events. Even I cannot go against it. Rage against the stars. But all you will find is heartache and grief."

Hera clamped her mouth shut, her anger simmering just below the surface of her pale skin. "You always take everything from me.

My love. My loyalty. And burn it down."

Zeus' laughter filled the hall. He signaled Hephaestus' mechanical women to serve the wine. "I wish to hear no more from either of you. I wish to enjoy Apollo dragging the light into the sea."

TROJAN CAMP

The dim of night spread across the sky. The fighting fell silent as men on both sides retreated to their camps and fires. Hektor surveyed his men from the platform of his chariot. The day's battle had worn them down, despite the victories and ground covered. Every face was smudged with dirt and blood. He signaled the heralds. "We must camp here. We can't chance heading back for the city gates. Make sure the wounded horses are tended. And set twice as many fires as needed. Let the Greeks believe our numbers are greater than what they are. They won't be able to rest worrying about the morning's fight."

The messengers sprinted off to spread Hektor's commands.

Hektor grabbed one young boy by the elbow. "Is your mind sharp?"

The boy nodded.

"Are your feet quick?"

The boy nodded.

"Are you afraid of the dark?"

The boy shook his head.

"Do you love Troy?"

"Aye, Prince Hektor."

"I need you to run straight for the city gates. Don't stop. Tell the king to gather all the old men and brave boys, like you, and set fires along the ramparts of the Great Wall. Can you carry that message?"

"Aye."

Hektor ruffled the boy's tangled hair. "I pray Astyanax grows to be as daring as you. Now, go. Run as if your life depended on it." The boy took off in a sprint. "Run," Hektor shouted after the boy, as he disappeared into the darkness.

Hektor had hoped that today would be the day the war ended, but victory eluded him once again. If the boy made it, and the fires were lit, maybe the Greeks would lose sleep as he planned and tomorrow would be the day. He couldn't fathom how much longer Troy could hold out, or the Greeks could keep fighting. Surely, the end of days approached both sides.

TROAN PALACE

Hecuba held Astyanax in her lap. She kissed the black curls on top of his head. "He reminds me much of Hektor, when he was a babe. The seasons have passed so quickly, yet I can recall them so readily."

"I pray my son grows up with his father at his side. As Hektor has had Priam."

"I pray the same, Andromache."

"I only wish he had brothers to keep him company."

"There is yet time." The lie slipped easily from her tongue. She knew the anguish Andromache suffered to carry children. She placed a hand on the hardening bulge gifted her by Apollo. "The gods show favors at the oddest of times."

"Do you think there is a chance that the Greeks might breech the wall?"

"I try not to think of that outcome." Cassandra's warnings rang in her ears. The ancient prophecy continued unfolding before her eyes, no matter what her efforts were. In the end, even Hektor's bravery and victories produced no clear and final victory.

Andromache persisted. "My mother told me of the heinous deeds of Achilles and his army."

The queen set her grandson down to crawl on a blanket. "He'll be walking soon enough."

"Achilles will show us no mercy."

Hecuba reached for Andromache's hand. "I have no intention of being taken by that murderer. And neither will you. Besides, he has withdrawn from the war."

"For how much longer?" Andromache knelt beside her son on the floor. "How can you be certain of your fate?"

"Apollo has promised me that Achilles will die."

"Before or after Hektor is forced to face him? Mother, we both know that every day it comes closer to that. And I am afraid, because I don't know who the gods will favor."

Hecuba understood Andromache's fear all too well. The gods had no answer for her, other than Apollo. It was all she clung to as each day passed, that it would be Achilles' last. "All that is clear to me is that Achilles will never see his home again. We must pray that Hektor does."

Helen reclined on a couch on her balcony. Crickets chirped softly. Dogs barked in the distance. The orange light from oil lamps glowed in windows and small fires burned in clay pots near refugee tents. The faint smell of jasmine and shit filled the air. It was the smell of siege war. When the city began to fill with the destitute, they were easily absorbed into life in the citadel. But, now, there were too many. Men relieved themselves in dark corners, and sometimes not so dark corners. Women emptied piss pots wherever they could. Helen was grateful for the manicured gardens with fragrant flowers and vines below the chamber she and Paris shared. Otherwise, the stench would be too much to bear.

Paris had left for anywhere away from her, and she was glad to be alone. She knew somewhere out there the Greeks were plotting their battles against the city. And Menelaus was stewing in his cups about her leaving, probably pitying himself. But he was no coward and whatever attachment he had to her wasn't a spell cast by Aphrodite. Even though he repulsed her mostly, she tolerated his grunting and sweating. She'd birthed Hermione. *Was life so horrible in Sparta?*

She believed, in the beginning, that Sparta's very air choked her. Paris appeared and it was as if the gods had sent her a savior. But it was all a lie. Without Aphrodite's interference, she would never have left Sparta. This never ending war would never have happened. She might have had a palace full of children with Menelaus, surrounding her with love and acceptance. *Maybe I should give myself up?*

Helen sat straight up. *I could give myself up. Go home.* But, would Menelaus take her back? By rights he could kill her for what she'd done, but … he was always too proud to claim her as his wife. She might be able to persuade him. She got up from the couch. *What are you thinking, Helen? Stop, you can't go back and you know it.*

TWENTY FOUR
the pride of Achilles
TROY—1238 BCE

Gusts of wind swiped at the tent. The flaps snapped despite being tied down. Above, the heavens rumbled with Zeus' displeasure. Agamemnon sat dejected in his chair surrounded by his captains of war. "How could Zeus be against us? Hera …" He drank deeply from his wine. "I *know* it was the goddess in my ear."

"The gods do not always favor us," Nestor offered. "Perhaps, when dawn comes—"

"What then, Nestor? We lose more men? Burn more bones to bundle for home?"

"I have led us to disgrace, dragged you through countless battles. Zeus has tricked me once again. The gods fuck us with this war."

Nestor stood. "We've conquered cities, my king."

"Achilles has conquered cities." All eyes turned to Patrokles who sat alone and apart from the others. "You cannot win without him. You know it. We all know it."

Nestor sat. Patrokles' words were the undeniable truth. He tugged at his white beard.

"Some of us have half grown sons and daughters in the camp," Odysseus said, eyeing Menelaus from across the table.

Agamemnon continued drowning his defeat in more wine. "We should return home. I can divine no other message, but that the walls of Troy were never meant to be breached. I was ... wrong."

Menelaus fumed in a darkened mood. "But *my wife*—"

"Has no use for you," Odysseus muttered loud enough for all to hear. "And we tire of hearing you complain on that account."

Diomedes threw his cup; it thudded against the tent side. "Look at you, you greedy bastard. King of Mycenae. Wallowing in self-pity. Achilles was right to speak up when he did. You've been crowned with honors since the day we left. The day you sacrificed your daughter for our success."

An audible gasp sounded around the table. Agamemnon's mouth was agape.

Diomedes kept ranting. "You would let her death mean nothing, because you don't have an easy victory? My rewards pale in comparison to yours. Where is your gratitude? What about the rest of us? If you want to return to Mycenae, have your men ready your ship. Go. But I am staying until Troy's fate is sealed, one way or another. Whether that be going home or Hades."

The captains applauded ... all except Odysseus. His thoughts bent fiercely on Ithaka.

Nestor stood again. "Although the youngest among us, Diomedes' words land on wisdom. But before we discuss anything further," he turned to Agamemnon, "is that roasted meat I smell, my lord?"

Agamemnon grinned, gathering Nestor's intent. "It is."

"Then, let us eat together. Bring the wine from your ships, my lord, and let us all enjoy the evening. I'm certain wise counsel will follow the wine."

Odysseus leaned into Diomedes' shoulder. "You spoke well. Honest. True."

"I did not come all this way to leave as a dog with its tail between its legs."

Odysseus spoke behind his wine cup. "Look at the poor bastard. Sulking because his whore wife chose someone else."

Diomedes smirked. "I would kill her as soon as I laid hands on her, if it were up to me. All the loss of good men on her account."

"Agreed. Why would he wish her back? A faithless wife is no wife at all."

"Maybe she has a golden cunt."

They both laughed loudly. Menelaus scowled from across the table, sensing their mirth was at his expense.

Odysseus said, "And he has been fortunate enough to father a son ... a bastard perhaps, but more comfort than some of us have had. I haven't seen Telemachus since he was a babe. He's half grown by now."

Nestor purposely cleared his throat. "My lord, Agamemnon, I wish to suggest something you may not wish to hear."

"Go on, old man. You have been ... mostly on my side."

Nervous laughter floated around the gathering.

"You expressed a desire to return home because you fear you have lost Zeus' favor."

Agamemnon shrugged. Men nodded.

"But you have forgotten our secret weapon."

The Great King scoffed and tossed a date in his mouth. "What are you talking about?"

Nestor glanced quickly at Patrokles, took a deep breath, and answered unflinchingly, "Achilles."

All eyes were on Agamemnon.

Diomedes leaned over to Odysseus and whispered, "This could go either way for Nestor."

Odysseus whispered back, "This may be the last day the old man draws breath."

"My lord, we all know you treated Achilles poorly. You dishonored him because you were mad about the priest's daughter. I can't even recall her name that's how unimportant she was. Yet, because of your anger you disgraced Achilles, who clearly has the gods' favor. Who *Zeus* favors. We all know who his mother is. Make your peace with him. Win him over to fight with us again. We can't lose if he is with us. Patrokles is right."

Agamemnon drained his wine cup. "I have heard you, Nestor. Every word."

Diomedes whispered to Odysseus, "Here it comes."

Agamemnon was weary of war, as much as any of his men. He was also tired of the humiliation of losing, and the prospect of returning empty handed. And most importantly, he could not let Iphigenia's death be for nothing. "You are right, Nestor. My anger has blinded me. I should atone for that with Achilles. Win him back to our cause."

An audible gasp sounded among the men.

Odysseus said to Diomedes, "That was *most* unexpected."

Nestor sat heavily in his chair, relieved his head was still attached to his body for another day.

"I have been thinking about this for days," Agamemnon said. "It seems clear that without Achilles we will fight, until we are all dead, and there's no one left to carry on but our bastards." He looked around at the men. "And they do not know the way home, nor would they be welcomed after delivering our bones."

Menelaus asked, "What do you intend to do?"

"When we defeat Troy … and we will once *he* is with us, I will let him fill the hull of his ship with treasures. Give him seven of the most beautiful Trojan women we capture. And my daughter's hand in marriage." Agamemnon looked Patrokles dead in the eye. "And I will give Briseis back to him. Untouched by me."

Nestor smiled, folding his hands atop the table. "Who should we send with this news?"

Patrokles broke his silence. "I will go."

Ajax stood. "I will accompany Patrokles."

Odysseus elbowed Diomedes. "We will also go."

Agamemnon drained his wine cup. "So be it."

The generals walked along the beach in the moonlight, heading toward the far end of the Myrmidon's ships where Achilles had secluded himself. They all prayed that Achilles would accept Agamemnon's proposal. Before they left Aulis, even reluctant men secretly longed for the adventures and the wealth this war promised.

But, now, the very notion of returning home was a siren's song worth more than gold.

"Do you think Achilles will listen to reason?" Diomedes asked Odysseus.

"Depends on how much wine he has drunk already. My last encounter with him did not go so … smoothly."

The sound of a man singing while plucking a lyre caught their ears, as they approached Achilles' ship.

Fat king, fat king
bastard coward cur
takes his portion
and leaves our ship hulls bare

Ajax turned to Odysseus, "That doesn't sound promising."

Achilles called down to them, "I hear you clucking about down there like a bunch of hens. What do you want?"

"I will go first," Patrokles said. As he pulled himself over the rail, he saw Nax mending a tunic by a fire burning in a bronze cauldron. The other captains poured over the side following Patrokles.

"What do you want?" Nax asked.

Achilles stepped into the pale circle of light. "It is late." He set his lyre down against the ship's side. "Have you decided to leave this forsaken place?"

"No, not yet," Odysseus replied.

"All the good captains have come at Agamemnon's request I think. Nax, get more wine. Pour some for my fellow kings and princes. There is meat and bread, as well."

Patrokles stepped to help Nax. "How is his mind this night?"

Nax's face soured at the question. "He is drunk. I think. But when is he not these days?"

"I expected as much, but let's hope he can hear reason."

"Is that why you brought a small army? To convince him of whatever you want him to do?"

"Something like that," Patrokles said.

Achilles tossed the first cuts of meat into the fire to honor the gods, and then sat on a fur opposite Odysseus. "I assume you are the mouth piece of Agamemnon?"

Odysseus, careful with his words, said, "You honor us with wine and bread ... and yes, we come with heavy news. The Trojans are camped on the plain. We can see thousands of campfires. Zeus has shown them his favor."

"Why should I care who Zeus favors? He is a god. He may do as he chooses."

The men looked nervously to Odysseus, who did not flinch. "With the dawn, we will likely see our defeat. Hektor has threatened to burn our ships to the ground."

Achilles shrugged. "That will make sailing for home more difficult."

Undeterred, Odysseus pressed on. "Save us, Achilles. Surely, your father or Chiron counseled you on the dangers of divided loyalties in war?"

"What you mean is that without the Myrmidons, you will lose."

"Listen to reason, Achilles. Agamemnon has promised to give you gold, bronze, women, horses. Whatever you can carry in your ships, if you join us."

Achilles threw his head back and laughed. "He offers me what I offered him ... and he refused?"

Odysseus said, "And also to return Briseis, who he swears by all the gods, he has not touched."

Achilles stared blankly at Odysseus.

"When we return home, he will make you his son by marriage."

Achilles' jaw clicked in agitation. "He offers me a daughter?"

"Aye."

"He promised another daughter my hand, so he could slit her throat in front of all of us. Why would I wish to join a family so cursed as the House of Atreus?"

Odysseus back-tracked. "Think of all the men. Your Myrmidons. The other Greeks. They all tire of war. Whether you like it or not, they have always looked to you for courage. Hektor has grown bold, too bold. He would challenge you, and we know … you know you would defeat him."

Achilles leaned back on his hands. "I will speak from my heart. I am not afraid of Agamemnon or his threats. The man has no honor in my eyes, or in yours. I can see it. He speaks one way and does the opposite. This fat king wants to persuade me with the very treasure I won for him? If my presence was so valuable, if his actions were so regrettable, why is he not here himself? I will tell you why." He took a swig of wine straight from an amphora. "If he showed his face here, I'd kill him for the disrespect he showed me. You all honor him as if he bloodied himself alongside you in war as often as I have. Odysseus, how many raids did we make in the south? How much treasure, how many slaves did we bring to Agamemnon's coffers? He is still the same. Wanting honor and glory for himself alone."

"But, surely you—"

"What? Wish to fight? Risk death? Even you don't fight for the fat king. You fight to return to your Penelope, do you not, Odysseus?"

Odysseus' backside ached from sitting on the hard wood. He shifted on his haunches. "I do."

"How many of you benefitted from my conquests? I lost count of the treasure I laid at Agamemnon's feet. He kept the largest portion, even though he made the least contribution of blood. Some, he rewarded generously ... but it was only from me, he demanded more than I should have been required to give."

"He wants to give her back," Odysseus said.

"If he had taken Penelope from you, would you accept the gesture?" Achilles threw the clay jar in his hands across the deck with such force it shattered into a thousand pieces against the rail. Lesser men would have startled at the sound, but these hardened men did not even flinch. "You have the gall to sit across from me and demand I do less than any of you. Briseis was my wife, not by law, but by *right*," he roared angrily. His eyes caught Patrokles' heated stare and his guilt took hold of him, forcing a long overdue admission. "You all guessed long ago that she holds my heart."

Men murmured their acknowledgment.

"Are Agamemnon and his brother the only men allowed to love their wives? I loved Briseis, even if she was my slave before I loved her. To me she is as Penelope is to you, Odysseus. Would you stand beside a man who took her from you?"

"I'd slit his throat."

Achilles shrugged. "I would have slit his throat if Athena hadn't stopped me. You of all men should know how persuasive Athena can be. I will not rejoin the fat king's war. He is a liar. Nothing to me. And tell him I would never marry a daughter of his after Aulis." Achilles laughed wickedly. "Iphigenia deserved a better father than him. Tell him that as well."

A terrible silence wrapped around everyone.

"He used my name to lure her to her death. Of all the unseeing eyes that haunt my sleep, hers I see the most. If I return to Phthia, my father will choose a queen to rule beside me when he is gone. Remember this, all of you, it doesn't matter the geras you acquire. This is war and no one knows their fate."

Patrokles asked, "What of Briseis?"

Achilles lowered his voice, his sharp tone softening. "There is so much more in the balance for me than to choose to love her or not. My mother counseled me years ago that I bore the burden of two fates. If I remain at Troy and fight, I will die. My song will be eternal. If I chose to sail home … marry Briseis or a woman of Peleus' choosing, I will live a long life. But no one will remember Achilles the Sacker of Cities. Who am I, Patrokles, if all these years of war mean nothing? If no one remembers what I have done here? Agamemnon seeks to steal it all away from me. He cannot have my woman and my fate, as well. I cannot live knowing that all of this will fade to a whisper. But you may all sail home. Do you really care what happens to Troy more than returning to your wives and children?"

Ajax spoke up, "Why do we bother with him, Odysseus? He won't change his mind. Achilles' heart will not be moved. All because of Briseis. A slave girl, no matter what he calls her."

Achilles' anger rose to his face. "Your words only remind me why I hate Agamemnon so much. Go tell him what I've said. I won't lift a finger until Hektor storms your fucking wall and starts burning your fucking ships. If he makes it as far as my camp, rest assured he will be stopped." Achilles looked to his second in command. "Patrokles, stay. I have missed your company."

Odysseus stood, making for the rail. Passing Nax, he said loud enough for Achilles to overhear, "Your master is as stubborn as an ox."

Ajax followed him overboard. Their arguing voices faded into the night.

"Pour fresh wine, Nax." Achilles' servant quickly refilled their cups, before sitting down to mending once again. "You may go, Nax. What Patrokles and I have to discuss is for us alone and no other ears."

Nax glanced at Patrokles and then set down his work. "As you wish."

For several long moments both men sipped their wine, avoiding each other's eyes.

"What do you want, Achilles?"

"Why have you stayed away?"

"You know why."

Achilles rubbed his bottom lip, narrowing his eyes at his companion. "There was a time when I knew your mind as well as my own. But, now, I cannot say what you are thinking. It is as if ..."

"As if what?"

"As if our bond is broken. *Betrayed.*" Patrokles stiffened just slightly, but Achilles caught the tiny movement. "Have you seen her? Briseis?"

"Once."

"How does she fare?"

"How do you think, Achilles? She is a slave in a whore's tent in Agamemnon's camp, while you sit here drunk and more preoccupied with your glory and honor than her."

The truth of what Patrokles said was not lost on him. Being perpetually drunk was the only way he could cope with the stalemate with Agamemnon. He could hear Chiron's voice scolding him for stubbornness, and loving a woman he probably should not. "Why have you been to see her only once? Did I not command you to see to her well-being?"

"Your commands carry little weight while you sit about your ship sulking like a child."

"What are you keeping from me, Patrokles? I can see that much at least."

"Nothing. You're drunk, Achilles."

Leaning back on his hands, Achilles studied Patrokles' indifference. He wouldn't let him off the hook so easily. "I should have killed Briseis the day I captured her in Lyrnessus. Then none of this would be happening. We might have been halfway way home by now."

"I don't understand you. Just take her back. Is your glory worth her life? Her happiness? How can you say you love her as a wife and let her languish as she is? Odysseus would kill any man who stood between himself and Penelope. Even Agamemnon. What you feel isn't love. It is twisted and selfish."

Patrokles' words stung. He knew he was not worthy of Briseis or her love. The struggle had always been the same. He was made for war, not love. "We both know who I am. What I am. I have never pretended to be other than what you see. Maybe, she is better off with someone else … you, perhaps?"

Lifting his face to Achilles, Patrokles revealed nothing of his inner turmoil. His friendship with Achilles filled what felt like half his life. He no longer wished to argue, when death swept so close to all of them. "If Hektor breaches the barricades in the coming days, none of this will matter to any of us. We will be nothing more than shades roaming the Underworld wishing we'd had more time."

Patrokles stood. "I leave you to your wine. It is good, Achilles, to hear you do have your wits about you."

"Tell Briseis …" Achilles' voice trailed to silence.

Patrokles waited. "What? Tell her what?"

"It doesn't matter." Achilles waved his hand as if shooing a fly. "Never mind."

Loneliness was a cruel companion for Briseis. She found her mind preoccupied with the life she had before Achilles. The prophecy of her birth, that she'd marry the greatest warrior, had driven her parents, especially her mother, to solidify her betrothal to Hektor. It felt like a dream now. How her mother had wept when Hektor married Andromache from the south. It was ironic how close she came to being on the other side of Troy's Great Wall.

But she married Mynes and had a beautiful daughter, Phila. She would have been a woman married by now. Briseis closed her eyes and willed an image of Phila's sweet face to rise from the ashes of her memory. But she found she couldn't hold it for but a brief moment. It had been so long ago …

"Briseis," Patrokles whispered at the back of her tent.

She pressed her ear to the tent wall. "What is it, Patrokles? Why do you stay away?"

"You know why, Briseis. Take this." He stuffed a rolled papyrus and charcoal beneath the tent. "Remind Achilles what is between you both."

Briseis' heart sank. "What has happened?"

"He rejected Agamemnon's offer to return you unharmed."

"Why? Why would he do that?"

"Only he knows all the reasons. Promise me, you will do as I ask."

"I promise."

"I will come before the dawn and take your message to him."

"Patrokles?"

"Aye?"

"I miss you," Briseis whispered and pressed her hand against the heavy cloth wall. Patrokles pressed his hand to hers from his side. Then, he was gone.

TWENTY FIVE
thieves in the night
AGAMEMNON'S CAMP—1238 BCE

"Have you seen the fires?" Agamemnon stared at Odysseus, Diomedes, and Ajax. "There are thousands of them. Scouts report that even the distant walls are lit up. How are the Trojans multiplying before our eyes?" Neither man uttered a word. "Tell me what Achilles said. Is he going to fight with us?"

"No," Odysseus said. "Not until Hektor's forces reach the Myrmidon camp."

Agamemnon paced his tent, clenching and unclenching his fists. He hated Achilles more than any man in the army. He secretly wished Achilles would sail home. Then, they would figure out some way to destroy Troy without him. Prophecy be damned. "I should have known that disrespectful dog would refuse my offering. What else did he say?"

Odysseus said, "He suggests you figure out what you're going to do. He intends to sail home tomorrow. He suggests we all do the same."

Diomedes chimed in, "Achilles has too much pride for his own good. What does it matter if he stays or goes? We should all rest. In the morning, we should take up this battle."

Agamemnon's face soured, his exasperation evident. "You told him I have not touched his woman? About marrying my daughter?"

Odysseus looked at his feet. They needed washing. He recalled how Penelope would wash his feet after a long day in the field, and how such intimacy led to other *pleasures*. "Aye, we told him everything."

"How can he refuse my generosity?"

"He brought up ... Aulis," Odysseus didn't want to say it, but there was no way around it. Achilles would not take a daughter of Agamemnon's to wife for a ship full of gold and silver. Because of Iphigenia.

Agamemnon acquiesced for the moment. "There is nothing to be done now. You may leave."

Sleep eluded Agamemnon. The mention of Aulis started the wheels of regret turning over and over in his mind. Had there been a clear and swift victory over the Trojans and heaps of gold and geras abounded, he could stare that terrible day's images down into the darkness. However, there had been no certain victory, and they now faced returning home as defeated cowards.

He threw off his linen blankets, grabbed his cape, and slid on his sandals. He ventured out into his camp. In the distance, the Trojan fires still burned brightly against the night. Walking among the tents, he heard men debating the day's events around dying embers and the muffled sounds of those choosing to lay with women over talking. At the edge of his camp, he found Menelaus staring off into the direction of the Trojan's camp.

"I should have realized you'd be here, as well."

"Why is that, brother?" Menelaus asked.

"You have the most to lose, if we are defeated tomorrow."

"You mean Helen?"

"Aye. You will have lost your wife and your dignity."

Not a single day passed that Menelaus hadn't been reminded of his unique troubles regarding Helen. Men snickered and women whispered when he strode passed them. Not even a bastard son had relieved him of this particular humiliation. "What's the plan, brother?"

Agamemnon pulled his cape tighter about his broad shoulders. "Zeus is deaf to our plight. My bones and heart are certain of his indifference. Hektor has us pinned at the beach. At dawn, I have no doubt he will try to burn us out of any passage home."

"Should we do as Achilles suggested? Should we sail home? Or do we stay and fight? Die in the end." Menelaus rubbed his hands together against the growing night chill. "Have you ever wondered what would happen if all this comes to nothing?"

The Great King stood in silence for a long while. "No." It was a lie. "We fight in the morning. We defend our camp to the bitter end. Death may be the only way I will ever have peace."

"Maybe you should send scouts to the Trojan's camp."

"Why would I do that?"

"There may be something to learn, some element of surprise we might make that will turn the odds in our favor."

Agamemnon clapped his younger brother on the shoulder. "Not a bad idea." Clasping his hands behind his back, he said, "I know just who to send."

The mournful cry of an owl sounded near Odysseus. "Athena is with us," he whispered over his shoulder to Ajax. "Dawn approaches."

They crept along in the dark, zigzagging carefully through the corpses from the previous day's battle. There had not been time enough to gather all the dead. Those that remained with their arms and legs twisted and bent unnaturally had begun to stiffen and stink. A flash of bronze in the moonlight caught Odysseus' eye. "Get down, Diomedes," he whispered harshly. "Someone approaches."

Crouching low, they pulled dead bodies over them like blankets. A lone man passed near them. When the footsteps grew distant, Odysseus said, "Must be a Trojan spy."

Diomedes agreed, "Aye. No doubt."

Together, they stalked the unsuspecting man heading straight for the Greek ships. The anticipation of wringing the spy's neck surged through Odysseus. He signaled for Diomedes to circle around their intended victim.

Within a few quick steps, Odysseus was behind the man with a blade pressed to his throat and his free hand smashed against the man's mouth. "Don't make a sound."

The man's neck strained against the sharp edge of the knife and his eyes bulged in their sockets. When Diomedes' giant frame appeared from behind a tangle of bushes, the man squealed into Odysseus' hand over his mouth.

"Do you know our tongue?" Odysseus asked

The man slowly nodded.

"What's you name?"

"D-Dolon." His body shook in fear, while he pissed down his leg.

"Where are you going in such a rush?"

"Please. D-Don't kill me. I have a wife and children. My father. H-He has gold and bronze for a ransom. I am his only s-son."

"What are you doing out here in the middle of the night? Stealing armor off dead bodies? Or spying for Hektor?"

"Hektor offered a reward to anyone who brought news of the Greek's plans."

Odysseus and Diomedes looked at each other. Odysseus mouthed, 'Athena,' to Diomedes, who nodded.

Odysseus pressed the trembling Trojan. "Where's Hektor's tent? How many guards are posted? Does he sleep or is he making plans for the morning?"

"Hektor is with his advisors. We watch the perimeter."

"What about the allies? Are they camped or did they return to the city?"

"In camp. Asleep. Only Trojans do not sleep."

"That makes it easier," Diomedes said.

"Please," Dolon begged, "leave me here. Let them find me bound and disgraced in the morning."

A low, wicked laugh escaped Diomedes' mouth. "So you can escape and try again to spy or kill us?"

Dolon put his hands up to protest, but Diomedes' blade glinted faintly in the dark, slicing through tendons and bone. Dolon's head hung gorily dripping blood in Odysseus' hand, which was now clenching the dead man's hair.

"A little warning next time," Odysseus said, tossing the head to the ground where it thudded like wet clay. "Fuck these Trojans."

The thrill of killing flooded through Odysseus and Diomedes, as they entered the unsuspecting camp Dolon had stumbled from. Creeping into tent after tent, they slit men's throats while they slept. They gathered as much armor as they could steal from the dead. Bloodied and laughing, they headed back to report to Agamemnon.

Odysseus washed the blood from his hands and stared at the red tinted water swirling in the bronze basin. *Who have I become?* He thought of Penelope back home. Gentle Penelope. The young woman he convinced to marry him, so shy she stood behind a pillar when Helen danced for all the suitors. She had blushed so sweetly, he thought his heart would burst. *How will she ever love the killer I've become? How can I hold her innocence in these filthy hands?* He splashed the water through his hair to wash the blood out. *I know more of killing than of making love now.*

TWENTY SIX

where heroes fall

AGAMEMNON'S CAMP—1238 BCE

Pale dawn bled across the heavens, mirroring the death and destruction below. The Goddess of Strife, on a mission from Zeus, cried out into the crisp morning air, urging the Greeks to forget their homelands and fight.

Agamemnon wiped the sleep from his swollen eyes. He stared up at the gently billowing tented roof. His body ached in every joint. "Age is closing in on me with every rise of Apollo." Slowly, he sat up and stretched. When his leg touched something, he glanced to his side. He'd forgotten about her. "You." He kicked at the sleeping slave woman. "Get out."

Without a word, the woman gathered her clothes and disappeared through the tent slit.

Rising from his bed, he thought of Briseis. She was what he truly wanted. To plow her deeply like a yoked beast plowing a field just to prove to Achilles he could. He grabbed his piss pot, but his cock had its mind on the fucking not relieving his bladder. "Fucking, Hades." He shook it. "Come on, damn it." He took a deep breath and closed his eyes. The image of Achilles rose up with eyes boring holes of hate and murder right through him. A thin stream sounded against the pottery. "Thank the gods."

Menelaus called from outside the tent. "Brother?"

"Enter."

"The men await you. They are ready to face whatever the day may bring."

Agamemnon scratched at the matted hair between his legs. He walked to the low table where the wash basin sat, and splashed water on his now flaccid member. "How do you judge the men?"

"They are ready to fight. More ready to go home."

Agamemnon continued to dress, pulling on a fresh tunic and slipping into his sandals. "Help me with these buckles."

Menelaus lifted his brother's breast plate jingling with bronze rings. He secured the leather straps over Agamemnon's shoulders and at his sides. "You have grown thinner."

Agamemnon laughed. "You lie. I know they call me the *'fat king'* behind my back."

"I only meant—"

"No matter. The greaves." He sat waiting for his brother to strap them over his calves. "I have hope the day will turn in our favor."

Lifting his brother's meaty leg, Menelaus secured one greave, then the other.

After rising from his seat, Agamemnon strapped on his sword

and grabbed his ash spear on the way out of his tent. Menelaus followed close behind him. "May the gods be with us."

Menelaus added, "And against the Trojans."

From the bow of his ship, Achilles watched the cloud of dust rise in the distance, signaling the initial clash of arms. He grabbed an amphora of wine and jumped from the rail to the shallow surf inching up the shore. The sand was firm and wet beneath his bare feet. He couldn't remember when he had last walked the camp.

Myrmidon shields stacked one against the other formed a short, black wall weaving through their camp. It brought relief to be in the crisp air walking among his men. As he passed by, they nodded and gave greetings but no one dared approach him. Once, he could be found among them, breaking bread and drinking wine, but the whispers of his foul temper kept them away now.

He made his way to the shore, hoping his mother might appear. Or Patrokles. The sea was calm, so Thetis was away. Her voice in his head was silent. He knew where Patrokles would be, so he made his way in that direction. More than a few startled faces greeted him as he wove through the camp, making his way to the edge where the sick and wounded were taken. Stray dogs barked as he passed, and young children oblivious to his mood circled him, questioning him as he walked.

"Achilles," they whispered, "it's Achilles!"

But he ignored them all. Eventually, they trailed off, disheartened and disappointed that they had failed to engage his attention.

Achilles peered into several tents before finding Patrokles, who was tending a man with a nasty gash across the back of his head. He stood for several moments watching Patrokles remove small pieces of rock from the man's scalp with a thin blade.

"What do you need, Achilles?" Patrokles asked without looking over his shoulder.

"What do you know about the fighting?"

"We've gained the upper hand. Agamemnon fights boldly. Uncharacteristic, I know. He has his men stripping the Trojan dead naked."

"Defiling the dead. There will be consequences."

Patrokles threw the filthy cloth in his hands into the clay basin. Water splashed over the edge onto the instruments next to it. "You are shocked? Why? You have done worse. I can remind you—"

Achilles sharply cut him off, "I know what I have done. What more do you hear?"

"Agamemnon was struck in the arm by a spear and carried off the field. Diomedes managed to get a good hacking at Hektor's helm, but Paris shot an arrow into his foot. Odysseus helped him uncork himself from the ground, but then he, too, was surrounded by the enemy. He suffered several wounds, before Menelaus and Ajax helped him escape. Last I heard Ajax was slaying the Trojans in all directions like a madman." His hands worked deftly, wrapping his patient's head. His fingers paused. "Nestor is wounded. That's all I know."

"That is quite a lot of information for someone not engaged in the battle itself."

Patrokles patted the wounded man's shoulder. "You should lie down for a while. Rest." Turning to Achilles, he said, "I am surrounded by information from the field. So are all the Myrmidons.

You're the one who chooses not to know anything."

"Until now."

"Until now," Patrokles said tersely.

"Agamemnon and most of his valued commanders do not fight. Maybe the fat king will humble himself and realize his mistake with me. Menelaus and Ajax, do they still fight?"

Patrokles paused, looking at Achilles as if he were a stranger. "Cousin, for many seasons I thought I knew you. But in recent days, you are practically a stranger to me. To the Myrmidons."

Achilles crossed his arms over his chest. "The blood tie. I hear your reproach without the words actually falling from your lips."

Patrokles glared at Achilles, saying nothing.

"Have you seen her?"

"Aye. I have." Patrokles stood to leave. "I'm going to check on Nestor. You can join me, if you like."

Achilles' temper simmered just beneath the surface. It had been too long without wine to tame it properly. He had no patience left to endure a scolding by the old man. "No. See to him and send word to me of any news you might discover."

Patrokles bowed his head, slightly. "Very well then." He exited the tent, feeling Achilles' eyes on his back until he passed beyond the last cluster of tents.

Patrokles poked his head into Nestor's tent, expecting him to be alone. The old man motioned him in with a wave of his wrinkled hand. "I'm surprised to see you, Patrokles. We all are. Come, join us." All the wounded commanders sat shoulder to shoulder, cramped around a small table. Agamemnon. Odysseus. Diomedes. Only Menelaus and Ajax were absent.

Taking a seat across from Diomedes, he asked, "How is your foot?"

The youngest captain shrugged off the injury. "I could have stayed in the fight—"

Odysseus scoffed. "Paris' arrow had you pinned to the ground. You would have lost half your toes the way you were tugging and screaming at your foot."

Diomedes shoved his plate away. "I'll never hear the end of it, will I?"

Odysseus shook his head and laughed. "It was a scene. You should have been there Patrokles."

Diomedes said, "Odysseus exaggerates. It's not that bad."

Nestor called to his woman, "Hecamede, bring the Pramnian wine and something to eat for our guests. Something sweet, I think, to dull our aches and pain."

Hecamede brought a basket of fresh bread to the table and poured the wine. "Here is honey for your bread. It is sweet." Her tone was amiable, but sharp. It did not escape the men seated, as they glanced sideways to each other, each questioning the nature of Nestor's relationship with his war prize.

Nestor patted her soft hip as she passed. She swatted his hand away. Undeterred, Nestor said, "You always know what is best."

"There is work to do, Nestor. I'll leave you men to talk of *your* war."

Ignoring Hecamede and turning to Patrokles, Nestor asked the question they all wanted answered, "Speaking of war, how much longer will Achilles remain idle?"

"He is stubborn. I doubt even Zeus could force him to join Agamemnon. He was curious about the wounded from this morning's fray."

Nestor tossed a hunk of bread on his platter. "Why does he care, if he has no intention of helping us? Is he waiting until Trojan torches burn us out? His camp is farthest from danger, so perhaps he thinks he will just shove off and leave the rest of us here to fend for ourselves and die like neglected dogs."

The war had certainly lasted beyond the expectations of everyone. Achilles' self-imposed exile had only exacerbated the tensions within the tiring army. Yet, Patrokles could do nothing. When they had first set out, Patrokles was privy to Achilles' mind. He shared his memories as a boy chasing rabbits and then deer on Chiron's mountain. It was where he credited his unusual speed and agility. He trained his Myrmidons to sprint and leap as he did, gifting them a weapon of their own body to stun the enemy with. Achilles spoke about his love and reverence for his mother. And the crystal thread between them. Achilles could hear Thetis when he called upon her in his thoughts. He also shared his joy and confusion upon becoming a father. His heart beat most strongly for battle and blood, but Neo rested in a soft place within his breast. He'd asked Patrokles once if that was love, and declared that if it was, he wanted nothing to do with it beyond his son, because it felt like weakness. But the days of late night fires and wine talk were over. Patrokles had no idea if the rift between them would ever be repaired. "Achilles has always done as he wished. Why do you expect him to be something else, when your king has taken everything he held dear?"

It was a bold statement. All eyes shifted to Agamemnon to

gauge his reaction, but the Great King sat stoically, unmoved by word of Achilles, for once. They counted it a small blessing and exhaled in relief.

Nestor folded his hands together, the wheels of his mind turning over what Patrokles said. They were in a precarious position, between retreat and defeat. Personally, he felt it reckless of Achilles to withdraw as he did, and for so long. "As his second, I am not surprised you hold such sentiment. But Achilles is part of this army, even if he doesn't wish to be. He took city after city in Agamemnon's name and for the sake of our cause. Not his own."

"That is his reasoning for withdrawing. You do not have to agree with him. He has already done it."

"I know what Menoetius advised you before you left for Aulis."

Patrokles flicked a pesky fly stalking the perimeter of his wine cup. "What did my father say that anyone here would be interested in hearing?"

"He reminded you that even though Achilles was superior in strength that it was your duty as his elder to give him good counsel."

Patrokles rubbed his thumb along the rough wooden plank of the table. The commanders eyed each other, worried that he would explode in a temper like Achilles. "As I have said, Achilles keeps his own counsel." Glancing up, he caught Nestor's eyes like a hawk snatches a rabbit from a field. There was nowhere for Nestor to hide. "Aren't you supposed to be closer to the gods than the rest of us? Perhaps, you should *pray* louder ... on our behalf. You might have better fortune with them, than Achilles."

Odysseus nearly spit his wine back into his cup. Diomedes raised his eyebrows.

However, Nestor would not give up. "He will listen to you,

Patrokles. Persuade him to help us, unless there is something else that keeps him away from battle? Why don't you go in his place? If the men see you, as Achilles, followed by the Myrmidons, it will bring hope back into our ranks. I can hear the Trojans quaking in fear thinking Achilles has returned to battle."

"Will you be able to defeat the Trojans without Achilles?" Patrokles asked.

Agamemnon—who'd sat silent through the entire conversation—voiced the dreaded answer, his tone grave and hopeless, "No. He presses us, even now, to our ships. When we gain the upper hand, the gods take it away again in favor of the Trojans. Final victory eludes us."

Patrokles drained his cup of wine and stood. "I will think on it. That's all I can promise. Achilles is not himself these days, and if ever my word held sway, I can't say to what extent it remains." He abruptly exited the tent, leaving the commanders stewing in their thoughts.

Agamemnon said to Nestor, "I can't help but wonder if the gods are against us and Hektor may defeat us. What if Achilles is not the only one in my camp who wishes me dead? Our defenses have been of little use."

Odysseus snapped, "Shut up before anyone hears you. If you want to lose the war, keep talking. If we leave now, like you suggest, the world will know we are all cowards. Who will fear us after that? We will return home to fight the rest of our lives to keep our worlds safe from invasion."

Agamemnon threw up his hands. "I am not commanding we leave, Odysseus. Our options are thin, unless you have a better plan?"

As the youngest captain, Diomedes was often ignored for war

advice, but he had had enough of the bickering. If Patrokles could speak his truth, then by the gods so could he. "It makes me sick to hear you old men even considering retreat. I did not come all this way for so long just to run like a scared dog with my tail between my legs. Did any of us imagine death would be a beautiful woman waiting to fuck us to sleep?" His looked hard at each man. "If we are fortunate enough to die in battle, death should greet each of us with fury in our hearts and blood on our swords. Wounded or not, I say we get back to the fighting. Find Hektor and kill him. I am tired of battle, too, but I refuse to run."

A chill wind touched Agamemnon's ear. *"Hear me, son of Atreus. I have not abandoned you."*

"Poseidon," Agamemnon whispered.

"Can you hear Achilles laughing at your fear?"

Agamemnon bristled.

"Let him be cursed among the men and the gods. Keep courage. I am with you."

"My men run. They fear Hektor."

"Let my voice fill them with bravery and fighting spirit."

Hektor stood with Kebriones on the deck of his chariot, surveying the palisade and ditch the Greeks erected around their camp. They'd lined the perimeter of the ditch with hundreds of sharp spears and heavy posts, close enough the Trojan chariots and horses couldn't pass through.

"Quite a barricade they built in very little time," Kebriones said.

"I wish Zeus would give us clear victory and send these fucking

Greeks back to their own lands. The only way through this maze is on foot." Hektor stepped down from his chariot. He kicked at one of the spears embedded in the ground. "It's deep. We will have to dig them out to make a wider pathway."

Kebriones followed his older brother. "It is more dangerous on foot. Without horses, we have no advantage. Our spy was found … without his *head*, so we have no knowledge what dangers await us beyond their gate. And Achilles is in their camp somewhere."

Paris joined his brothers with his bow in hand. The quiver of arrows jostled at his hip. "Do you have a plan, Hektor?"

"Break down part of this barricade. Then, storm their gate. Burn their ships."

"They will run for their ships once we get passed that gate. Cowards that they are," Paris said.

Hektor scratched at his scruffy chin. He missed the comforts of home. He could use a soak in hot water and a glass of wine … and Andromache. His brother was one of the reasons he could have none of that. "We've underestimated them too many times. They've proven they aren't cowards. Or have you forgotten how Menelaus tossed you around like an untrained boy?"

"Aphrodite—"

Hektor snapped, "Don't you understand it doesn't matter if Aphrodite saved you or not? It's that she *had* to in the first place."

Kebriones said, "The gods are fickle with their favors. That is the true weakness in any plan you make."

"Aye. The gods dole out favors and just as quickly yank them away," Hektor agreed. It was unnerving to engage in a battle knowing that the strength of your army and your sound strategies may come to nothing, if the gods decided against you. "Paris, dispatch men to start digging out these spears and posts we need to get a larger force through to avoid being picked off by their arrows. The breach we made earlier proved too narrow."

A shrill cry overhead caught their attention. Squinting into the sun, they saw an eagle soaring above them clutching a bright red snake. The serpent struck the eagle with its fangs. Screeching, the eagle released its prey. The snake writhed midair as it fell to its death near Hektor and his brothers.

"It's a god-sign," Kebriones said in awe. "Perhaps, we shouldn't fight the Greeks? Wait for a more auspicious omen?"

Hektor wanted nothing so much as to end the war. His faith waivered, but he would not give up. Not yet. "We're on the edge of battle. They can see us from behind their wall. They would think us cowards. No, we can't turn back now. It's a god-sign that we must defend the citadel and crush their hopes."

Paris shook his head, uncertain Hektor had interpreted the god-sign correctly. "It's an omen we will not win the battle. The snake dropped on our side of the wall."

Grabbing Paris roughly by the arm, Hektor whipped his body around to face him. His eyes bore fiercely into his brother's face. "Shut your mouth, or I will finish what our father could not. I don't think you understand that the people, the men, think you a coward for what happened with Menelaus. You can't afford to utter words that will instill fear or doubt in their minds. Then, all would be lost."

A gust of wind caught the length of Hektor's sea-blue cape, whipping it around his legs. "Strange," he muttered. Pulling it free, he glanced up at the sound of a distant howl. Behind his army a cloud of dust was moving rapidly toward them. The men hunkered down, shields and capes pulled over their heads, as the unexpected dust storm rolled over. Hektor rubbed his eyes and squinted in disbelief. The image of a giant in a chariot flashed for a moment inside of the storm. "Zeus," he whispered. He grabbed Paris by the arm. "We must charge the gate now. Zeus is with us."

Paris nodded and disappeared into the pale yellow air. The Trojans mobilized within the shroud of the storm, the Greeks blind to their movements.

"Pick up that rock, Hektor."

The hairs on Hektor's body rose, and his skin tingled with power. "Zeus."

"Pick it up."

"It would take five men to lift that boulder."

"It is not wise to doubt me, Prince Hektor."

Hektor nodded. He walked to the boulder and wrapped his arms around the middle of it. The rock was oddly warm and smooth. With all his strength, he easily hefted the rock up to his shoulder. "By the gods!"

In his ear, Zeus said, *"By me. Throw it."*

Hektor launched the boulder with all his might, smashing the center of the gate into a thousand pieces as if it had been nothing more than fragile clay and sticks. He stood in awe as the dust cleared and the gate was gone. The confidence of Zeus filled him, and he charged with a spear in each hand. "Kill them all!"

The Trojan army's battle cry filled the air as they flooded through the breach, scattering the Greeks like ants seeking holes and crevices to hide.

From above, Poseidon's feigned disinterest faltered and a wicked scowl marred his perfect face. He'd spent an eternity bending to his brother's will as a subordinate, relinquishing his own authority. Watching Zeus assist the Trojans in pinning the Greeks to their ships, he made up his mind to help the Greeks. Zeus be damned.

Poseidon flew like lightning to his sea-realm where Zeus had no power. The high-walled halls built of rocks and shells provided solace beneath the ocean waves, when he could bear the weight of bowing to his brother no more. Zeus had taken everything he loved, including Thetis, by decree and prophecy. He'd been humiliated by being forced to live as a mortal, building the very wall the Greeks were so desperately trying to crash. He was glad of his palace beyond the peering eyes of Zeus, because now he would do as he willed, not as Zeus commanded.

He gathered his gleaming armor from his great hall glittering with mother-of-pearl and gold. After pulling his breastplate from the wall, he buckled it across his broad chest. The silver steel, unknown to mortals, shone as brightly as a stunning star set against the ink of night. "I will bow no more."

Poseidon harnessed his magnificent horses with their golden manes to his chariot. Snapping the guide straps, he roared, "Rise! Rise from the sea! Fight with me!"

The horses jolted and cried out, their hooves pawing the sandy ocean floor. He snapped the reins again, and the chariot rose through the murky waters, the horses galloping as if on land. As they neared the surface, Poseidon commanded the sea to make way and the waves parted, revealing a frothy valley walled by water. He flew through the opening swirling with mist and sand, his chariot skidding across the shore amidst the startled Greeks. The god unleashed a terrifying roar.

A thousand voices uttered, "Poseidon!" And a thousand men fell to their knees and covered their faces.

"Rise up and fight!" the God of the Sea bellowed like a storm. "Rise up and fight!"

Ajax spun in awe to see the god with his own eyes and cried out, "Poseidon! Help me! Lend me your strength and I will break the Trojans and force their women to wail with grief."

Poseidon's glittering eyes fell on Ajax. "As you wish, mortal."

The power of the god filled Ajax's limbs, and confidence swelled in his heart. His keen eyes caught Hektor blazing a bloody path through the camp. He ran like a lion to meet his mortal enemy, the man even Achilles had not been able to kill while he still stood with the army.

Ajax screamed out, "Hektor!" His breath burned in his chest and the ground quaked as he ran. "The storm of Poseidon comes for you!"

Hektor's face contorted with equal rage; the essence of Zeus still lingered in his veins. "Come at me, you fucking Greek!" Blood spattered and smudged by gore, Hektor launched himself at Ajax who was barreling toward him. The clash of their arms sounded as thunder. Both armies charged, renewed by their commanders' vigor. The fighting was fierce, but indecisive. Sweat glistened across men's faces and the heat slowly sapped their strength. Swords once held high, lowered. Men pushed and shoved, as Hektor and Ajax hacked at each other.

A spear whizzed passed Hektor's ear, stabbing dead center of

Ajax's shield, followed by another and then another. The fourth spear twisted Ajax's helmet to the side, temporarily blinding him. Ajax took a step back to right it, but not before a ring of heavily armed Trojans swarmed around Hektor, pulling him to safety within the larger body of the army.

Kebriones gripped his eldest brother's arm with fingers of iron. "We must pull back."

Ajax's angry roar carried over the din of men fighting and struggling in battle. "We are not finished, Prince of Troy!"

A severed head tumbled to the ground, rolling to a stop at Hektor's feet.

The god's gift faded from Hektor's eyes. He surveyed his men fighting on the left and right. "How did we become so scattered?" His mind cleared of the blood lust. He shook his head in disbelief. "We had Zeus' favor. But now, we are pinned between their ships and their ditch. We can't pull back yet."

Every hair on Idomeneus' body stood on end. He turned but saw no one beside him. He'd heard the shouting from the shore and knew the god was near him. "Poseidon," he whispered. "We welcome your aid. Zeus turns from our pleas, favoring the Trojans, no matter how hard we fight. No matter how much we tire of war and yearn for home."

"I am here. Arm yourself. Fight."

Poseidon's words slid icily down Idomeneus' spine. "Aye." Then, from the chaos of battle, a man appeared, running wild eyed and frantic. As he neared, Idomeneus shouted, "Where are you going,

Meriones?"

Meriones skidded to a halt. "My lord, I need weapons. My spears are thrown or broken."

"Do you know my tent?"

"Aye, my lord. I do."

"Go. Grab anyone who can help you. Bring all the Trojan arms I've collected. And take what you need to keep fighting. Poseidon is with us."

"I heard the rumor, my lord, that he rose from the sea, but I didn't believe it. Are you certain?"

"The god has spoken into my ear. It is true. He fights among us."

"Then I will hurry before we lose his favor!" Meriones sped off.

Idomeneus grabbed another man running by him. "Have you seen Teucer and Ajax afield?"

The man whose eyes were as large as a moons, nodded.

"Good. Find them and tell them to hold the center of Hektor's attack and send men to hit Hektor on the left flank. The day is not over yet."

Hektor had plowed through the center of the fighting, testing the odds stacking against them. Ajax the Giant commanded his ranks flawlessly, emboldening the Greeks who'd repelled each Trojan advance. Realizing he faced a bloody stalemate, Hektor signaled for his army to fall back.

"How did this happen, Kebriones? We had a clear advantage, now we're surrounded."

"Some of your men have given up. Look." Standing next to

Hektor on the chariot's platform, Kebriones directed his brother's attention behind them. "They run because they have no weapons. See, men are picking up spears from the dead and dying. And over there." He pointed far in front of them. "Others are trapped inside of the Greek's camp. We must pull back now, or make a hard push for the ships. If you choose the latter, the war will be decided by nightfall."

Hektor watched his men scavenging for weapons and armor. Andromache's face flashed before his eyes. If he lost the battle, risking everything at this moment, she and Astyanax would be slaves by nightfall. His heart sickened at the thought. How many Trojans would suffer, if he pressed the Greeks without the gods' favor? "Why did Zeus abandon us so readily?"

"The gods do as they wish. Besides …" Kebriones' voice trailed off.

"Speak."

The battle sounded around them. Men screamed in victory and agony. The stench of fresh blood and shit filled the air. "I don't think Achilles will stay away from battle much longer. And when he emerges from his discontent, we do not want to be this close to their camp."

"I agree." Hektor knew what Achilles' eventual return would mean. The final days of the war would be upon them and the outcome of Troy's fate would be decided soon after. It was a moment he longed for, yet dreaded. Peace was an elusive lover, enticing men to taste the sweet nectar of her breasts, only to pull them away when their appetite for more grew. "We must regroup and push them back to the ships if we hope to burn them out, before it's too late. Gather men beyond that rise, over there." He pointed not too far away. "Spread the word. We make one last effort before Apollo's light fades."

Moving to the rear of the army Hektor passed dozens of dead bodies, familiar faces of men he'd spoken with and fought alongside. This was not the day he had been promised when Zeus whispered to him of victory. He could not let Troy fall today. All could not be lost. A spear whistled passed his shoulder and he dove to the ground, rolling behind a ruined chariot for safety. "Paris."

Loosing an arrow, Paris quickly nocked another. "Get behind me," he hissed. "I can't see who's throwing the fucking—" Another spear thumped against the chariot's side, bouncing off it and clanging to the dirt. "Fucking Greeks," Paris muttered, loosing the second arrow and nocking a third.

"Are there no commanders left?"

"You mean commanders you respect?" Paris shook his head and loosed the third arrow, as a return arrow twanged into the chariot. Another skidded across the ground in front of them. "Only me." He glanced sideways at Hektor. "My men are scattered. Some fighting at the ships. Trapped because your men couldn't push through the center as planned."

"Come with me," Hektor said between clenched teeth. "We are regrouping."

By midday, the Trojans and their allies again marched toward the Greek's defenses. In the midst of the ranks stood Hektor, the bronze rings of his breastplate and his shield flashing like tiny suns in Apollo's golden light. In a booming voice he cried out, "Who will stand against me?"

Ajax of Telemon, standing tall as a mountain, stepped forward. "Let's finish what you started. I don't fear the likes of you. But know this, Hektor of Troy, soon you will be prince of nothing but rocks and ruin."

"Soon enough the dogs will eat your rotting flesh and the birds will peck your bones clean. And your ships will be burnt to ashes mixed into the sand."

The ranks of Greeks and Trojans faced one another, standing bravely behind their commanders. Bronze blinked in the light. Spears quivered in the hands of men eager and fearful to do battle. Hektor raised his spear, unleashing his terrible battle cry. The clash of bronze floated to the heavens.

TWENTY SEVEN

Hera's guile

OLYMPUS—1238 BCE

Hera gazed down from her perch on the sacred mountain, pleased that Poseidon was helping the Greeks. But, she knew Zeus' attention would soon turn to the chaos below. If his anger was ignited, it could mean the end of Olympus as they knew it.

In the gleaming halls of her abode, she called the mechanical maidens gifted to her by Hephaestus. They drew her bath in a great crystal basin, easily carrying the heavy amphorae of steaming water. The goddess sprinkled rose petals and jasmine blossoms onto the water's surface. Lowering herself into the water, she eased into the bath, continuing to scheme how to keep her husband from the mortal combat below.

When she stepped from the bath, the maids dried every inch of her fair skin flushed pink from the water. They brushed her silver hair until it gleamed. She slipped into a gossamer gown of spun silver, sheer enough to reveal the slim perfection of her form. Hera crowned herself with a simple circlet of gold to contrast the pale beauty of her hair. The final piece was Aphrodite's belt. The small lie she told to obtain it, she reasoned, was worth the power to enchant Zeus. She tucked a vial containing a sleeping potion into the belt and made her way to Mount Ida where she knew her husband had sequestered himself.

Hera walked softly across the meadow, knowing within the woods in front of her, she would find Zeus. Flowers blossomed beneath each step, as even nature was helpless to give up its treasures in the presence of her beauty. The power of Aphrodite's belt surged through her. For a moment, she forgot her anger and jealousy concerning her daughter. Wielding such magic was indeed intoxicating, even for her. She almost pitied the mortal woman, Helen, for carrying the slightest touch of Aphrodite's power, but then Zeus turned his eyes to her and Helen was instantly forgotten.

"I want no company," Zeus said, standing beneath a giant oak. However, his eyes lingered on her, hungrily devouring her as she crossed the last of the meadow.

Hera smiled slightly, recognizing the familiar tone of desire in his words. She swept a strand of her silver hair from her shoulders. "I have come to make amends." Zeus stared at her a long enough a sliver of doubt crept into her mind. "Believe me."

Zeus' eyes darkened with carnal desire. "Why must you fight me at every turn?"

"You made me this way."

The god's upper lip curled into a wicked grin. "You wound me, Goddess."

Hera slipped lithely to his side and placed her elegant hand on his hardened cock. "Let me heal the wounds I have inflicted." She brushed her lips against his, before playfully biting his bottom lip.

Zeus growled, and the mountain shook. He wrapped Hera up in his huge arms, pulling her close. Kissing her hard. Lifting her from her feet, he laid her down in the soft grass. With a wave of his hand, he pulled a shroud of mist around them. "What I am about to do to you—"

Hera's mouth stifled the god's words. True longing replaced her earlier pretense. Her body needed the full power of the god inside of her. It had been too long. Zeus pulled up her gown, exposing her glorious naked flesh. Bending his head to her delicate folds, he licked her there until she trembled. He positioned himself between her thighs and thrust into her with all his strength. Hera cried out with pleasure as much as pain. When the god was finished, he collapsed beside her with one leg resting heavily over her hips. He closed his eyes to sleep.

Hera slowed her breathing and regained her senses to focus on her true purpose. She felt for the vial she'd tucked away in her belt. It was still there. Grateful, she pulled it from its hiding place and opened it. She let a drop of the elixir touch Zeus' lips. She waited to see if he would wake. Only when his chest quietly rose and fell, did Hera dare to slip from beneath him. Standing beside her husband's peaceful form, she tilted her chin up. She had done what no other god would dare. Confident Zeus would be none the wiser, she left him to his magical slumber.

Apollo's light swept across the blue heavens, raising sweat on the men below. Both sides fought furiously for victory. The clash of arms and agonies of men at war, crying out to him by the thousands, woke Zeus from his unnatural sleep. He rubbed at his eyes. His limbs felt heavy. He scowled as it slowly dawned on him what Hera had done.

Zeus peered through the clouds down the mountain at the raging battle. The Trojans pressed the Greeks to their ships, but the Greeks repelled every advance. The tug-of-war continued with no clear winner. It was then that he saw Poseidon, rushing the Greeks as he yelled from his chariot. Zeus' anger rose in his chest like a storm. Lightning flashed across the midday sky.

He scanned the ground, searching for Hektor. The favored Prince of Troy lay on the ground, mortally wounded. Blood gushing from his mouth. His armor scattered all around him. Without a second thought, the god flew to Olympus, catching Hera in the crystal gardens. He grabbed her roughly the elbow. "You deceitful bitch! How dare you plot with Poseidon against me? My own brother! I warned all of you to keep away from the war."

As Hera's tongue licked at her bottom lip, a lie formed. "I have not spoken to Poseidon or urged him on in any way. What he does, he does of his own accord. He pitied the Greeks trapped at their ships."

Zeus narrowed his eyes to burning slits. "I don't trust a single word falling from your lips. Send word to Poseidon that he must quit the fight. Tell Apollo to heal Hektor. The field must be leveled after Poseidon's help." He pressed his face close to his sister-wife's. "If you disobey me, I will destroy you and all your beloved Greeks."

"It shall be as you say." Hera's lower lip trembled. Fear surged through her being. "I promise."

Zeus grabbed her arm, squeezing it tightly as his flaming eyes bore into hers. "Know this, wife; there is a purpose for all things. You do not know everything in my mind, nor will you ever. Not one of you will help either side, until my promise to Thetis is fulfilled."

Hera bristled at Thetis' name. Her arm burned with pain, but a sliver of defiance remained. "What did you promise the nymph *this* time?"

Zeus released her arm, shoving her backwards. "That Achilles' honor would be restored. My plan has already been set in motion, and none of you will stop it."

Hera fled to the Great Hall and took her seat among the gods already partaking of the evening meal. Her face was reddened. Her eyes panicked. She rubbed at her aching arm. "Let us feast. I have news."

Ares, Athena, Aphrodite, and Hephaestus sat silently trading awkward glances. Hera held her chin high. "We all know the risk of defying Zeus. Yet, we do from time to time."

"We have no choice," Ares said, stuffing a thin crusted sweet into his mouth.

Hera pressed her lips into a tight line. "We must stop … for now."

Ares rose up violently from his heavy chair, striking the table with his fists. "Why must we always do what he wills? Are we not gods as well?"

Hera cautioned, "We must not continue to intervene."

Ares remained defiant. "Zeus can kill me with a bolt of lightning if he chooses."

Athena spoke up, "Brother, you must think of the consequence. If war breaks out among us, and we lose, we could find ourselves in a *worse* place."

"Tartarus," Aphrodite whispered. The very name of the place sent shivers through her body. "I have no wish to join the Titans in that dark place."

Hephaestus cut a hunk of roasted meat on his silver platter. He looked at each of his siblings in their glorious bodies. He alone was the gimp of the gods. The immortals sought him for his skills in metal working, but considered him so ugly and undesirable none offered him any true affection. "Or he could simply throw you down the mountain."

No one said a word. Zeus could maim and kill them all.

Aphrodite was the first to relent. "We were never going to save all the mortals anyway." Her wine cup refilled itself of delicate nectar. "I'm not sure why we believed any of us could. It is an easy decision."

Hera sighed in resignation. "I'll send Iris to bring Poseidon back."

Athena asked, "Do you think it wise, Mother, to summon Poseidon back to Olympus? Isn't it better he returns to his halls below the sea?"

"That would be more prudent." Her eyes found Apollo's. "You are to heal Hektor."

Apollo bowed his head and left without a word.

Hera sipped her wine. "It's over for us."

"For now," Athena said. "For now."

Hektor struggled in the dirt. The force of Ajax's sword had knocked him to his back and sliced through his breastplate. His men stood helpless around him like a wall. There were no physicians close by and no way to send word for one. Hektor propped himself up on an elbow, gasping for breath. "This … cannot be … the end," he said, as he desperately clung to life. He slumped back to the ground beneath the heavy hand of a god.

"Rise up, Prince of Troy. Why do you lay here in the dust?"

Hektor stared up into the fading day, a shadow creeping over his eyes. "Ajax struck me …" His voice trailed off to silence.

"He had the advantage of an immortal blow. Poseidon gave him the strength of two dozen men. But you have survived the onslaught. A lesser man would be dead."

Hektor closed his eyes to the pain. "Apollo." His chest heaved mightily. Blood dripped from the corners of his mouth. "Am I dying?"

"Not this day, Hektor." Apollo placed his hand on Hektor's chest, filling his mortal frame with life and power. *"Zeus finds favor with you yet. Stand, Hektor, Golden Prince of Troy. Have courage. Zeus commands me to fight beside you. Call your men. Victory will be yours."*

Hektor rose like a lion, free of pain, and unleashed a ferocious battle cry, renewing the spirit of his army. "Apollo is with us!"

The astonished Trojans took Hektor's miraculous recovery as a god-sign and joined behind him to storm the enemy at the gates. Hektor and Apollo strode side by side, the god a mere shimmer to mortal eyes. The enemies rushed at each other, as the song of swords clashing filled the air.

Apollo roared, as his sword cut men to the bone. The Greeks fell to the ground, covering their ears—some wept, and others ran for the ships. They despaired because the courage of Poseidon had abandoned them.

Hektor's voice thundered across the carnage, "Take the ships!"

Apollo flattened the offending ditch with his heavy feet, clearing a path through the trench for the Trojans to ride their chariots. With delight, he smashed the flimsy mortal wall on both sides of the gate, pushing the Greeks into the heart of their camp.

When the noise of war drew too close, Patrokles stepped outside of the physician's tent. Chaos swirled around him. Trojan warriors had ascended the far beached ships, burning and killing everyone in their path. Black smoke filled the air. Men ran with wild-eyed faces. Others dragged wounded comrades to safety.

Patrokles grabbed a bleeding man running passed him. "What's happened?"

"My lord, the Trojans have destroyed our defenses. The wall is gone. Hektor is coming for us."

He released the man's arm. "Go." The frightened man ran, disappearing into the maze of tents. Standing alone, watching the destruction of the camp, Patrokles knew it was time. It was time to get Achilles back into the fight, or they would all die.

PART THREE
Ashes in the Wind

blood soaked ground
feet slipping in the muck
mercy is sliced away
by crimson dripping blades

bones crack and crunch
shields splinter and
spear points find homes
in soft flesh

dark eyes close forever
mothers and daughters
weep and weave shrouds
dyeing threads with bitter tears

mothers, wives, sisters weep
at the foothills of pyres
mercy now in hungry flames
floating through Hade's gates

bones to ashes settle on the wall
across the gory plain
revenge blossoms beneath their breasts
the rage of queens does reign

TWENTY EIGHT

catch a falling star

AGAMEMNON'S CAMP — 1238 BCE
DAY 19 LATER IN THE DAY

Acrid smoke filled Patrokles' nostrils. He coughed the stinging air out of his lungs, only to inhale more of the same. Making his way to Achilles' ship, he prayed to the gods that his cousin wasn't too far into his wine for logic and reason. He had been sewing men's wounds and closing their eyes when their spirits soared to the Land of the Dead, since Achilles abandoned the war. Patrokles could not fathom how Achilles, so attuned to his men's needs, could be so heartless for all the others. *How can he remain so hateful?* When he reached the rope ladder, he climbed to the rail and hopped onto the deck. It was unusually quiet. "Achilles?"

From behind stacked jars and baskets, Achilles stepped into view, once again disheveled and barefoot. "I'm here. What do you want?"

"A favor, cousin."

Achilles groaned, "The blood tie. Every time you seek to persuade me, you address me as *cousin*. It's a bad habit."

A moment of silence hung between them. Patrokles took in the deep circles under his cousin's eyes. "You look the beggar."

Achilles laughed, and then quickly sobered, his mouth falling into a scowl. "There's a greeting that will surely get you what you desire. Ask now or get off my ship. I have better things to do than stand here *not* drinking."

An angry tear slid down Patrokles' cheek. "What might that be, Achilles? What pressing matters do you have besides your next jar of wine? Can't you see that the Trojans are near our camp? Can't you hear the sound of our brothers dying? Smell death in the air?"

Sneering, Achilles replied, "What do I care if Agamemnon loses this war?"

Patrokles hardly knew the man before him. This was not the warrior who roared across the field, joyfully singing the song of war, inspiring the men around him to do the same. He knew first hand the magic of Achilles' dance with Ares, and the surge of strength it gave. Where had that Achilles gone? "They are *our* people, Achilles. Years we have fought alongside them. Now, without us, they lose hope. Cousin, you must get back into the fight. By Ares' sword, I beg you."

Achilles picked up a nearby open amphora and swigged the bittersweet nectar. "You sound like a little girl lost in a market, crying because she can't find her mother. Tell me ..." he tilted the jar to his mouth again, gulped more wine, then wiped his lips on the back of his free hand, "do our fathers yet live?"

"Of course."

Cocking an eyebrow, Achilles asked, "What reason do you have then to be moved to begging? Surely, you don't concern yourself so much with Agamemnon's army? Although, I do pity them for following an arrogant king."

"When you pulled us from the war, you devastated everyone. Even the Myrmidons. You think your warriors are happy to sit around fires and swim in the surf, while others go to battle?"

"Do not presume to speak to me of the Myrmidons. I know my men."

"Do you? Do you truly? When was the last time you walked among them and looked them in the eyes? Ate with them? Laughed with them? Sat drinking wine while they fucked their women?"

"You push me too far, Patrokles."

Undeterred, Patrokles asked, "How can you be angry with men who have loved you? Been inspired by you? One glance of your helm from across the field was all the inspiration they needed to fight on. How can you abandon them now, when the Trojans have them pinned against the shore?"

Achilles walked to the railing behind his cousin, setting the amphora on the edge. "I have no pity left for anyone."

"That is a *lie*. Look at you. You're full of pity." Grabbing Achilles' shoulder, he turned him so their faces nearly touched. "Diomedes lays wounded, as well as Odysseus. Both are in the physicians' tents where I should be. But, I am here, begging you to join Agamemnon. Put your pride aside, cousin. Don't let the Trojans beat them back. Or all these years of fighting will have been for nothing because you refused to fight. What will your song be then?"

Achilles remained silent, but his eyes fumed.

"Who is there to inspire the men to fight on if not you?"

Taking in a long breath, Achilles stared out across the bay. He exhaled. "I hear your words, cousin, but where would my honor be if I go back on my word?"

"By all the gods! How can one man be so stubborn and full of pride? What is it, Achilles? What is it that you want?" His heart pounded, and angry tears fell. "Briseis?" He laughed in spite of himself. "If you'd truly wanted her, you would never have let her go in the first place."

Lightning cracked behind Patrokles' eyes; his knees buckled beneath him and he fell to the deck. Slowly, he rose to his feet, wiping the blood at his lip. His gray eyes blazed. "I hope the gods *never* harden my heart as they have yours."

Achilles turned away. "It's all Agamemnon's fault."

"Agamemnon? You truly believe you shoulder no part in any of this chaos?"

"*You*, of all my companions, know the truth. Agamemnon is a greedy whore's dog. He could have had Troy laid at his feet, but he chose a slave woman over gold. Then, when he could *not* have *her*, he took my woman." Achilles leveled his eyes at Patrokles. "And you know better than anyone that I love her. You can't imagine the pain of *knowing* the woman you love lies beneath another man."

If Agamemnon touched Briseis, Patrokles would kill him in cold blood. It wouldn't be the first time he'd murdered a fellow Greek. If, however, Achilles ever found out that he had lain with Briseis, well, that would be his end. Grinding his teeth, Patrokles answered, "You should never have let her go."

"I couldn't go against the goddess." Achilles softened with understanding. "But, I can't blame you, cousin, for believing so. Love makes cowards even of the brave."

"Then, win her back with your honor intact. Fight with Agamemnon and beat the Trojans once and for all. And if you won't, then …" Nestor's words came back to him. He could take Achilles' position; a false hope planted could sprout to true victory. "Let me fight in your place. Wear your armor. Bear your shield. Lead the Myrmidons into battle. Give the men a sign of hope."

"I swore to the gods I would not fight until my own ships were threatened—"

"Can you not hear the sound of war in the air? Smell the burning ships from the other side of camp? If you do nothing, the Trojans will catch us without armor or shields to defend ourselves."

"That will never happen." Achilles walked to a chest and opened it. "Come, Patrokles. Arm yourself." He pulled his breastplate out first, and then his helmet. Even without Apollo's light, Achilles' armor glinted with untold glory. "Take them. Take it all, except my spear. For only I can wield it."

Patrokles was taken aback. "Are you certain?"

"My father was right to put you beside me. Your counsel is more often wiser than my own. I think of … other times when you advised me against my own stubbornness … had I listened my regrets would be less. Lead the Myrmidons to war in my stead. You're right, cousin. We can't let the Trojans win by pushing us back into the sea."

As Achilles buckled Patrokles into his gear, he said, "I'll do my best to honor you and our men."

Achilles slapped Patrokles on the shoulder. "Keep the ships from burning, cousin, or else how will we ever reach home when the war is done?"

Patrokles grinned. "*Home.* Is there a sweeter word than that?"

"Your victory will be mine. And then the Greeks will know how wrong Agamemnon was. They will send Briseis back to me with gold. And because they haven't wronged me, as you have made clear to me, I will accept their gifts and end the feud between me and the fat king." Achilles grabbed Patrokles by the shoulders, digging his fingers into his flesh. "But you must swear by the gods that you will not push the men on to Troy. Don't let your victory carry your heart away in rage and lust for more blood than I give you permission to take. Apollo loves the Trojans, and if you do more than save our camp, you will call his attention down upon us. Make no mistake, Apollo is a vengeful god."

Patrokles made a short bow. "I promise, cousin. I will do as you command."

Achilles adjusted the shield strap. "You resemble me, but not as tall." He touched Patrokles' dark braids falling below the helmet. "The Trojans will not know to notice your hair." He embraced his cousin. "Take my horses and my chariot. Ride with fury."

"I will."

"Go now, and kill them all."

Patrokles nodded and jumped lightly to the rail, despite the heavy armor. He longed for battle, as much as any other Myrmidon. He missed the dance of war, and the fighting would release his guilt over Briseis. Patrokles' heart was free for the first time in ages. He turned and said, "I love you, Achilles. More than a blood brother could ever know." Grinning widely at his cousin, he leapt to the sand and disappeared from view.

Achilles listened to Patrokles' voice, like a lion roaring across a desert plain, calling the Myrmidons to battle. The wind chilled his skin as a dark cloud passed over head. He glanced up at the sky.

Circling carrion floated high above him. He shivered. *Mother, I pray you protect him.*

He shouted to the sea, "Do you hear me, Mother? Protect him."

A warm breeze wrapped around his shoulders and whispered, *"I cannot ... you know what you must do."*

Achilles nodded silently. Turning, he walked to the back of the galley where he kept the chest his mother had given him years ago. Opening the lid, he reverently pulled out the silver challis. His were the only mortal hands to ever touch it.

He poured wine into the shining cup and set his eyes to the sky. "If ever you favored me, Zeus, I pray you hear my words now. I've sent Patrokles to fight in my stead against the Trojans. I've given him the sacred armor which only I have worn. I pray you put your thunder in his heart. Let Hektor feel his wrath, a gift from you. And when the threat to our camp has been extinguished, bring my cousin safely back to me."

After returning the cup to the chest, he leapt from his ship, making his way atop the beachhead's rolling hills where he knew the Myrmidons would assemble.

Patrokles stood tall in Achilles' chariot as the men formed their ranks under their captains. "Myrmidons! The day we've waited for has come!" His voice boomed above their shaking helmet plumes.

"It has indeed!" a voice roared from behind Patrokles.

"Achilles," hundreds of voices whispered like a breeze through tall trees.

Patrokles turned, uncertain. Behind Achilles walked Odysseus and Diomedes released from the physicians' tents.

Achilles flashed a stunning grin, as he leapt onto his chariot's wheel, balancing easily on its edge. "I know many of you blame me for what has happened to Agamemnon's army. Many of you wanted to go home if we weren't going to fight. But now I ask you to remember the rage you have in your hearts for all your lost companions."

The Myrmidons shook their shields and spears, and cheered their golden champion's winning words.

"Although, I can't break my word not to fight, I urge you, follow the only man worthy to wear my armor. Follow Patrokles as you would me. He will lead you to victory."

The Myrmidons' united voices thundered through the air.

Jumping from the chariot, Achilles strode from the gathering without looking back. In his heart, he longed to fight, but settled instead to wait and watch his Myrmidons win the day. He'd find some high ground to keep his eye on them. *Soon, Hektor, the God of Death will whisper in your ear.*

Patrokles' gray eyes matched the tumultuous sky above. Looking out over the shaking helms of the Myrmidons and the sea of bronze tipped spears, he allowed himself to think of Briseis. Her shining eyes. Her mouth. Her skin. Then, he pushed the thoughts back into the dark of his mind. He would fight this day to kill the Trojans to a man, and rid his heart of love for Achilles' woman. Turning to his charioteer, Automedon, he signaled the advance. "Gods be with us," he shouted, raising his sword, then slashing it downward.

With that, the Black Shields marched out of their camp to

the fray. Beneath their feet, the ground shook. Their hearts desired nothing less than a river of Trojan blood. Their battle cry carried on the air, and Patrokles' voice the most ferocious of them all.

As the wall of Black Shields approached the melee, the Greeks cheered and the Trojan forces faltered, when dozens of soldiers ran shouting in fright.

"Achilles has returned!"

"It's Achilles!"

"Run! He'll kill us all with his spear!"

"His death spear!"

"We're doomed!"

The Myrmidons crashed over the Trojan forces, scattering their ranks. Patrokles, with the blood of war pounding through his veins, hefted his heavy ash spear, hurling it into the shoulder of a Trojan, pinning the man to the ground where he squirmed like a fish out of water. His agonized screams were drowned out by the din of battle.

Around them the Greek ships were ablaze, sending black smoke into the air. Patrokles bellowed to the captain at his left, "Eudorus! Take your men and put the fires out before they destroy all the ships." From the corner of his eye, Patrokles saw his commands being carried out. "Kill them all!"

Bronze sang against bronze, while men groaned and screamed, filling the air with war song. Dust and smoke choked down throats, yet men from both sides fought on. The thirsty ground drank their crimson blood as a sacrifice to Ares. Patrokles leveled his spear time and time again, crashing through the ranks, smashing bones and severing limbs. The dead lay in a crooked path behind his chariot, broken and bleeding, guts leaking into the muck of war.

Fighting like lions caged for too long, the Myrmidons' bravery infused the Greeks with renewed courage. Penelos nearly severed a man's head off; it dangled by a strip of skin before he fell, his blood spurting a thin river winding around him in the dirt. Idomeneus jabbed his sword into a Trojan's mouth. The dead man's teeth lay scattered about his head like grains of wheat to be planted.

And in the midst of the carnage, Ajax hurled his spear at Hektor, but the killing point skittered across the wide shield of Troy's prince. Hektor whirled in his chariot and dashed back across the ditch that surrounded the Greek encampment. Many of the Trojan captains followed, some crashing their chariots into pieces in the attempt. Horses loosed from their restraints galloped wide eyed with manes flying from the fray back to the city.

Forgetting Achilles' words, Patrokles ordered Automedon to follow. Leading a small contingent of cavalry, Patrokles headed off the fleeing Trojans and pushed them back, trapping them between Troy and the Greek ships. Red fury filled Patrokles' chest, as he carved a path through the enemy. He took the first Trojan with his sword, hacking his limbs cleanly off. Another man he speared through the teeth like a fisherman stabbing a fish in shallow waters. Splattered in blood and dirt, Patrokles laughed as he laid waste to every Trojan in his path. *I will kill them all to get to Hektor.*

From across the skirmish, a challenge rose to Patrokles' ears. He turned to see Sarpedon, a mighty warrior rumored to be a son of Zeus and a Trojan ally, leaping from his chariot.

"Achilles! Come and fight a worthy man!" Sarpedon shouted.

Patrokles leapt from his chariot and charged with Achilles' shield slightly tilted just as Achilles would do. Running like a god, he slashed a warrior standing between him and Sarpedon in half. The man's guts spilled into his hands, slipping to the dirt. He fell to his knees screaming while frantically trying to gather his innards up in his arms. Sarpedon hurled his spear at Patrokles, missing wide and striking a startled horse nearby. The beast screamed and reared before it fell on its side, heaving heavily, blood pouring from its nostrils. Before he could grab another spear, Patrokles hurled his spear, striking Sarpedon through his armor, sending him to the ground.

Sarpedon lay immobile, but cried out, "Don't let the Greeks strip my armor!"

Patrokles, covered in blood and war muck, stood over him, laughing. "You won't need it where you're going." Grasping the spear shaft with both hands, he plunged it deeper until the point pierced the ground. Sarpedon gasped once in shock, as blood poured from his mouth and nose. Patrokles put his foot on the dead man's chest, yanking the spear out followed by a bloody lung.

The clamor of war mixed with swirling dust, and Patrokles' fury increased. It was a death gift from Zeus. "Strip Sarpedon's armor," he bellowed. "Take it to the ships."

Patrokles' sword flashed and glinted as bodies piled up around him. When Hektor turned his chariot from the fight, Patrokles pursued him through the haze of war. As Automedon pushed Achilles' horses like the wind, a chilling breath pressed against Patrokles' ear. *"It's not your destiny to conquer Troy. Not even Achilles will take the shining city."*

"Apollo," Patrokles whispered. He grabbed the reins from Automedon and slowed the chariot.

"What are you doing?" the charioteer asked. "Why are you pulling back?"

"Apollo is among us."

Automedon shivered. "That is a bad omen."

"It's a warning. Achilles told me not—" Patrokles relaxed the reins and looked around him. His entire life had come to this very moment. He had not been a true contender for Helen, because he had nothing to offer. He would never have Briseis' love, because again he had nothing to offer her. And her heart belonged to the only man he would *not* kill for her. It dawned on him that this was the first time in all the long years of war that he faced battle without Achilles at his side. "No matter. It's too late now."

From across the fighting, through the hazy air, Patrokles saw Hektor approaching by chariot at breakneck speed. His heart filled with renewed hate, forgetting completely Achilles' caution. Handing the reins back to Automedon, he said, "Fly like the wind to Hektor." His charioteer snapped the leather, and the horses bolted forward.

Reaching for a sharp stone in a basket at his feet, Patrokles threw it with all his strength, hitting Hektor's charioteer between the eyes. The force of the blow knocked the man from his feet; his body tumbled from the platform. Hektor's chariot careened wildly through the chaos on the ground, running over the fallen and the fighting men.

Patrokles leapt from the moving chariot, racing to the body to strip the warrior of his armor. As he bent to unbuckle the breastplate, he turned to see Hektor charging on foot toward him with sword raised.

"Kebriones! You'll not take my brother's armor, Achilles," Hektor roared. "Not while I live."

Patrokles sneered beneath the glittering helm and stood. He unsheathed the sharp blade at his hip. "Then you will die."

Their swords clashed, singing the silver song of war, as the blades slid down to the hilts and parted. Both men, sweeping their weapons above their heads, put all their strength behind another blow. The resounding crash caught the attention of warriors from both sides. Men stopped mid-swing to watch the best of their respective worlds.

"Look, they fight over Kebriones' body!"

"Achilles will slay Hektor."

"Take the bastard's armor, Achilles!"

"Our prince is more honorable!"

Hektor reached for Kebriones' head to drag him away from Patrokles' murderous intent. "I won't let you defile my brother."

"Your brother?" Patrokles laughed, circling to grab the dead man by the feet. "How many whores does Priam have?" The gathering horde of on-lookers smashed their spears on their shields. Patrokles clawed the dead body from Hektor's grip and dragged it into a section of Greeks. The Trojans pushed forward, but a contingent of Myrmidons muscled to keep them at bay.

Kebriones' was stripped of his armor and spirited away to the beached ships. His naked and mutilated body lay in plain sight, covered in blood and shit. Fighting resumed, but confusion and chaos surrounded everyone.

Hektor cried out, "You will pay for this, Achilles!"

But Patrokles, fueled with war-rage, swept through a sea of Trojans, leaving more mutilated bodies behind. He hefted his spear for a fatal throw, but it shattered to splinters in his grasp. Then, without warning his shield fell from his shoulder, followed by his belt, taking his swords with it. Patrokles whispered in disbelief, "Apollo?"

"You should have listened to Achilles." Apollo undid the breast

plate and that clanged to the hard ground. *"Look around you. Where are your Myrmidons?"*

Patrokles quickly glanced around him. *I'm alone.* "Why, Apollo?"

With a swirl of mist to cloak him from mortal eyes, the shining god slammed his palm into Patrokles' back, stunning him and sending Achilles' helm to the dusty ground. *"Who are you to question me? Or the will of Zeus?"*

Nearby Trojans and Greeks stood aghast at an astounded and helpless Patrokles.

Murmurs rippled across the armies.

"That's not Achilles."

"Where is Achilles?"

"The gods trick our eyes."

A young Trojan warrior, whose beard barely darkened his chin, was emboldened to strike knowing that it wasn't the living god-like warrior beneath the shining armor. He stepped forward and hurled his spear deep into Patrokles' back below the dark braids. Achilles' companion fell to his knees. The youth sprinted to pull his spear out before returning to the circling crowd. Patrokles struggled to his feet, stumbling about the cleared center, looking for friendly eyes.

A mighty roar ripped from Hektor's throat, as he barreled through the throng with murder in his heart. "Prepare to meet the dead." With great precision, Hektor's spear caught Patrokles from behind, the blade sticking out from below his unprotected collar bone. Hektor then pierced Patrokles through the lower back.

Patrokles crashed to his knees, staring disbelievingly at the bloody bronze tip protruding from his stomach. He touched it with a shaking hand. The crowd of Greek and Trojan warriors fell silent. Hektor ruthlessly pulled his weapon free of its target. Leaning back, swaying like a drunkard, Patrokles tumbled to the ground. The circle widened and whispers of disbelief traveled like smoke through the throng.

"You're a fool to think you could storm my city." Taking his spear in his strong hand, he swung it in a wide arc. "Where is the mighty Achilles? Afraid to face me in combat, so sends *you* instead? A poor second."

Patrokles sputtered blood, trying to speak.

Hektor laughed wickedly. "Your companion can't save you now. No one can."

"Apollo ... stripped my armor. Knocked ... me ... to the ground. Without his help ... I would've killed you ... twenty times over." He coughed up more blood, as a burning pain shot through him. "You ... won't live long, Hektor. Your death song is already on Achilles' lips."

The Prince of Troy kicked Patrokles. "You're wrong. It will be *me* who kills Achilles."

Patrokles lay on wings of blood, his mouth opening and closing like a fish out of water gasping for breath. Looking up at Hektor, he watched the fire of war devour the prince's eyes. He tried to speak, but blood gurgled over his lips and at the corners of his mouth. His limbs became heavy. Coldness filled his body. *I am at the end.*

As shadows closed around his eyes, images floated before him in the growing darkness. Achilles laughing over a cup of wine. Achilles' heels kicking up sand as they raced along the shore. His fingers stitching a wound closed. Flies. The tang of salty air stinging his nose. Standing on the ship's railing. Dark birds flying above Lyrnessus ... Thebe.

Achilles, forgive me ... for everything. For her. I could not help but love her, too. A flash of light startled his eyes open. *Briseis? What are you doing here?* Bending over him, smiling, she leaned to kiss him. Reaching a hand to her cheek, as the God of Death stole him to the Underworld, Patrokles whispered, "Briseis …"

As Patrokles lay dead in the dust, Hektor stabbed him once more with his spear, stepping on the dead man's chest to yank his weapon free.

"Gather his armor … *Achilles'* armor, and take it to Troy." Several Trojans rushed to do as Hektor commanded.

The prince leveled his spear at a stunned Automedon, the unfortunate charioteer. Hektor's throw fell short. Automedon snapped out of his stupor and whipped the immortal horses to a frenzied flight. Hektor sprinted to his chariot, slipping here and there on slick, bloody mud. Reaching his transport, he leapt onto the platform, and bolted after Patrokles' retreating man.

TWENTY NINE
battle over Patrokles
AGAMEMNON'S RANKS—1238 BCE

"Get to Patrokles!" Menelaus screamed to his men. "Don't let the fucking Trojans steal his body!" Charging like a bull in an arena, the Spartan king rushed to Achilles' companion. He'd watched as Hektor stripped the armor, but had been too far afield to stop the atrocity of the final jab. With his sword slashing and glinting in the light, Menelaus carved a crimson path to the slain Myrmidon. He skidded to a stop when he reached him, holding his shield up to protect them both from stray arrows.

A young Trojan warrior dared emerge from the melee, confronting an enraged Menelaus. "I was first to fell that man we thought was Achilles. Stand aside so I can take my spoils."

Menelaus sneered. "You think I'll give Patrokles' body up to a scrawny fuck like you? I'll send your ass to the Underworld, boy, if you cross me."

"You're the one who killed my brother. Made his wife a widow. His children fatherless. If I bring your head on a pike, my family will have some satisfaction."

The Spartan King threw his head back, laughing. "Try me, boy." He positioned his feet and leveled his shield. "But be prepared to die."

The youth charged Menelaus with his spear held tight. At close range, he slammed the spear into Menelaus' shield but the tip merely bent against it. His eyes widened and the shaft slipped from his grasp. Like a lightning bolt, Menelaus' bronze spear shot over the rim of his shield, ripping the young man's throat open. The Trojan stumbled backward a few steps, before falling straight back, bashing his head against the hard ground. Blood quickly seeped into a lake around his head, his lifeless eyes still wide open, staring into the sky.

The King of Sparta ripped the man's armor off like a ravenous raven ripping flesh from bone. As he tossed the bloody bronze and leather into a pile, a cold finger ran up his spine. Knowing the godsign, he looked about him frantically. "Apollo," he whispered with a slight sneer. "Always fucking us."

"Hektor is coming for you, Red King. Can't you hear him?"

The icy whisper sliced across Menelaus' ear.

"Get this armor out of here!" he bellowed to some Greeks near him. Three men scurried to do his bidding. Picking up the gory prize, they ran with it toward the ships. It was then that he heard the furious roar of Hektor tearing through the air. "Fuck me. Where is Ajax?" Scanning the field, he searched for the Giant of Telemon.

When he saw Hektor's chariot riding roughly over dead bodies and men yet alive coming straight for him, he glanced at Patrokles' corpse. Menelaus frowned. "I will return. I promise." With that he abandoned Patrokles.

Once in earshot of the giant, Menelaus yelled, "Ajax! Come! Help me keep Hektor from stealing Patrokles from us."

Ajax sliced a Trojan almost in half with a single stroke. The unlucky man toppled over with his innards leaking like ghastly snakes from his belly. "Who's guarding Patrokles?"

Menelaus didn't want Ajax to think of him as a coward. "Apollo is on Hektor's side."

"Fucking gods," Ajax muttered. "You left Patrokles unguarded?"

"No time to argue, Ajax. Will you help me? You know I can't defeat Hektor alone, with a god backing him."

Together they shot across the grim ground, making their way back to Achilles' dead companion. Ajax bellowed, "Not this day, Hektor!"

Patrokles nude body was bent over Hektor's knee and one of the Trojan's hands was wrapped into his dark braids, the other held his blade high and ready to hack Patrokles' head from his shoulders. "By the gods," he mumbled. Still fueled by Apollo's word, he pushed Patrokles' body to the ground with a thud. "The King of Sparta requires aide, I see!"

The Giant of Telemon bore down on Hektor like rocks sliding down a mountain. Hektor let loose his spear. Ajax swiped the weapon away with his shield, as if batting away an annoying fly. The Prince of Troy pulled his sword from his belt, as Ajax tilted his shield, a lethal battering ram. The crash of bronze on bronze sang in the air, and Hektor fell back a step.

"I'll tear you in half," Ajax growled.

"You can try, Greek."

Ajax swept his shield around like a giant scythe, slamming it into Hektor's chest. Falling flat onto his back, Hektor winced when he drew breath. He ran his hand down his side, checking for a wound, and then rolled over, struggling to his knees. Before he could fully stand, Ajax brought his sword down on Hektor's helmet, cracking the mighty crest, sending Hektor back to the ground. Several Trojans rushed forward and pulled their prince to safety behind them.

"Coward," Ajax bellowed. "You're not worth the effort!" Returning to guard over Patrokles' body, he took position next to Menelaus once again. "The Trojans are cunts."

HEKTOR'S RETREAT

"Prince Hektor!" Glaukos yelled from the flank of retreating Trojan soldiers. "Prince Hektor!"

Hektor slowed his chariot. Seeing Glaukos, commander of the Lycian allies, he signaled his men to stop. His horses pranced nervously. "Easy, boys. Easy."

Glaukos rode his horse alongside the prince's. "Why are you leaving the field? The battle isn't over."

"I've taken Achilles' armor. Killed his second-in-command. Isn't that prize enough for one day?"

"No, it isn't. While the Greeks fight like wolves against your men for the body of Achilles' man, you would leave your dead, *our* dead, to their hands? What kind of coward are you? I didn't leave my homelands to follow a king or a prince who hasn't the stomach to finish this shitty war. I should take my men home, and mind you, if I do, your city will fall. Why don't you kill those fucking Greeks, grab Patrokles' body, and drag it into the city? Maybe then we could ransom Sarpedon's armor. But you're too afraid to stand against their giant."

Hektor resented his honor being questioned. But the truth of Glaukos' words wormed its way into his mind. He didn't fear Menelaus, but with the giant at his side doubts seized his bravery. "Zeus shifts his favor between both sides? The god decides who wins and loses. It's not up to men. I'm no coward, if that's what you're implying."

"Your actions speak otherwise, Prince Hektor. I won't follow a coward."

"Do as you wish, Glaukos. The Trojans have no need of you." As he signaled for his attendants to move forward, an icy chill ran down his spine.

A cold whisper pressed against his ear. *"Death is near, Hektor. Put Achilles' armor on. Win the day ... but soon Andromache will pay the price."*

Hektor shivered. *The gods.* "Hold," he bellowed. "Hold." The column came to a grinding halt again. He straightened his back. "Fetch me Achilles' armor."

"At last, the warrior emerges," Glaukos said. "Yes, put on Achilles' armor and fight them."

Within moments, the shining armor of Achilles was set before Hektor. Glaukos dismounted to help him don the stolen gear. The greaves. The breastplate. The shield. Golden and shining and still smeared with Patrokles' blood. The spirit of Ares shot through

Hektor's body. His courage surged. *This is what it feels like to be Achilles.*

Zeus whispered, *"Achilles needs no armor. Go. For I am done with you."*

The hairs on Hektor's body stood on end. He whispered defiantly beneath his breath, "This isn't the end." Mounting his chariot, Hektor wheeled around and galloped back to the front and addressed the allies and his men. He shone like a god in the stolen war-gear of Thetis' son.

"Men! You've come to fight alongside me. To send these fucking Greeks back to the sea. Back to whatever god-forsaken cities they came from. And I say this is the day we live or we die."

A mighty cheer rose from the gathering army. Spears and swords slammed against bronze shields.

The Prince of Troy rallied his army for another charge at the enemy. Hektor's shrill call to war thundered over his warriors. Heading straight for the ragged group protecting Patrokles, the Trojan forces startled the Greeks struggling to hold their ground over the dead body of Achilles' man.

Menelaus pulled his shield tighter to his chest. "Don't break the wall. Keep your shields held fast."

Ajax spat into the dirt at his feet. "He's wearing Achilles' armor, that fucking bastard. Men! Circle up. If we don't get Patrokles back to camp, Achilles will be far fiercer than these fucks."

A mist rose around the fighting.

The full force of the Trojan charge crashed on the Greek shield wall like a stormy wave breaks on a rocky shore. In the pushing and shoving of shields, the Trojans grabbed hold of Patrokles and pulled him within their ranks.

Ajax broke formation, wading through the disintegrating battle to get to the man dragging the body of Achilles' beloved by the ankle. Raising his sword, he brought down all his hatred in one swing. The ill-fated Trojan fell to his knees with half his helmet falling to the ground with half his brains. As he bent to lift Patrokles, a spear shaft whizzed passed his ear. He turned to see Hektor reaching for another.

Heaving the dead weight over his shoulders, Ajax ran toward the Greek circle. "Fucking, Hektor!"

The Greeks circled tighter around Patrokles, three circles of men deep. In the center stood Ajax, barking commands and threats. "No retreat! No retreat! Stand close. Be unbreakable, men. Think of Achilles' rage if we should fail. Fear him more than these dog-faced Trojans!"

Groans of agreement sang through the men.

Someone muttered, "If they take him, it would be better for us to die where we stand than face Achilles' wrath."

Someone else grunted, "I pity Achilles. He has no idea Patrokles was slain or his armor taken."

As the Trojan forces crested over the Greeks' shields, their bodies soon littered the ground as shells scattered on a beach. The ground greedily drank their blood and the battlefield became a consecrated temple to Ares.

Menelaus' arms tired. His foot slipped. Sweat dripped and burned into his eyes. "Ajax," he huffed, "they're going to push us back."

"Stand your ground, Menelaus. Stand your ground!" Ajax bellowed from behind.

"Do not give up, King Menelaus."

"Athena?"

"It is I."

The cold words warmed Menelaus and strengthened his limbs. "Why does Zeus favor them, not us?"

"Think of your reputation."

"Ajax! We can't win when Zeus is against us." Dust choked down Menelaus' throat. "We must retreat."

"We should send word to Achilles. He doesn't even know what happened." Ajax, taller than the rest, scanned beyond the close fighting. "We need a messenger. A Myrmidon. I can't see the field beyond us. This *fucking* mist blinds everything."

As if on command, the air cleared and sunlight drenched the circle fighting to protect Achilles' dead companion. "Menelaus, the Black Shields are to the east of us. Send a man to find someone Achilles trusts to carry the news about Patrokles."

"To what end? He will not come and fight. He has no armor."

Ajax roared, "Let Achilles decide what he will do. Send your man. We need to move Patrokles' body from this fight or—"

"Or all is lost."

Ajax grimaced. "Agreed."

Easing himself from the men at his left and right, Menelaus backed to the center of the men around Patrokles. Meeting Ajax's eyes, he said, "If I fail …"

Ajax clapped the king hard on the shoulder. "Have faith. You won't. We may die on this foreign land, but gods be damned if we die like cowards."

Menelaus nodded.

"Now, pick him up and run. I'll keep the Trojan dogs occupied long enough for you to escape."

Groaning under the dead weight, Menelaus mumbled, "You're

heavier than I thought you'd be." Positioning a lifeless Patrokles over his shoulder, Menelaus muscled his way through the back of the circle out of Hektor's line of sight.

Ajax yelled, "Push them back to Troy!" The shoving of shields renewed with vigor. "That's it, men!" Dust filled the air as the Greeks shuffled their feet to defend the empty space where Achilles' second had lain. But without the body, they lost heart and strength.

With one last charge, Hektor broke the ferocious line. The Greeks fled in all directions of the melee.

THIRTY
the shield of Achilles
AGAMEMNON'S CAMP—1238 BCE

Achilles paced the deck of his ship, the sun-faded planks warm beneath his feet. Three empty amphorae lay scattered about, yet even deep into his wine solace eluded him. Thetis' warning echoed in his ears. *Was I wrong to let Patrokles go?* He recalled his cousin's eagerness to fight in his stead. *How long has it been?* He scanned the distant horizon where a dust cloud hung like a dark omen. The battle continued, he knew, as long as men could kick up the dirt. *What if Patrokles—*

No! He pushed the thought down. *What if—*

"My lord."

Startled from his thoughts, Achilles glanced below the railing to see Antilochus standing there wringing his hands. "What news from the field?"

Antilochus choked. "My lord, I ..."

Dread fingered its way up Achilles' spine. He inhaled sharply.

"Where is Patrokles?" He narrowed his eyes. "Where are my Myrmidons?"

"They continue fighting."

"And Patrokles with them?"

Antilochus dropped to his knees, tears streaming clean lines down his dirty cheeks. "He … he … *fell*, my lord."

Achilles leapt from his ship to the shallow surf. He grabbed Antilochus by the neck, squeezing his fingers into his flesh. Antilochus' face reddened, and then purpled. "You are mistaken. He had my armor. My shield. My blessing. Where. Is. Patrokles?"

Antilochus shook his head. Achilles roughly tossed him to the sand where he gasped for breath. He choked out, "Menelaus sent me. The battle rages. He thought you should know." Antilochus wept bitterly. "Hektor stripped him of your armor."

Achilles stiffened. "He went beyond the ships?"

"Aye."

Fear flooded Achilles. He whispered to himself, "That was the only order I gave him. Not to go beyond the ships. Not to challenge Hektor man to man."

"Patrokles was glorious in battle, my lord. He fought as you. The Trojans never knew, until the end."

The truth tore through Achilles' heart. His voice broke when he asked, "Then, he has truly fallen?"

Antilochus nodded, wiping blackened snot from his nose. "Aye. Menelaus and Ajax fight to keep the Trojans from stealing his body. Hektor … Hektor stabbed him over and over again."

For the first time in his life, Achilles weakened and sank to his knees in the sand. He murmured bitterly, "I have killed him." The weight of Patrokles' death slowly filled his chest. "Who am I without him?" The grief of war rattled his bones. He looked to Antilochus. His voice cracked once again as he said, "I have killed him." He stood abruptly and walked to the nearest fire pit with Antilochus anxiously trailing behind him.

Kneeling before the cold ring of blackened stones, Achilles released a mournful howl. A wave of grief, as deep as the raging sea, shook Achilles to his core. He was helpless to stop the gathering storm. "I have killed him," he cried out again. After scooping up handfuls of the gray ash, he smeared it over his head. "I have sent him to his death." Tearing out several ratted braids, he made a bloody mess of his scalp. He ripped the front of his tunic open and wept like a lost child.

Antilochus ceased weeping at the sight of Achilles' in such a state. "I never—" Quickly, he leapt to Achilles' side, just as the flash of bronze gleamed at Achilles' throat. "No!" He grabbed Achilles' wrist. "No!" He clung to the Myrmidon commander, refusing to let go.

Achilles mourned aloud against Antilochus' shoulder. As tears streamed down his cheeks, Patrokles' image rose before him. His dark eyes dancing with mischief and scolding. His tender hands sewing an open wound. His shoulder pressed next to his in battle. His hardy laughter when deep into his wine. "What have I done? What have I done?"

With a stinging pain, his mother's veiled words returned to haunt him. *"This war will take everything from you."*

"I never thought to see a day without him, Mother. Half my heart has been torn from my chest."

Antilochus said, "My lord, you must save what remains of Patrokles. Give him all honor."

Sinking heavily into the Myrmidon, he said, "I have no armor." Achilles screamed up at the sky, "Why do you curse me? Why?

You've taken the better part of me. He wasn't supposed to die here." He wept until his voice was hoarse and his eyes were dry. "He wasn't supposed to die before me." Antilochus held his commander until the initial grief abated. Slowly, Achilles got to his feet. Surveying the empty camp, he said, "Now, I'm dead, before I die."

SILVER CAVE OF THETIS

The strand of pearls in Thetis' hands dropped, sending the beads bouncing along the rocky cave floor. She closed her eyes and bowed her head. The wail was unmistakable, though she'd never heard it before. It was Achilles. Without second thought, she raced to the sea and dove into the surf, swimming as a flash of light beneath the waves to the shore of the Myrmidon's camp. Emerging from the water, she saw her son—a wretched heap of rags and with a bloodied scalp. Behind him a half-circle of Myrmidons stood, watching and waiting. They fell to their knees in her presence.

She approached Achilles, her feet barely impressing on the soft sand. Kneeling beside him, she tenderly caressed his temple. "Achilles, I am here."

"Mother," he cried out in a tone foreign to her ears. He reached for her. "Mother, he is gone."

Pulling her son's head into her lap, she thought of the small child she'd tried to burn in the sacred fire. Burn him to save him. Save him from all that would ever pain him. But, she'd failed. Her precious son was now sprawled in the sand, weeping like a little boy. She carefully stroked his head, avoiding the bloodied spots where he'd mutilated his head.

"What has happened, Achilles?" For the first time in her immortal life, she feared the words he would say. Her heart cracked with a pain she'd never felt before. She wept quietly, tears spilling like liquid pearls down her cheeks. She knew this was the beginning of the end. The end of her son. The boy she'd loved above all things in this mortal world. She tried to protect him, but clearly, she realized now, she could not. His mortal shell would pass and she would live an eternity with the growing ache of his loss. "Achilles," she whispered softly. "My sweet boy."

"He's dead, Mother. Patrokles is dead."

She bent her graceful head to his and kissed his filthy cheek. "I am sorry, Achilles."

"Hektor stripped my armor from his body. It is my fault he has died."

All the moments leading to this terrible scene crashed into Thetis' mind. The dual fate of her son was always meant to be a curse. The gods would never allow a mortal so beautiful and terrifying to survive long in the world. Fate always beckoned him down the shorter road. She realized now that Achilles never really had a chance at the long life she so desperately wanted him to grasp. Thetis cried aloud to the heavens, knowing Zeus would hear her, "You have betrayed me. You restore his honor, only to take his life."

"I want to die, Mother. Take me beneath the waves."

"Once you kill Hektor, the gods will take you." The words fell from her lips like rocks tumbling down a mountain. How long ago had fate spun this web of grief? Achilles was made for war, yet he had been allowed to love. And it had destroyed him. Love for a woman had cost him his honor, and love for a man would cost him his life.

"I can hardly remember my life before Patrokles. Everywhere I turned he was there. Now, he is gone."

Thetis resumed stroking Achilles' cheek. Words failed her.

"I drank myself into oblivion for the sake of my honor. How cheap did I hold Patrokles' life? I have done nothing but drink. Feel regret. Drink more."

"Shah, Achilles. In your heart, you already know what you will do. As do I. Hektor may have your armor, but he won't have it for long. His death is coming for him. I see it in your eyes. I will go to Hephaestus myself. Beg him to forge you new armor and weapons. Do you have your father's ash spear and his horses?"

"Aye."

Taking her son by the chin, she sought a promise in his eyes. "Do not seek your revenge, until I return at dawn." She could hear the God of Death approaching and she was helpless to stop what was coming.

"I will wait, then," Achilles said, tears breaking anew down his cheeks. "What else can I do?"

Thetis disappeared into the sea.

Achilles collapsed to the sand again, his limbs too heavy to walk to his ship. His heart too heavy for life. His mind bent on Patrokles and his regrets. "I am lost."

Above him the sky swept by. Before him the surf crashed. Behind him war raged on without him still. And he did not care. He closed his eyes, empty of tears, willing the darkness to fill him.

"Achilles."

"Leave me be, Athena."

"I cannot. Hektor is chasing Menelaus who carries Patrokles' body. He is calling for Patrokles' head on a spike."

The world stilled. Then, the flame of rage slowly pushed

Achilles' grief aside, filling him with slow burning hate. He sat bolt upright. "He must not defile his body."

"Only you can stop Hektor now. Apollo's power fuels his fighting."

Achilles scoffed, grabbed a handful of sand, threw it in the air, and then screamed aloud, "I have no fucking armor." He held his head in his hands, defeated and frustrated. "I could borrow Ajax's, but he is in the battle … wearing it. No one else is big enough." As his mind strategized a way to fight, he remembered his words to Thetis. Achilles hesitated. "I promised my mother I would wait until dawn. Help me, Athena."

"Do you trust me, Achilles?"

Athena's words raised every hair on his body. He remembered every moment of his life when the gods aided or thwarted him. Every decision he'd made had brought him here. To this sandy spot. To this torment. To this grief. He stood, brushing the sand from his arms. "Men have no choice but to trust the gods."

The goddess whirled about Achilles in a golden mist. The nearby Myrmidons fell back in fear, murmuring protective prayers. *"Go to the highest hill."* She turned Achilles' head. *"There. Show yourself to the Trojans."*

Without question, Achilles strode through the camp, stepping over dead bodies and ignoring surprised Myrmidons gathered around their ships. Standing on the eastern edge of camp, Achilles hiked to the top of the hill made from the dirt the Greeks had piled up when they dug their massive ditch. The sky raged red and orange. Achilles watched the fighting for a moment. "They are losing badly, Athena. Hektor fights like a god. Why do you care about me now? Why not go to Odysseus?"

"You are the key to defeating the Trojans. You have always known

that truth." Athena touched Achilles' forehead. The goddess' power filled him. "*Speak.*"

Achilles spotted Menelaus running with a body draped across his shoulders, dodging spears and arrows. He saw Hektor bearing down on him in a chariot. He opened his mouth and his voice rose as a thunderous roar echoing over the heads of every warrior in the camp and beyond. Sparks of fire and gold shot from around Achilles' head. Startled horses bolted, tossing riders and charioteers to the ground. Men fell to their knees, covering their ears, weeping that a god was among them. Hektor's chariot careered dangerously close to tipping. Achilles shouted, "A storm of blood is coming!" He unleashed an anguished howl again and again. The Trojans and their allies fled from the ships back to the plain and their own camp.

With the enemy hastily withdrawing from the camp, Menelaus was able to get Patrokles' body to a waiting litter. The wild fire of Patrokles' death had already spread through the army, but not a single tear could be shed while death hammered at them. Seeing Patrokles' broken body laid before them was enough to break every heart. Men gathered around and wept like lost children. If Patrokles could be taken, then death was surely waiting for them all.

A long, dark shadow fell across Patrokles' body, and the gathering hushed. Achilles approached with heavy footsteps. He stopped, Patrokles just beyond his reach. His iron heart once again broke with the heat of his anguish. "I have done this to him," he said in a whisper of shock. "It is my fault." Achilles stepped up to Patrokles' side, his eyes taking in the gory wounds. "I loved you above all men." The once steady hand that had murdered thousands now shook as he brushed the black blood crusted with sand from Patrokles' face and neck. "You are so pale." He closed Patrokles' dead eyes. Then, he passed his hand over Patrokles' shoulder that was nearly cleft from his body. Blood and filth and shit covered the dead man's thighs. Overwhelmed, Achilles fell over Patrokles' chest. "I should have never let him go," he sobbed, as a mother who has lost a child.

Achilles' grief shocked those standing nearby, and they could not help but cry watching the great warrior unravel before their eyes. Their tears fell unchecked for the fallen best of men, Patrokles, and for their own losses. The war had stolen their youth and robbed them of their families. It had also taken beloved companions of them all to the Underworld.

Achilles lifted his head, his mouth a gaping black hole of misery. "I have done this to him." Greeks and Myrmidons alike fell to their knees, keening and groaning with him. "I promised him he'd return home with glory and gold. Now, we will both die in this fucking place. Neither of us will ever see home again."

"You must, my lord," whispered a dozen of Myrmidons.

"Now I understand what the gods intended all along." He kissed Patrokles on the forehead. "I promise you, Patrokles, I will not hold the sacred fire to your bones until I lay Hektor's armor and bloody head at your feet. I will drench the pyre wood with Trojan blood. Our tears will be unceasing until I do."

Briseis startled as an anguished cry rent the night air, echoing across the camp. The hairs on her arm stood on end. She was certain it was a man keening not a woman. Earlier she'd heard the commotion of thousands of feet dragging through camp. She stole a glance through a crack in the tent flap. The guards remained posted on either side of the opening. The camp itself was strangely still. A few women and children walked here and there. Another wail ripped through the air. Braving the guards' anger, she pushed her head through. "What's happening?"

The guard on the left eyed her cautiously. "The Myrmidons have returned with the army."

"The Myrmidons? Achilles fights?"

Annoyed, the guard hit at the tent flap with the butt of his spear. "No, not Achilles. Now, shut up and get back in the tent."

Retreating, Briseis stood alone in the middle of her prison. The shabby linens rumpled on the makeshift bed, the reeking piss pot in the corner, and the bare table all reminded her of who she really was. "I've been a fool all this time." A third blood-curdling scream ripped through the night. She relieved herself in the piss pot.

Something is wrong. Soon, the droning grief of hundreds of men's voices hung in the air. She called out again, "What's going on? What's wrong?"

One of the guards answered, "Someone has fallen."

"Who?"

The guards shouted back, "Shut up."

When she lived in Achilles' tent, she knew everything that was happening between Achilles' evening talks and Nax's gossip. Since she'd been taken as Agamemnon's, she'd been isolated and was told nothing. She surveyed the shabbiness of her tent. It was hard to imagine she'd been a queen once, living with fine linens, gowns, and jewelry. It was truly another lifetime ago. She sat on the lumpy mattress, scratching at several sand flea bites.

The war for the Spartan princess had lasted longer than anyone believed possible. It had changed all their lives, and as far as she could tell, mostly for the worse. The wailing continued for a while longer, and then faded into the distance.

A breath of chill air brushed her cheek. She shivered, pulling the blanket to her chin. A shadow in the corner of her eye caught her attention. "Patrokles?" Briseis sat up, straining to see in the dark.

A familiar voice whispered, *"I could not help but love you."* But no one was there.

"The gods wouldn't dare …" Briseis pressed her hands together and beat her forehead. "Not Patrokles. By all the gods, not Patrokles."

Achilles' cheek was smeared with a mixture of Patrokles' and his own blood, so he refused to wash. He tenderly scooped up Patrokles' body in his arms like a mother carrying a sick child and walked in silence to his tented ship, each step a painful stride into the unknown. A fog clouded his mind. Patrokles' cold weight in his arms. Patrokles' face pressed against his chest. The truth was a nightmare from which he wanted to awaken, but the God of Dreams refused to release him. One step, then another. The women and Myrmidons trailed behind him like tears.

Achilles gently laid Patrokles on the table that had been hastily prepared for his body's final preparations. "You did not deserve this end. I should have been your shield against death, but …" he whispered, as he positioned his companion's arms along the torso. His hand lingered on Patrokles' bloody thigh. "The gods are cruel to take you in your prime."

Myrmidons wiped tears from their eyes. How many tragedies had unfolded? How many more were to come? If Patrokles could fall, perhaps they were all doomed. But no one uttered a word. Under a cloud of sorrow, the women filled a bronze basin with scented water to wash the filth of war from Patrokles' body. They moved with ritualistic grace. Their skilled hands purified Patrokles of dried shit and blood.

Achilles startled the woman who'd begun to wash Patrokles' hair. "Stop." She stepped back and she handed him the water jug. He tipped it, spilling the water over Patrokles' head. One by one his hands deftly worked the blood and dirt from each braid. He worked in silence, stifling his tears. Achilles kissed Patrokles' cold cheek when he was finished. The women rubbed perfumed oil on his skin and filled his wounds with bittersweet rosemary. Finally, they wrapped him in a linen shroud.

"He is no more," Achilles said. His eyes stone cold. His voice certain. "Only vengeance remains."

TROJAN CAMP

Across the plain, in the temporary safety of their camps, the Trojans dreaded the dawn. For when the pink fingers of the day raked the sky, Achilles would be leading the enemy. God-like. Shining. Murderous. The boisterous talk of the day was silenced. A cloud of doom settled over their tents and fires. Men talked of abandoning the battle and fleeing to the far south. Some gathered around fires, wringing their hands. Others took to wine and women.

In the center of the main encampment, Hektor paced with his racing thoughts. His brothers and commanders waited. "Did you see him standing there like a god?" Hektor groaned. "Kebriones.

What Achilles' second did to our brother …"

Paris looked at Hektor. The other men shifted their weight. They all feared the gleaming image on the hill.

Hektor asked aloud, "Which god favors him now?"

Paris' brow furrowed. "Why does it matter? He has returned to the war. We knew that one day he would. Now, that day is here."

The Prince of Troy shook his head in disbelief. "If we sacrifice to the right god, the favor will once again be ours. We were so close to final victory."

Paris spoke the words no one else dared utter. "You killed his companion. We all know what he will become. We have all seen it happen before."

Hektor's face soured. "I had to do it. Kebriones may have been our father's bastard, but he had our blood."

Paris' voice was somber when he replied, "There will be no mercy now. We should retreat to the city. As long as Achilles was angrier at Agamemnon than us, we had hope of victory. But after what happened, he will not be satisfied with victory on the plain. He will want our city; take our women and our children. Rape them. Make them slaves. Tonight, he weeps for his companion, but make no mistake his wrath will be unstoppable come the dawn. It's best we defend ourselves from the ramparts."

"Those are the words of a coward," Hektor said. "Haven't you all tired of sitting behind the wall? Hiding like small children behind their mothers?"

"Do you mock me on Helen's account? Aphrodite took me—"

"Shut up, Paris. We will have Zeus' favor once again. I know it. I will order the sacrifices. We can't retreat now. I will face Achilles come the dawn. Only then will we know who the better man is."

"This is the beginning of the end," Paris said quietly.

"It has been long enough," Hektor said. "Go, the rest of you. Spread the word. We fight at first light."

OLYMPUS

Thetis arrived at Hephaestus' forge on Olympus. She knew the way inside. The stone floor was cold under her silent feet. She brushed her hand along the glittering walls, smooth to the touch. Above, the purple sky was dotted with stars. She'd always marveled that in Olympus the halls of all houses had no ceiling but the deep heavens. The clang of metal on metal drew her inward toward the forge chamber.

"Thetis, I knew you were coming," Hephaestus said, not bothering to look up from his handiwork. "It is not safe for you to be here."

"I was careful."

The god looked at her now, wiping the soot and sweat from his brow. "No one is careful enough where Hera is concerned." He stepped toward Thetis, limping on his bent leg. "I should know."

"Apologies, Hephaestus. I had to come."

"Charis, we have a guest."

A woman of dark skin and eyes appeared. An aura of golden light surrounded her, enhancing her beauty. She reached for Thetis' hand. "What has happened that you would take such a risk coming here?" Charis ushered the nymph to a silver chair. "Please, sit. Ambrosia?"

"If it pleases you, my lady Charis."

Charis clapped her hands, and three mechanical maidens appeared. Smooth gold was their skin. Their bodies were shaped with the modest curves of women. Their heads were bare of hair and their eyes were sparkling sapphires. They wore no garments and walked without shame. "Bring the ambrosia and cups. Help my husband prepare for his guest."

"Yes, lady Charis." The maidens spoke in unison with voices as rich and as smooth as their exteriors. They moved with unexpected grace. Forged of gold by Hephaestus' own hand, he'd endowed them with the gifts of speech and presence of mind.

"They are exquisite," Thetis said.

"They are quite helpful," Charis replied, as the maidens returned with the god's nectar and cups. "Hephaestus, come. I believe Thetis is in need of your services."

The golden women washed the forge god and dressed him in a fresh tunic. He wrapped a simple belt of leather with a silver clasp about his waist. Joining his wife and Thetis, he took his seat. "You are not yourself. I can see it in your eyes. What has happened that you require my service?"

"So many things …."

"You alone cared for me when I was cast down from this place. You showered me with motherly affection when I had none. Whatever you ask, I cannot refuse."

The nymph fingered a gem-encrusted pin in her long, black hair. "I kept all your lovely gifts."

Hephaestus leaned forward in his chair, resting his massive forearms on his thighs. "Thetis, why have you come?"

"You know the hardship I endured married to a mortal man. Forgotten by Zeus."

"I do."

"Peleus resents me. His anger toward me festers. He did not understand immortal ways. Our ways. Our reasoning." Tears threatened to spill. "I was blessed with a son, Hephaestus. A son whose fate is now set—"

"In the war below that Zeus has forbidden us from interfering in." Hephaestus' chair creaked under his weight. Charis placed her hand on her husband's. "The love I bear you cannot set me at odds with Zeus. I cannot intervene."

"Achilles will never return home to his father. Or to me. His days grow shorter now because he is my son. He has offended no gods."

"What has happened to Achilles now?"

"Agamemnon took his woman. Achilles was angry. Who could blame him? He has wallowed in grief and wine, staying away from battle. Forbidding his men to fight. But Patrokles, his most beloved, convinced Achilles to let him wear his armor and fight in his stead."

"A deception for the Trojans."

"Hektor killed Patrokles and stripped his armor as a prize. Now, when Achilles' grief moves him to fight, he has no protection. No armor to guard his mortal flesh."

Rising from his chair, Hephaestus said, "Have no fear, Thetis. Achilles shall have the most splendid armor ever forged for a man."

Hephaestus worked the entire evening and into the night without rest, hammering and shaping the shining armor. In the morning as the stars faded, he brought the armaments to Thetis. She held up the great shield with its images immortalizing the war and Achilles' fate. Circling the outer edges were the earth, the sky, and the sea. The sun and moon and stars symbols of Achilles' fate foretold by prophecy and set in motion by Zeus' hand. Two great cities. A wedding. Thetis thought of Peleus. The apple cast by Eris. Fields and orchards ready for harvest. A peaceful life Achilles would never know. The legacy of two houses and the battle between them. The war that Achilles now fought.

Thetis' trembling fingers traced the image of one man standing, with a dead man being dragged by the feet. "Which one is Achilles?" Until this moment she hadn't thought about *how* he would die.

"Does it matter, Thetis? In your heart, you have always known it would come to this."

"If only he'd remained in Skyros."

"Achilles was not made for the quiet life you wished for him."

Brushing the rim of the shield, Thetis sighed. "I don't know if I can live forever without him."

"No matter his choice, Thetis, your hands were always meant to bury him."

"It is a final cruelty, is it not? Giving me a mortal son? Being a childless mother to mourn forever."

THIRTY ONE

AGAMEMNON'S CAMP—1238 BCE

A restless night broke to a red cloud dawn. Thetis moved swiftly through the Myrmidon camp. Their fires smoldered with blackened wood and ash. The drone of anguish had hushed. Dogs stirred as she swept in a magical blur. Men lay awake, contemplating their mortality. How swiftly mortal life moved at the end of all things.

Thetis found Achilles by his ship, weeping over Patrokles' body. She approached with caution. She laid Hephaestus' sacred gifts at his feet. "Achilles?" She touched his shoulder. "Achilles, I have returned as promised."

Achilles' breath hitched in his throat. He lifted his gaze to her. His eyes were clouded and unrecognizable. His face swollen.

"My poor, sweet son."

Achilles picked up the shield first, admiring the intricate work with his eyes and hands. He leaned it against the table beneath Patrokles. Then, he hefted the glittering helm. "These are more than I hoped for."

"Try them on," Thetis said. "You can mourn for Patrokles when the day is done."

Achilles' dull eyes now sparked with rage. "I will kill them all, Mother. Every last one. May I ask one last favor?"

Thetis' heart grew heavier with the word *last*. "Ask what you will."

"Keep his flesh from rot and worms … and the flies, until I can send him properly to the Underworld."

"I will do as you request," Thetis said, then slipped beneath the water in a mist.

With that, Achilles fastened his newly forged armor on. Each piece fitted with perfection. He donned the mighty helm and unleashed a terrifying war cry, startling the entire camp awake. Men ran from their tents, thinking the battle had begun without them, only to glimpse Achilles followed by a contingent of Myrmidons heading toward Agamemnon's camp.

Outside of the Great King's tent, two guards nervously faced Achilles. "Let me pass," he demanded. One guard slipped inside. "Agamemnon! I come to make terms with you."

A young slave boy appeared and held the tent flap open. He put his head down as Achilles' enormous frame passed him. Agamemnon was already seated at his table. Achilles sat opposite him.

"Wine?" Agamemnon offered.

"I've had my fill of wine. I thirst only for blood."

The king held up his cup in salute. "Achilles has returned."

"I see now that my absence caused much suffering among the

men. Something they are not likely to forget. And over a woman."

"I should never have taken Briseis from you. Zeus made me too bold."

"It would have been better if some sickness had taken her." He told himself that if Briseis had died long ago, then he would not have loved her. In his mind, he could hear Patrokles scolding him. *Lies, Achilles. Lies.*

"We can't change what burdens the gods have already bestowed on us. They have played us both for fools. I will give you all I promised before, and ... I will return your woman *untouched* by my hands. Let us feast before we fight."

"I will feast once I have satisfied my revenge."

The tent flap opened, startling Briseis who was huddled in a wretched heap on her mattress. She'd hardly slept all night, waking several times to piercing cries and the drone of mourning. With swollen and bloodshot eyes, she squinted into the torch light, lifting a hand to shield the glare. Three of Agamemnon's men stood before her in their faded and frayed crimson capes with their helmets in the crooks of their arms.

The stockiest one commanded, "Get up, woman."

Briseis froze. Her throat squeezed tightly around words. Slowly, she rose from the bed. "Where are you taking me?"

"Agamemnon has called you to a private assembly."

Before she could stop herself, she asked, "Why?" It didn't matter why. She knew why. She'd dreaded this day since they dragged her from Achilles' tent. Patrokles had warned her that eventually

Agamemnon would claim her as his proper prize. *Enough time has passed. He's given me no word. Not responded to my letter. Even Patrokles has abandoned me.* Briseis slowly rose from the bed. "I'm ready." *Agamemnon will never know that I'm frightened. I will not scream and weep for his pleasure.*

The king's guard led her through a maze of tents to the great pavilion in the center of camp. Fire cauldrons burned brightly at its entrance. Smoke from spits roasting meat filled the air. Briseis' eyes darted about the camp. Women busied themselves at cook fires and soldiers polished and sharpened their weapons. She was surprised to see Myrmidons among Agamemnon's men. Myrmidons had gathered around fires, speaking softly to one another and some openly weeping. *He means to take me with an audience?* Her knees quaked, and she stumbled in the soft sand. One of the guards caught her by the elbow and steadied her. Despite her resolve to be brave, a hot tear escaped down her cheek.

Two century guards opened the pavilion's draping, pushing her through the entrance. She tripped on an edge of carpet and stumbled into the center of the gathering. Agamemnon sat at a large table laden with bread and cheese and wine, maps and stratagem pieces were scattered about the platters. Menelaus stood across from him drinking a cup of wine. All eyes were on her as she stood shaking under their scrutiny. She saw Odysseus, Diomedes, Ajax, Nestor … and Achilles sat alone, apart from the rest. She did not see Patrokles.

She dared another glance at Achilles, who looked as wretched as she did. His scalp was a dark, bloody mess of raw skin where chunks of his hair were missing. His golden face was swollen and filthy. He gave no sign of acknowledging her.

Agamemnon motioned her to come closer. "I've good news for

you, woman."

Briseis remained mute. Every hair on her body rose in fear.

"Don't you want to know, Briseis? What's in store for you?"

Her eyes nervously darted from Achilles to Agamemnon then to her feet. *How can he just sit there? Even if he chooses to discard me, he begged me to remember him that night. Why is his head a bloody mess? Has he been beaten?* She brushed that thought away, for no one could lay a hand on him unless he allowed it. And that she couldn't imagine was even possible.

Agamemnon twisted a golden ring around his thumb. "Have I treated you poorly?"

"I've been treated as any other slave."

"Have I defiled you? Harmed you?"

Briseis looked up and folded her arms across her chest, painfully squeezing her fingers into her flesh, willing herself not to cry. Her mouth twitched. "Other than taking me from Achilles? No."

Menelaus coughed with a mouthful of wine. "You dare speak to the king with disrespect?"

Agamemnon eased back into his chair, as he signaled a slave boy to clean up Menelaus' wine. "If I was your master, I'd beat the sharpness from your tongue."

I'd rather be beaten than raped. Please, Athena, let him beat me. Don't let him take me in front of all these men. She braved a quick glance at Achilles, aloof and uninterested in her plight. *He is not the Achilles that I knew. Patrokles would never allow this. Maybe Achilles keeps him away on purpose, so Agamemnon could do as he pleases with me.*

Pushing away from the table, Agamemnon addressed the small gathering of men. "I'm sure you are all waiting to hear why you've been summoned under the … circumstances. I've reached an agreement with Achilles. He's agreed to fight with us once again." A small cheer echoed around the tent. "We begin the final assault after we fill our bellies and fuck our women. Boy!"

A young slave, in a long line of nameless slaves since Palamedes, appeared from behind a partition. His squeaky voice quivered in the king's presence. "Yes, my king?"

"Go to the heralds and tell them Achilles has rejoined the fight. Tell them we feast before the battle. Tell the men outside to bring Achilles his gifts."

The boy nodded and darted off. It wasn't long before the sound of cheering rose from the camp. Women draped in little more than scarves with silver and gold bracelets lined up their arms were brought into the tent. Baskets of jewels and coins and shimmering fabrics followed. Amphora after amphora of wine was set before Achilles. Briseis could see that Achilles' mind was elsewhere. Her mind reeled with reasons to explain Achilles' behavior. He should be pleased to fight again. He is rid of her, as she always feared he would do. Nothing she conjured seemed that catastrophic. Maybe something happened to his mother. They were closely bonded. Or Patrokles?

Briseis dared voice her question. "Achilles, where is Patrokles?" Achilles said nothing, but the assembly grew quiet. "Patrokles … Achilles, do you hear me? Where is he?"

Achilles slowly turned his face to her, as if the very effort of lifting his head caused him great pain. His blue eyes had lost their fire. "He's gone," he said quietly.

Patrokles would never leave Achilles' side, not even for an army of his own. And the Myrmidons had not been to battle on account of her … and Agamemnon. But then she remembered the Myrmidons were in Agamemnon's camp. "To Phthia?"

"He's dead." Achilles looked right through her, before he cast his head down. "That is enough talk for me. Feast as you all see fit. Send my portion to my ships. My men will dispense with it there." Achilles stood, and without looking back, headed out. Achilles stood, waving his hand for Agamemnon's slaves to follow with his treasure.

Two of Agamemnon's guards grabbed Briseis roughly by the elbows, ushering her out behind the other women. "Wait! Where are you taking me?"

"You crusty bitch. Back to Achilles you go," one of the guards said gruffly.

"I'd have thrown her into the whores' tents and left her there to rot. It's her fault Achilles left and so many of us died."

"No, it was Agamemnon's. He shouldn't have taken her in the first place. We all knew it. But still," he tugged Briseis' elbow, "so many of *us* did die on her account."

As the guards argued, Briseis processed the news Achilles so gravely and unexpectedly delivered. She wanted to deny it, scream to the heavens that it wasn't true. Couldn't be true. She stumbled again and the guards dragged her until she found her footing. The nightmare of Patrokles' death unfolded with each step. *Patrokles. My sweet, dear Patrokles. What will become of me without you?* For endless days her anguish over Achilles' betrayal had haunted her, broke her in ways she had not thought possible. Her grief over Achilles' absence now paled against this sudden ache for Patrokles. She wept freely, hopeless now of happiness in any form.

Agamemnon's slaves carried the extensive wealth he'd gifted Achilles, while the female prizes trailed behind, huddled in a little group for protection. The walk to Achilles' tented ship lasted an eternity. She wondered what would happen to all of them and if her life with Achilles was nothing more than a lie she believed to survive. Achilles had barely acknowledged her presence since she'd been returned. Now, she knew why, but also worried it might be more than that. If he discovered what she'd done...she shuddered to think what might happen then.

Over the last crusty sand dune, the entourage came to a halt. The jolt pulled Briseis back to the world she wanted to forget. Not far off, she saw him. *Patrokles*. A glittering gauze shroud covered him. Fires burned in massive bronze basins circling his body. Lit oil lamps and flowers littered the ground. And Achilles was already at his side, head bowed and shoulders sagging. Dozens of Myrmidons gathered around their commander, openly weeping. Briseis noted that many had torn out locks of their long hair and ripped their tunics, as Achilles had done.

"Briseis, come," Achilles commanded.

The guards released her. Fear seized her. Finally, a guard pushed her. "You heard Achilles. Move."

Briseis approached slowly, her eyes focused on Achilles' back. Who would he become without Patrokles at his side to temper him? Who would she be to him now, if anything? Did he suspect their betrayal, because she knew he would see it that way?

In a few steps, she stood looking down into Patrokles' face. Gold coins on each dead eye. She raised a trembling hand to touch his chest. It was cold and hard. She inhaled sharply. "How is he so beautiful even in death?"

In a voice hoarse from weeping, Achilles said, "Thetis protects him."

"Patrokles … Patrokles," Briseis whispered over and over.

"How can you be dead?" The anguish of all the days since Lyrnessus washed over her, as new grief pulled the old to light. "Only you thought to comfort me when I was alone and frightened. The day Achilles claimed me, and I had lost my husband and brothers ... my entire life. You saw me. You knew." She wiped angrily at the tears she could not stop from falling like rain. "You promised you would make Achilles take me for a proper wife. That we would finally have peace in Phthia. Look at you now. How will I endure without your true kindness?" When she leaned to kiss him, her warm lips touching his cheek, the raging storm within broke free of its chains. She threw her head back and screamed at the gods until her sorrow was a silent spasm stabbing beneath her breast. She wept, and the other women wept, though not for Patrokles, for they had never known him. They wept for their own husbands and brothers and fathers lost to them because of war.

Achilles took her hand and led her to the tent they had shared together. It was dark and smelled of soured wine. She stood in the center, taking in the dank surroundings. She tried to remember that not long ago she was content beneath this cover. "What do you want of me, Achilles?"

He stripped Hephaestus' armor off and set it on the table. "I don't know."

"What will happen now?"

Achilles sank into a chair covered in the fur of a mountain lion. "I will kill Hektor." His lips settled into a grim line. "And then I will die."

Briseis fell at his knees. "Then, do not fight, Achilles. Let us flee to Phthia. Live." Despite the current agony, she did not want to lose Achilles or be forced to serve another man.

His fingers pushed her chin up and searched her eyes. The blue fire within them was dimmed and cold. "You deserved love, Briseis. He deserved to be loved." Achilles released her face. "I always knew he loved you, but I would not give you up to love him."

Briseis' chin quivered with the truth. "What?" She was confused. He knew Patrokles loved her? *He knew?* A new question burned inside her mind and heart. The truth she was only now beginning to understood. "Did you never love me?"

Achilles' face softened. "Not the way Patrokles did." His eyes begged her to understand. "I never meant to hurt you, Briseis. I wanted to love you more than I could. You gave me comfort."

Briseis crumpled at his feet. If Patrokles had taken her, none of this would have happened. He would have always been kind. Protected her. Kept her from Agamemnon. He would have lived and returned with her to Phthia. Married her. Grown old with her. She could have endured a life with him. Loved him with a whole heart, because Achilles would never have taken root inside her. "You have truly taken everything from me."

"Did you let him love you, Briseis, when he came to you?"

Briseis stared dumbfounded back at Achilles.

"I go to die. I need to know if he … if he …"

"Aye," she whispered hoarsely. "He loved me." She no longer cared if Achilles plunged his sword into her chest or hacked her head from her shoulders in a rage, because then all her pain would end.

Achilles said nothing. He sat still as stone. She sensed his mind turning over his thoughts. "There is nothing more I require."

Briseis could not help but pity him. "You don't have to die in this war. Go home. Raise your son. Take me with you. We can live as Patrokles would have wanted us to."

"War and glory are a siren's song to me, Briseis. You have always known this. I will find Hektor on the field. Rip his head from his shoulders and feed his body to the camp dogs. Then, I will burn Troy to the ground."

Briseis placed her cheek on his knee. She closed her eyes. The burden of war and death had exhausted her. "What will happen to me, when you're gone?"

He stroked Briseis' hair, as he stared off into his own thoughts. "You will go with my treasure back to Phthia."

"What if I do not wish it?"

"Where else would you go? You have no other place, but here."

"Aye. I have nowhere else."

"Vengeance is a desert, empty of love, Briseis. I will send word to my father before the end that you are not to be hurt in any way. Once, I had hoped you and Patrokles would sail home. Foster my son, so he would know some small part of me through you both. But that dream has been stripped away by Hektor and this war over Helen who doesn't even want her husband. Patrokles was the best among us, not me."

"Aye. He was."

In the middle of the night, Briseis woke to the sound of uncontrollable sobbing. She reached for Achilles in the dark, but his side of the mattress was cold. The weeping continued. She rose from the bed, wrapping one of the blankets about her shoulders, and walked outside. It was Achilles.

A ring of Myrmidons surrounded the makeshift altar where Achilles had laid Patrokles' body. The men parted, opening a gap like a narrow river for Briseis to wind her way through to their leader. Standing at the rim of the inner circle, she froze. Never in her life had she thought such a scene possible. Not even if Zeus had pinned this to the stars could she have imagined it.

Achilles had pulled the body from the table. He sat in the sand, wretched and weeping, his face blotched with grief, clutching and rocking Patrokles like a mother cradling her limp child to her breast. "See what I have done?" he cried out, his mouth a gaping hole of grief. With one arm flailing to the sky, he screamed, "Look what you gods have made me."

Briseis realized then that it wasn't just Patrokles' death haunting him; it was all the deaths he himself had caused. The heartache of a thousand mothers and wives weighed on him here in the end.

Briseis stepped toward him, unsure of her safety. Achilles' eyes were wild and dark. *He is not himself, now. He is someone else. Something else.* "Achilles?" she whispered.

He reached his hand to her and she fell to her knees beside him, clasping her arms around them both. Achilles' warm frame against one arm and Patrokles' cold one against the other.

"How can this be happening? Only I was supposed to die in this fucking war. Not him."

"Shah, Achilles." She leaned her cheek against his head, careful not to press against the bare wounds. Briseis knew words held no power against the sting of a loved one's death. Time would lessen the pain, but the scar would remain. And after years of war, she'd begun to wonder if they weren't all held together by scars with only patches of unblemished skin. His agony broke her heart all over again.

Achilles' grief broke like a stormy sea against her shoulder. She held him as he wept like a child in her arms. "Shah," she whispered over and over until he calmed. "Come, my love," she finally said. "You must rest. At dawn, you go to war."

Slowly, Briseis guided them both to their feet, Achilles leaning heavily on her. The Myrmidons silently parted for their commander and the woman who'd pulled him from the war. Not a single man uttered a word, but their angry eyes bore into her. She knew many blamed her for the events that led to Patrokles' death and the death of hundreds more. Had she not existed, Agamemnon would never have found a way to insult Achilles. Then he would never have left the war. And Patrokles would still be alive. She understood them, because she blamed herself, too. She allowed her heart to be captured by Achilles. Had she never given in, he would not have risked so much and Patrokles would still be alive.

They walked back to the tent where she laid him down on their bed. She curled up beside him, cradling his wounded head in her arms, and his wounded heart in hers.

Achilles whispered hoarsely, "He loved you most."

Sighing, Briseis kissed Achilles' head. There was nothing to say. She pulled him closer, and he wrapped his arms around her tighter, clinging to her comfort as he had done countless times before. Her tears for a lost life fell in hot trails down her cheeks. The man who truly loved and desired her as a woman, who wanted her for a wife, and who respected her was dead. The end brought more clarity in a single moment than years of living had done.

When the sun broke the sky opened with a new day, Achilles rose with murder in his eyes. Without speaking, he donned the gleaming armor of Hephaestus, slung the mighty shield over his shoulder, and picked up his father's great ash spear. Briseis knew he would kill every Trojan who was unfortunate enough to cross his path. She watched his broad back disappear through the tent flap. She wept quietly for everything she'd lost and had yet to lose.

THIRTY TWO

the red river

PRIAM'S PALACE—1238 BCE

Hektor's messenger arrived just before dawn. His words brought Andromache great relief. He promised to be in her arms by nightfall and that he'd put an end to the Greeks and the city's suffering once and for all. Standing at the threshold of Astyanax's nursery, hope surged through Andromache. The young prince stirred in his little bed. She crossed the room and scooped Astyanax up in her arms. His weight filled her arms and heart with joy. The babe nudged her breast. She opened her gown, and his hungry mouth found her nipple. "You will never have to worry about wars, little prince." Andromache gently stroked a silky lock of black hair at her son's temple. She swept her thumb over his cleft chin. "So much like your father."

"My lady?" a voice came from the doorway. "Shall we fill the bath?"

"Aye. I'm certain my husband will want to soak the aches and pains of the day away."

"And for the food, my lady?"

"Bring up the best wine. Slaughter the fattest goat. Bread. Olives. Something sweet."

"As you say, my lady." The servant woman disappeared to carry out her chores.

Andromache sat on the soft couch near the window overlooking the courtyard below. She leaned back against the wall and closed her eyes. *Soon, life will be all we desire. Peace. Prosperity.*

"I thought I would find you here," Queen Hecuba said, gliding into the chamber. "You've heard from Hektor?"

Andromache opened her eyes. Hecuba always moved with unnatural grace; it was unnerving at times. This morning she was wrapped in a himation of dark purple wool. She looked every bit the cold queen people whispered her to be behind her back. "He promised he'd be home by evening. And the war would be at its end."

The queen sighed heavily, rubbing her arms to ward off a chill. "I pray to the gods he is right."

"Are you well, Mother?"

Hecuba shrugged. "As well as I can be." Her hand smoothed over Apollo's growing gift. She took a seat next to Andromache. Astyanax glanced at his grandmother, smiling up at her with his mother's nipple still in his mouth. The queen tugged his little foot. "What were you thinking about, Andromache?"

"Hoping really. That the gods might bless us with more children once the war is over." Andromache looked at Hecuba. "Do you think it possible?"

"Why wouldn't it be?"

"I am … getting older. Perhaps, too old. Maybe Hektor will need to find another—"

"Think no more of that. I bore children into my later years. As long as you flow, you can conceive. With the stress of war behind us, I have no doubt you and my son will have many blissful years ahead."

Astyanax squirmed in her arms, so Andromache shifted him to the other side. He held his mother's heavy breast in his chubby hands and sucked the warm comfort of his mother's milk. "Will you weave this afternoon?"

The queen offered one of her rare smiles. A smile so rarely bestowed because of her grief, but it was capable of lighting the darkest corners of Hades. "Perhaps." She patted her grandson's foot and stood. "Perhaps it *is* a good day to weave. Hope is in the air."

BATTLEFIELD

Hektor rode through the camp on his chariot, inspecting the men and their weapons. They were ragged and tired, but he knew they would follow him to the Gates of Hades if he asked. He stopped here and there, exchanging greetings with his warriors, testing the sharpness of their spear points and sword blades. His mere presence uplifted the men's spirits and determination.

From his platform, Hektor addressed them. "We all witnessed Achilles last evening. Clearly, a god favors him. We know what we are up against. Just remember, we also find favor with the gods. I have sacrificed to Zeus. He will be with us. Of this I have no doubt. Remember, as well, that no man, not even Achilles, can defy the will of the gods. All our fates were cast into the stars before this day. No one knows what the days ahead will bring. Nothing is certain, until the end. Take comfort and draw courage in that."

A heavy hand pressed down on his shoulder. "Apollo," Hektor whispered. "You gods toil mightily on our behalf."

"That is why I have come, Prince Hektor. Zeus no longer restrains us. I come to warn you, the gods will be afield, lending their aid to those they favor."

"Welcome news, Apollo. Gratitude."

"You do not understand. Achilles and his Myrmidons march on you already. Athena is beside him ... and Ares."

"Are you with us, Apollo? Or do you only come to give warning?"

"I am with you, but Achilles will not rest until he kills you."

"What am I to do?"

"Stay away from him, if you can. His sword heralds the only clear threat to your life."

"I will obey."

As the sun rose in the sky, the rumble of a thousand pairs of feet filled the air. Achilles stood shining like a god on a small hill, opposite the Trojans, with a sea of Black Shields behind him. Hektor turned to his army and shouted, "We win or we die this day!"

Achilles stared at the Trojans waiting across the gap. The helm pressed painfully on his head where he'd yanked his hair out, but he didn't care. Pain fueled his fury to fight. A line of thin trees and shrubs and rocks were all that stood between him and the revenge burning through his heart. He could see Hektor on his chariot barking orders at his men. He sneered to himself. Whatever Patrokles' killer said would mean nothing in the end. By the time night fell, Hektor's head would be on a spike and his armor at Patrokles' feet.

The Myrmidon commander unleashed a terrifying shout and his men charged down the embankment and headlong into the advancing Trojans. Achilles hefted his spear in one hand, and in the other he held his sword. He stabbed and slashed at the enemy as he ran, sending showers of blood in every direction. Over and over his crazed screaming sent even more Trojans fleeing for their lives. The terribleness of his grief only grew with the blood dripping from his blade. He had nothing left to lose or gain from war. Achilles wanted an end to everything.

A young boy fighting with Hektor's protection caught Achilles' eye. Several times the boy dipped beneath the prince's shield while he let loose his arrows. Achilles sneered with anger. "He protects him as I did Patrokles."

Honing in on the target, Achilles' spear shaft sang through the air and pierced clean through the boy's back. He watched the boy pause, uncertain of what had happened as he looked down at the spear protruding from his middle. The boy's hand shook as he tested the sharp tip of bronze. His entrails slipped through the gaping hole. With wide eyes he reached out to Hektor as he thudded to the ground.

Hektor turned just in time to see his youngest brother fall and Achilles bearing down on him. Forgetting Apollo's warning, Hektor wheeled to meet Achilles face to face.

Achilles' eyes flared hatred. He screamed out, "I will kill you before the day is over."

Hektor shouted back, "You are but a spear tip from Hades."

With that threat, he hurled his mighty ash spear.

Achilles' grace and speed in battle was legendary. He easily avoided the spear as it whizzed past his head, skidding to the ground behind him. He laughed wickedly and pulled his shield from his shoulder. Raising the blinking bronze blade of Hephaestus, he barreled straight for Hektor, shield tipped. As he closed in for the death blow, a mist rose, confusing him of any direction. He skidded to a stop, blindly slashing about. "Fuck!" he yelled. "What god steals my revenge?"

"It is I, Achilles. Apollo. You are a wraith walking among the living."

Achilles groaned and screamed again, "You fucking gods! You will not take this revenge from me."

"I have already done so ... for now." The mist cleared, and Hektor was gone.

Achilles' anger cracked his spirit open. He pressed dozens of Trojans to the Xanthos River nearby. Trapping them in the cold water, he slashed and decapitated every last one of them. The river ran red with Trojan blood as if Gaia herself were mortally wounded. A man with curly, dark hair thrashed in the tainted water, desperate to escape the wrath of Achilles. But the mad warrior grabbed him by the head, yanking him back. He bent the man's head, exposing his throat, and looked down into his wide, bulging eyes. "You."

"Please," the man begged, his arms flailing about.

"I remember you. Patrokles sold you years ago."

"I beg you, let me go. My father will pay for my life."

Achilles sneered. "A son of Priam. The man is a whore-king. What is your name?"

"Lykaon. Please, I beg you. I have only returned to my father's house—"

He thumped his chest with the pommel of his sword. "You think I care when the gods returned you? Mercy does not live here."

"Please, please—"

Achilles' blade flashed like a star across Lykaon's neck. A thin line of blood opened to a gaping, gory hole. Lykaon's eyes rolled back in his head and his arms went limp at his sides. Crimson gurgled and gushed over his chin. Achilles roared with the power of killing. He tossed the body aside, and the spirit of Priam's son drifted to the Underworld, finally freed of war as only the dead can know its end. As Lykaon's body floated away, many less fortunate Trojans struggled against the current, scrambling to reach the opposite side and run for the city.

Achilles yelled, "Myrmidons! Seize a dozen of these pathetic Trojans. Take them back to camp." His men obeyed without question. His return on the battlefield had made all the difference. Achilles refused to stop until every last one of them was dead or enslaved.

High above the melee, Apollo watched Achilles slaughtering his favored people. He narrowed his flaming eyes to mere slits. His lip curled up in an evil grin. Achilles was a challenge, but no match for him. He flew down to the plain with a plan to thwart the Golden Warrior right beneath the other gods' noses.

A mist twisted around Achilles, squeezing his arms and stealing his breath. He dropped his sword to the ground. "By the gods!" He writhed against the cloudy fingers. "Show yourself!" And just as suddenly, the binding air released him to face the figure of Agenor, a Trojan warrior, emerging from the haze.

"You will not take Troy so easily, Achilles, Sacker of Cities. Prince Slayer. Murderer."

Achilles laughed in his face. "You dare to challenge me? Alone?"

"I do."

"Draw your weapon and steady your shield. We will see what your bones are made of, Trojan dog."

Agenor disappeared into the mist. "Catch me if you can, Achilles of the Iron Foot."

Achilles roared in frustration, but took off with the speed of a god, his sword slashing indiscriminately at the air. Agenor's laughter spurred Achilles on, until his legs tired.

"Achilles." A voice floated about his ears.

"Fuck!" Achilles skidded to a halt. "What trick is this?"

Apollo's laughter spiraled around Achilles' head. *"Your rage will be your undoing."* For a brief flash, Apollo revealed his sacred form. Flaming hair and eyes, beautiful, yet terrifying to behold. "You are too easily led by your heart, Son of Thetis."

Achilles seethed and ground his teeth. "Apollo." He was no match for the Sun God. With a growl, he said, "You cannot stop fate."

"Nor do I wish to. Not on your account, at least."

Achilles sped back to Troy, cursing himself that he'd allowed the god to deceive him and take him so far from the fighting.

THIRTY THREE
the undefended
RAMPART OF TROY—1238 BCE

Queen Hecuba's fingers burned with small abrasions from gripping the rampart edge. The distant dust cloud drew closer. "Priam, what is happening?"

"The fighting is moving toward us."

She noted the dismay on his face. "What should we do?"

"Open the gates," he called down to the guards. "Open the gates on first sight of Hektor. Or any of my sons."

Priam moved to Hecuba's side and put an arm around her shoulders. In a rare display of acceptance, Hecuba reached a hand to his. "I never believed we would live to see the end of Troy."

"There's still time, Hecuba."

The cloud was moving quickly now. A few horses appeared

ahead of the main army. As they drew nearer, the watchers on the wall could hear the riders screaming, "Achilles is coming!"

Hecuba's eyes filled with tears. She leaned into her estranged husband's chest. "Hektor must live." She turned in Priam's arm to gauge his face. "Can he defeat Achilles?"

The king's eyes saddened. "I don't know."

Chariots raced through the gates followed by men on foot. Women and children who'd been out gathering wood and hunting small game ran frantically alongside the army, desperate to find safety behind the Great Wall. Bringing up the rear, Hektor shouted for men to hurry inside. Hecuba prayed thanks to Apollo for bringing her eldest son safely back to the city.

"By the gods," Priam whispered with horror in his voice.

"What?" Shielding her eyes, Hecuba looked in the direction of Priam's gaze. "It cannot be." She held out a shaking hand, but her voice was as steady as a cold stone. "They were right. Achilles is coming."

Squinting toward the horizon, Priam watched the blinking flash draw nearer. "Quickly," he yelled at Hektor below. "Quickly," he yelled again, but his eldest son was too far away. "Come, Hecuba. He can't hear us from here." He practically dragged her to the lowest guard tower. Hanging over the rampart, Priam hollered, "Hektor! Achilles is coming!"

Hektor looked up and waved.

"Get behind the wall! I beg you!"

Hektor took off his helmet, cocking his head toward his parents. A nearby soldier approached him, and they spoke briefly. Hektor nodded.

"Is he refusing to come within?" Hecuba asked, confused. "Why would he refuse?" She dug fingers into the king's arm. "Make him listen, Priam."

"How?" Priam hit his head in frustration. "Is he determined to die today? Of all the sons I have lost, his death will break me." He screamed again with his ancient voice, its power already faded with years. "Hektor! Hektor!" As Priam's voice reached him, Hektor looked up.

Hecuba was desperate to reach him, reach his heart. Was it just a moment ago he was a babe nursing at her breast? A boy learning to walk and ride a horse? When did he become this man, hard and distant? "Come behind the wall," she screamed frantically.

Hektor shook his head, the wind catching his long horse tail crest. She remembered the boy who loved his horse, Ares, and the man who wept when that horse died in his arms. Hektor had the hair of Ares' tail set into a new helmet crest. In all his life, he'd never battled without some part of his beloved warhorse. Now, she could not watch him die at the hands of Achilles. Alone. Where was Apollo? She despaired for everything.

Out of sheer terror and desperation, Hecuba ripped open the front of her gown, exposing her naked breasts. "Please, I beg you, Hektor! My son!" She sobbed uncontrollably. "I nursed you my son, gave you life! A mother's sacred bond is forever. Do not break it now, like this. Please, please, come to safety."

Hektor shouted up at his parents, "I must face Achilles. We all know I must." He put his helmet back on and snapped the chin strap.

Hecuba pulled the front of her garment closed and wept for so many reasons. When she beseeched Apollo to bring down Achilles in revenge for Troilus, she did not think to beg for Hektor's protection.

She'd somehow believed him invincible against Achilles. If any of her sons could survive against him, she thought it would be Hektor. Now, she knew she was wrong. *How could I have been so blind to this?* "He may be ready to die, but I am not ready to let him go."

Priam wept beside her as well. "We cannot change what fate has set into the stars. No matter what we say or how we entreat him, Hektor is right. He is the one to face Achilles. All the years have come to this moment. I can hardly bear to watch."

Achilles' blood-curdling screams carried on the wind. The killer rapidly advanced. Without warning or shouted word, Hektor bolted, disappearing from sight around the curved tower wall and into a tree line.

Hecuba pointed. "Where's he going?"

"I don't know," Priam answered.

By now, the Myrmidons were straggling in from the plain, having followed Achilles. They stood leaning on their spears or sat using their shields to block the heat of the day.

Everyone, Trojan and Greek alike, waited to see what would happen. A long while passed before Hektor came running swift as the wind directly toward the city gates.

Priam yelled down, "Open the gates if he gets close."

But before Hektor could get close enough, Achilles cut him off, not once but twice. After three passes around the city walls, Hektor unexpectedly stood still.

"Why has he stopped? Achilles will catch him." Hecuba tugged at her veil. "What is he doing?"

They watched as their son and Achilles exchanged words. Achilles' golden armor flashed like a silver star in Apollo's light, and his angry words floated up to the rampart. "There can be no promises between lions and men." Hecuba wilted against Priam, but he caught her before she hit the ground.

"What's wrong, Hecuba?"

Clinging to Priam and the rampart edge, she asked, "Do you remember the nightmare I had before Paris was born?" She'd almost forgotten it herself, until Achilles' threat pulled the memory to light. "This is the battle from my dreams. *Lions and men*. How could I forget?"

"By the gods," Priam whispered. "By the gods."

Hecuba cried miserably. Her body shaking to the core. "It was always meant to be Hektor and Achilles."

Priam clutched his chest and ripped the silver and gold hanging from his neck, tossing his regalia to the ground. "It has all come to pass, Hecuba. We tried to defy the gods, but … Hektor was always meant to die and Troy will fall. How many sons have we lost because we could not let one go?"

Hecuba wheeled on Priam, her face contorted in rage and grief. "It was never a choice to kill any of our children. Don't you understand? The gods have cursed our house from the beginning." She turned her eyes to the fight below, brushing aside the horror that would come after. Achilles and Hektor circled each other. Achilles cast his spear. Hecuba held her breath, as Hektor ducked. Hecuba watched wide-eyed as Achilles charged with shield tilted and spear leveled for a fatal strike against her son. The men crashed into one another, splintering their shields and tossing the remnants to the ground. With a roar, Achilles circled and attacked like a lion. The song of the God of Death rang out with their silver swords clashing. The queen's heart pounded, knowing it was Hektor's day to die. Any warning dusted on her tongue. The macabre dance of death continued, until with a graceful lunge Achilles' spear found the soft flesh of Hektor's neck. Hecuba shrieked.

BELOW THE WALL

Hektor's eyes widened in shock seeing his blood splattered across Achilles' armor. His legs buckled. He collapsed to his knees, his chin bobbing precariously close to his chest. Blood gurgled up his throat as he tried to speak. The bitter taste of death was undeniable. "I beg you. Allow my father the right to ransom me." He coughed up more blood. "Give me proper rites."

Achilles spat into the dirt. "Your body will rot in the sun. No one will mourn you or give you the sacred rights. What mercies did you show Patrokles, my kin, my beloved? The dogs will rip the meat off your bones and the seabirds will pluck your eyes from their sockets."

"But my mother—"

Achilles laughed then. "I do not care about your mother's pain. She will never see you properly mourned. There will be no honor for you in death. If the gods allowed, I would rip the flesh from your bones and eat it raw just to shit you out as the stinking fuck you are."

Coldness spread through Hektor. Until this moment, he had not allowed himself to think about what would happen if he fell. Death was inevitable now. He gasped for air, even as Andromache's sweet singing filled his head. Here at the end of all things he could find no lingering regrets. "I will die at peace. My song will be one of honor, but yours, Achilles, will not. Apollo will help Paris cut you down. Even you can't stand alone against a god." Hektor, the Golden

Prince, breathed his last and toppled over.

Achilles kicked the corpse. "I welcome death whenever the gods wish it." He turned his attention to the watchers on the wall. "Here is your prince!" he yelled up to them. "He took the best of us and I have paid the debt in kind. You Trojans will remember it was Achilles who brought down your mighty Hektor."

Myrmidons and Greeks circled the dead body of Prince Hektor like vultures and wolves. One of them stripped Hektor's armor—Achilles' armor—from the body. Dead, the prince posed no threat to them, so they took turns stabbing the corpse with their spears and swords. Achilles grabbed one of Hektor's feet and pressed his sword tip through the heel tendon. He did the same to the other foot. He dragged Hektor's body to his chariot where he threaded leather thongs through the fresh cuts. He tied the straps to his chariot. And when he struck the lash on the horses' backs, they bolted straight across the plain, Hektor's body bouncing on the hard ground and his head bashing against every rock and dip.

On the wall, everyone stood in stunned silence, horrified by what the gods had allowed. Hecuba was the first to cry out, "No! No! Nooooo!" She screamed and ripped at her hair; clumps tangled in her fingers. Leaning over the rampart's rail, she cast her arms out, shrieking for Achilles to bring him back. To bring back the boy who used to sit beside her and comfort her with his smile. A smile she would never see again. Her son who loved horses. Who had a son of his own. A loving wife. Hecuba shrunk under the pain. She could not *unsee* what she had seen. It was not enough time. She pulled her headdress off and flung it from the wall. It fluttered to the dust below.

"My son," Hecuba wept, over and over. "My son." She collapsed with one arm still clinging to the rail. The anguish of the moment pushed a gush of warmth between her legs, reminding her that the gods would steal every piece of joy she clung to in this life. "It is wrong that I lived to see this day. Better that I was dead already. Hektor was everything to all of us." She pulled herself up with some difficulty. The blood flowed down her inner thighs. The queen walked stoically from the wall, leaving a thin trail of blood behind her.

Hecuba's grief had ignited the wailing of other women, and soon the citadel was filled with the high-pitched songs of mourning. The city had grieved before, but this was a darker sorrow. Hektor had been killed, and without him, Troy was doomed. If anyone had ever doubted the rumors swirling about Paris' curse, they did not do so now. The city had lost its champion, because a babe was allowed to live a life span ago.

Priam threw himself at the rampart's edge, but his men grabbed his robes, pulling him to safety. "Let me go!" He struggled against the hands holding him back. "I must go to Achilles. Beg him to return my son." He groaned and cried aloud, his pain shaking the bones of everyone around him. "No father can bear this torture. Of all my sons, I cannot bear the loss of this one." He pulled his beard out in bloody chunks. "We are cursed. My house is cursed. We are lost now. Troy is lost."

From her weaving chamber, Andromache caught the shrill sound of women's sorrow through the window. She dropped the needle from her hands. The air stilled, and the fine hairs on her arm rose with knowing. Tears stung her eyes. "By the gods, no … not *Hektor*. Not my love." Throwing her threads to the floor, she raced to the wall. Rounding a corner, she slipped on an uneven cobblestone. Skidding hard into the ground, she cried out. Blood oozed from a gash on her palm. She scrambled ungracefully to her feet, running until her legs ached and her lungs burned. Her veil billowed behind her like a sail caught in a strong wind.

Andromache stopped at the gate tower wall above the lower wall where she saw Priam weeping and wailing. She scanned the faces below for Hecuba, but the queen wasn't there. A distant roar drew her attention to a dust cloud moving quickly around the city. She grabbed the edge of the wall, leaning out to see more clearly. Achilles was dragging a body behind his chariot. The terrible truth crashed in on her. "No!" she screamed. "Noooo!" She ripped her veil from her head and tossed it over the wall and fainted.

She woke with her household women surrounding her, tears in their eyes. "I wish I had never been born. What will happen to my son now? My love will be eaten by worms."

Andromache pulled herself up with her women steadying her on her feet. She stumbled down to Priam in her disbelief and shock. "Father, what will happen now? How could you let Achilles take my husband's body? You must make him return Hektor to us. For proper rites."

"No matter the cost, I will convince Achilles to return what belongs to Troy. To us. To the gods. Achilles has brutalized my sons and shredded my legacy before my eyes. I will, on whatever honor I have left, bring Hektor home for you to mourn … before the end of all things." The king was once again lost in his grief; his eyes unseeing and his voice crying out to the gods.

Andromache walked in a daze to the home she shared with Hektor, the Prince of Troy and Breaker of Horses. Crossing the threshold where he once carried her as a young bride, a profound loneliness struck her. Her chest heaved with an ache she'd never experienced until now. The once joyful and bustling halls of her home were now dark and filled with the sound of weeping. Desperation hung in the air like a foul odor.

She walked to her weaving chamber and stared blankly at the crimson cape edged with an intricate design of interwoven shields. It was to be a masterpiece welcoming the peace Hektor promised to bring. A peace that would now never be. She crossed the chamber and sat before her work. Her fingers touched a stray thread. She tugged at it, unraveling a tiny section of her work. Andromache stared at the handful of threads in her palm. Without any clear thought, she savagely assaulted the garment on the loom. Threads flew in all directions.

As Andromache lashed out at her loom, a servant, hearing her cries, came running. "My lady! Stop. What are you doing?"

"My husband is not coming home. I don't even know if I will be able to wash his body and offer a sacred farewell." She brushed the yarn from her lap. "What use are his fine garments to me or Astyanax, if he is not garbed within them? And burn his clothes so I don't have to look on them. Burn everything belonging to your master. Take what you want and run if you dare. It will be less for the Greeks to take. They will have my life as well as my son's in their hands. That will be enough." Andromache collapsed in a sobbing heap on the floor. The maid left her there, shutting the door behind her. The prince was dead and so, too, were the dreams of all Trojans.

THIRTY FOUR

the shade of Patrokles

MYRMIDON CAMP—1238 BCE

Achilles stood on the platform of his chariot before his Myrmidons. He was still covered in the dried blood of Hektor and the Trojans he had slain earlier in the day. His eyes flamed with rage, as he scanned their weary faces. "You fought bravely. All of you."

Behind him, the twelve Trojan captives from the river wept and begged for their freedom or a quick death. They'd been stripped of their garments and lashed to posts. Achilles was oblivious to their suffering.

"Tonight, we feast and mourn Patrokles. He was the best of us. Of me." He snapped the horses' reins and his chariot exploded forward, dragging the mutilated body of Hektor behind it.

Three times Achilles circled the camp with his men standing there, watching with wide, horrified eyes. Yet, not one of them had the courage of Patrokles to speak against what their commander was doing to offend the gods. When Achilles tired of dragging the corpse, he returned to Patrokles' body. Stepping down from his chariot, he yanked Hektor free from the leather straps binding his heels so hard the tendons popped. The body was hardly recognizable as a man. Achilles dragged Hektor's corpse by the leg and kicked it face down next to Patrokles' altar. Looking down into Patrokles' cold, ashen face, he said, "I did what I said I'd do. Hektor is dead. His body belongs to the dogs. I have Trojans for your funeral pyre. Their blood will not restore you to life, but will make my life more bearable until I am dead." A company of Myrmidons kept a watchful vigil over Patrokles body as the day faded to night.

Briseis met Achilles as he entered the tent. She'd lit the oil lamps to chase some of the gloom away. "Drink, Achilles."

Achilles brushed passed her without even a glance. The wine in Briseis' hand sloshed over the cup's edge. He tossed his shield to the corner and let his spear fall to the ground, then took a chair at the table. "I don't want any wine. Why have you lit the lamps?"

"It was dark—"

He brushed her words away in the air. "I am beyond consolation, Briseis."

"You are filthy."

"I don't care." He stood and stripped his garments off, tossing them across the tent. For a brief flash the old Achilles returned ... the man who didn't care who saw him in his naked perfection. He splashed some water on his face at the basin.

Briseis stepped toward him, uncertain if he would strike her or not. Some aspects of him were the same, but he was not the Achilles she had known. It was as if her captivity had reset to begin again.

"My lord, please." She offered the cup again. "I mixed some herbs to ease your sorrows. True nothing can take away the pain of losing …" Briseis couldn't even say his name. *Patrokles.* "Please."

Achilles searched her face, his blue eyes now revealing his agony. "If I could but sleep, however briefly …" He took the cup, drained it dry, and set it loudly on the table. "I am for bed. Come, lie beside me."

Together they found comfort. Briseis pulled Achilles' head to her chest and she gently swept the side of his cheek with her fingers. The wine took effect, and Achilles' breathing slowed. She kissed the top of his head. "Sleep well, my love." Briseis closed her eyes. Nothing would ever be the same. Love and the war had killed all three of them. She willed sleep to take her away from the truth of her waking world.

Sweet and restless slumber pulled Achilles' eyes shut. He was slightly aware of Briseis' fingers brushing against his face. His scalp throbbed where he'd pulled his hair out. He inhaled her essence, salt and honey. His shoulders relaxed. He had missed her, but found that now he hadn't the strength to voice any tender words. He was not even angry she had shared her body with Patrokles. They had found each other while he had raged against Agamemnon, drunk and mindless on his ship. *If only I had killed Agamemnon, then …*

"Achilles."

"Leave me alone."

"Achilles, open your eyes."

"I am too tired."

"I am here."

Across the darkness of a dream, Achilles recognized the voice calling to him. "Patrokles? Is that you?"

"Aye."

A strange heaviness held his eyes shut and he struggled to open them. "How?"

Finally, Achilles' eyes fluttered awkwardly open. There he was. Patrokles shimmering like a god. He could only stare at the specter.

"I haven't known you to be at a loss for words."

"You are beautiful. How did I not see before?"

Patrokles' smile was so bright that Achilles had to shield his eyes. *"Your light dims all those who stand beside to you in life."*

"I loved you."

"And I loved you."

Achilles' eyes filled with tears, melting slowly down his cheek. "Why did you follow Hektor? Why? I should not have let you go."

"Peace, cousin. I do not blame you. But you must live a while longer without me."

"I do not wish it."

Patrokles' face darkened with a shadow. *"You will join me soon."*

"Take me with you, now."

"Bury me, Achilles."

"I cannot."

"You must. I am wandering in the gray and can't reach the dead. I am denied the peace that only comes with death. Rest our bones together."

"We have shared everything I have ever valued in life. I will not deny you in death."

"I loved her."

"I know."

"Promise, you will not leave her without means for a life we ruined for her."

"I promise." Achilles reached for Patrokles, but embraced only a cold mist. He sat up with a start. His tent was cold and dark. Briseis stirred beside him. Patrokles was gone. A hard lump tightened in his throat.

"Farewell, Patrokles." He lay back down, pulling Briseis into his chest. Her breath was warm on his bare skin. He and Patrokles had both loved her in different ways for different reasons. Patrokles was right. She deserved a life other than the one he'd forced on her as his war prize. He would make certain she had gold and treasure. And her freedom. Patrokles' visit gave him a small comfort knowing that he would live after death, that the stories Chiron told him were true. He fell back to an uneasy sleep.

Another red dawn broke. Achilles dragged himself to Patrokles' resting place with a company of Myrmidons following him. Hektor's body lay as he had left it the night before—mangled, bloodied, and covered in dirt and sand. Achilles laid his hand on Patrokles' thigh. Death had yet to mar his flesh. His countenance was one of a peaceful sleep despite the violence of his final breath. After his vision, it was clear what he must do.

With a heavy heart, he turned and addressed his men, "We must build a great funeral pyre as a message to the gods that we will not forget what they have allowed."

As the men moved to obey without question, Achilles resumed his vigil by Patrokles' side. Briseis joined him. An uneasy silence passed between them, as he slipped his hand in hers. All around them, the Myrmidons worked, stacking hundreds of tree trunks and branches together until they raised a mountain in the midst of their camp. And as the men labored under Apollo's heat, the groans of Achilles' prisoners from the river could be heard. They knew they were not long for life, yet their pitiful prayers stretched skyward.

"He came to me, Briseis."

"Who?"

Achilles didn't answer. Briseis didn't ask again. The end of their beloved had ushered an understanding between them they hadn't shared while the war raged. As Troy's demise grew nearer, somber more quiet voices grew stronger. After a time, Briseis returned to their tent to mourn in private.

PATROKLES' FUNERAL PYRE
MYRMIDON CAMP

All day the Myrmidons had heaved and sweated on account of Patrokles, completing the pyre by nightfall. Without being called, the warriors of Phthia gathered around the great hill, donned in their armor with their shields proudly hanging from their shoulders. Briseis was among them. Some men cast her disparaging glances, but most ignored her and for that she was grateful.

As stars blinked against the darkness, they waited on Achilles standing beside his companion with his head bowed low. A gentle wind stirred, as he reached to lift Patrokles' body from the altar. He cradled him in his arms as a mother carries a sick child. Agony etched Achilles' golden face. The Myrmidons parted before him, as he walked with the body to the pyre. Before their eyes, their leader had transformed into a man they had never seen before. Darker. Angrier. Ethereal. The blood of his mother shone through him, transforming him before their eyes into a god. Unfeeling and remote.

Achilles gently laid Patrokles on the pyre's peak. With the tenderness of a long-lost lover or a bereaved mother, he arranged Patrokles' hair about his shoulders. He leaned his head down and kissed Patrokles' forehead.

"Farewell, beloved," he whispered loud enough for only the dead man's ears to hear. He pulled a small knife from his belt and cut a long lock of his remaining hair and placed it on Patrokles' chest. "Until I see you once more." He descended from the pyre, his broad shoulders wider, his eyes wilder, and his mood darker. The change in him was palpable by those he passed by. He lifted his hand and signaled for the sacrifices to begin.

While his men slit the throats of untold thrashing sheep and cattle, Achilles raised his blade to the frightened horses. One by one he grabbed their manes in his hand, as he pulled his blade across their thick necks. One by one they snorted and screamed, then stumbled and crashed to the ground in pools of gory crimson. Their black eyes wide and glassy. He slit the throats of two dogs who fed from the Myrmidons' tables; one had been Patrokles' favorite. A brown, short-haired hound whose head reached a man's hip. It had come to Achilles tail wagging, head slightly bowed, but instead of a rough scratch to his ears, he was met with a cold blade. Achilles eased the hound to the ground, its blood running through his fingers. It tried to raise its head to him before dying. He turned to the Trojan captives with red and sticky hands.

Briseis watched in horror and disbelief as one by one he killed each man, nearly severing their heads from their bodies. They fell at his feet in sharp, awkward poses. There was no hesitation or joy. The strength of his need for revenge increased as the blood flowed. A sinister shadow passed over Achilles' face. In all the years of war, she'd never beheld the blackness she saw in this moment. Tears melted her cheeks, because in her heart she knew that the Achilles she had loved was gone. Perhaps, forever. She feared nothing could stop him in his quest, not even the gods. Only death held that power now. When the last prisoner laid a mutilated corpse at his feet, Achilles surveyed the assembly. His flaming blue eyes were a sharp contrast to the blood smeared across his face. "It is done," he said.

The Myrmidons watched in mortified silence as their commander pulled a torch from its staff in the sand and set it to the bottom of the wood stack. Achilles stood alone as the flames slowly licked up the wood. Soon, it was a raging inferno against the dark night.

"Farewell, Patrokles. Part of me is already with you. Keep it well until I join you."

One by one the Myrmidons left the funeral site, seeking the shelter and comfort of their own tents and beds. Achilles chose to bed beside the burning pyre. Briseis left him there. It was no use trying to persuade him to rest in comfort. She could see he preferred the torture of his pain as his new companion.

TROAN PALACE
PRIVATE QUARTERS OF QUEEN HECUBA
THE SAME EVENING

Hecuba stared into the hearth fire's dancing flames. The crackle of wood burning to ash was oddly soothing. The groans and wails of the city mourning the brutal death of Hektor floated over her balcony into her chamber, but she remained numb. Her grief no longer had a voice, and her eyes had no more tears to shed. In all her days, she never thought to see the death of Hektor. She closed her eyes to ward off the image of him being dragged behind Achilles' chariot. His death ushered her own and that of the entire city. Everything was lost.

She rubbed her aching abdomen. The loss of the holy child began at the wall with Hektor's death. "It was best," she whispered to the fire. The flames sparked higher, responding to her words. The hairs on her arm rose. Hecuba smiled in spite of herself. "Apollo."

The god emerged from the fire like a specter, transforming into the image of a young Priam. "How do you fare, consort mine?"

Hecuba looked up to see the Priam she'd almost forgotten. "Of all the guises you are capable of, why choose his?"

"Did he never hold your favor once?"

"Years ago, perhaps." She smiled wanly. Her hands drifted again to her abdomen.

"You have bled out the child."

"I could not stop it from happening."

Apollo poured Hecuba a cup of wine and added a pinch of the

herbs from the pouch suspended across his chest on a golden rope. "It is as I thought. Drink this. It will ease your pain."

"Nothing can do that now."

"Drink, I said. The god does not ask twice."

Hecuba drank the bitter brew. Slowly, warmth spread through her body. "I didn't know I was so cold, until now."

Apollo raised his dark brows. "It is working."

"I am tired, Priam," Hecuba said as her heavy eyes closed.

"So be it," Apollo said. He scooped the queen up in his arms. Against his strength, she rested as light as a feather. As he laid her on her bed, he looked on her. She was as pale as death. Silver strands contrasted sharply with her dark tresses. Even the age of mortals had only slightly dimmed her beauty. "It is sad, Hecuba, that our children did not survive this war. I recall Troilus' conception. Your unbridled passion. You raised my son in secret, as I requested." Where most mortals disappointed him, Hecuba pleased him.

The queen moaned in her unnatural sleep. "Apollo, is that you?" Her whisper was barely audible. "Priam?"

"It is Apollo."

"Why did you allow Hektor's death?"

"I did not wish it. Athena tricked your son at the last."

Hecuba sighed. "More is the sadness."

Moved by her loyalty, the god asked, "What is your heart's desire?"

"To kill Achilles."

Apollo's smile curled wickedly up one side of his beautiful mouth. "So be it." He brushed the side of her cheek gently. "I can heal you ... if you wish."

With her eyes still closed in a dream-like world, Hecuba nodded against her pillow.

The god stripped the clothes from his body and lifted Hecuba's thin gown. Gently, as was not his custom, he mounted her. Within a few measured thrusts, Apollo released his silver seed within Hecuba, restoring her womb to health and staunching her flow. He kissed her forehead.

"Your lips are small fires."

Apollo pulled the linen blankets up, tucking them in around her. He brushed his thumb across her lips. "I should have come to you more often."

"Perhaps."

"I give my word; I will come once more before the end."

"Farewell …"

"Farewell, Hecuba," Apollo said, then vanished into mist.

THIRTY FIVE

the unraveling and the rival

MYRMIDON CAMP—1238 BCE

Ashes ceased falling by dawn. The air reeked sweetly of burnt human and animal flesh. Apollo's light fought through the haze lingering near the ground like a gray fog. Achilles slowly opened his eyes. They were dry and burned. He rubbed them with his palms and rolled to his back in the sand. The deep ache beneath his ribs reminded him of where he was. "I wake only to walk in darkness once again."

Achilles stood, surveying the remnants of the great pyre he'd built. Chunks of charred wood smoked in small piles on the ground. Tendrils of thin smoke fingered toward the sky. The gloomy day had begun. Drawing breath hurt. He knew the footsteps behind him before he turned around. "I wish it had been me."

Briseis just stood there, waiting. "I have brought you a basket … for—"

"*His* bones," Achilles finished for her.

"Aye." Briseis' chin quivered. She pressed her lips together. "And wine."

"I always believed it would be him gathering my remains. Take them back to my father." Achilles turned to her, his face pained and pale. "I never dreamt this …"

"I will help you," Briseis said.

"As you wish."

Side by side they walked to the center of the smoldering ashes where Patrokles' bones would be. Briseis handed the wine jug from the basket to Achilles. He pulled the wax plug, tossing it into the charred rubble of cinders. It wasn't long before they found the skeletal length of their beloved. Achilles poured the wine over the hot white bones, cooling them to the touch and tinting them faintly rose. He plucked the skull first, examining the eye sockets. "Do you recall how gray his eyes were?"

"And fierce when crossed."

"That he was. He was never afraid to stand up to me. Others cowered at my demands. But never him." He glanced sideways at Briseis. "Nor you."

Achilles brushed the charred ashes from the rib bones and shoulders. He placed them in the basket with the skull. He picked up the bones of Patrokles' hands. "His fingers were strong. Graceful."

"He had no equal," Briseis said, quietly.

"We were fortunate to know him. Love him. Though, I am not sure which of us loved him more."

Skirting the topic, she asked, "What will you do with Patrokles' remains?"

"He asked to be buried with me, when the time comes."

"I see."

"For now, I will have rocks piled here to mark his passing. Funeral games. I intend to give my geras away. Soon enough, I will have no need of any of it."

Briseis touched Achilles' arm. "I am not ready to lose you, so soon … so soon after …"

His eyes softened, and for a brief moment the old Achilles returned. "I will provide for you, Briseis. I promised *him*."

"Gratitude, Achilles." She had no idea what he intended, and she hadn't the strength to ask.

"Take the basket to the tent. I will see his remains properly stored when I am finished."

Briseis stared at the basket on the table for a long time. The sounds of mourning filtered through the tent, as did the muted light of day. She gathered the courage to touch the stacked remains. Her fingers caressed the smooth side of his skull. "It is just us, now." She lifted it to her lips and kissed the cool flatness of his cheek bone. "Farewell, Patrokles. Know I did love you, even if it was not enough."

A blood-curdling scream rent the air. Briseis fumbled the skull in her hands, before placing in back in the basket. She rushed from the tent.

"By all the gods," she said, covering her mouth with her hand in disgust and fright. Circling the Myrmidons stacking stones for Patrokles' monument was Achilles in his chariot. He'd lashed

Hektor's body to the platform again and was dragging it through the dirt. "What madness is this?" she whispered. "What curse?" She turned back to the tent, having no wish to witness Achilles unraveling like a thread violently tugged from a tapestry.

TROY
THE PALACE

The horror of Hektor's death ran through Andromache's mind. She could not stop the dark and bloody images from haunting her. She wept silently in her chambers. The bed linens were in disarray from tossing and turning into the night. An oil lamp burned low on a side table. A sliver of light touched the stone tiles. The agony of Hektor's loss was blissfully lost on Astyanax, who slept sweetly across from her. Her worst fears unfolded moment by moment, paralyzing her from doing anything other than sit, weep, and stare. A knock at the door startled her. "Enter."

Queen Hecuba swept into the center of the room in a cloud of dark linen. She paused before taking a seat next to Andromache. "This is a loss none of us can bear, my dear, but we must." She brushed a messy curl of hair from Andromache's face. "For your son, you must find a way."

Andromache's face contorted in agony. "I don't know how to go on, Mother." She sobbed, as Hecuba held her close. "It is too much. We are alone, now."

"You are not alone, Andromache. You are a true Princess of Troy. Never forget that."

"How will we defeat the Greeks without Hektor? Who will rise up to replace him?"

Hecuba held Andromache's eyes in her own. "Rage, my darling. The rage of queens."

"What do you mean?"

"What Achilles did to Hektor—" Hecuba's voice sharpened. "For all the sons he has taken from me ... Troilus, my beautiful boy ... for so many tragedies of the Trojans. Achilles will pay. I have assurance."

Andromache sensed the darkness behind Hecuba's words. She was a cold and sharp woman, one who should never be crossed. Andromache believed Hecuba capable of slitting a man's throat in his sleep, and had often wondered if that's why Priam chose to sleep elsewhere most nights. It was hard to imagine the warm and sad mother Hektor assured her she was. "How? How do you know?"

"*Apollo* has promised me." The god's visit had reassured her.

"Apollo," Andromache whispered with a hint of fear. "He is—"

"Our means to ending the war. And ending Achilles' reign of terror over our city." Hecuba clicked her tongue. "You must get up, Andromache. Wash your face."

"I would rather throw myself from the wall." She looked to her son. "But, of course, I cannot."

"No, you cannot." The queen extended a hand to Andromache. "Daughter, don't give up."

Andromache brushed the queen's hand from hers. "I ... it is not so simple for me."

Hecuba stepped back, taking the measure of her son's widow. She folded her arms, hoping Andromache possessed the will of iron she would need in the days to come. "Nothing about this war has been simple. Revenge will not be simple. There will be a time to mourn, but it is not this moment. However much your heart is breaking, you must find the strength. If not for yourself, then for your son."

"But you ... you are—"

"What? The cold queen who haunts Priam's palace? I hear the stories. Do you think that because I am old, the pain of Hektor's loss does not rip my heart in half? He was my first born. The Golden Prince of Troy. He was to inherit all of this. He understood me, as no other ever has." Hecuba's face darkened; her eyes narrowed to angry slits. "And Achilles took him in the most brutal way. Defiled him." Her voice cracked. "Keeps him from proper burial. Yet, with every loss, I have remained steadfast in my duty as queen. I promise you, when the day arrives as Apollo has promised me it will, Achilles will fall, and we will be free."

"What of Astyanax? His future?"

"He will be king someday. So get up and be his strength, as Hektor was yours."

Helen paced her chamber; turning over the reality she'd grown certain of with each passing day. Hektor's cruel passing days ago only made the news she had to deliver more tragedy than joy. In the beginning, she never expected Paris to discover her plan, but now that he knew the underlying truth there would be no denying it.

"You wished to speak with me?" Paris said from the threshold of their room. "You have been avoiding me since Achilles ... since Hektor—"

"Do you think we have a chance to win the final battles to come?

I mean without *him*. Who will take his place?"

"The duty falls to me. May I enter?" He crossed the space without waiting for Helen's permission. "Is that why you asked for me? To speak of war?"

Helen wrung her hands together. "Yes. No. So many things."

"Which is it, then?" Paris poured himself a cup of wine from the table. He drained the contents and poured a second before he sat on the couch near the fire. "Well?"

"I don't know how to begin." She rested a hand on her lower abdomen. "I … you know we talked of children …"

"It is too late for us to speak of making a family. Too many things have passed between us. What you did to my son …"

Helen stopped pacing, frozen by insinuation. "What I did?" she scoffed and shook her head. "Oh, Paris, what I did was … reprehensible, but you … what *you* did surpassed anything even the gods could forgive."

A shadow crossed Paris' face. When he looked up at Helen, he sneered. "You slept with my son, Helen. You've bewitched me with a longing for you that disgusts me. Even now—"

"Even now, what?" She let her hand stray toward her sex. "You want this? Despite the fact your son plowed the fertile fields you could not?"

Paris' cock began to stiffen. "No! No, you can't fix this with …" Paris groaned miserably. "By the gods you arouse me against my will. Wait? What are you saying, Helen?"

"I have only recently confirmed it. But I am with child. *His* child."

"By all that the gods hold sacred, how can you be certain of that? We are fucking every day."

How many times she'd prayed for a different life, Helen had lost count. Hoping that she and Paris would have a family of their own would have made the sacrifices they both endured sting less. Perhaps, a family would bind them with something natural. As the years passed, it became more obvious to her that Aphrodite would never allow their union to be blessed. The goddess had no desire to grant them peace or joy.

Helen stepped closer to Paris, close enough to feel his mounting desire pressed against her thigh. She looked up into his stone blue eyes. "You have been taking me for years and my womb has never quickened. He is the father. I am carrying your grandchild."

Paris stumbled backwards. "I despise you," he screamed like an injured animal.

Helen's voice was ice. "Then we are well-matched, indeed."

They stood staring angrily at one another, frozen in their mutual contempt. Then, Paris reached a hand to her arm. "Even still," he pulled her into his embrace, and she melted into his hungry kisses, "I cannot stop myself."

Tears spilled over Helen's lower lashes. "Neither can I."

In an angry tangle of loathing and longing, they took each other like wild beasts rutting in a field. Gone was the pretense of love. All that remained was the curse of desire and the regret of giving into it. They grunted to their climaxes and fell sweating on the floor, when a distant scream pierced the air.

Helen brushed her hair from her eyes. "What was that?"

Paris sat up on his elbows. "It can't be."

"What?"

"Achilles." Paris scrambled to his feet, grabbing at his chiton. "Get up. Get dressed. We must go to the wall."

As they raced to the ramparts, the cries grew louder. Dozens of citizens were already lining the wall. Some crying out to the gods, others openly weeping and wailing. The crowd near them parted, so they could reach the edge. Helen looked down to see Achilles dragging the mutilated body of Hektor around the city fortress. "By all that is sacred," she whispered, and then fainted.

THIRTY SIX

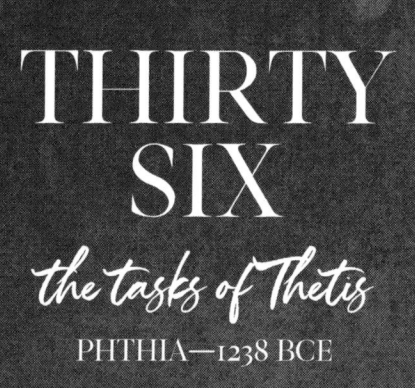

the tasks of Thetis

PHTHIA—1238 BCE

The light of Apollo stretched golden across the heavens, as Thetis approached Peleus in his gardens. "Peleus," she said softly, "I have a message from our son."

The king froze. Closing his eyes, he slowly turned around. When he opened them, he sighed loudly. "I never thought to see your loveliness again."

Thetis' message strained her smile. "Greetings, husband."

"*Husband*. I had almost forgotten," Peleus said quietly. "I have lost track of the time." His eyes lingered on her face. "You are unchanged. As always."

"What did you expect?" Thetis held out her hands. "Come. I have much to share."

"Is the war over? Does Achilles live?"

"No, the war rages its last days. Achilles lives—"

"Thank the gods. He will come home. He must come home."

Sweeping to Peleus' side, Thetis lifted a graceful hand to her husband's bronze and weathered cheek. "Shah, my love. That is a dream we *must* release to the Fates."

Peleus grimaced, his chin quivering against his will. "No." A stray, hot tear breached Thetis' hand. "No."

"Peleus … he will never return. I knew it years ago. It is why I …" Thetis sighed. "No matter now. The past cannot be changed. Knowing one's fate only encourages a futile struggle."

"Why?" Peleus broke down after a lifetime of fighting wars and keeping the peace. The legacy he'd crafted his entire life now hung in the balance. His son was soon to be bones wrapped in a dusty shroud. "Why now when I am helpless to save him? I cannot bear his loss." He melted against Thetis' chest.

When his grief slowed, she said, "No one can save him, Peleus." Thetis gently stroked his gray beard. "I do bring a message from him. Would you hear it?"

Peleus lifted his head, his face but a short distance from hers. He nodded. "Tell me everything."

"There is no way to soften the blow of this. Patrokles is dead."

"How?"

"He donned Achilles' armor. Hektor slew him thinking it was Achilles."

Peleus stumbled as comprehension swept over him. "Has he taken revenge?"

Thetis steadied him, steering him to a nearby bench. They sat silently for a moment. "He has taken revenge beyond what is reasonable, Peleus. He … defiles the corpse. Drags it behind his chariot. Even as I left his side, he was determined to let Hektor's body rot, denying Hektor's family the privilege of proper rites."

"Can you not reason with him?"

"He will hear nothing."

"Then, you are right. I will never see my son again. The gods will punish him." Peleus patted Thetis' warm hand. "I am old. I expect the gods will take me soon enough."

"He did send a message for you."

"What is it?"

"He said to tell you, you were right to send Patrokles to guide him. He also bid me say farewell to you. And begs you take in Briseis, the woman who he loved second to Patrokles."

The king's breath caught in his throat, as a small shudder of grief shook his chest. "I can deny him nothing. I will see it done."

Thetis kissed her husband on his cheek. "You are soft in your old age."

Peleus chuckled quietly. "We mortals tend to do that."

"It's a pity there's no remedy for that."

"Oh, but there is. Wine. Join me in a cup."

In the dark hours of early morning, Thetis rose from the bed she shared with Peleus. He snored slightly with old age, but remained beautiful, like a rugged mountain, in her eyes. She wrapped a thin, shimmering cloak of silver about her nude body and walked out to the garden alone. The damp grass beneath her feet grounded her to a life she never truly wanted, but for love of Achilles, she'd accepted.

In the beginning she abhorred Peleus' mortal nature. After years of loving her son, Peleus' mortal flaws seemed less so. It surprised her that she found their lovemaking oddly satisfying. She plucked a white flower from a bush, inhaling its sweetness.

"Thetis, I have been searching for you," a voice boomed behind her.

She spun around. "Zeus! What are you doing here?" Her eyes scanned the sparkling skies for signs of Hera. A bird. A moth. A low hanging cloud. "What do you want? Quickly, tell me before Hera discovers you."

"I did not think to find you here among mortals."

"You mean with Peleus."

"I believed you content to be among your sisters."

"You have not answered my question."

The god approached her slowly, his power shimmering in the waning moonlight just beneath his skin. "You must stop him, Thetis. By any means. I cannot hold back the anger of all the gods at once. Achilles has desecrated Hektor's body long enough. He violates the sacred rites of the gods."

"He grieves deeply for Patrokles who Hektor slew."

"Apollo killed Patrokles, not Hektor. It was the god who unbuckled Patrokles' armor, leaving his mortal joints exposed. If Achilles wishes revenge, he should take up against Apollo."

"That is impossible."

"Is it? Your son has lost control of his emotions. His anger now borders on madness."

Thetis worried that Zeus would strike Achilles himself if angered by her refusal. She studied his black, shining eyes. The universe reflected in his large pupil, but there was no hint of trickery.

"What should I do?"

"Twelve days have come and gone since he fought Hektor at the wall. Stop him from further desecration of the body. Persuade him to return Hektor's corpse to his father. It is right that he do so."

"I will try. I cannot force him to listen."

Zeus stepped toward Thetis, and his face hovered above hers. His eyes stared hungrily at her mouth. "That is all I ask, Thetis."

"I must go."

"As must I." Zeus disappeared in a flash of light.

Thetis stood for a moment before returning to Peleus' bed. Zeus' visit confirmed that Achilles' death was imminent. All her efforts had been in vain. Death chased her son with gods' speed. She flew to Peleus' side and kissed him lightly on the lips. He stirred, but did not awaken.

"No time for farewells," she whispered against his ear. Then, she was gone.

Thetis emerged from the sea mist gathering along the shore of the Myrmidon's camp. The beach was deserted except for one man standing against the shadows of early morning. She pulled her shimmering dark veil about her shoulders and approached him on light feet. "Achilles."

"I heard your call, Mother."

She embraced him tightly with her elegant arms.

"You needn't worry, Mother. I am prepared to die."

Thetis released him quickly and grabbed his shoulders. "I am not prepared to lose you. You have just begun to taste the sweetness that mortal life can bring."

"And yet it is enough."

"There is life after grief subsides." Achilles' face softened, but Thetis marked the pain in his blue eyes.

"I have lost enough of myself with war. With Patrokles gone … what remains longs for vengeance and death. Peace eluded me in life, perhaps in death I will find it."

Thetis took his face in both of her hands and looked deep into his eyes. "You have been my entire life. I have loved you as I have loved no one else. Happiness can be yours, Achilles." She brushed a hand gently over his bruised and scabbed scalp. "Why not take Briseis as wife before the end? Don't push away the joys of life, even though your days are short. Enjoy what you can, while you can."

Achilles smiled wanly. "I am content. Tell me about Peleus."

"He wishes you to return home. Take his place as King of Phthia. But, he knows that is not to be."

"After I am gone, you must not abandon him. Promise me, Mother."

"I promise." Thetis sighed. "There is something else. A message from Zeus."

Achilles' eyebrows shot up. "Zeus?"

"He came to me in the garden with a command for you."

"I am almost afraid to hear it."

"You may not like it, but you must obey. It is about your desecration of Hektor's body."

A shadow crossed Achilles' face. The desperate anger returned. "What does he say?"

"He demands you return Hektor's body to King Priam. The gods are angry that you continue to … drag the body. That it is improper and stirs the Olympians to contend with one another. Zeus commands that your grief be satisfied."

His rancor was visible in his clenched jaw. "If that is Zeus' will. I will obey. What choice do I have?"

She took Achilles' hands in her own. "Before the war is over, find some happiness in this life. However small and short-lived it may be."

THIRTY SEVEN
the beggar king
PRIAM'S PALACE, TROY—1238 BCE

Queen Hecuba listened to every word Priam said with disbelief. Surely, it was a ruse to strike the fatal blow at Troy. If Priam's plan went awry, there would be no second chance. "Are you certain, Priam?"

"Hermes spoke to me directly. The vision was very clear. Take a ransom, face Achilles myself, and ask for our son's body."

"Have your wits abandoned you? You're no match for Achilles. You will put all our lives in jeopardy if you do this. No one wants Hektor's body returned more than his own mother, but not at the expense of the living. If you die, all is lost within the day. There must be some other way."

"Hecuba, I must do this."

The chamber grew cold. A shadow passed between them. Hecuba shivered, pulling her himation tightly about her shoulders. Each day since Hektor's death was colder than the one before. "You're inviting more senseless deaths. Hektor should have listened and stayed behind the wall. He would still be alive. Andromache would not be a widow. And Astyanax would not be fatherless. Why do the gods curse us so?"

"I don't know."

"How different our lives would've been if Agelaus had obeyed you. If we'd never known about Paris. Because of his fate, we've all suffered more loss than one lifetime should yield. If I could tear Achilles' heart from his chest with my bare hands, well, perhaps then I would have some small vengeance."

"I will return with our son. And if I am wrong and do not, I will have Hektor in my arms and can pass to the Underworld in peace. Help me into this tunic."

Hecuba lifted the soft, white garment over his head and smoothed the neckline and shoulders with her shaking hands. She picked up a golden belt, but Priam pushed it away. "No adornments."

"If you are leaving in secret, under cover of darkness, why have you called all your remaining sons to the Great Hall?"

"Come, my wife, and you will hear."

The sons of Priam gathered at the south end of the Great Hall, waiting impatiently and murmuring amongst themselves. When Priam entered with Hecuba on his arm, an uneasy silence settled on the assembled group. They glanced left and right at one another with worried eyes and faces.

Priam's disapproving eye looked them all over, each and every one. "You are all worthless." His sons shuffled their feet and looked down in shame at the insult, but no one said a word. "Hektor's death but preceded our own. Troy will fall without him. I wish that any of you had died instead of him, you worthless cunts. He was a true warrior, ready to be a king." Priam spat on the floor. "Look at the lot you! Not one of you compares to the son I have just lost." His angry gaze landed on Paris. "And you … you most of all. If I had known what my city would suffer at your hands, I would have ripped you from your mother's womb and fed you to the dogs. And Helen. I was blinded by your beauty and soft words like everyone else around you, but you are nothing but a worthless whore cowering behind my son. I wish you'd never stepped foot in my city, or that I'd sent you packing back to Menelaus years ago. Now, ready me a wagon with a ransom fit for a king. I will face Achilles myself. I might be an old man, but I have more courage than any of you cowards." The brothers, except for Paris, dispersed to quickly carry out their father's commands.

Hecuba saw Priam now, for the first time as the old man he was. She realized that she, too, was old. Sorrow and time had ground her spirit into dust. Paris stood back, waiting for her. She approached him with heavy steps. Her eyes slowly met his. It was difficult knowing she'd been wrong all along, and that her weakness in obeying the god was partly to blame for Hektor's death and the shadow hanging over the city.

"Mother, I—I will do all in my power to bring Achilles down."

Hecuba placed a hand on Paris' cheek. "Defying the gods only brings suffering. They revel in our misery. You, my son, were never meant to live a peaceful life. You also lost a son, your only son, because of *her*."

"More so than you will ever know."

Hecuba kissed his cheek. "Do what you can to save us, for as long as you can. As for Achilles' death, I pray Apollo brings it swiftly." She watched Paris walk away and sighed.

Priam touched her shoulder. "Hecuba, it is time."

Inhaling her grief, Hecuba said, "Bring my son home." Not until she was alone in the hall did Hecuba weep. She pulled her dark himation closely about her head and face and made her way through the palace to the streets overflowing with refugees to Apollo's temple. She knew the way to the inner sanctum. Not a single priestess moved to stop her. The black marble was cool beneath her feet. She stripped her garments and knelt before the god until her knees ached. She prayed for the return of her son and her vengeance against Achilles.

Priam urged the oxen pulling the heavy wagon on with measured snaps of the reins. The uncollected dead of both sides littered the ground. Putrid fumes filled the night air. He pulled his cloak around his nose to ward off the stench. By midday it would be unbearable. He could make out the shadowy form of scavengers moving like wraiths among the bodies, taking what little treasures as they could. The sorrowful song of women and children weeping for the fallen stirred his old, aching heart. The war had taken everything he held most precious from him. He was about to put his life in the hands of his mortal enemy, and he was fully prepared to die before dawn.

Out of the gloomy, early morning, a young man appeared in

the middle of the road. Priam pulled up the oxen. "Easy. Easy." The wagon creaked to a halt. "Who are you?" The hairs along his arms stood on end. "Where did you come from?"

"I am returning to the Myrmidon camp."

"That's not an answer."

"Why are you going in my direction? You are not one of us."

"No." Taking a chance, Priam said, "I need to speak to Achilles."

Raising an eyebrow, the stranger replied, "There's a risky deed."

"If you help me, I will give you a gift from this ransom."

The stranger glanced around Priam at the wagon piled high with baskets and chests. He shook his head. "A ransom intended for Achilles? Misfortune follows anyone who dares take from Achilles what is his by right."

"Can you tell me if Hektor's body still lies by the ships?" Priam's heart pounded wildly against his ribs. His voice quivered. "Or have the dogs devoured him?" His shaking fingers touched a scabbed-over patch on his scalp.

"You must be King Priam." The stranger bowed his head. "I can tell you Achilles continues to defile the body. The dogs refuse to go near it. It is strange that the body does not rot. Almost as if a god protects it."

Priam exhaled without realizing he'd been holding his breath. "I am grateful, then."

"Come, then, king. I will take you to Achilles myself. Keep your eyes down and speak not a word to anyone, but Achilles. If anyone were to recognize you—"

"I give my word."

The stranger hopped into the wagon and took the reins. With a quick snap, the oxen strained to start the roll of the heavy load. The compacted sand gave way to softer patches, causing the wagon to sway, jostling the treasure. The clinking of gold, armor, and bronze bowls reminded Priam of the first time he'd tried to ransom a son. He hoped he was more successful at reclaiming Hektor's body than he was at appeasing Apollo for the life of Paris. In his heart, he doubted he would return home. He was prepared to die with his efforts. A fight with Achilles would surely bring a quick and easy death. The years had left him an old, frail man. He hadn't held a sword aloft in years, let alone headed into battle, since Hektor assumed his place as the head of the Trojan forces.

Before long, they passed by rows of black shields lined in the sand, leaning against tall spears. Behind the shields were scattered groups of tents and low-burning campfires. A few dogs roamed around, sniffing for scraps of food. The cries of children pierced the quiet. They kept moving toward the center of the camp, nearer the shoreline. Priam prayed it wasn't a trap.

The stranger pulled the reins up tightly, slowing the oxen to a halt. He jumped down and slapped the side of the wagon. "This is Achilles' tent. Choose your words wisely. He's known for his quick temper these days." He disappeared into the shadows.

"By the gods," Priam whispered, for he had no doubt one of them had just helped him in his quest. He got down with some difficulty and stood for a long time at the entrance of Achilles' tent contemplating his words. A thin line of light edged the gap where the tent flap overlapped the siding.

"Who's there?" a deep, gravelly voice called out from within.

Priam swallowed hard, reaching a trembling hand to part the entry. He slowly stepped into the darkened interior. A single oil lamp burned against to gloom. "I have come to beg your mercy,

Achilles, Prince of Phthia."

"Briseis, get up and light the lamps."

The silhouette of a woman rose from the bed. Priam could see her outline as she pulled a chiton over her head. She took the oil lamp from Achilles' hand and lit the other lamps. A golden hue filled the tent. For the first time, Priam clearly saw the face of the man who'd terrorized his lands for so many seasons; he'd almost forgotten what peace was like. He looked into the blue eyes that were the last thing Hektor would have seen. Achilles was the biggest man he'd ever encountered. Priam realized how terrifying it would be to face him on the battlefield. He stole a glance in Briseis' direction. She was much older now than when he'd seen her last. After Achilles had sacked Lyrnessus, he mourned the passing of Briseus, her father. He'd heard that princess Briseis had been made Achilles' prize. The irony of the gods wasn't lost on him. He remembered that she was destined to be the wife of the greatest warrior who ever lived, and that he knew now was Achilles, not Hektor.

"I have come for my son."

Achilles took a seat at the table. "Briseis, wine." The woman filled two cups and handed one to Priam without saying a word. Achilles pulled her close, whispering something in her ear. "You may leave us, Briseis." The woman nodded and bowed out of the tent, leaving Priam alone with the man whose name was synonymous with death throughout the Troad. "I am surprised you've come without a guard. It would be an easy thing to take your life." Achilles fingered a space between the wooden planks of the table.

Priam shrugged. "It would be, but little honor in killing an unarmed, old man. Even a king. As for a guard, why risk another man's life, when mine clearly hangs in the balance?"

"You are either very brave, or foolhardy."

"Broken. I am broken by the loss of my sons. I am a desperate man, not a brave one."

"I vowed your son would never see proper burial. You expect me to break my sacred word?"

"When your word goes against the gods, aye, I do. The gods do. They can forgive folly, but not blatant disregard." Priam fell at Achilles' feet, taking his knees in supplication. "Look at me, damn you. Do you not see your father's pain reflected in my face? It is an agony for a father to bury his son. I have laid more sons than any father should have to on their funeral pyres."

Achilles studied Priam's wrinkles and deep-set eyes. "I can scarce recall my father's face."

"He waits for your return, I am certain. What father would not?" Priam grabbed Achilles' hands and kissed them. "These hands have robbed me of my legacy. Soon, I fear, of my entire city. Yet, I kiss them with humble lips and beg you think of your own father's pain. Please, return my *son* to me."

"My mother told me I will never see home again, nor rest my eyes on my father. He already mourns my passing, for it is imminent."

Priam's grief broke and his shoulders shook violently. He wept on Achilles' bare knees. The weight of war had won, finally, in the end. He didn't care for his power or glory, just the body of a man whose life meant more to him than anything else. This time, he would be a father before a king. Perhaps, if he had to do it all over again, being a father instead of a king may have saved everything and everyone he'd ever loved. He would never know now.

A tear trailed down Achilles' cheek. "I think you are brave to come. Your pain has made you so. We must accept that the gods are the needle and fate is the thread of our lives. We exist to live out the design they weave in the stars for us. The life I had before … with a father, with Chiron … is no more than a dream with bits of fleeting light shining on one memory, then another. Do not weep, old man, I will return your son to you."

Briseis prepared a table in a vacant tent to cleanse Hektor's body as Achilles had directed her. It took four women to heft his dead weight inside. She placed a cloth over his privates. Once he was laid out, Briseis called for the water basins. Pouring water over his head and face, she gently cleansed the dirt and sand from his skin and hair. It surprised her that for all the desecration Achilles had inflicted, that Hektor's face sustained only a few minor scratches. "You were once so handsome," she whispered. "And kind to a young girl." Her hands worked with grace and tenderness as she continued the sacred ritual, wiping the grime of defilement away. She winced as she passed the cloth over each cut and bruise on his torso, still not as horrific as she'd expected. When the body was cleansed, the women anointed Hektor with scented oil, pulling a freshly bleached tunic over his nakedness and wrapping him like a newborn babe in a deep blue himation.

One by one, the women left the tent, until Briseis stood alone with Hektor's corpse. She leaned to kiss his cheek. It was cold and stiff. "You deserved better. I pray you enter the Underworld in peace now."

The tent flap flew open. It was Achilles. "Is he ready?"

"Aye."

Priam pushed passed Achilles' shoulder. His breath caught in his throat when he saw his son. "Hektor. Hektor." Rushing forward, he threw himself over Hektor's chest and wept fiercely. "My son. My son."

Achilles just stood there, watching; his face resigned, cold. "You must leave before dawn. I have been generous with you, but if Agamemnon discovers you in camp, he will show you no mercy."

Priam wiped his eyes and nodded. Achilles scooped up the body, and Priam followed him to the cart. Together, executioner and father, pulled up a gray blanket and covered the Golden Prince of Troy, who was no more.

"How many days will you require for his burial?" Achilles asked in such a matter-of-fact voice, Briseis thought he sounded more like a farmer bartering for wheat than a man handing over a dead prince to a king.

"We must gather wood for his pyre. If your men would not attack our efforts. Nine turns of Apollo. Trees have grown scarce since …" His voice trailed off. Briseis sensed his mind gauging how much to say and if Achilles would care. "We need time to prepare a feast. Bury his ashes in a tomb. At least twelve days. If you still wish to fight, we can resume the war."

Achilles simply nodded. "Twelve days. So be it."

Priam climbed up the wagon and took the reins. "Farewell, Achilles. You have my gratitude. And the city's, as well."

A cloud of thinly veiled anger colored Achilles' face. Briseis knew his patience was waning. "Offer no gratitude to me. When your mourning is complete, I will raze your city to the ground." He slapped the haunches of the ox closest him, and the cart jolted forward, taking Priam from view.

Briseis stood staring after the cart long after it had disappeared. She wondered how different her life would have been if Hektor had chosen her. She knew all too well what the Trojan women would face once Achilles decimated their city and killed all their men. "Achilles?"

He glanced down at her. "What is it, Briseis?"

"It's almost like *he* was never here, isn't it?"

"I pray Patrokles will forgive me this. I promised to let Hektor's bones bleach in the sun, after the dogs and birds had gorged on his flesh."

"He would understand your mercy … you dole it out so sparingly."

Achilles scoffed, rebuffing the sting of honesty. "I see Patrokles taught you how to sharpen your tongue."

"Among other things."

"I am restless."

"As am I."

"He will always be between *us*."

"Aye," she said. They walked to their tent, letting the day begin without them. As they lay wrapped around one another, Briseis asked, "How will you die?"

"Only the gods know."

"Are you sure you will … die, I mean?"

Achilles pulled her closer to his chest, inhaling the sweet and saltiness of her. "I will miss this, I think." He kissed the top of her head. "Thetis has said so. And I believe her. She would never speak of such a painful thing if she was not certain."

"I wish there was a way—"

"Shah. Let us not waste the time I have left." He kissed her softly, his tongue lazily sweeping through her mouth. "Our time is short."

Briseis gently held the back of his head, pressing her forehead to his. "You are right. Let's not waste it."

THIRTY EIGHT
three laments

TRO AN CITADEL—1238 BCE

Apollo stretched a gloomy dawn with a bitter sun across the sky, as Cassandra paced the ramparts, waiting for a sign of her father's return. Every moment of uncertainty was an agony. She couldn't help but wonder, now, when Troy's fate hung in the balance, how different the world would've been if she'd pleased the god. Her prophecies would have been heeded and the war avoided. She squinted into the distance at a small, dark dot. Cassandra held her breath, sending up a prayer. As the image drew nearer, the spark of the divine filled her. She blurted out, "Priam returns with Hektor's body. Gods, have mercy on us."

Cassandra's call brought Hecuba and Andromache to her side, along with Helen and Paris. In the belly of the citadel, mourners spilled into the streets, sending the song of sorrow skyward. When Priam drew near, Paris commanded the gates be opened. Priam's head hung low to his chest as he crossed the threshold of the mighty gate. At the sight of their king, the crowds parted like water over a boulder and grew so quiet the creaking of the wagon wheels filled the silence. The oxen pulled their burden to the citadel's center, through the inner gates, and into the palace grounds.

Paris and Deiphobus lifted their brother's body from the wagon and solemnly placed it on a litter draped in bleached linen edged with purple. They carried their brother to a waiting altar adorned with wildflowers from the Trojan fields and delicate garlands of laurel and olive from the city's gardens. Frankincense burned in silver bowls, perfuming the air. Every citizen, highborn and the lowly, struggled with Hektor's farewell. He'd been the strength and security Troy had clung to these many seasons. The Defender of the City had fallen, been brutalized before their eyes, and now, every man and woman feared their world would crumble.

Andromache's stoic face cracked with grief. She handed Astyanax to his nursemaid, steeling herself for the gruesome figure she was certain she'd see. The babe reached for his mother, squalling for the comfort of her arms. The crowd of onlookers blurred. There was only Hektor. With each step she recalled a moment compelling her to love him. When his fingers gently pulled the pins of her chiton on their wedding night. When he sought the comfort of her arms after Ares died. When he laughed with joy once presented with their son. Her last memory was her beloved being dragged behind Achilles' chariot. She stumbled, as tears stung her eyes. Raw grief tugged at the thin thread of her strength and she unraveled. Nothing would be the same. No one could save her or her son, their son, from what would come. A thought pricked her heart that she had somehow caused his death with her own worry, so in despair, Andromache grabbed a lock of her long, dark hair and violently yanked it out with a mournful scream. She tossed the bloody mess to the ground. Astyanax cried louder, but his mother was lost in her anguish.

Standing beside Hektor's body, Andromache lifted the golden shroud to see his face. She was astonished to see only a few scratches, and he looked otherwise peaceful. "Oh, Hektor," she whispered, taking his head in her hands. She kissed his gray lips. They were cold and stiff beneath her warm ones. "You've been taken too soon. There was so much more joy to share. Life to live. Love. However, the gods are cruel. Haven't we agonized in life enough to satisfy them? What a blessing Astyanax is. With you by our sides, there was nothing to fear. Everywhere I look without you, all I see is danger and suffering. He will not survive the war … You know what will happen to him, to me. I will be forced to lie beneath a man, a master. I know he will be cruel, because I am the widow of the man the Greeks feared most. I will be raped, and if I am fortunate, killed mercifully." She rubbed at her burning eyes. "We had no final words, Hektor. Did you think of me? Of our family? I would have comforted you, as you did for me so many times. I did not get to say good-bye … There are no loving words to comfort me in the long, dark days ahead." Andromache threw herself on his body, weeping.

Hecuba put an arm around her son's widow. Watching Andromache's agony pulled her own ancient wounds to the surface. "He gave strength to all of us." Andromache leaned her head into Hecuba's shoulder, her sobbing catching in her throat. "He was my favorite son." She looked each remaining son circled around

Hektor in the eye. Her voice trembled with the sharp truth. "You all knew it was so. None of you could complain, because you loved him more than any of your other brothers." Hecuba turned her gaze back to Hektor's face. "Look at my poor son. Favored among us and the gods. Achilles sent many Trojan princes to slavery, but you, he plucked from us with his murderous spear. Stealing your life to ease his guilt about his second in command. Your death did not bring back that other man." She kissed his cheek as her tears flowed. "You have the look of peaceful slumber despite the ravages Achilles put you through." Hecuba kissed Andromache's head so close to her own. "You will never be alone, my dear. Ever."

Andromache clung to Hecuba and sobbed anew.

To the surprise of everyone, Helen stepped forward to offer a lament on Hektor's behalf. Standing at his feet, separate from his widow and mother, she said in a silvery voice, "You were the jewel in Troy's crown, a prince among princes. Even above my own husband, your brother. I wish that I had died before I lived to see you struck by Achilles' hand. All these years, you offered me kind words. Stood up for me for Paris' sake."

Hecuba hissed, "You lying bitch."

"He was kinder to me than you have ever been, Queen Hecuba. Than the lot of you, save Priam. I am sad, Hektor, for it seems we are both doomed souls. There is no one left to comfort me. Everyone blames me. Hates me."

Paris came forward and awkwardly pulled Helen behind the familial circle. She wept against Paris' chest for her own sadness and burdens. His eyes cast his apology to his mother and father, but he dared not look at Andromache.

"You have no honor spilling such lies over my husband's dead body, when he can't rise to defend himself. He had only contempt for you. Blamed you for the war. For everything."

Priam, in his grief and sadness, raised both arms for peace. "We have twelve days to prepare Hektor's pyre and feast. I will not have us fighting amongst ourselves, when the true enemy remains a spear toss beyond our gates."

"I will prepare the gathering of the wood," Paris said.

"Aye. Go, Paris. See that it is done."

GREEK CAMP

Agamemnon's grand pavilion was packed with his commanders around the heavy center table, while their seconds, with worried faces and darting eyes, lined the perimeter. The platters of bread and roasted meat were mostly untouched. Achilles' news had stolen everyone's appetite, except for young Diomedes. Agamemnon paced the carpeted floor, while Achilles reclined in a chair. "You had no right to release Priam without my consent."

Achilles leaned forward with his forearms against his thighs. He shrugged. "He came to me. It was my right to grant or deny his request."

"I do not wish to cause another rift between our camps."

"Then don't. What more do you want, Agamemnon? My certain deference or victory?"

Agamemnon grunted.

"I will take the city," Achilles said, indifferent to Agamemnon's growing irritation.

Menelaus blurted out, "If we held the king, the city would fall by the time Apollo dragged the sun to the sea. I am sick of this place."

Odysseus mumbled into his wine, "We are all sick of this place."

A heavy silence settled over all the men. Achilles rose from his seat. "Consider this ... they have twelve days to mourn. We have twelve days to rest our men and contemplate how we will divide the plunder of Troy's treasury. I have given my word." The tent flap snapped closed behind him.

Menelaus clicked his tongue. "After everything we've endured on account of that man's wounded pride—"

"That man is the key to victory," Odysseus said. "Don't you want to go home?"

"Of course, I do. Achilles speaks as if he *alone* will take down the city."

Odysseus narrowed his eyes at Menelaus, his lip curling angrily. "You open your shit mouth and words fall out ... words no one wants to hear. If you had kept a better eye on your wife's pleasure, none of us would be here at all." He stood and stepped around the table. His temper shook. He squared his shoulders, daring Menelaus to challenge him. Odysseus scoffed, "Have you misplaced your courage, Menelaus?"

The other commanders sniggered; Menelaus roared in exasperation.

Agamemnon raised his voice above the disagreement, "We all know without Achilles we will lose. And what then? Those of us not rotting on the ground or being eaten by wild dogs return home empty handed? No. No one is more offended than I by what he did. But I agree with Odysseus. It's time we go home."

THIRTY NINE
the Amazonian princess
TROAN PLAIN—1238 BCE

Behind the Great Wall of Troy, masses of refugees gathered in the streets with more arriving, as word of the tenuous truce spread. Songs of mourning resounded throughout the city, as did the playfulness of innocent children. Stray dogs roamed free, sniffing out discarded morsels or a head scratch. Merchants shouted to sell their wares. The stench of urine and shit soured the air. The king's counselors argued about how long the city could sustain the strain of so many inhabitants. They surmised that the stores of grain wouldn't last long, and neither would fresh water. Starvation and disease would not be far behind a food shortage. When people became desperate, dangers of another kind would arise. King Priam reminded his counsel that refusing entry to refugees would be their certain death, because the Greeks were still out there waiting for their opportunity to strike on the twelfth day. He asked them what kind of king he would be if he just pushed their allies to their common enemy to be decimated.

Despite the masses, Priam designated the city's lower central court for the building of Hektor's pyre. It was the only area large enough to build and accommodate the crowds. For days, wood gathering parties scoured the hillsides for trees; felled them and dragged them back to Troy. A crew of several dozen men built the pyre stack. Dozens more children scavenged for kindling to stuff between the gaps. As the mountain grew, so too did the weeping and wailing of women. Hektor's death was seen as a sign of Troy's impending doom. Rumors of Achilles grew into tales of his invincibility and a growing belief he was actually a god disguised as a man. The remaining brothers of Hektor also heard these stories and fear took root in their hearts.

The somber days of funeral preparation dragged on, until on the fourth day, a lookout raised Troy's alarm. A cloud of dust appeared on the horizon. It was no storm, but the telltale sign of an army on the move. Many cried, fearing the Greeks and Achilles had broken their promise. People cleared the streets, scurrying into shops, gardens, anywhere they could. The princes of Troy lined the wall to assess the imminent danger. Paris called to close the gates, while his brothers organized a defense from the parapets and ramparts.

With Hektor's death, the command of the Trojan army fell to Paris and Deiphobus, who took their positions at the center of the wall. Paris gripped his bow in his hands. "Do you think Achilles would break the truce?"

"He could've killed our father. It makes no sense to break his word after such an act of restraint."

"He is ruthless and untrustworthy," Paris said.

"If it is Achilles, he comes with only his Myrmidons. There are not enough to be the united armies." As they stood waiting, a small contingent pulled away from the main horde. "Look, Paris. They've sent heralds."

Paris narrowed his eyes suspiciously. "We shall know soon enough who threatens us."

Three tall riders approached on horseback, stopping just beneath the main gate. Their skin was sun-dark and their bearing regal. They wore short tunics and coverings about their legs. Their clothing was adorned with glittering bronze scales and beads of bone. "Queen Penthesileia sends her greetings. She heard of Prince Hektor's death, and has come to join Troy's fight against the foreign invaders," a rider announced in a clear, commanding voice.

Paris looked at Deiphobus. "They are women, brother."

"Amazons," Deiphobus said. "Fierce fighters. We may win this war yet."

Paris shouted down, "We welcome all allies committed to destroying the enemies of Troy."

One of the riders removed her helm. Long, dark hair fell about her shoulders. "Is the one they call Achilles yet living?"

"Aye, he lives," Paris answered.

"Our queen will be pleased. She wishes an audience with King Priam and Troy's commander."

"We are honored and extend our hospitality, but our city can't hold your army. Our refugees are too many. You will have to set camp outside of the walls. Head northeast. Our allies' encampment is nearby. It is the safest place outside of the city. We will send an escort for your queen at dusk."

"Very well," the herald said, refitting her splendid helm. The riders spun their horses around and headed back to their horde.

Priam's Great Hall warmed with the glow of oil lamps and blazing torches. Trestle tables were spread with platters of roasted boar and lamb and warm bread baked with rosemary. There were dipping pots of olive oil and bowls of sweet blood oranges. Household slaves hurried to pour fresh wine, while a lyre player struck soft notes in a corner. A fire burned brightly in the central hearth.

Queen Hecuba's black garments wrapped about her like a winter storm, setting the tone for the somber reception. Andromache's scalp had healed slightly, but she chose not to wear a head covering, preferring the world to know the depth of her grief. The other women of the royal family followed suit by donning dark attire. King Priam's black tunic was unadorned by precious metals or jewels, and he'd ripped the front as an expression of his burdened heart.

Hecuba leaned to catch Priam's private ear. The gold bangles on her wrist clanking against the table. "Paris and Helen are not here. It is disrespectful."

"I will send someone to fetch them." Priam signaled a thin slave with stooped shoulders standing in the shadows. "Find my son, Paris. Tell him his presence is expected at once." The man nodded and limped away without as much as a scrape of his sandal on the stone.

The music of the hall hushed as Queen Penthesileia entered, flanked by a dozen women clad in dark leather tunics trimmed with golden scales and leopard skin capes. The queen was taller than anyone else in her entourage. The hem of her sleek, black leather cape swept the tile, and a collar of luminous raven feathers framed her chiseled features and golden eyes. Her long hair, black as the darkest night, cascaded in curls about her shoulders. A wide, flat circlet of gold set with an emerald adorned her head. She wore a ring on each finger, including her thumbs. As she walked, the silver rings layered across her chest piece shook, sounding the music of war. She approached the dais where Priam and Hecuba sat, her head held high, and her neck unbending. "We come to grieve the loss of Prince Hektor, and to fight alongside you for his revenge."

King Priam acknowledged her with a small nod. "We welcome you as our guest and as our ally."

"Please, accept these gifts from my people." She raised a long, elegant arm, and wide-shouldered men with bare chests brought forth stacks of seasoned ash spears and curved bows. "During war, a king may find well-made weapons more valuable than gold."

"You have our gratitude, Queen Penthesileia," Priam said. "You are most welcomed in our hall. I have reserved you a place of honor at my right."

The queen took her place at the high table, while her commanders posted themselves strategically around the room. "One must be ready when the wolf paces outside of the door."

"How fare your troops after the long march?"

"We are used to the hardships of war. We will be ready, when the enemy takes to the plain." Penthesileia sipped her wine and ripped a hunk of soft bread for her trencher. She poured the olive oil over it. "I have heard stories of your son, Hektor, since before the invaders came. It is hard to recall a time when our lives were not burdened by their presence. The loss of Hektor is a tragedy for everyone who depends on Troy's victory for survival. Who have you named as his successor?"

"No man could replace him. His brothers, Paris and Deiphobus, are now joint commanders of our forces."

Penthesileia bit into her bread, licking the spicy oil from her fingertips. She wrinkled her brow. "Two commanders?"

"They each have their skills and strengths."

"You know your men best. Tell me about this Achilles. Is he as ruthless as the stories say?"

When the Greeks first arrived, Priam believed the incursion would be short-lived, and that the Greeks would soon retreat for easier prey. But, as each season stretched to the next, his confidence began to wane. No siege war had ever lasted so long. Those who dared in the past had given up and left empty handed. Then, there was Achilles. No warrior had ever fought like he did, like a god. At first, he'd brushed tales of Achilles aside as soldiers' exaggerations. He had been wrong. They had all been wrong. For every decision they had executed, the Greeks countered with an exceptional strategy of their own. However, it was Hektor who paid most dearly for his failings as King of Troy. In his indignation and grief, he wanted to kill Paris and Agelaus, as well, for disobeying a direct command. It was too late for his regrets.

"Achilles is everything you have heard. And worse. He fights without honor and defiles the dead."

"I am the daughter of Ares. I will not fail you, King Priam."

The mood of the city was as gloomy as the sky, as King Priam and Queen Hecuba led Hektor's funeral procession through the winding streets of Troy. Behind them, Andromache—veiled in the blackest gossamer—walked with Astyanax clinging to her neck in fear of the noisy crowds. Paris and Helen followed after, then Deiphobus, Cassandra, and Helenus, and the remaining royal household. Five hundred Trojan soldiers followed in their shining armaments and tall spears knotted with silver and blue ribbons. Thousands of mourners cast flowers and garlands at the golden litter bearing Hektor's body as it swayed by. Women wept without shame and bared their breasts. Men rent their garments and tore out their beards. Children cried because they were afraid and hungry. Dogs howled. Not a living soul was immune to the sorrow of the passing of Hektor and what it meant for all of them.

The procession wound its way to the lower central square where the marketplaces and bazaars were usually erected with colorful tents and long carts pulled by fat oxen and strong horses. Hektor's family gathered around the pyre, while Paris and Deiphobus, their brother's successors, led the litter bearers to the pyre's peak. The litter was carefully secured on the wooden altar. They placed Hektor's spear beside him and his great shield at his feet. In the days it took to erect the giant structure, the grieving had stuffed bits of embroidered cloth, oranges, chiton pins, and garden flowers into the stacks. The war had robbed most of them of their wealth and possessions, but they would not leave their prince without some tokens of their affection and sadness.

As Apollo pulled the sun to the sea, the torch bearers lit the bottom of the pyre stack. Weeping and moaning grew louder, as the fire climbed higher. Fingers of flame reached for Hektor's body. A gust of warm wind whipped 'round and 'round the great stack, until the fire became an inferno. The ritual flames crackled and roared as they consumed Hektor, the Golden Prince of Troy.

The gray of the day had given way to a deep purple sky blinking with silver stars. The pyre still burned, but less eagerly now. The grieving crowd had returned to their homes and tents to lay down their weary heads. It was a lonely place, now, the pyre where Hektor had been. A solitary figure remained, her long gown fluttering from time to time in the night air. Hecuba. She had brought him squalling and pink into the world of men, and she would see him to the bitter end, a stack of wine-tinted bones resting in a box. She sweetly caressed every memory of Hektor. A mother's song for her son is mostly the quiet joy she shares while he lives. When he no longer needs her hand to hold. When he finds enduring love. When he presents her with a child of his own. All this she sings in her heart, forever.

Hecuba prayed to Apollo with her aching soul and heart of ash, until the new dawn broke. "Hear me, Apollo. For my son. For our son. Be my instrument of rage and vengeance."

Apollo's icy tongue licked at Hecuba's ear. *"Is your desire for revenge deep enough, I wonder?"*

"I will do whatever you ask of me, if Achilles suffers as Hektor did."

"Promise that on the day I command, send Polyxena in a yellow gown to my temple. I will do the rest."

"I promise."

Apollo burned her lips with a kiss. *"It is done."*

FORTY
a growing madness
TROJAN PLAIN—1238 BCE

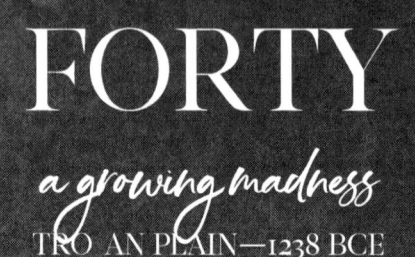

Achilles towered as a god before the ranks of Myrmidons. His black cloak snapped in the breeze behind him. An angry scowl was fixed on his lips, as he gnashed his teeth. His eyes blazed ice. His Myrmidons were uneasy facing an army of mostly women, but Achilles commanded them to fight them as they would men, because they were warriors who had come to fight and risk death for their efforts. The black horsehair on his helm crest shook, as he shouted across the distance between the armies, "You have come to die, Queen of the Amazons."

Penthesileia stood unflinching as his words rolled like thunder over her head. Her army stood brave and bold at her back. Since she arrived in Troy, she'd heard the stories of how Achilles slaughtered his enemies, how he relished the bloodbath of war. She knew he was made for combat and that made him a worthy challenger. Her sword was deadly, for in her chest beat the heart of a lion, not just a queen.

The bones of her victims adorned her helm's crest and clattered as beads against the bronze. She wore paint of grease and ground, bleached bones smeared across her face and arms. Her breastplate gleamed in Apollo's light. "Your words do not frighten me, Achilles. I am the daughter of Ares," she roared. "We shall see who my father favors this day."

She held her sword aloft, unleashing a fearsome war cry. The Myrmidons leaned forward, trembling with their need to fight. Penthesileia's army flew behind her as they charged the Myrmidons at breakneck speed. Once more, shields clashed on the Trojan Plain.

Penthesileia and Achilles crashed into each other like storming waves against a rocky shore. Grace and death danced for blood and victory. Each strike brought one of them closer to the Underworld. The Amazon gripped her sword in both hands, ready to strike a fatal blow, but instead her chest heaved for breath. She stumbled one step, and then two. Her sword clattered to the hard ground. Looking down, her shaking fingers touched the bloody spear point protruding from her middle. Penthesileia's surprised eyes met Achilles'; he poised, ready to strike, but he made no move to do so. Neither of them had heard the fatal song of the spear until it was too late.

Thersites, an ignoble and undistinguished Greek, thrilled at his triumph. "I have felled the Amazon queen. Her armor is mine."

Achilles' blood boiled at being denied his fight. "You are a fucking fool, Thersites." Quickly, he moved to Penthesileia's side, removing her helm. "You deserved better. A champion's death."

Penthesileia tried to speak, instead blood gurgled at the edges of her mouth. Achilles held her upright, as she closed her eyes and died in his arms. His days were growing shorter; he knew it, felt it in his bones. Each victory so close to his last. He laid the queen gently down on her side and turned with fury in his eyes to the thief of his glory. And unexpectedly, the haunting grief of Patrokles' death crept into his chest, and his new rage blinded him to reason.

"Her armor is mine by right," Thersites goaded from behind Achilles. "I killed her."

Achilles seethed at Thersites' arrogance. "You won't have it. She was meant to die at my hand, not yours."

Wiping his filthy hands on the hem of his chiton, Thersites replied, "I suppose the gods thought otherwise."

"You. Won't. Have. It."

Thersites' temper snapped. "You aren't so different from Agamemnon."

The old indignation rose from Achilles' dead soul, mixing with the raw grief of Patrokles' death. A voracious lust for blood flooded through Achilles' veins. He drew his sword without second thought, attacking Thersites. In three swift strokes, the man lay in pieces with Achilles breathing heavily over him. His anger blinded him to all else. As if in a cave, Achilles heard a muffled voice calling his name.

"Achilles! Achilles! What have you done?"

Achilles' senses cleared and he found himself face to face with Odysseus. He glanced down at Thersites, whose dead eyes stared blankly into the sky from his severed head. Achilles felt nothing. The rage was gone.

"Why did you kill him? He's one of us. What madness grips you?"

Stabbing his sword into ground, Achilles surveyed the aftermath of his wrath. "Whoever I was, I am that man no longer."

"Your defilement of Hektor was barely tolerated in the end, but he was our enemy. He'd cut down many of us over the years. I could argue he deserved most of your ... punishment. However, you can't expect to kill one of us without impunity. You must purify yourself, Achilles, before your mind is lost completely."

Achilles' jaw clenched as he turned over Odysseus' advice. Since Patrokles' death, he'd lost his way. He could feel his soul drifting directionless on an endless sea. He no longer cared about anything. Only the brief slivers of light Briseis cast shone through the growing darkness. "Where should I go? Who will stand for me before the gods?"

"Which god favors you the least?" Odysseus asked.

"Without a doubt ... Apollo."

"Then, we head for Lesbos. Make your sacrifices to Apollo. I will sponsor you."

"Why the god who works against me for love of the Trojans?"

Odysseus rested a reassuring hand on Achilles' shoulder. "If you should win *his* favor, your good fortune is assured."

Achilles growled his discontent, but he relented. "We sail at dawn. On one condition."

"What is that?"

"Briseis comes with us."

"As you wish."

LESBOS
BEACHHEAD CAMP

Apollo's light stretched gold across the blue sky, and a light wind scattered downy clouds as far as the eye could see. Achilles lay naked with Briseis at his side on the deck of his beached ship, the sea gently lapping at its hull. Achilles' eyes were closed, while his fingers lazily twirled a strand of Briseis' dark hair, streaked with silver since Patrokles' burial. She shifted to face Achilles. "What was it like being purified? Why haven't you spoken of it?"

He opened his eyes and stared into the sky for a long while. Briseis could see his thoughts churning like the sea. "I know that look of concern on your face. What are you afraid to tell me?"

"I sacrificed to the god. And Odysseus washed my body with the sacred blood. We went down to the beach. I scrubbed the blood off with sand. Then, we drank wine and bathed in the ocean."

"Is that all?"

Achilles sat up, pulling her with him. A lone seabird cried above them. The sound of his crew talking carried on the breeze. He reached a hand to her cheek. "Briseis, what do you wish most?"

"Peace from war."

"Even if it is for a short while?

Briseis twisted to look at Achilles, eyeing him suspiciously. "Something has changed." She reached for his hand. "I see it. Feel it."

Achilles smiled down at her and entwined their fingers, bringing her hand to his lips. "Purification has many benefits. What about peace? Would you have it, if only for a while?"

"If war has taught me anything, it's that nothing lasts forever. Aye, I would have peace, even if it was not everlasting."

"There are no words to tell you how ... broken my soul has been since Patrokles—" Achilles' voice cracked. "I cannot even bring myself to say the words aloud."

"I know," Briseis whispered.

"Marry me, Briseis. In Apollo's temple."

Briseis sat up, stunned by his question. "Why now? Why this

change of heart?"

"We honor Patrokles by doing so."

"Because he would have married me, had he lived and you died?"

"Isn't that reason enough?"

She thought of all her losses, her agonies, and her defeats. There was nothing left to lose anymore, except life itself. Everything she'd ever held in tender regard had been stripped from her hands and heart. "We will have peace?"

"For a time."

"Aye. Then, I will marry you."

Achilles pulled her down to him. "Had I taken you as a wife years ago, Patrokles would still be alive. Whenever I contemplate why he needed to die, I find myself at fault."

"There is guilt enough for us both."

"He was under my protection, Briseis. I am the one who failed him. It was my pride that killed him."

They lay together in silence, for a long time.

When the first star appeared in the sky, Odysseus called to them, "I've brought wine."

"Come up," Achilles said, propping himself up on his elbows. He shrugged sheepishly. "I cannot pass up wine."

Briseis stood and stretched. "I know."

Odysseus hopped over the railing, balancing the amphora of wine. He'd tucked three cups into his belt. "What are you two lovebirds doing?"

"Pour the wine and I will tell you," Achilles said.

Odysseus passed the first cup to Briseis, then to Achilles and himself. "They have good wine here."

"Do you remember the day you told me I should take her to

wife?" Achilles asked Odysseus.

Odysseus cocked an eyebrow. "Aye, but do you recall my advice?"

"I am taking your advice. We will wed come the dawn."

"That calls for more wine." Odysseus refilled their cups. "It's about time you made her your proper wife."

"I had no idea you held me in any regard, Odysseus. You've rarely even spoken to me," Briseis said.

"I do not talk with many women, Briseis. I observed how Achilles changed after he'd taken you as his own. There had been no other women, after you. I am of a like mind. There is only Penelope for me."

Achilles groaned. "Everyone knows that."

Odysseus drained his cup. "A man cannot choose who he loves."

Briseis agreed, "Neither can women."

"Well, that settles it. In the morning, you and Achilles will marry." He glanced between them. "I'll leave the amphora. I'm sure you would rather have your privacy."

Achilles waved his hand at Odysseus. "In the morning, then. Sleep well."

Their guest stepped over the rail and was gone. They were alone once again.

"Are you certain, Achilles, that you want this?"

He answered by pulling Briseis into his arms and kissing her. "Let's sleep beneath the stars."

With the dawn, Achilles took Briseis to Apollo's temple accompanied by Odysseus and the Myrmidon crew. A priest, draped in robes dyed saffron and trimmed in gold threads, led them to a sacred chamber of black obsidian and marble. A golden statue of the god had been erected on a bare, black marble altar. A silver bowl of wine had been placed at the god's feet.

"Remove your sandals," the priest commanded.

Everyone stooped to untie their shoes.

Achilles led Briseis to the altar, while the witnesses stood back and watched. Briseis' eyes locked on Achilles' face as he drew his blade across her palm. A thin, red line blossomed against her skin. "Your blood in exchange for his blessing," Achilles said quietly.

The priest took Briseis' hand, tilting it so a single red drop fell into the bowl, sending ripples in the wine to the bowl's edge.

Achilles repeated the ritual on his hand. "We ask for the blessing of peace," then added, "while my time remains."

Apollo's priest stirred the blood and wine with a silver rod, and then set the bowl before the god's statue. He spoke in the divine tongue, as he bound the bride and groom's freshly blooded palms together.

"You are once again a princess, Briseis," Achilles said. "As it should have always been."

Briseis said nothing, but smiled.

Achilles kissed her before his men and Odysseus. They cheered and clapped their commander on the back. For the first time since Achilles' had claimed her as a prize, they looked on her with true respect, bowed their heads, and called her "my lady." The merriment continued at the beachhead and Achilles' ship.

The warm sun sparkled on the clear, blue water. Briseis and Achilles sat on the soft sea grass against the low bough of a twisted tree. Achilles' men splashed one another and ran races. A few gathered wood for later. Their unbound laughter floated on the sea air. "Your Myrmidons are cheerful."

"As I am."

"What happens when we return?"

"I go to war, Briseis." Achilles stood up abruptly. "But this day is my gift to you. I wish to live as I have never lived before." He grabbed her hand, pulling her to her feet and toward the beach. "I wish to see just how swift Odysseus actually is."

Briseis laughed. "You intend to challenge him?"

Achilles' eyes danced with joy, and his grin widened. "His pride won't let him refuse. He believes Athena helps him win everything, since she helped him win his wife."

"How did she do that?"

"She whispered in his ear, or so he says." Achilles took off, sending up a shower of sand behind him. Briseis laughed again. She'd never seen him so lighthearted. It was a balm she didn't know she needed until that moment. Odysseus was laughing and stripping his clothing, when Briseis caught up with Achilles. The men headed down to the hard, wet sand, waiting for their commander.

Achilles kissed her cheek. "Wish me the speed of the gods, *wife*."

"You already have that, *husband*."

"When I was a boy, I raced Chiron and won, but don't tell Odysseus."

"I heard that Achilles," Odysseus shouted over his shoulder, tapping the side of his head. "What are you waiting for, Achilles?" Odysseus turned and ran, his heels kicking up to his bare buttocks.

Achilles tossed his tunic to the sand and ran like the wind after him. Caught up in the merriment of sprinting, the Myrmidons cheered and stripped their clothes as well. They raced one another and swam in the clear blue water, until Apollo pulled the light to the ocean's edge. Briseis wove a crown of sea grass for each man. For the first time since she'd fallen into Achilles' world, her heart swelled with hope. The pains of war washed away.

As the light dimmed, Achilles' men lit a towering bonfire on the shore and roasted a goat on a spit. The flames reached for the stars, and the sea crashed against the shore. The spell of the day had touched everyone. The ease of leisure relaxed tired bones and hearts. Before the blazing fire, Briseis crowned each man for his efforts, while Achilles presided over them from a reclined position on the sand. Each man knelt for his turn and rose, grinning. A few winked at Achilles. Soon, the wine flowed as did bawdy talk and stories of home. The only thing missing was Patrokles.

Taking her place nestled at Achilles' side; Briseis dug her bare feet into the sand. She noticed Achilles' eyes slipping to the silver path of light on the water. "What is it?"

"Nothing."

"You can't take your eyes from the sea. Are you so eager to return to war?"

"It isn't that. I look for a sign of my mother is all. Did I ever tell you why she left me in Phthia?"

"No."

"She wished me to be immortal. She tried to burn me in a sacred fire with her magic, but Peleus stopped her. My father believed she was trying to kill his only son. He cursed her, and then banished her."

"What a sad story."

"It is the reason I am here now. At war and mortal."

Briseis kissed Achilles' chin. "Will she be pleased with our marriage?"

Pulling her tighter into the circle of his arms, he said, "It was her wish that I find joy with a woman before—"

"Don't say it." He'd promised her peace from war, but the thought of it was never very far from the edges of her mind. It was as if the camp, the constant skirmishing was all life had ever been. "I wish we could sail to Phthia from here. Never go back to Troy."

"That is a dream, Briseis. One which will never happen. No more talk of Troy." He lifted Briseis in his arms. "Men, I am off to take my wife to bed." They cheered their commander on with wine-drunk words. Throwing his head back, he laughed. "Make camp on the beach. I have need of the ship until sunrise." Then, he carried her off.

With the stars sparkling overhead, Achilles and Briseis climbed over the side railing. The deserted deck would be their wedding chamber. Oil lamps were already lit. Achilles pulled several furs from a basket and spread them out. "Your bed, my lady."

Briseis settled on the makeshift mattress, running her hand across the soft furs. "Bear?"

"That one, yes. The other is stitched rabbit."

From another basket Achilles procured an unopened amphora of wine. He pulled the wax plug and drank from it, before handing it to Briseis. "A gift from Odysseus. He had the lamps lit, as well."

"He was very quiet this evening."

"The nights have always made him ... *darker*. I believe thoughts of home haunt him when he is alone."

"Is it true he tried to trick Agamemnon, so he wouldn't have to come to Troy?"

"It is."

"He must love his wife very much." She extended her hand. "Come lay with me."

Achilles knelt beside her. Briseis caught the slight trembling of his ever steady hand, as he slipped the shoulder pins from her chiton. The plain, bleached linen fell to her waist. He bent his head to her breasts, kissing each mound with tender lips. "What is it, Achilles?" she whispered near his ear.

"Come the dawn, I will no longer be yours. I will belong to war and death."

Briseis embraced him, fiercely kissing every part of his face. She had known a confident, arrogant lover. Passionate. Eager. With every word, with every touch, with every kiss, he fulfilled his promise to her. But knowing it would all burn to ashes broke her heart in ways she was unprepared for. Their love was doomed, as was everything that crossed Achilles' path. Her future depended on his victory, but his victory demanded his death. "The gods are cruel, my love," she said quietly. "Cruel to keep the pleasure of old age from you."

"Did I ever tell you I once asked Odysseus for advice about you?"

"Whatever for?"

"I wanted to conquer your heart, but he told me a man can't take what should be given freely."

"He was … is right."

Achilles took her hands in his, leveling his eyes with hers. "My words have been hurtful to you. Patrokles would have been a better husband to you. From the beginning, he loved you. We fought about that once. That is when I knew for certain." Achilles smiled sadly. "I think he wanted to kill me that day, but of course, I could not allow that. And we forgave each other. Now, I wonder if perhaps in his heart he never truly did."

Briseis sat stunned by Achilles' revelations. He was speaking her private thoughts into existence. Loving Achilles had taken her by surprise. She'd hated herself for it. A life with Patrokles would have given her security, and love as well, but he was gone. Even so, Achilles would have always been between them. Now, on the verge of losing Achilles forever, she knew Patrokles would always be between *them*. The only cure was for Achilles to consume her very essence.

"My regrets are many, Briseis, but a mortal cannot undo what has been done."

"Can your mother persuade the gods—"

Achilles placed a finger on her lips. "Shah. Do not call the gods down to spy on us. I would take you without their prying eyes." He pulled her chiton over her hips and tossed it to the deck. His eyes lingered on her naked skin. "You are so beautiful." He kissed her softly on the mouth, nipping her bottom lip in his teeth. "I have wronged you. Forgive me." He kissed her cheeks. "Forgive me." He kissed down her neck. "Forgive me," he whispered, before his mouth came up to devour hers.

His confessions tore every wall down. There was nothing to fear anymore. They both knew what the next few days would bring.

Achilles disrobed, revealing his glorious perfection. Briseis gave in to his embrace and kisses. As he swept his tongue into her mouth, she melted into knowing they were bound to one another if only for a short time. Pressing her face to his, she inhaled the salty, smoky scent of his skin.

He ran his fingers lightly down her spine. "Let me love you both."

Briseis pulled her head back. "What do you mean?"

"You and Patrokles were bound, when I abandoned you for pride. I would touch him one last time by loving you the way I never loved him in life." Achilles eyes lingered on her lips, before his mouth descended on hers. Her body trembled under his desire, a hunger she'd never known him to possess. "Do you trust me, Briseis?"

"Aye," she said in a shaky voice. She regretted not speaking the words to Patrokles that he wanted to hear, and now Achilles presented a way to honor him that could only happen between them. "Let us both love him one last time then."

Together, they entered into an unspoken dream world. Achilles gently flipped Briseis over, pulling her hips into his. "Trust me," he whispered over her shoulder, as every hair on her body rose in delight. He pressed his cock between her buttocks and thrust into her tightness.

Briseis cried out. Achilles moved slowly, easing into her. A thin sheen of sweat covered her body, as the exquisite pain turned to intense pleasure. One of Achilles' hands held her hips steady, while the other traced each nodule of her spine. She filled her mind with images of Patrokles. His beauty. His kisses. His sly glances. Soon, her body craved what she had only held for a brief night. Her entire body shook with her release.

As Achilles' pleasure mounted, his thrusts quickened until finally he cried out their lover's name, "Patrokles." He collapsed against her back, weeping with ecstasy and sadness. "I loved him, Briseis. I loved him."

Twisting gently beneath him, she gingerly broke their physical bond. She pulled him down to her, bare chest to bare chest. Achilles wrapped his arms around her, cradling his head against her shoulder. He wept quietly like a child needing a mother's comfort. "Shah, Achilles. Shaaah." Briseis kissed the top of his head. "We have had our peace. And it was enough." It was a lie, she knew it as soon as she said it, but it was all she could think of saying. As Achilles' breathing slowed, she knew sleep had taken him. In the coming days, he would be stripped from her and there was nothing left to do but accept it. Closing her eyes, Briseis pressed her cheek to Achilles' head. He mumbled in his sleep, trapping her beneath a heavy leg, but he didn't wake.

Briseis whispered, "It was all either of us could do *not* to love him."

Sailing back to Troy, the mood of the entire crew grew somber, as Achilles withdrew from all conversation. Odysseus grumbled and brooded in his wine. The men rowed in silence. The spell of the past few days was broken. The war awaited their return.

FORTY ONE

a golden death

TROY—1238 BCE

Under a gray and heavy sky, Achilles took his position at the edge of the plain. Despite the gloomy dawn, his armor gleamed and flashed with his every movement. He planted his feet shoulder width apart and stabbed the butt-end of his father's great ash spear in the dirt, sending up a small cloud of dust. He waited. To honor Patrokles, Achilles chose to stand alone, for no other man could take Patrokles' place in life or death. Behind him his Black Shields gathered ready to charge at his command. Odysseus and Ajax of Telemon positioned their troops on the left, while Agamemnon, Menelaus, and Diomedes would circle around on the right. Not since they'd landed in Troy had the full force of the united armies been poised to strike the Trojans and their allies.

Achilles' eye caught the panoply of armor glittering with a light of its own among the enemy's ranks. "It is as you foretold, Mother." Thetis came to him as he bathed in the ocean, after his purification. He had welcomed her in a joyous embrace, but her appearance brought a troubling revelation. She told him that on the day of his death, he would face a worthy adversary, the son of Eos, called Memnon. He would know this new adversary by the armor he wore, a set of armor forged by Hephaestus. They would meet as equals. Thetis had wept not knowing if Achilles' death would come at this new foe's hand or not, only that his appearance marked Achilles' final day. With sadness swimming in the aqua pools of her eyes, she kissed him, before darting away beneath the waves. Achilles realized every step he took this day would be the last in that direction. He would not return to camp a victor, but as a dead man. Briseis had been right to question him in Lesbos, but he had caused her enough pain, so he kept this knowledge to himself. Death was a passage to reunite with Patrokles in the Underworld. And for that reason, he was not afraid to die.

The war horns sounded as if the gods themselves held them to their holy lips. Achilles listened to the rustling of leather and bronze weapons and the angry breath of his men stirring restlessly at his back. One spear butt hit the earth, then another, and another. Soon, the pounding of their ash spears rolled like thunder across the plain.

Achilles held his spear aloft. "Death is coming for you Trojans," he roared. "Prepare to die."

Hundreds of frightened Trojans ran for their lives, because they secretly believed the rumors flying around the city that Achilles was a god. They knew no mortal could stand against a god.

Memnon returned Achilles' war cry with a challenge of his own.

"One of us will die!" He held his broad shield before his chest and leveled his spear. "Come for me, Son of Thetis!"

Achilles charged with all his speed, leveling his spear as he ran. He cocked his arm back, his muscles straining, for the lightning quick toss. He launched his spear like an arrow at Memnon. The bronze tip nicked the shield, bouncing off the center to the ground. Memnon threw his heavy spear, but Achilles dodged the wicked spinning shaft. Each man pulled his sword, circling one another, eyes seeking a vulnerable point of entry. Their blades sang, sliding against each other. They grunted with effort and blind determination. Achilles fought his fate, as much as he fought Memnon. He fought for every last moment of his life, determined his executioner would have no easy task. Achilles would die fighting, or kill until the end.

Around the heroes, the two opposing armies clashed and broke into pockets of vicious struggle. War song filled the air. Men screamed. Men Grunted. Men fell over dead. Blood spilled into the dirt with the shit and the piss of the dying, turning the ground slick with putrid muck. The stench of death filled men's nostrils, so they fought more desperately to keep the haunting darkness of the unknown at arm's length.

Achilles swung his sword in a wide arch, spinning to catch Memnon at the narrow gap between his belt and breastplate. Memnon stopped in his tracks, threw his sword to the ground, and reached for his innards spilling from his body. He looked to Achilles in confusion. "How—" Then, he toppled over like an old, mud brick wall.

Above the fight, thunder rolled through the dark clouds.

"To the bitter end," Achilles yelled. "Myrmidons! To Troy's gates!" He stormed toward the city with his troops close behind.

Wild. They ran with the speed of gods, leaping over dead men and horses and overturned chariots. Wolves. War filled them with an insatiable hunger, and Achilles was their god. Beside him, the Myrmidons were invincible. They slashed every Trojan in their path, broken bones and guts littering the earth behind them. When they reached the city gates, no one was left to stop them. The lurkers on the ramparts fled in fear.

"Take the palace," Achilles ordered. "The truce is over." The Myrmidons killed every man, woman, and child unfortunate enough to be standing in their way. As they moved through the winding streets, murdering helpless refugees, their untamed madness slowly cooled. Foot soldiers and chariots and mounted Myrmidons pushed toward the city's center, passing the temples of the gods.

"There will be no desecration of the holy," Achilles commanded.

His men marched on, eager for plunder and the soft thighs of victory.

But the flutter of a saffron gown caught Achilles' attention as it vanished around an ornate column. A girl with long, dark hair peered from behind it, laughing before running into the temple. With his waking eyes, he could not believe that it was ... *her*. All those years ago, Agamemnon's lie took her life and ended his innocence of war. Her death began the burden of killing in his name. Patrokles had warned him of Agamemnon's plan. He never asked Patrokles how he knew, but he had been correct. Unfortunately, he'd been too late. All these years, her frightened eyes and red, gaping neck and the stains on her yellow gown haunted him. That he should see her, here, at the end surprised him.

"Go to her," a voice whispered passed his ear.

"By the gods, it cannot be." Achilles abandoned his men,

compelled to follow her. He ran to the temple. "Iphigenia? Is it you?" His voice echoed through the sleek, black marble hall.

The young woman's silver voice rang out, "I am here." But it sounded from all directions.

Achilles ventured deeper into the center of the temple, and farther away from his men. He stepped through a curtain of dark silk floating above the floor and into a chamber built entirely of polished black marble. The god's golden image rested on a black altar across from him.

"Apollo," Achilles whispered. Every hair on his body rose in alarm. "Why have you led me here?" he asked the god. "You purified me and blessed my union."

"So you would truly know regret," Apollo whispered coldly.

The shouting of soldiers skirmishing sounded behind him. Achilles spun to leave, but his feet were rooted to the floor. The scuffle of leather and the clang of bronze weapons drew nearer.

"Achilles!" It was Odysseus shouting. "Achilles!"

The woman in yellow glided into view from behind another curtain. She was smiling, but her eyes were dark and deadly.

"*You* are not Iphigenia."

"Do you not recognize me, Defiler of Innocents?"

"Should I?"

"You killed my brother as he sought Apollo's protection."

It was long ago and done in obedience to Athena, who threatened his son, Neoptolemus. Regardless, his reasons would not matter now. He could still feel Troilus' slender neck bent over his knee and his warm blood spilling over his thigh. He had not wanted to take his life. "The boy called Troilus," Achilles said quietly. Surveying his surroundings with a soldier's critical eye, he realized he held an undesirable position. "What is your name?"

"Polyxena."

"A Trojan princess." Peisidike's face rose up before him. He'd used her to take Methymna. Patrokles had warned him against it, but he refused to listen in the name of war. He'd stoned her before her father's eyes. Now, he wondered if a Trojan princess was being used to take him. "Are you here to fight me, Polyxena? Or fuck me?"

"You disgust me," Polyxena said, even as she admired his broad shoulders and the chiseled features of his face. "Never."

"You would be the first to refuse me."

Odysseus skidded into the chamber, tearing the sacred curtain from the wall as he scrambled to keep his feet beneath him on the slick floor. "Fucking Hades, Achilles! What are you doing? There's no time for women! The Myrmidons have made it to the palace gate."

Have you ever wondered, Achilles, how Patrokles fell so easily to Hektor? Apollo's wicked tongue sliced through Achilles' mind. *It. Was. Me.*

"We have to go, Achilles," Odysseus bellowed. "Wait, is that—"

"No, it is *not* Iphigenia's ghost."

Deiphobus and Paris, who the god had concealed, stepped from thin air behind Polyxena. The truth settled on Achilles. His wide shoulders fell with a sigh. "So be it."

"By the fucking gods!" Odysseus yelled. "Achilles, fight!" Odysseus charged, but was repelled by an unseen wall. His spear and sword as useless as children's playthings.

Achilles pulled his shield from his shoulder, as Deiphobus' spear, gleaming with unnatural light, struck like a bolt of lightning. Achilles' shield spun away, and he stumbled backward.

"Achilles!" Odysseus yelled desperately. "Nooooooo!"

Surprise crossed Achilles' face. Never had he known the despair of disadvantage. Never had he lost. His body stilled. There was nothing left to fight anymore. He was no match for Apollo. And it was the god who lured him here and guided the Trojan brothers' weapons.

Paris held his bow at his shoulder, nocking the arrow at Achilles' heart. Apollo stepped behind him, placing his arm over Paris', and pulled the bowstring back … the bow curving dangerously close to snapping in half. Paris held Achilles in his eye. His arm shook.

"*Loose,*" Apollo whispered in Paris' ear. "*Loose the arrow.*"

With a loud twang the arrow flashed like a small sun, its path a thread of gold suspended in the air, then shimmering to dust. By bringing down Achilles, who'd slain his brothers and defiled Hektor, Paris hoped his personal failings would fade. Now, at least, his mother's vengeance was complete. His life was more than just a story of doom. But Paris hated Achilles not just for the atrocities against his family, but because *he* was everything Paris was never meant to be. Achilles was never a coward in life or death. Paris hated Achilles, because he feared to face him without a god at his side. As he lowered his bow, Apollo's power faded quickly from his aching arm.

Odysseus caught the flash of golden light as Paris let the arrow fly. He knew a god hovered at Paris' side, but he was powerless to intervene. "Achilles!" he shouted over and over until his voice was raw. By now a large group of Greeks and Myrmidons crowded behind him. With weapons drawn, they stood in shock as Achilles dropped to his knees. Paris loosed several more arrows at Achilles, before being whisked away in a mist with his brother and sister.

Achilles' fingers fumbled at the golden shaft lodged in his chest. Blood ran in thick streams down his breastplate where it pooled on the floor. He could feel his strength ebbing away. Until now, he'd never known the searing truth of a fatal injury. He'd sent thousands of men to the Underworld without a second thought, but as he toppled over, he wondered what awaited him there.

Apollo's heavy hand squeezed his shoulder. Achilles groaned. Cold words hissed into his ear. *"Did you think I would let the death of Troilus, my son, go unpunished?"*

Achilles' voice strangled in his throat; blood gurgled up instead of words. His eyes fixed ahead of him. Gathering all his strength, he struggled awkwardly to his feet.

"Your song is over, Achilles."

With defiance in his eyes, Achilles sputtered, "It has … just … begun."

Odysseus and the men leaning on him tumbled forward without warning. He rushed to Achilles, catching him as he fell backward into his arms. "By the gods! Ajax! Where is Ajax?" With disbelief on their faces, men crowded Achilles and Odysseus. The same terrifying thought ran through all their minds. If Achilles died, would they all be doomed? In anger, they tossed the golden statue of Apollo to the floor where it clanged and tumbled face down. They ripped the sacred curtains to shreds, forsaking their beliefs, daring the god to stop them.

"Ajax," Odysseus screamed. He broke off the arrows in Achilles' legs and the one in his chest. And he plucked the one sticking out of his heel. "Hold on, Achilles. I will get you to the camp. The physicians will heal you." He pulled Achilles from the floor, hefting him over his shoulder. "They must heal you."

Achilles groaned, "It is … too late."

Odysseus held Achilles' legs tight behind the knees and ran as if the wild hounds of Hades nipped at his heels. They were behind the enemy's gate without their hero to see them through. Without Achilles, Odysseus knew they must retreat. Word spread quickly of Achilles' fall, and with it, the Myrmidons backtracked through the city, abandoning their bloodlust. The Greeks also succumbed to the growing confusion, because Achilles was supposed to conquer Troy. If he died, every man knew he himself was lost. If he died what did any of their suffering and sacrifice mean? If they returned home empty handed or rotted on the Trojan plain, their lives will have held no purpose. They would have no legacy. They would have no songs. Men cried as they raced to retreat for the camp.

The sharp sounds of Trojan horns heralded the imminent return of her army, pushing Odysseus beyond a mortal's pace. His feet pounded the winding stone street, his knees ached, and his shoulder was on fire under the hero's weight. Myrmidons, catching sight of Odysseus carrying their wounded commander, sped to surround him with their strength and black shields. They flew like a cloud of dark-winged birds swirling this way and that until they cleared the Trojan gate. Three of the swiftest runners broke off from the group and sprinted ahead to the beach camp.

Odysseus prayed to Athena for a sign of hope or a plan, while his lungs burned for breath and his legs grew tired. As he rounded an uphill curve in the path, Ajax and a contingent of ruthless fighters flew from behind the hill. A splinter of the Trojan army was in pursuit. *Not the fucking sign I wanted.* His lungs still burned. He heaved for each breath. *Fucking Trojans.*

"Odysseus!" Ajax shouted, startled to find Odysseus along the fringe of battle. He had planned to pull the enemy deeper into the chaparral, swing around and take them by surprise. But, the pursuing

Trojans, recognizing the Black Shields of Achilles' forces, turned tail and bolted for their lives. Shoving Myrmidons out of his way, Ajax raced beside Odysseus. Crimson stripes covered Odysseus' arms and back. "By the gods, it's true! Is he alive?"

Achilles' blood mixed with his sweat beneath his tunic and breastplate. The open wounds oozed crimson, making it difficult to hang on to the dying man. Odysseus grunted, "I hope so."

"My legs are fresh. Give him to me." Ajax reached for Achilles, and Odysseus reluctantly surrendered his burden without breaking stride. If Achilles was to survive, they could not stop. The Myrmidons circled protectively around Ajax, Odysseus, and their fallen prince, and on they ran. Only the God of Death could stop them from reaching the beach, and even he they would fight for Achilles' sake.

FORTY TWO
the farewell
MYRMIDON CAMP—1238 BCE

The dark clouds swirled above camp, and a mournful breeze stirred sand and dust. When the Myrmidon sprinters arrived carrying the grim news of Achilles' fall, Briseis refused to believe it. The whisper of despair swept like a wild wind through tall pines, before the storm breaks from the skies. Men were already tearing out their hair, renting their garments, and weeping. Briseis had survived worse, she reminded herself, much worse, and so refused to bend under the weight of this fresh anguish. She toyed with the gold bangle at her wrist that Achilles had gifted her on their wedding night. He had warned her that this day was coming and to be prepared, but she had prayed until her soul ached that Thetis was wrong, or that Achilles was wrong, or that the gods would change their fickle minds. Her thoughts would not calm. What would happen now? Would the Greeks depart empty handed? Was she truly a Princess of Phthia, or just a spear-won prize? She crossed her arms over her chest, willing herself to remain on her feet, and waited.

Briseis' heart leapt against her ribs at the sight of a mob of Myrmidons moving quickly down the beach. *They have him*, she thought. *By the gods, they have him*. Her world fell away. Sea birds cried shrilly above her. Waves tumbled against the shore. They had spotted her and shifted in her direction. "Achilles," she whispered. "Oh, Achilles, what wicked games the gods play with us."

The circle of Myrmidons halted before her, some falling to their knees, like petals of a dying flower. Having reached their destination, their fierce hearts broke and they wept their first tears. From their midst, Ajax emerged with Achilles draped over his shoulder. The giant gently laid Achilles on the sand and sea grass at Briseis' feet. "My lady," he said miserably.

The once dazzling armor of Hephaestus was dulled by Achilles' dried blood. His arms and legs were covered in it. His skin was pale. His lips were gray. "Briseis …" His voice cracked.

She knelt beside him. The storm of grief was building, but she held it tightly to her chest, refusing to unleash it for fear she would lose herself completely and irrevocably. "What are you waiting for? Take him to the physicians' tents," Briseis commanded the Myrmidons.

"No. It is over," Achilles said weakly. His hand trembled to find hers. She took it in her own, covering it with kisses. She frantically searched the faces of Odysseus and Ajax for hope, but they only shook their heads. Briseis recognized the shocked look of despair and sadness that had settled there.

Achilles' eyes rolled open. "We knew ... Briseis," he groaned, as he heaved his broad chest.

She unbuckled the breastplate, careful of the gaping hole still oozing his life away. He struggled for each breath, and *that* broke her resolve. She had lost everything because of him, and more of herself than she'd ever intended. She no longer knew who she was without Achilles at her side. He had become her entire world in this war, and the only thing that anchored her. And Patrokles. Fierce, sweet Patrokles. She'd lost him, too. She couldn't bear the unknown, and grabbed Achilles by the shoulders, shaking him with all her desperate fears. "Don't leave me, Achilles. I beg you, don't leave me alone." She collapsed against his chest, weeping uncontrollably.

With great effort, Achilles touched her salt-stained cheek. "Shahhh."

Odysseus knelt beside her, placing his strong hand on her shoulder. "Briseis," he said, gently. "Say farewell, before it is too late."

With her scarred heart ripped open, she cupped Achilles' face and leaned to kiss his lips. Lingering above his bloody mouth, she tasted the bitterness of war and loss. As Achilles' breath grew more ragged, Briseis realized that only the brightest, sharpest truth would honor his passing. They had nothing left to hide from one another. "You are a difficult man to love, Achilles, but I have loved you."

Achilles closed his eyes. "He could not help but love you. We could not help but love him. Remember, the ashes."

"Together," she whispered. It was their most private moment he called forth at the end. Not war, not glory, but a single night of passion that bound the three of them together. "Forever."

Gathering the last of his strength, Achilles cried out,

"Myrmidons!"

His men roared like thunder, "Achilles!"

And then he was gone.

A thousand Myrmidons gathered around Achilles' pyre draped in their black cloaks with their shields on their backs. Even the wounded limped from their beds to pay their respects. They numbered so many that those in the back were pressed to the sea's edge. Many held their glittering helms in the crooks of their arms, because their scalps bled with fresh wounds. They'd tossed their locks of hair upon Achilles' pyre to honor him.

Briseis wore an unadorned, dark blue chiton with simple gold pins at the shoulder and the gold bracelet from Achilles on her wrist. In her hand, she gripped Achilles' great ash spear. She woke to find her hair almost entirely silver now, so she wore it unbound as a sign of her sorrow. Drums beat a lament into the air. Odysseus stood ready with the torch to send the fallen prince to the Underworld.

Achilles was laid out on the pyre's flat altar fitted in the scratched and dented armor he'd stripped and reclaimed from Hektor. It had been worn by Patrokles, and so seemed a fitting shroud. Thunder rumbled above them through heavy, dark clouds.

Odysseus shouted, "Here lies Achilles. Fiercest among us. May he be greeted in the Underworld by the companions he lost along the way." He lowered the torch to the wood pile. Small flames caught and crackled to life, weaving between the dry stacks. Briseis braced herself, as the fire licked toward Achilles' body. She would never be ready to watch him burn.

Out of the gloomy sky, a giant sea gull swooped and screeched above the gathering. A wave washed high up the beach, sending men scrambling to find their footing. When the water retreated, it pulled farther out than it should have, stranding small crabs scurrying for shelter, octopuses slipping from exposed rocks, and silver fish gasping for breath. Confusion rippled through the crowd. Poseidon's name fell from the lips of some, but Briseis knew in her heart which immortal had come. The only one who could never have stayed away.

The surface of the ocean dimpled with thousands of tiny bubbles as the fifty Nereids rose in a salty, shimmering mist. Achilles' men fell to their knees in awe and reverence. They whispered her name, "*Thetis*," as she passed through them followed by her sisters. The Nereids wore gowns of glistening gossamer and sea foam. A crown of pearls and shells and treasures rescued from the sea sat upon each of their heads.

Thetis and her sisters circled the pyre with joined hands, and raised their faces to the sky. They called down the rain to douse the offending flames with their silver voices singing in the gods' tongue. The heavens opened and the rain fell. The assembly stood in amazement of the miracle. The flames sputtered, smoked, and died out. A sliver of sun pierced the gloom surrounding Achilles alone in its light. "Zeus," some whispered.

Achilles' mother approached Briseis, standing beside the pyre, head lowered. She slipped a cool hand to Briseis' cheek. "I will not allow mortal fire to take my golden son."

Briseis dared to meet the deep pools of Thetis' blue-green eyes with her own. "My lady," she whispered reverently.

Thetis smiled slowly, her elegant shoulders rising and falling with sadness. "You have the bones of Patrokles?"

Briseis retrieved the golden box embossed with a star of many rays. It was heavy. She kissed it before handing it to Thetis, who handed it to one of her sisters. The Nereids slipped back to the sea, sending the water to glide gently against the sand.

"Where will you go, Briseis?"

When Thetis spoke her name, it sounded like music floating in the air between them. Achilles' mother was mesmerizing in every way. The very air around her swam. It was no wonder Achilles' beauty was flawless. "I don't know, my lady. Achilles killed my first life. Paris has killed the second."

"Go to Phthia. Peleus will welcome you. You are a Princess of Phthia. No one else can sing the song you know. Not even Deidamia."

Thetis took Briseis' face in both her smooth, cool hands. "If only Achilles had been gifted more time … an immortal blinks an eye, and a mortal's life is dust."

"Where will you take him?" Briseis asked.

"To the White Island." Thetis turned to Odysseus. "It is time, King of Ithaka."

Odysseus climbed the pyre, lifted Achilles from his funeral bed, then placed him in his mother's arm. Thetis did not falter under the weight of her son's body, but cradled him effortlessly. With great tenderness, she kissed his cheek. "My beautiful boy."

The throng of Myrmidons watched silently as Thetis carried Achilles in her arms, as if he were once again the golden-haired babe seeking comfort at her breast. Off shore, her sisters waited with leaping dolphins. Thetis glanced back at the men whom Achilles led in countless battles, and at the woman he had loved at the last, and was satisfied his short life had brought him honor and happiness. It was all she could have ever hoped for a mortal child. She turned and walked into the foamy sea and disappeared.

CAST OF CHARACTERS

THE GREEKS

Achilles: Phthia, son of Thetis and Peleus, Captain and Commander of the Myrmidons

Aegisthus: Sparta, half-brother to Agamemnon and Menelaus

Aethra: Aethra, mother of King Theseus, forced to serve Helen

Agamemnon: Mycenae, King of Mycenae, husband to Clytemnestra

Ajax the Great: Salamis, also known as Telemonian Ajax, he is son of king Telemon and the Prince of Salamis, cousin to Achilles

Anticlea: Ithaka, mother of Odysseus, wife of Laertes

Antilochus: Pylos, son of Nestor

Caster: Sparta, son of Tyndareus, brother to Helen

Chiron: Mt. Pelion, centaur, half-brother to Zeus, mentor to generations of warrior-kings

Clytemnestra: Sparta, Mycenae, daughter of Tyndareus, widow of Tantalus, wife of Agamemnon and mother of Iphigenia

Deidamia: Skyros, princess of Skyros, daughter of King Lycomedes, wife of Achilles, mother of Neoptolemus

Demius: Gythium, friend of Patrokles, helped Patrokles escape Gythium murder

Diomedes: Argos, king of Argos, immortal weapons granted by Athena

Elektra: Mycenae, daughter of Clytemnestra and Agamemnon

Eurycleia: Ithaka, nursemaid to Odysseus

Helen: Sparta, daughter of Tyndareus and Leda, Queen of Sparta, wife of Menelaus and Paris

Hermione: Sparta, daughter of Menelaus and Helen

Hesione: Troy and Salamis, sister to Priam, taken captive by Herakles and given to Telemon of Salamis. Her sons fight against Troy.

Iphigenia: Mycenae, daughter of King Agamemnon and Queen Clytemnestra

Kalchas: Mycenae, seer for Agamemnon and the Greeks

Knaxon: Aulis, Achilles' servant and mentored by Thetis

Laertes: Ithaka, retired king of Ithaka, father of Odysseus, husband of Anticlea

Leda: Sparta, Queen of Sparta, mother of Clytemnestra, Pollux, Castor, and Helen

Lycomedes: Skyros, king of Skyros, father to Deidamia, grandfather to Neoptolemus

Menelaus: Sparta, brother to Agamemnon, husband of Helen

Nauplius: Euboea, father of Palamedes

Neola: Mycenae, trusted servant of Clytemnestra

Neoptolemus: Skyros and Phthia, son of Achilles Nestor, Pylos, old king of Pylos, in Messenia, wise council warrior

Odysseus: Ithaka, King of Ithaka, husband to Penelope, father to Telemachus

Orestes: Mycenae, son of Agamemnon and Clytemnestra

Palamedes: Mycenae, personal servant to Agamemnon

Patrokles: Phthia, guardian and elder cousin of Achilles

Peleus: Phthia, King of Phthia, father of Achilles

Penelope: Sparta and Ithaka, cousin to Helen and wife of Odysseus

Phoenix: Phthia, friend to Peleus, guardian of Achilles

Pirithous: Athens, helped Theseus kidnap Helen, he wanted Persephone as a wife

Pollux: Sparta, son of Tyndareus, brother to Helen

Tantalus: Mycenae, Prince of Mycenae, murdered by Agamemnon and first husband of Clytemnestra

Telemachus: Ithaka, son of Odysseus

Telemon: Salamis, traveled with Herakles, father of Ajax, took Hesione as concubine

Theseus: Athens, King of Athens, kidnapped Helen

Thrasymedes: Pylos, son of Nestor

Thyestes: Mycenae, King of Mycenae defeated by Agamemnon

Tyndareus: Sparta, King of Sparta, father of Clytemnestra, Pollux, Castor, and Helen

THE TROJANS & THEIR ALLIES

Aeneas: Troy, Trojan warrior, nephew of King Priam, and founder of Italy Agelaus, Troy, royal bull herder and breeder, foster father of Paris

Andromache: Hypoplakia Thebe and Troy, daughter of Eetion and Mira, wife of Hektor

Astynome: Chryse, daughter of Chryses, prize concubine of Agamemnon

Briseis: Pedasus and Lyrnessus, daughter of Briseus and Shavash, widow of prince Mynes, concubine and wife of Achilles

Briseus: Pedasus, father of Briseis, King of Pedasus

Cassandra: Troy, daughter of Priam and Hecuba, cursed priestess of Apollo

Chryses: Chryse, priest of Apollo, father of Astynome

Corythus: Troy, son of Prince Paris and Oenone

Eetion: Hypoplakia Thebe, King of Hypoplakia Thebe, father of Andromache

Eurypylus: Tenedos, Son of King Telephus and a physician

Evenus: Lyrnessus, king of Lyrnessus

Hapeshet: Methymna, Seer and wise man to King Mikares

Hecamede: Tenedos, war prize gifted to Nestor

Hektor: Troy, eldest son of Priam and Hecuba, the Golden Prince of Troy and Commander of the Trojan army

Helenus: Troy, son of Priam and Hecuba, twin brother of Cassandra

Hypsipylos: Methymna, Warrior commander of King Mikares army, betrothed to the Princess Peisidike

Kebriones: Troy, bastard son of Priam by Melita

Korei: Tenedos, distinguished warrior in King Telephus' army, father of Valparun

Lateke: Methymna, hand maiden to Princess Peisidike

Lexias: Troy, wife to Agelaus, foster mother of Paris

Lykaon: Troy, half-brother to Hektor and Paris

Megapenthes: Troy, bastard son of Menelaus by Teridae

Malina: Lyrnessus, handmaiden to Prince Mynes, mother of Yoruk

Melita: Troy, concubine to King Priam

Mikares: Methymna, King of Methymna, a kingdom on Lesbos

Mynes: Lyrnessus, prince of Lyrnessus, first husband of Briseis

Oenone: wood nymph married to Paris, mother of Corythus

Paris: Troy, second son of Priam and Hecuba, the Forgotten Prince of Troy

Peisidike: Methymna, princess and daughter of King Mikares

Polyxena: Troy, youngest daughter of Priam and Hecuba

Shavash: Pedasus, mother of Briseis

Sidika: Lyrnessus, Queen of Lyrnessus

Telephus: Tenedos, King of Tenedos, a province in Mysia

Teridae: Troy, concubine of King Menelaus, mother of Megapenthes

Troilus: Troy, youngest son of Priam and Hecuba

Valparun: Tenedos, son of Korei

Yoruk: Lyrnessus, prince of Lyrnessus, son of Mynes and handmaiden Malina

THE GODS

Aphrodite: Goddess of Love and Beauty

Apollo: God of the Sun and Healing

Ares: God of War

Athena: Goddess of War and Wisdom

Artemis: Goddess of Hunting and Chasteness

Cebron: River god, father of Oenone

Eleithyia: Goddess of Childbirth

Eris: Goddess of Strife

Hera: wife of Zeus'

Hermes: Messenger of Zeus

Poseidon: God of the Seas

Thetis: sea nymph, Goddess of Water; also, wife of Peleus, beloved of Zeus, and Achilles' mother

Zeus: father of the Olympians, true father of Pollux and Helen

TIMELINE FOR HOMERIC CHRONICLES

SONG OF SACRIFICE

1295 BCE   Hektor is born in Troy
Agamemnon is born in Mycenae
1290 BCE   Paris is born in Troy
1288 BCE   Clytemnestra born in Sparta
1285 BCE   Andromache born
1282 BCE   Briseis is born in Pedasus
Menelaus is born in Mycenae
1279 BCE   Odysseus is born in Ithaka
1272 BCE   Wedding of Thetis and Peleus
Paris fights Ares' Bull
The Judgment of Paris (15 years old)
1271 BCE   Achilles born to Thetis and Peleus
1270 BCE   Penelope born
Cassandra's Curse
Leda raped by Zeus
Clytemnestra (18) marries Agamemnon (25)
Helen born
1269 BCE   Briseis (13) meets Hektor (26)
1268 BCE   Hektor (24) meets Andromache (18)

1267 BCE   Briseis (15) meets Mynes (25)
1266 BCE   Iphigenia born to Clytemnestra & Agamemnon
Achilles (5) with Chiron the Centaur
Hektor (29) meets Andromache (19)
1265 BCE   Hektor (30) marries Andromache (20)
Briseis (17) marries Prince Mynes (27)
1263 BCE   Orestes born to Clytemnestra & Agamemnon
1262 BCE   Phila born, daughter of Briseis (20) and Mynes
1260 BCE   Elektra born to Clytemnestra & Agamemnon
1259 BCE   Phila dies of illness
1257 BCE   Achilles (14 yrs) returns to Peleus
Studies under Phoenix
Corythus born, son of Oenone and Paris
Achilles (14) sent to Skyros by Thetis
1254 BCE   Achilles (17) marries pregnant Deidamia (16)
Helen kidnapped by Theseus and Pirithous
1253 BCE   Neoptolemus (Achilles' son) born
1252 BCE   Helen (18) marries Menelaus (30)
Odysseus (27) marries Penelope (18)
1251 BCE   Hermione born to Helen and Menelaus
Paris quests to rescue Hesione
Menelaus attends funeral of Catreus of Crete
Paris (39) takes Helen (19)
Telemachus born to Odysseus and Penelope
Gathering at Aulis for Troy
Odysseus retrieves Achilles (20) at Skyros
Iphigenia (15) at Aulis

RISE OF PRINCES

1251 BCE   Iphigenia's funeral
Agamemnon's fleet at Lemnos
Paris farewells Oenone
Yoruk born to Mynes and the handmaiden, Malina
1250 BCE   Achilles attacks Methymna
1249 BCE   Agamemnon's fleet arrives at Tenedos
1248 BCE   Queen Leda travels to Mycenae
Agamemnon's fleet arrives at Troy
Ambush of Caster and Pollux
The united armies of the west threaten mutiny
Clytemnestra meets Aegisthus
1247 BCE   Odysseus' revenge
Nauplius seeks restitution
1246 BCE   Neoptolemus sent to Chiron
Penelope waits with Anticlea
Paris reveals the truth to Helen
1245 BCE   Penelope consults the Oracle
Orestes (18) promised to Hermione (6)
Aphrodite consults Zeus
Achilles takes Lyrnessus
Princess Briseis captured
Lykaon sold into slavery
1244 BCE   Priam marries Melita
1243 BCE   Achilles and Odysseus at Bay of Edremit
Menelaus takes Megapenthes as heir

1242 BCE   Refugee Camp established in Troy
1240 BCE   Aphrodite blesses Helen
1239 BCE   Corythus (17) to Troy
Achilles sacks Hypoplakia Thebe
Achilles ambushed Troilus and Polyxena
Astynome given to Agamemnon

RAGE OF QUEENS

1238 BCE   The events of book three span the year 1238 BCE. The events are told chronologically, and oftentimes a single day will span several chapters, as the end draws nearer …

MY MYRMIDONS

I want to thank everyone in my life who has endured my incessant talking about Greek mythology, whether it was about this series or my podcast. I love it so much. The passion. The glory. The messiness. There are days when it's all I can think about. I wish I was faster, but alas, I find my mind is like an old fashioned percolator.

The women whom I dedicated this book to have been in my life for decades. They knew me when I was, well, younger. Each one has contributed something meaningful to my existence in the world. Amber her mysterious ways and fire ceremonies. Anni her fierce truth about everything. Bre her gift of bursting out in musical tunes. Miss Macy (yes, I actually call her that and never by her first name) her resolute love of all things Spartacus. Vandy her sense of what is right. Verni her open door policy and embracing me as a family member. I am grateful for their support. They are the epitome of women supporting women.

If you enjoy podcasts, I invite you to give my show, Greek Mythology Retold, a listen on your favorite platform for free. You don't have to listen in any particular order. Become a subscriber if you want the bonus content and ad free listening by visiting: https://greekmythologyretold.supercast.tech/.

REFERENCES & INSPIRATIONS

Aeschylus, *Agamemnon*.

Alexander, Caroline. *Iliad*, translation. HarperCollins Publishers. Reprint edition (November 24, 2015)

Arnson Svarlien, Diane; Scodel, Ruth, translator. *Euripides: Andromache, Hecuba, Trojan Women* (Hackett Classics) (March 15, 2012).

Cassandra. Retrieved from https://www.greekmyths-greekmythology.com/the-myth-of-cassandra/

Claybourne, Anna. "Achilles." *Gods, Goddesses, and Mythology*. Tarrytown, NY: Marshall Cavendish Reference. Retrieved from https://search.credoreference.com/content/entry/mcgods/achilles/0

Cuypers, Martine, *Ptoliporthos Akhilleus: the sack of Methymna in the Lesbou Ktisis*, Hermathena, v.173-174, 2005, pp. 117-135.

Due, Casey and Mary Ebbott, *Mothers-in-arms: soldiers' emotional bonds and Homeric similes*. War, Literature and the Arts: An international Journal of the Humanities, 2012. Retrieved from Academia.edu.

Hanson, Victor Davis, *On Barry Strauss's The Trojan War: A New History*. Retrieved from www.newcriterion.com.

Hauser, Emily. 'There is another story': writing after the *Odyssey* in Margaret Atwood's *The Penelopiad Classical Receptions Journal*,

Hesiod, *The Homeric Hymns and Homerica*, H.G. translated by Evelyn-White

Higgins, Charlotte, *The Iliad and what it can still tell us about war*. Retrieved from www.theguardian.com.

Homer, *Iliad*.

Homer, *Odyssey*.

Hyginus, *Fabulae, Cassandra* 65. Retrieved from http://www.theoi.com/Text/HyginusFabulae3.html#65.

Hyginus, *Fabulae, Palamedes*105. Retrieved from http://www.theoi.com/Text/HyginusFabulae3.html#105.

Mark, Joshua J., *Oenone*, Ancient History Encyclopedia, 2009.

Mason, Wyatt. https://www.nytimes.com/2017/11/02/magazine/the-first-woman-to-translate-the-odyssey-into-english.html (On Emily Wilson's *Odyssey* translation)

Mendelsohn, Daniel, Battle Lines: A Slimmer, faster Iliad. Retrieved from www.NewYorker.com.

Muich, Rebecca M. *Pouring out tears: Andromache in Homer and Euripides* https://www.ideals.illinois.edu/handle/2142/16755

Ovid, *Ars Amatoria*.

Ovid, *Herois 5*, translated by R. Scott Smith.

Parada, Carlos, *Peleus*, Greek Mythology Link. Retrieved from http://www.maicar.com/GML/Peleus.html

Parada, Carlos, *Agamemnon*, Greek Mythology Link. Retrieved from http://www.maicar.com/GML/Agamemnon.html

Parada, Carlos, *Paris*, Greek Mythology Link. Retrieved from http://www.maicar.com/GML/Paris.html

Polyxena: *Encyclopedia Mythica* from Encyclopedia Mythica Online. Retrieved from http://www.pantheon.org/articles/p/

polyxena.html. Accessed March 03, 2017.

Reardon, Tyler (Dramaturge) https://pacifictheatrearts.wordpress.com/ancient-burial-customs/

Restrepo Documentary, June 2010. Directed by Tim Hetherington and Sebastian Junger.

Seneca, *Thyestes*.

Shay, Jonathan, M.D., PhD., Achilles in Vietnam" Combat Trauma and the Undoing of Character. Touchstone: New York: NY, 1994.

Stewart, M.W. *Achilles*. Retrieved from https://mythagora.com/bios/achilles.html (now available in Kindle format)

Strauss, Barry, *The Trojan War*.

Thyestes and Atreus. Retrieved from http://www.classics.upenn.edu/myth/php/tragedy/

Wilson, Emily. *Odyssey*, translation. W. W. Norton & Company; 1 edition (November 7, 2017).

Printed in Great Britain
by Amazon